# FRACKED TO DEATH

A Cortlandt Scott Mystery Thriller

Lee Mossel
April, 2017

Lee Mossel

**ISBN-13:978-1523498505**

**ISBN-10: 1523498501**

To Jennifer -

Thank you for your interest and congratulations for winning! I hope you enjoy the book. I would sincerely appreciate your <u>honest</u> review.

All the best!

Lee Mossel

## Dedication

*Fracked to Death* is dedicated to Jan without whom no words would ever be written.

# CHAPTER ONE

I was standing on my deck sipping a second cup of coffee when my "duck quack" ringtone frightened a very pregnant mule deer munching on the day lilies around the back yard. Caller ID read 'Siren E&P.' Siren Exploration & Production is Mercedes "Mercy" Drexler's oil and gas company. Mercy is the richest woman in Denver.

That's a call you take even at 8:05 a.m. Monday. I watched the doe springboard into the oak brush and answered, "Hello, Cort Scott speaking."

A pleasant sounding woman said, "Mr. Scott, this is Janelle Simmons, personal assistant to Ms. Drexler at Siren Exploration and Production. Would you hold the line for Ms. Drexler please?"

"Of course." I thought this should be interesting.

"Thank you, please hold." The connection clicked, but before any elevator music could start, it clicked again.

"*Good morning*, Mr. Scott. Thanks for taking my call." Mercy Drexler had a low, sultry voice with no discernable accent. It made me think of a cable news anchorwoman: good diction, good pronunciation, and probably good teeth and hair to go with the voice. "I was wondering if you would have time to come downtown and meet with me? I'm involved in a new project; it's going to involve a lot of travel and, hopefully without sounding too dramatic, possibly some personal danger. I believe I could use someone with your, uh…*special talents*."

I wondered what she meant by special talents? "Well, that's an intriguing introduction, Ms. Drexler; could you give me a few more details?"

"I'd be happy to…but not over the phone. Let's just say what I have in mind should appeal to you from several directions. You'll have a chance to use your background in petroleum geology as well as your experience as a private investigator. Still interested?"

"You've certainly piqued my interest, Ms. Drexler. I---

"First condition, Mr. Scott: you'll need to call me Mercy."

"Turnabout is fair play, *Mercy.* You need to call me Cort."

She chuckled, "Deal! Could you come by my office today? I'll explain what I'm doing and we'll have lunch at the Petroleum Club. Would 11:00 a.m. work for you?"

"Works for me; I'll see you at 11:00 a.m."

"Do you know where my offices are located?'

I silently laughed to myself. "As a matter of fact, I do. Everyone in the oil business knows you're on the top floor of the old Colorado National Bank building at Seventeenth and Champa. That's still correct, isn't it?"

"Yes, that's correct, although it's been renamed the First Colorado Energy Bank building. I'm looking forward to meeting and talking to you."

I'd never met Mercy Drexler, but like most people connected to the Denver oil business, I was familiar with her story. She'd graduated from Colorado School of Mines with a PhD in geological engineering, gone to work for Amoco, and after a rapid ascent through their engineering department, left to start Siren. The company had hit it big in Wyoming in the mid-nineties and Mercy had parlayed her oil and gas successes into a multi-faceted conglomerate with real estate, banking, Denver urban renewal projects, construction, and some other investments. She even had a minority interest in the Colorado Rockies baseball team. Everything she touched turned to gold.

In the process, Mercy Drexler had become one of the city's most generous philanthropists, supporting causes large and small. According to what I'd read, her time and effort contributions were nearly as valuable as her cash.

How do you dress to talk business and have lunch with a billionaire? I knew the Petroleum Club had a dress policy including a jacket, although they no longer required a tie. That was a good thing. I had very few ties left from my days in the corporate world and I tried to avoid places requiring the damn things, reserving them mostly for weddings or funerals.

I settled on a pair of tan slacks, a blue, button-down collar shirt, and my trusty navy blazer. I brushed my Bass Weejuns, pulled on a pair of black and burgundy argyle socks, and checked out the result in the floor length mirror. Good enough! My girlfriend, Lindsey Collins, would be pleased--probably astounded.

The clock read 9:54 a.m. I had time to give Linds a quick call and tell her what was up. She's a crime scene technician and DNA testing supervisor for the Arapahoe County sheriff's office. I'd met her during the murder investigation of my first client as a PI. Unbelievably, during that investigation, my girlfriend at the time, Gerri German, was also murdered. Lindsey's immediate boss, George Ivins, the Arapahoe sheriff's lead homicide investigator, helped me run down the gang of scumbags who'd murdered Gerri. Meeting Lindsey had been totally serendipity, but a blessing I had come to recognize.

In the aftermath of that horrible time, Lindsey, George Ivins, and my best friend Tom Montgomery from the Denver Police Department had supported me and kept me sane, although not sober.

She picked up on the second ring. "Hey, Linds, what's happening?"

"Hey yourself, sleuth, this is a pleasant surprise! You don't usually call me at work."

"Yeah, I know, but I wanted to tell you I'm going downtown to meet Mercy Drexler. She wants to talk about a job."

"Who's Mercy Drexler? That name sure sounds familiar."

I laughed, "Just Denver's only female billionaire!"

"No kidding? And she wants to hire *you*? Damn! You *swore* you were done with the gigolo bit." I could picture the silly grin spreading across Lindsey's face.

"Well, maybe just one more time--if the money's right, of course." I laughed and heard Lindsey do the same.

"Okay, but don't enjoy yourself too much. Will you be back for dinner?"

"I plan on it, although she's buying lunch at the Petroleum Club, so I probably won't be too hungry. Why don't we just go over to Pradera Country Club for a salad and glass of wine? That okay with you?"

"You bet…I like the view from their deck. I know it's only May, but it should be warm enough to sit outside. Are you coming home first or should I meet you there?'

"I should have plenty of time to come home."

"Okay, thanks for the call; see you later."

# CHAPTER TWO

I backed my Corvette out and waved at the neighbor lady who was walking her giant Doberman on the path toward the open space behind our houses. The damn dog was big as a pony. I considered putting the top down, but regardless of what Lindsey had said, it was still a little cool.

I hit the media button on the sound system, pulled up a bluegrass album by Trampled by Turtles, and cruised slowly through the subdivision. Although I continued to keep an office in downtown Denver, I enjoyed the fifty step commute from the kitchen or deck more than the fifty mile roundtrip from Parker to downtown.

Traffic was heavy but moving and I made good time. Using the E-470 express toll road and I-25 put me in the parking garage at 10:42 a.m. I had eighteen minutes to make the three-block walk to the First Colorado Energy Bank building; no problem.

The original building had been constructed in 1915 as Denver's and Colorado's premier regional bank. The Ionic columns fronting both Champa and Seventeenth Street set it apart from the high-rise metal and glass boxes stretching up and down Seventeenth Street, the Wall Street of the West. Originally four floors, the top had been popped during the renovation and a fifth floor added. The new fifth floor now housed the offices of Siren Exploration & Production. The bank occupied the first floor, mezzanine, and two basement levels. The third and fourth floors were offices, many of which were leased to independent oil and gas exploration companies.

Inside, I glanced at the monumental murals on the façade of the mezzanine which depicted the Plains Indians. The murals had been a Great Depression era WPA project and I'd read the story of how they had been lovingly restored. Mercy Drexler had financed their restoration and received numerous awards from the Denver and Colorado Historical societies for leading the effort.

The elevator doors slid open on the fifth floor; I was facing a floor-to-ceiling glass wall separating the elevator foyer from Siren's reception area. The glass was covered with laser-engraved oilfield scenes: old time derricks, bull wheel pumps with wooden walking beams, modern rigs, and pumping units. I wondered if they were by the same glass artist who'd done the windows and doors of the spa room in my house.

An efficient-looking receptionist wearing a single ear headset raised her head at the gentle chime that sounded when I opened the door. "Good morning, sir. You must be Mr. Scott; right on time for your 11:00 o'clock appointment." The digital clock on her credenza read 10:59 a.m.

I smiled and said, "You win the prize; I'm Cort Scott; I'm here to see Ms. Drexler."

She returned the smile. "Yes sir, I'll ring for Mrs. Simmons; she'll escort you to Ms. Drexler's office." She touched the keyboard, waited a couple of seconds, and said, "Mr. Scott is here." She closed the intercom call, looked up, and said, "She'll be right out."

Everything seemed very formal; more so than Mercy Drexler had sounded on the telephone. A stunningly attractive, well-dressed black woman, probably a thirty-something, emerged from the hall, strode toward me, and offered her hand. "Good morning! I'm Janelle Simmons. Thank you for coming *and* for being on time. Ms. Drexler appreciates promptness."

I took her hand, noting the firm grip and the warmth of her skin. "It's a pleasure to meet you, Janelle. Lead the way." I thought I'd try the first name only approach.

She turned and led the way down the hallway. As we walked, I noted the well-appointed space: each office had a window to the hall as well as an exterior window with a view. The interior spaces looked like filing and conference rooms. I remembered my first year at Shell Oil when I'd had a windowless interior office the size of a broom closet with a rubber-tile floor and metal furniture. I'd made a childish drawing of a four-pane window with a potted plant on the sill and stuck it on one of my walls. The district geologist I worked for hadn't been pleased.

At the end of the hall my escort opened the door to a corner office, stepped to the side, and said, "Mercy, Mr. Scott is here." It was the first time I'd heard a first name used; I took it as a good sign.

I stepped inside a surprisingly Spartan, moderate-sized corner office with modern wood and metal furnishings: a rather uncomfortable looking chrome and leather couch in front of the table-style desk, and a round conference table with four chairs. There was no corner post to block the magnificent view of Longs Peak through the floor to ceiling windows.

Mercy Drexler was standing in the middle of the room, near the couch; she took two strides forward and extended her arm. "Hi, Cort, it's good of you to come! May we offer you something to drink: coffee, juice, water, or something stronger? We have most everything, I'm sure." She also had a firm, warm grip.

Mercy was medium height and weight and attractive: maybe five-five and a hundred and thirty pounds, curly, coal-black hair, brown eyes, and a broad smile showing a mouthful of nice teeth. Her appearance matched her anchorwoman voice. She was wearing tan slacks, a long sleeve, black silk shirt, and a pair of brown-patent pumps with low heels. Mercedes Drexler looked like a person comfortable in her clothes--and her skin.

I returned the grip and replied, "Nice to meet you, Mercy; maybe just some water--for now."

She shot me with her index finger and thumb, "Got you covered." She turned to Janelle, "Would you be so kind?"

Her assistant nodded and left without speaking, leaving the door open.

"Well, come in, come in! Have a seat." Laughing at my hesitation and pointing toward the couch, she said, "It's a lot more comfortable than it looks."

She was right, the couch wasn't bad. I sat near the end so I could use the side table for my water. Janelle returned carrying two large glasses with ice. She placed one on a coaster near my right elbow; the other on Mercy's desk who said, "Thanks, Janelle." Simmons left and, this time, closed the door behind her.

I glanced around and said, "Nice digs; great view of the mountains."

"Yes, it's remarkable to have any view at all considering all the high-rise buildings. Luckily, they're aligned just right to leave an opening to see the mountains. I thought about that a lot before I agreed to purchase the building and add this floor. But, if you don't mind, I didn't invite you here to discuss the view; I've got a business proposition for you."

So much for small talk.

"Cort, what do you know about Siren Exploration & Production…and me? Did you do any research?"

Luckily, her question didn't catch me totally off guard. After her call and before stepping in the shower, I'd done a Google search: found Siren's website, clicked on "Management," and then on CEO and Chairperson, Mercedes Drexler.

I pondered what I'd learned before replying. My first thought was she didn't look 54, her listed age. Her profile and curriculum vitae were impressive: undergraduate degree summa cum laude from Colorado School of Mines; PhD thesis on stimulation of non-traditional oil and gas reservoirs; Wyoming District and then Rocky Mountain Division production manager for Amoco; vice president of the national Society of Economic Petroleum Engineers.

She'd left Amoco in 1992 and formed Siren E & P with five million dollars from a stock offering. Less than a year later, the company sold a drilling prospect to her old employer for a 12,000-foot wildcat in the Green River Basin of southwestern Wyoming. Siren had been "carried," in the deal, meaning they didn't put up any money for a twenty-five percent interest in the first well. They would have to pay their twenty-five percent share in any subsequent wells on the huge lease spread--nearly five hundred thousand acres in the prospect.

As the old saying goes, "The rest is history." That first well, the Amoco #1-25 Federal GRB, was completed producing five million cubic feet of gas per day. At the time, natural gas was selling for about $1.25 per thousand cubic foot which equated to over $6,000 revenue a day. But production was limited due to a lack of pipeline capacity. Two years later, a gas pipeline was completed to carry Wyoming and Rocky Mountain gas to energy-starved northern California and the Pacific Northwest. By that time, twenty wells had been drilled and completed. Whale Field, as it had been named by Wyoming, was destined to become the biggest onshore U.S. gas field drilled in more than fifteen years. With the pipeline in place, natural gas prices had climbed to $4.15 per thousand cubic foot; Siren's twenty-five percent interest in the producing wells was bringing in over two and a half million dollars a month. The stock had surged from its $1.00 per share offering price to nearly twenty dollars a share.

While still on Google, I'd leapfrogged around to get an idea of what Mercy's net worth might be. She was the largest individual shareholder in Siren as well as being the 100% owner of numerous other assets: a drilling company with five rigs; an oil well service company; three ranches in Wyoming and two in Colorado; plus some downtown Denver office buildings, including the one we were sitting in. She had founded First Colorado Energy Bank and was Chairman of the Board. I had multiplied numbers until my eyes began to cross, finally settling on a net worth somewhere north of two billion…with a capital "B."

Now, I studied her carefully as I replied, "Well, I Googled you and got some information; there's quite a bit on the internet. Pretty impressive--which makes me wonder what you might need from me?"

Picking up her water, she stood and walked from behind her desk taking a seat at the opposite end of the couch. "I want you to be my bodyguard."

I was disappointed. "I'm sorry, but I don't do that kind of work. I investigate criminal activity related to the oil business: I look at shady operators, crooked deals, fraud, oil field theft, stuff like that. I'm not hired muscle; I haven't done it and don't want to."

She smiled and said, "Don't dismiss it out of hand just yet; there's more to it. I told you I had something that would appeal to your petroleum geology background and I do. Want to hear the rest?"

I sighed but said, "Why not; it's your office."

"Good! Okay, here goes: As you well know, Gerri's Dream Field, the gas field your friend Gerri German discovered, was the tip of the iceberg for the Green River Basin. It was just a big buried sand bar, twelve thousand feet deep and over-pressured, but it was a 'conventional' reservoir--nothing exotic. It didn't need to be fracked; you just shot some holes in the casing and stood back.

"But when I, or I should say 'Amoco,' drilled the discovery well for Whale Field, it was a completely different animal. It's a whole bunch of individual thin sandstone layers, as many as twenty or twenty-five of them, scattered up and down over almost a thousand feet of drill hole. *I* was the one who figured out a way to conduct multiple frack jobs and get all those individual zones opened up. Before we developed the technique, an operator could only frack one or two zones and had to produce them completely to depletion before going back in to frack another two or three zones. My frack innovations allow an unlimited number of zones to be fracked and placed on production right from the start."

I interrupted, "Mercy, I'm fairly familiar with all this; I don't want to seem rude, but what's your point?"

She blinked a couple times and paused before continuing, "My, my…a little impatient are we? Okay, here's the deal: the biggest oil and gas resources in the U.S. are now *horizontally* drilled, shale plays. I've figured out a way to run multiple frack jobs *in a horizontal hole*. What's more, I've patented the technology and started my own service company to run the jobs using *my* proprietary information. In essence, no one else can use this technology! I can charge whatever I like for the service, but what I'm really after, what I'm going to *demand,* is a royalty on every single well I frack!

"And here's where it goes off the charts--I intend to travel to every damn oil producing country in the world, give them a dog and pony show on what I've got, and then tell 'em if they want to use it, they've got to come to me with royalty assignments in hand. Cort, if I can pull this off, I'll have a royalty interest in nearly every new well drilled anyplace in the world!"

I was staggered by the audacity and scope of her plan. If she could, indeed, "pull it off," it would be like someone had patented the idea of an automobile and collected a fee on every car ever built. I asked, "Where does a *bodyguard* figure in this? Why are you talking to me?"

Her friendly demeanor and smile faded and her tone sharpened, "I've made five presentations so far: four to US exploration companies who are big time horizontal players and one to the national oil company of a European country. I gave only a barebones outline of the technology and you could practically hear the wheels turning in everyone's brains during the concept phase; they were already figuring ways to adopt--or more accurately stated--*steal* the technology. I would finish up each presentation by showing them copies of my patents and warning them not to try and go around me. Then I'd hit them with the proposal.

"And that's when, as my father would've said, 'The shit hit the fan!' Cort, you could literally feel the resentment, I'd even call it *hate*, emanating from some of them. Within two weeks of the last presentation, I started receiving threats and--

I interrupted, "What kind of threats?"

"Some were financial, you know what I mean: 'you can't do that'; 'you can't patent something like that'; 'you'll be sued in anti-trust actions'; the sort of stuff you'd expect. But then it got personal. I've received two untraceable faxes threatening my life."

I nodded and said, "I can understand why you'd be worried, but I need to ask again: Why me?"

"Because I checked you out from several angles and came to the conclusion you're *exactly* who I need. You're a knowledgeable, technically oriented geologist who's been successful, found production, *and* you ran your own company. Now you're making a name for yourself as a PI and, according to some people, have been involved in some damn tough scrapes.

"I don't know exactly what caused you to take up the PI business, but I know you got off to a rough start when Gerri German was murdered. You tracked down her killers and sent every one of them to prison or death row. I also know you had an ownership position in Mountain West Gas Exploration, the company she founded, and a share of Gerri's Dream Field which would have made you a multi-millionaire. But instead, you sold or assigned everything to charities or universities.

"Basically, I've got it on good authority you can be a hard-ass, but are better known as a wise-ass. Does that about sum it up?"

I was forced to laugh; I took a sip of water to gather my thoughts. "You do your homework, Mercy. Mind if I ask you who you've talked to?"

"I've talked to a bunch of people, but always confidentially. I *will* tell you I've spent a lot of time with your buddy, Tom Montgomery, from the DPD. I met him through the chief of police who's a friend of mine. Tom's the one who recommended you for this."

"Good to know, but I'm still not clear where my geology background and supposed 'technical skill' come into play? If I would accept the job, I don't want to just stand around in the corner trying to look tough."

She nodded and said, "If you're as sharp as I suspect, you'll be a quick study on the science of what I'm doing. After you pick it up, we'll be making 'team' presentations of the technology; you'll be right beside me--not 'standing in the corner.' I'll feel safer, you'll be doing your job, we'll be partners, *and* it would get you back in the game, so to speak. Plus, I think it'll be a lot of fun and we'll make a *ton* of money to boot." She smiled at the last.

I considered her words before saying, "I'm not sure I want to 'get back in the game.' At this stage it's not much of a motivator. But I've gotta ask, How much money is a 'ton'?"

She smiled, "For starters, I'll put you on a retainer at $15,000 a month plus expenses. If the company--Frack Focus Inc.--makes any 'sales' during the first six months you're on board, I'll assign you one percent of the company's share. Since I'm asking for a one percent royalty for the company, *your* share would be one percent of one percent…that's one hundredth of one percent; it's 'point' zero, zero, zero, one. That doesn't sound like much, but to put it in perspective, if you'd had that deal on the Bakken play in North Dakota, you would have already collected over $9,000,000 because they've just produced their one billionth barrel of oil! Of course, the damn Saudis are trying to drown the world in crude; oil prices are a third of what they were last year. That won't last forever though, thank God!

"But, if you can find a calculator with enough digits, multiply the Bakken production by all the oil shale basins in the world--getting the picture, Cort?"

The numbers were shocking. I said, "My old friend, Hedges, along with almost every farmer I've ever met, says 'If it looks too good to be true, it probably is.' And this looks too good to be true. What's the downside?"

She laughed out loud. "Well, the deal is off if somebody kills me! And the same thing applies to you--of course if you're dead, who cares, right?"

"When do I start?"

Mercy leaned across the couch and offered her hand, "If you're armed, you start as soon as we walk out the door and go to lunch."

We shook hands.

# CHAPTER THREE

We entered the lobby of the Anaconda Building and waited in front of the express elevator for the Petroleum Club on the thirty-seventh floor. The doors slid open and we stepped in. As they started to close, an arm thrust inside and banged against the bumpers. The doors retracted and a heavyset man barged into the car.

"Thanks a lot for holding the car, although if I'd known it was you, Mercy, I probably would have waited for the next one." The guy's voice was heavy with sarcasm. He was wearing a well cut, obviously expensive, dove-gray suit, a white shirt, and a pearlescent silver tie. His shoes looked expensive too.

"*Always* nice to see you too, Guilford." Mercy's tone matched the new passenger's in sarcasm.

I assumed from the unusual name the newcomer was Guilford Rockson, founder, CEO, president, and chairman of Rockson International. I knew him by reputation only and that wasn't exactly sterling. His company was known for cutting every corner it could and spending almost as much time in court as it did drilling. Regardless, Rockson had grown from a small contract driller to an international production company. They'd managed to sign lease concessions and production-sharing contracts with several Asian and African countries and were rumored to be pursuing similar arrangements with some of the smaller national oil companies in the Mideast and Eastern Europe. They'd been early players in horizontal natural gas drilling and, at last count, had become the largest independent gas producer in the U.S. They'd recently announced moving their head office to Houston, so I was surprised to encounter Guilford Rockson himself in a Denver elevator.

Rockson gave me a quick once-over, turned to Mercy and said, "You come down off your fuckin' high horse yet? You get over that bullshit about wantin' a 'royalty' for fracking a goddamn well?"

I started at the profanities and watched Mercy's face color. She stared back at Rockson before replying, "I guess everything I've heard about you is true, Guilford. You really are a pig--and that's probably an insult to a good pig. You know, I regret having even shown you my methodology. *I* have the final say on which companies I work for and you can be sure you're *not* going to be one of them. Too bad, too…all your horizontal plays scattered around the world would benefit, but that's not going to happen."

Rockson bristled, leaned forward, and hissed, "You bitch! We'll see about that. I'm goin' to--

I arm barred his chest and pushed him back a couple of steps. "That's enough! You need to back off a couple notches, pardner."

Rockson looked surprised, but blustered, "Who the hell are you? You ain't got no stake in this! This bitch is trying to extort money from--

I slammed him against the elevator door. "*I told you to back off!* Ms. Drexler and I are having lunch at the Petroleum Club and unless you want to have your prime rib sandwich served through a straw, I suggest you keep your voice down and maintain a civil tongue. I'm Cort Scott by the way; I work for Ms. Drexler, so I *do* have a stake in this."

Rockson seemed to settle. I took my hand off his chest and stepped back beside Mercy. He surveyed me carefully for a moment and said, "I've heard of you, Scott. You're the washed out geologist who got rich off your dead girlfriend's gas discovery. Now you're running around saying you're some kind of detective or some such bullshit. I've got half a mind to--

I retraced my step to get up in his face. "You're right about one thing, Rockson--you've got half a mind. Now, like I said before, '*back the hell off!*' We're almost to the Club; when the door opens, you need to step out and not look back. We're going to our table and enjoy a nice lunch. I'm not one to make idle threats, so listen up. If you *ever* address Mercy Drexler like you just did, I'll be coming to see you. If I have to do that, I'll kick your ass so far up between your shoulder blades, you'll have to take your teeth out to shit! Got it?" I grabbed him by the shoulders and spun him just as we arrived at the 37th floor. The door opened and I shoved him out.

The girl at the reservations stand jumped as Rockson stumbled out. He had to catch the podium to keep from falling. I heard him mumble, "single's table" as he rushed into the Front Range Room, turned right, and continued to the twelve-place table in the north end of the room reserved for lone diners.

We stepped up and Mercy said, "Reservation for Drexler." The girl nervously flashed a smile and said, "Yes, of course, Ms. Drexler; nice to see you again. I have your regular table."

Mercy returned the smile, "Thank you, Willa." The hostess picked up two menus and led the way to a round four-top in the southwest corner of the big room. There were two place settings arranged side by side with our backs to the room to take advantage of the unobstructed view of the Front Range.

As soon as we were seated and Willa departed, Mercy began laughing. I could see she was struggling to stifle herself. Her face contorted and she brought both hands up to cover it. Laugh tears welled up as she gasped, "Oh my God, Cort… '*take your teeth out to shit!*' That's the funniest thing I've ever heard! Where in the world? Did you *really* say that? Oh my God! Did you see the look on his face? I'll bet no one has spoken to Guilford Rockson like that in thirty years! Thank you *so* much! I knew I was hiring the right man. That calls for a celebratory drink for sure; what'll you have?"

Her mood was infectious and I laughed myself. "It's another 'Hedge-ism' from my long gone and dearly-departed friend. He had a saying for almost anything; some of 'em didn't make much sense, but they were always funny and strangely appropriate. I'll just have a beer, a Bud, if that's all right."

She giggled again. "Of course it's all right; I'm having a glass of chardonnay, a 2009 Jordan. They keep a case or so around for me."

A waiter appeared and Mercy ordered the drinks. She looked over each shoulder before quietly saying, "You know Rockson has a reputation for getting even. I'd keep an eye out and be careful for a while if I were you."

"I'll do that. He's kind of rough around the edges isn't he?"

"I guess that's a nice way to put it. Do you know his story?"

The drinks arrived and the waiter poured my beer in a tall lager glass before I could stop him. I prefer it out of the bottle. I raised the glass, tapped it against Mercy's, and said, "Here's to 'getting back in the game', I guess. No, I don't know much about Rockson other than he's rich as Croesus and becoming a big player worldwide."

She sipped the wine and nodded her head in silent appreciation. "He's a devious bastard from the original school of hard knocks; started out as a roughneck in southern Illinois and worked his way up to toolpusher on one of Charlie Rexall's rigs. The first thing you know, he married Rexall's daughter, Helen. She was probably twelve or fifteen years older than he was and ugly as sin; had a face that would make a train take a dirt road. Old Charlie knew what was going on, but he was just so damn glad to get rid of her, he never said a word. It lasted about seven or eight years, until about a year after Charlie died. Rockson was running the company by then and when Helen inherited everything, he did all he could to piss her off. He was openly campaigning for a divorce and eventually she gave in.

"He went to a bank, mortgaged the company, gave her several million in cash, and promised her a share of the profits for twenty years. She agreed, gave him the divorce, moved to Santa Barbara, and has had a series of 'boy friends'…and I do mean *boys*…ever since.

"Rockson started taking working interest positions in the wildcat prospects he was drilling by giving the operators a discount and the lucky bastard started hitting. Eventually, he bought some more rigs, moved into the Rockies doing the same thing, and kept finding oil. He hired some geologists and began generating his own prospects, concentrated on natural gas, and figured out horizontal drilling was the way to go. Long story short, he's gotten rich, expanded all over the world, but has about tapped out the gas plays. He desperately wants to get in the shale oil plays, but that requires horizontal drilling *and* multiple frack jobs…my technology.

"The very first presentation of my new technologies was to his general manager and we were just getting started on the proposal stage when Rockson flew into their conference room. He must have the room miked because he'd obviously been listening. He raced in yelling and cussing about how he wouldn't stand for it; how he'd sue me on all kinds of restraint of trade issues, plus a whole bunch of other bullshit. When he finally shut up long enough to catch his breath, I dropped the fact on him that *everything* was patented and copyrighted and he couldn't do a damn thing about it. I thought he was going to have a heart attack right on the spot. Today is the first time I've seen him since; it doesn't look like he's cooled down much."

I took a pull on my beer and asked, "Do you think he's the one who threatened you?"

She thought for moment before answering. "I don't know. Like I said, the physical threats have been anonymous."

"What's your gut feeling?"

"Frankly, even as much of an ass as Rockson is, if he was going to threaten me, I think he'd tell me face to face…like in the elevator. But he's a hard guy to figure and there's no telling what is in his mind. I heard a rumor he was even getting involved in all kinds of weird military stuff."

That got my attention, "What do you mean?"

"Nothing concrete, but a friend of mine told me Rockson has a small ranch down in Texas, somewhere close to Dallas I think, and he was fortifying the place and stockpiling all kinds of military equipment. My friend said Rockson was 'preparing for when the government tried to take over' or some sort of BS like that."

The waiter reappeared and we ordered lunch: a tuna melt for me and a Monte Cristo sandwich for Mercy. I turned to glance the length of the room and saw Guilford Rockson sitting alone at the head of the singles table. He was looking our way and talking on a cellphone. "I've already agreed to take this on, Mercy, but I'd like to ask a couple more questions; that okay?"

"Sure, ask away."

"First, I have a girlfriend, Lindsey Collins. She's a crime scene investigator in the Arapahoe County sheriff's office. If it's convenient and she can get the time off, I'd like to take her along on some of our trips. If you'll pardon the pun, will that fly?"

Mercy grimaced at the pun, smiled, and said, "No problem; Siren owns a Gulfstream G280; we can seat eight to twelve for domestic flights or six with sleeping berths for international travel. Lindsey would be welcome anytime, plus it might be nice to have another woman along. What else?"

"Kind of relates I guess; I haven't seen any mention of a husband or significant other in any of the stuff I've read about you. Is there one?"

Another smile, "There's no husband and, currently, no 'significant other'. No real reason, I just never seem to find the time and now, believe it or not, it's tough to meet men. Frankly, I'm too rich and that makes me intimidating, I suppose."

I was modestly surprised at both her answer and frankness. "When do classes start?"

She raised her glass and we clinked. "Tomorrow. We have four days this week and that should be enough time to get you up to speed. We'll be flying to Houston first thing Monday morning and meeting with Shale-Ex in the afternoon." She double clinked, "Here's to a great relationship; I'm looking forward to it!"

## CHAPTER FOUR

When we finished lunch and turned to leave, I looked toward the singles table. There were five or six men seated at one end but no sign of Rockson. We exited the Petroleum Club, took the elevator to street level, and strolled two blocks up Seventeenth Street toward the Equitable Building where my office is located. I asked Mercy if she wanted me to walk the additional block to her office, but she declined. We shook hands and I confirmed I'd be in Siren's office first thing next morning to start my instruction on the revolutionary fracking techniques we'd be presenting.

At Champa Street, I turned and walked the half block to my parking garage. Since I'd been slacking off on morning runs and needed the exercise, I decided to take the four flights of stairs to my reserved parking spot.

As I exited the stairwell on the fourth floor, somebody clocked me. He knocked me back through the doorway onto the landing. I saw points of light and flashes, but didn't go all the way down. I got my left arm up just in time to block another blow from the leather sap my assailant, a big white guy, was swinging. He managed to hit me on the forearm and it felt like my arm muscles were paralyzed. He moved in for another shot, but that was a mistake. I threw a short right uppercut and caught him in the pit of the stomach. His breath left in a rush. He gasped and staggered backward into the garage.

I stepped through to finish him off, but that was another mistake and this time it was mine. Another attacker, a black guy this time, was standing outside the door. He grabbed my arm and spun me to the side. I noticed the back of his right hand was covered with vitiligo spots…white splotches. The first asshole recovered and had time to smash me up against the cement block wall. My left arm was dead; I couldn't summon the strength to break away from the second man and he kept pulling me off balance. After that, it was ugly. The original slugger moved in and deployed the sap on my shoulders and neck. Every blow rocked me to the core. As I started to sag, they both began throwing punches. My last conscious thought was that these bastards are pros; they know what they're doing.

*****

"Just keep still, don't try to get up, we'll be at the hospital in under a minute." The disembodied voice sounded like it was coming from an echo chamber miles from wherever I was. I opened my eyes enough to make out a couple of faces floating above me and realized I was inside a moving vehicle, an ambulance. I could hear the siren whooping as we approached an intersection, but it quickly began to wind down and I felt the wagon decelerate and turn. The voice, a little closer now, said, "Hang in there, buddy. We're at emergency. We've got you. You're strapped on a gurney; we'll wheel you out and get you taken care of."

I blinked, trying hard to focus, but wasn't doing much good. I had the coppery taste of blood in my mouth. I ran my tongue over my lips; they were split and crusty. I used my tongue on my teeth. It felt like they were all in place.

The ambulance stopped, the doors opened, and the gurney lurched into motion. The legs snapped down and we started rolling. The sunlight was bright in my eyes as the EMTs rolled me the short distance to the automatic doors at the entrance to emergency. I heard the whoosh of the doors and the ceiling appeared along with more faces. They all seemed to be talking at once.

"BP?"

"One-twenty-four over eighty-nine."

"Pulse?"

"Seventy-eight."

"That's damn good, all things considered."

"Yeah, somebody worked this guy over pretty bad."

One face came into clear focus, a woman with blonde hair and a purple streak through it. She actually smiled and said, "Hello there, are you with us?"

I licked my lips and swallowed, trying to get a little saliva going. My mouth felt like the inside of a wool sock. I managed to croak, "Yeah, I'm in here."

Miss Blonde and Purple smiled again. "Good! That's good! My name's Mickey. Can you tell me yours?"

"Scott. Cort Scott. Where am I, Denver Health?"

"That's right, Mr. Scott. Very good! We've got some tests to run, but it doesn't look like you've got a concussion. Let's get you in, clean you up, and we'll see what we've got. Okay?"

I tried to return the smile, but it hurt too much. I whispered, "Not much choice; would you call Lieutenant Montgomery, he's DPD Homicide?"

"*Homicide?* Is there something we should know?"

"No, he's a friend. There's no homicide to report…yet."

I opened my eyes to Tom Montgomery standing beside my hospital bed, a concerned look on his face as he stared across the room. I said, "No luck for you, pardsy; the will doesn't kick in unless I'm dead."

Tom shot me a dirty look, but the concern left his face. "Shit! And just when I was getting ready to turn in my papers. How ya feeling? What the hell happened?"

"I feel like hammered dog shit. What time is it?'

Tom glanced at his watch, "Ten after six; you've been out almost three hours. Hospital called me around three. I got here in fifteen minutes, but they'd just put you under to stitch up your face. Like I said, what happened?"

"I got the crap beat out of me! What the hell does it look like happened? I gotta call Linds; I was supposed to meet her at Pradera. She's gonna be--

"She's here; just went down to the coffee shop. She'll be right back."

"How'd she find out? You call her?"

"Yeah, I called right after I got here and they told me you'd be okay, but sleeping for a few hours. She got here as soon as she could. She's pretty shook up. Listen, dammit, tell me what happened before she gets back. Who stomped you?"

"I don't know; they didn't give me a business card and there wasn't a lot of conversation. It was a salt and pepper team: one black, one white. I don't know who they were, but I've got a pretty good idea of who sent 'em."

Tom raised his eyebrows, "Well, that'd be a good start. Who've you pissed off now?"

"I had a run-in with a guy named Guilford Rockson in the Petroleum Club at noon today. Doesn't prove anything, but I saw him talking on a cell while I was still having lunch and then two guys jumped me right after as I was going to my car."

"Why'd you get into it with him?"

I shifted positions and started to rise up on my elbows. It felt like someone hit me between the shoulders with a shovel. "Ouch! Son-of-a-bitch, that hurts! Raise the bed, would you?" Tom grabbed the bed control and raised the back to about thirty degrees. "I'm getting ready to start a job for Mercedes Drexler and she and Rockson have some 'issues.' She and I were going to lunch at the Club today and ran into him in the elevator. He started bad-mouthing her and I stepped in and shut him down. She told me later he's famous for getting even."

Tom didn't say anything for a moment or two, nodded in acknowledgement, and muttered, "Well, I guess it's my fault then; I recommended you to Drexler. She knows the chief, asked him for a recommendation on a bodyguard, and he asked me. I talked to her two or three times about you. To tell you the truth, I wasn't taking her too seriously about being in any kind of physical danger; guess I was wrong about that, huh?"

I shook my head, which hurt too. "I don't know about her, but it's not your fault, Tom. Actually, I appreciate it. It could be worth a lot of money."

"I gathered that. After she explained it to me, I told her if I knew anything about the oil biz, I'd quit DPD and do it myself. Hell, it only took her about an hour to quit laughing."

The door opened and Lindsey walked in carrying two Starbucks cups. Linds looked surprised to see me sitting up in the bed. She rushed in, put the coffees on the bedside table, and took my hand. I saw her eyes glisten, fill, and run over. The tears slid down her cheeks. "Hey sleuth, you don't look so good."

I tried a smile but that hurt too. "Well you do; I'm glad to see you."

"I got here soon as I could after Tom called. We've been watching you sleep for an hour or so; I'm glad to see you coming around. Rough day at the office, huh?"

I squeezed her hand and she squeezed back. "Well, it wasn't really 'in the office' but close enough I guess; couple of sluggers jumped me. I didn't manage to do much to stop 'em."

Lindsey used her free hand to wipe away her tears. "This didn't have anything to do with your meeting, did it?"

"I don't know. I'm not ready to make the connection, but there might be something there."

Tom interjected, "Save it for your statement; this isn't the time or place. I'll get a technician in here and we'll tape what you've got to say."

Linds pointed at the coffee, "Tom, I got you an Americano just like you ordered. Would you mind taking it out in the hall and giving us a second?"

Tom shot her a look but nodded, picked up the cup, and left.

I must have had a questioning look on my face. As Tom pulled the door shut behind him, Lindsey stared at me for several seconds before saying, "If that rich bitch you went to see has anything to do with this, I'll stomp a mud hole in her ass and walk it dry!"

# CHAPTER FIVE

Wednesday morning as Lindsey watched from the small visitor's couch, I shuffled to the bathroom and changed out of the hospital gown into the clothes she'd brought. My body felt like somebody had been pounding on me which, of course, was the truth. I studied my face in the mirror and thought about the old gag line of 'you should see the other guy.' But, it wasn't all that funny. Five butterfly stitches over my right eyebrow, three more beneath the eye, purple bruises at the hairline on the right temple and on the side of my neck. My entire face was puffy and swollen; my right ear was red. When I slipped out of the 'show my butt' gown, I could see more bruises and abrasions across my shoulders and along the collar bones. No wonder I was sore.

I was glad Linds had brought a button-front Hawaiian shirt rather than a golf polo. Getting my arms up and through the sleeves would've been a problem. I pulled on my pants, buttoned the shirt, and returned to the room to join her on the couch where I could get my socks and shoes on.

The door opened just as I painfully finished and a nurse entered pushing a wheelchair. "Okay, up and around, I see. Good! Ready to get out of here, Mr. Scott?"

"No offense, but that's an understatement! You 'all have been exceedingly kind, but I gotta say I prefer my own bed and, quite frankly, either my own or Lindsey's cooking. Plus no more 12, 2, 4, and 6 a.m. bed checks…I hope!"

The nurse chuckled and said, "Yep, I hear you. Well, let's go; you've completed all the paperwork and I assume you've got a pain prescription. Right?"

"Yes, I'm all set. Let's blow this pop stand." She turned the wheelchair, I got in, and she pushed me into the hall. We'd already had the argument about release procedures and Denver Health's requirement that *everyone* had to use a wheelchair. Truth be told, I wasn't unhappy about it, although I'd put up a strong defense to protect my manly image. I was pretty sure Lindsey knew the truth.

Linds said, "My car is parked in the circle driveway outside the patient discharge door. When we get downstairs, you'll only have about twenty steps."

I nodded my acknowledgment. "Sounds good. We need to stop by the garage and pick up the 'Vette. With the stick shift, it might be easier if you drive it and I'll drive your car."

"That's already been taken care of; George Ivins drove me downtown yesterday and I took it home."

"Ah, sweetie, that's great! Thanks!"

"I think among George, Tom, and I, we've got you covered. Tom called that Drexler woman on Monday night and told her what happened. She had a bouquet delivered to the house this morning that would look good around the neck of the Kentucky Derby winner. Goddamn thing fills half the living room." Lindsey's voice didn't sound pleased.

"*That Drexler woman*'s name is 'Mercy', Linds. You can't blame her for what happened. She's just trying to hire me; she can't control what other people do."

"She could've done a better job explaining the dangers of what you were getting into. I can't help it, Cort. I don't like this one bit and I'm afraid it's the tip of the iceberg."

We reached the elevator; the nurse pushed the call button and gave us both a quizzical look. "You must live an interesting life, Mr. Scott."

*****

When we arrived home, I felt like I'd been gone for two weeks not two days. My head had cleared considerably during the ride and I noted the bank thermometer in downtown Parker read eighty-four degrees. I told Lindsey I'd like to sit outside on the deck for a while. She gave me a disgusted look, but agreed. I said, "I think I'll change into some shorts and try to tan up these white legs. I feel like another of Hedges' old lines, 'Are those your legs or are you riding a chicken?'"

I finally drew a grin with that, but she said, "*I* think you should get into bed and rest, but you never listen to me anyway. If we're going to sit outside, what would you like to drink?"

"What I'd *like* is probably different from what you'll give me. To save an argument, how 'bout an Arnold Palmer?" Another disgusted look, but she nodded.

When I managed to shuffle outside, she'd arranged two chaise lounges side-by-side on the east end of the deck. They would be in the sun for half an hour or so before being shaded by the roof. The table separating them was covered with drinking glasses, newspapers, our cell phones, and sunscreen. I said, "Wow, this looks great, babe! Just what the doctor ordered, so to speak. I assume you're joining me?"

"Soon as I change clothes; I'm taking the rest of the day off and told George I'd call about tomorrow."

"I'll be fine. You can plan on going to work tomorrow."

"We'll see in the morning. That's the last word on the subject for today, got it?"

I nodded and lowered myself gingerly onto the chaise as she turned and marched into the house. She had just slid the screen shut when my phone quacked--I needed to think about changing the ringtone. "Cort Scott."

Mercy Drexler's voice sounded strained. "Cort, you're home! How are you feeling? I'm so sorry for what's happened. Is there anything I can do for you?"

"Hi, Mercy. Thanks, and thank you for the flowers." I'd seen the bouquet in the living room and Lindsey had been right--it was over the top. "I'm kinda stoved up for the moment. We just walked in and I'm gonna take it pretty easy for a day or two. Sorry

I'm missing out on Fracking 101; are you still going to Houston Monday?"

"No, I decided to postpone until you're back. With what happened to you, I've made a decision to be a lot more careful. If somebody absolutely can't wait to see the presentation, they'll have to come to our offices…at least until you're back up to speed."

"Are you sure you still want to hire me? My track record isn't looking too hot at the moment."

Mercy sighed. "I'm more determined than ever. Besides, I thought we already had a deal; we shook hands on it, remember? Do you think Rockson set this up?"

"I don't know, but he'd be at the top of the list. I don't know who else I've pissed off recently, although it could be a long list." I tried for a laugh, but didn't get a result. "Does it sound like something he'd do?"

"Like I told you, he's got a reputation for trying to get revenge. But, to tell you the truth, this seems like a big step even for him. Are you going to go after him?"

It was my turn to sigh, "I don't have much to go on, but I'll tell you this: he's not the only one who likes to get even. I'm sure as hell going to look into him."

"Be careful, Cort. If there's anything I can do to help, let me know. You can call whenever you feel up to it and we'll get started on the project, but there's absolutely no hurry."

"Thanks again, Mercy; I'll be in touch."

Lindsey slid the door open and stepped out on the deck. She'd changed clothes all right…into a bikini that left little to my imagination. I gave a low whistle, "That outfit's not very conducive to a restful afternoon, young lady! How am I supposed to relax and recover with you parading around practically naked?"

She gave me the lascivious grin that always stirred me up. "At least those assholes didn't bother your vision. But cool your jets; I'm just going to sit here and read and wait on you hand and foot. There'll plenty of time for other stuff when you're more 'up for it' so to speak." She laughed, did a couple of dance steps, and gracefully took a seat on her lounger. "Who was on the phone?"

"Mercy Drexler; she just wanted to check in."

Lindsey's smile faded. "She's not pressing you to come to work is she?"

"No, nothing like that. Like I said, she was just inquiring about how I'm doing."

"I don't want her bothering you. You need to tell her next time she calls. You shouldn't be thinking about working until you're completely healed."

I reached across the table and put my hand on her arm, "Don't worry; I'm fine."

She gently moved her arm away and fixed me with a stare. "We'll see."

# CHAPTER SIX

I managed to "recover" enough by Saturday night for some physical therapy due, in no small part to Lindsey's efforts, I'm sure. Tom Montgomery and Lee Anne LeBlanc, his new bride and a Denver cop, came by Sunday afternoon. It was unseasonably hot reaching the mid-eighties by 1:00 p.m. Linds brought a pitcher of margaritas out to the deck and as she poured into the salt rimmed glasses, glared at me. "This is your pain medication for today. Got it? No more pills!"

Tom grinned, "I see Nurse Ratchett is carefully monitoring your meds, huh?"

I faked a grimace, "Yeah and I'm suffering like hell."

Lee Anne snorted a laugh, "Oh poor baby! Don't forget we've heard about you trying to parlay the slightest injury into 'sympathy sex' before. I think you've played that card too many times, Cort." Lindsey didn't say anything but nodded her head vigorously.

The tone of Tom's voice changed. "I went over your statement about your beat down and then took a look at the video tapes from the garage's surveillance cameras. The tape for the stairwell on the fourth floor was black. Whoever got you planned it out beforehand because they put a piece of duct tape over the camera lens. Nobody monitors those cameras in real time; there are too many of 'em. It seems to me it was an awfully short length of time for Rockson to set something like that up from when you had your dust-up before lunch 'til you got mugged. How would he even know where you park let alone which floor? You sure you haven't stepped on some more toes recently? You have a knack for it."

I said, "Look Tom, I gave you everything I know. I don't recall pissing off anybody other than Rockson. Like I said, I saw him talking on his cell during lunch; he could have been setting something up then. He acknowledged he knew who I was. I've been parking in that garage for five years and my assigned space is up on four so it wouldn't have been that hard to figure, plus he's got 'resources' if you know what I mean."

Tom nodded, "Yeah, I get it, but I gotta tell you we don't have enough to even question him. I need something solid."

"Luckily, I'm not you."

"I don't like the sound of that. You bust his chops and you'll likely ruin any case we might put together. If it *was* him, he's proven he's got muscle available on short notice. You're liable to get your ass stomped…again."

"We'll see, I guess."

*****

Lindsey closed the door behind Tom and Lee Anne as they left, turned, and gave me a hard stare. "You're planning on going after this Rockson guy, aren't you? I can tell by your voice and the way you look. You didn't hear one word of what Tom was saying, did you?"

I shrugged.

"Damn it, Cort! Do you ever think about me…about how I feel, about what you mean to me? You can barely lift your arms over your head and you're already planning some kind of crazy payback! Can't you let Tom handle it for once?" I'd never heard the shrillness in her voice before.

Lindsey and I had been together since the year after Gerri German was murdered. We'd gone through a couple of tough scrapes together and had settled into a very comfortable relationship. We even used the "L" word. Maybe "love" was what she was thinking now, but it didn't seem like it.

"Tom said he doesn't have anything to go on, Linds. There's nothing he *can* do. If anything is going to get done, I'm going to have to make it happen. I'm not going to do anything stupid. I *do* think about you and care too much to go off half-cocked, *but* we need to get something straight: I'm not going to let this lay. I'm pretty sure Rockson was behind it and I'm going to prove it one way or another."

I'd spoken louder than I'd intended. Lindsey's face reddened and a veil passed over her eyes. She walked past me into the bedroom and through to the closet, closing the door behind her. I wanted to stop her and apologize, but I couldn't. I returned to the kitchen, emptied the last of the margarita pitcher into my glass, and went back outside. Ten minutes had passed when I heard the kitchen door to the garage open and close. I moved as quickly as I could but managed to open the door only in time to see Lindsey's Edge backing out. I didn't descend the steps into the garage; it wouldn't have done any good.

Lindsey had kept her Englewood condo after moving in with me. Periodically, when she needed a little "me" time, she'd spend a few days there. Usually we both benefitted from the time away from each other--and the homecomings were always glorious. This time felt different.

## CHAPTER SEVEN

It'd been three days since Lindsey stormed out; no calls, no emails, no contact. I was sorry as hell and my pride was wounded, but I felt too embarrassed to make the first move. Physically I was feeling much better, even managing a short jog on Tuesday, so I decided to rejoin the living and get started on Mercy Drexler's job. I hoped it would be informal; it had been a long time since I'd sat in a classroom.

"Janelle? Cort Scott calling; is Mercy available?"

"*Good Morning*, Mr. Scott. I'm afraid she hasn't arrived yet. She does an extended workout routine on Wednesday mornings and doesn't usually arrive until about 10:00 a.m. May I give her a message?"

"Sure, would you tell her I'd like to come in tomorrow and get started with my education on the frack techniques? I'm going stir-crazy sitting around the house; I might as well be trying to learn something."

"That's great news! I'm *so* happy to hear you're recovering. Mercy has been completely out of sorts since the incident. Speaking for myself, I can't believe what happened; I'm so very sorry."

"Thanks for that, Janelle. It hasn't been much fun. It'll be good doing something productive, plus nice to see some friendly faces. Tell her I'll be in at 8:00 a.m. tomorrow."

"Of course; see you tomorrow, Mr. Scott."

"One more thing, Janelle…would you mind calling me 'Cort?' We're going to be seeing a lot of one another and I'd be a lot more comfortable. Work for you?"

I could sense a smile as she replied, "Works for me…Cort."

*****

Two days later I was feeling overwhelmed but knowledgeable about Frack Focus and why Mercy Drexler felt comfortable demanding a king's ransom for her company's services. I'd been tutored by a series of the "best and brightest" petroleum engineers I'd ever met. Most were painfully young--compared to me--and universally enthusiastic about their work and the results.

At 3:30 p.m. Friday afternoon, Mercy strolled into the high tech conference room that had doubled as my classroom. She was followed closely by a tall, bookish looking guy wearing khakis and a light blue polo shirt. "Well, Cort, I see you've survived 'Frack 101!' At least, I hope you have…and you're still awake…that's always a good sign."

She laughed and gestured towards her companion. "Meet Clay Webb; Clay's the operations manager for Frack Focus and my right-hand man. Clay, this is Cort Scott. He's going to be joining us, at least for a while, as, let's see…what should we call you, Cort: Head of Security?"

I stood and offered my hand to Webb. He took it with a less than enthusiastic grip. "Good to meet you, Scott; Mercy's told me about you."

"My pleasure." I turned back toward Mercy, "Let's find something a little less formal than 'Head of Security'. That'll just raise eyebrows and suspicions. Why not just something in sales or marketing? That'll lower expectations and maybe keep some creep from watching me too closely."

She nodded in appreciation. "Good thinking--how about 'Business Development?' It covers a multitude of sins and is basically meaningless." She laughed again. "So, do you have questions for us?"

"Mercy, how in the world did you get patents on most of this? Most of the technology has been available and in use for fifty years. What's new about what you're doing?"

She looked pleased with my question. "Everything has always been done in vertical well bores. I figured out a way to get the fracking tools around the corner to horizontal, but more importantly, we literally invented some equipment allowing us to run several frack jobs consecutively. Before, you could only frack one small section of the wellbore, produce it to depletion, and fill the hole up with cement before you could do another section. With my way, the operator gets to produce the entire length of the horizontal hole right from the start.

"Instead of producing a few tens or maybe hundreds of barrels a day, new horizontal wells with my fracks can produce *thousands* of barrels. It completely changed the economics of drilling shale oil wells. But the most important thing was…I was first in line at the patent office to submit all the drawings and specs. I got patents issued before anybody else thought about trying."

I air toasted her with my coffee cup. "Okay, here's to being first in line. Next, what does a typical horizontal producer cost to drill, frack, and equip? And, how long to get your money back?"

"Well, first of all, there's no such thing as a 'typical' producer. You know as well as I every well is different: different depths; amount of shale section; number of natural fractures; angle of penetration; even the downhole pressures. For the Bakken producers in North Dakota, costs can run anywhere from eight to twelve million dollars. Using simple math, if we say a completed well costs eight million, at $100 a barrel it would take about 100,000 barrels of oil to get a payout. But crude prices have gone in the dump; they're about a third of that currently, so an operator needs anywhere from 250,000 to 500,000 barrels to get their money back. That's a hell of a lot of oil and we don't have enough production history to know for sure every well is going to make that much.

"Still, with the old way of doing things, a well might make a couple hundred barrels a day, so you were looking at four or five years before it became profitable. With my technology, it's not unusual to produce 5,000 barrels a day! You might have your money back in five or six months!"

I whistled, "I get it--a game changer!" Turning to Clay Webb, I asked, "When did you get involved?"

Webb glanced at Mercy before replying, "Relative to Siren Exploration and Production, I'm new. I came on board when she formed Frack Focus Inc., about eighteen months ago."

I nodded, "Where were you before that?"

"I was the Rocky Mountain Division manager for Halliburton."

That made sense; Halliburton was the biggest hydraulic fracturing company in the world. "I'd guess this is a little more lucrative, right?"

Webb nodded, "Yeah, it's a good deal."

Mercy Drexler looked at her watch and asked, "Cort, would you mind if we cut today's session short? I'd like to talk to you about something that's come up.  Clay, would you excuse us?"

Webb shot her a glance and said, "Sure, I'll see you soon, Scott."  He turned on his heel and left.

Mercy stared at his back as the door closed behind him, "Let's go into my office; I'm probably paranoid, but I have it swept for bugs every couple of days. We do the same in this room, too, but only once a month."

Back in the corner office, she motioned me toward the couch and took a seat at her desk. "Cort, have you done any more thinking about who mugged you? Or, more to the point, who ordered it?  Do you still think it was Guilford Rockson?"

I rubbed the shoulder muscles at the base of my neck. They were still sore. "I don't know. I have to believe he had something to do with it, although it seems way too obvious. Why do you ask?"

She exhaled slowly in a long sigh. "I've received another threat. It said, 'Let what happened to Scott be a warning. Unless you back off, you could be next.' Unless you or the cops have released the information, it had to come from someone involved."

I sat up. "Nothing's been released. How did it show up; any way to trace it?"

"A text; it was on my *private* cellphone this morning when I got up…about 5:30 a.m. I forwarded it to Tom Montgomery; he said it was from some kind of a disposable smartphone and there's no way to trace it. I didn't know there were such things! What's the fucking world coming to!" The F-bomb coming from the normally demure and low-key woman jolted me.

"5:30 a.m., huh? You're an early riser. Was there a date and time stamp?"

"Yes. Supposedly, it arrived at 3:17 a.m. I turn that phone off at night, so I didn't hear anything."

"How many people have your private cell number?"

"Not many--fewer than twenty-five. Mostly people from here at the office plus a few select friends."

"That's not such a long list; it shouldn't be too hard to start checking it out."

"*GOD!* I can't imagine someone I know, or trust, would be involved."

"Don't start jumping to conclusions. From everything I keep seeing in the news lately, apparently it's not difficult to hack into all kinds of data bases for personal information including telephone numbers."

Mercy slumped in her chair and sighed again. "I don't know if that's good news or bad news. I'd hate to think someone I know would try to hurt me, but it scares me almost as much to think virtually anyone can get my information."

I nodded, "I hear you. Do you still want to go to Houston?"

"Yes, I do! I've scheduled meetings for Monday and Tuesday. We'll fly down Sunday night and meet with Shale-Ex at 9:30 a.m. Monday; I've also set up a Tuesday meeting with SUDPET. That's the new national oil company of the Republic of South Sudan. The old country of Sudan split up with mostly Muslims in the North and a secular government in the South. I'm not sure how everything is going to work, but I *do* know the South has an absolute *ton* of reserves, they're new to the business, and it would be a great opportunity to get in on the ground floor. I don't have a time yet, but we'll meet at our hotel. Does all that work for you?"

I considered for a few moments and said, "Yeah, it shouldn't be a problem as long as you think I'm ready."

She smiled, "I *know* you'll be ready and Clay will make most of the presentations so you'll have a chance to observe. Do you want to ask Lindsey to come? It'd be fine with me."

"Probably not this time; it'd be kind of short notice and she's always really busy at the beginning of the week."

Mercy Drexler raised her left eyebrow slightly.

# CHAPTER EIGHT

The jet eased down at the Lonestar Executive Airport in Conroe which made for a short trip to the Hyatt Market Street hotel in The Woodlands. A stretch Lincoln limo pulled up a few steps from the airplane's stairs; the pilots quickly offloaded our bags and the limo driver stored everything in the trunk. The entire technical presentation was in Clay's laptop computer. It was a lot different from the "old days" when I'd had to lug around map cases with several pounds of rolled maps.

Half an hour later we were in the lobby lounge of the Hyatt, checked in, bags in the rooms, and relaxing over drinks: a Jordan chardonnay for Mercy, an Owen Roe pinot noir for Clay, and a bottle of Bud for me.

I asked Mercy, "Do you know Marty Gear? He's the head honcho for Mountain West Gas."

She nodded as she sipped her wine. "Sure, I've known Marty forever! Some of the acreage in our Whale Field play was adjacent to Gerri's Dream. Why?"

"I saw him Friday after I left your office…first time in months…and we had a drink. We talked about a lot of stuff but the most interesting thing he said was that he needs to diversify his production from over ninety percent natural gas; he wants to get into some international shale oil projects. But here's the bombshell, he told me he's thinking about merging Mountain West with Rockson's company."

Mercy choked on the Jordan, sat bolt upright, and set her glass down with a bang. "That's terrible! Marty Gear is one of the good guys and Rockson's a prick! As you well know!

"I think it's just a ploy by Rockson to get my technology. Even though it differs slightly for gas reservoirs than for oil, the general techniques are the same. Frack Focus has just signed a deal with Mountain West to frack some of their horizontal gas wells over on the Western Slope of Colorado. If Rockson gets a close-up look, I'm betting he will try to change things just enough to get around my patents and then use it in his shale oil projects.

"*Son-of-a-bitch!*

I'll have to figure a way to get out of my deal with Marty!" She picked up her glass and drained it in one gulp.

Clay Webb stared at his boss in amazement. Apparently, he had never seen her go ballistic before. "Holy Cow, Mercy, you don't really believe Rockson would merge his company just to get at our technology, do you?"

She signaled the waiter for another round and shot Webb a murderous look, "You're damned right I do! I think Guilford Rockson would make a merger with the devil to get back at me *and* get access to our proprietary information. I think we need to be more careful about who we show our technology to and even *more* careful who we sign contracts with."

She turned to me, "Would you have a talk with Marty about this? Maybe you can convince him not to make a deal with Rockson."

After finishing the beer, I said, "I can talk to him, but I'm not sure if it'll do any good. In some ways, he's been mad at me ever since I opted not to join him and help run Mountain West."

As the new round arrived, Mercy picked up her glass and looked across it at me. "That's not the answer I was hoping for, but it can't hurt to try. I'd appreciate it."

I offered her an air toast and nodded.

At 9:00 a.m. the next morning we were ushered into the main conference room of Shale-Ex where we met their entire executive staff: President, VP of exploration, VP of production, VP of land, COO, and CFO. As soon as we'd exchanged handshakes and business cards, Roger Hampton, the president, slid a thick folder across to Mercy. "There are all the signed nondisclosure agreements and proprietary information requirements you've asked for, Mercy. Man, getting a look at this stuff is like trying to infiltrate the Pentagon! You're really being extra careful, aren't you?"

She carefully checked the signature page of each document before smiling and replying, "Probably tougher than cracking the Pentagon, and, yes, we're being careful. This is so big, I've *got* to be careful…and, frankly, so will you if go with us and utilize our technology. Believe me, if anyone, and that includes companies we work with, tries to go around us, we'll drag them through every court in the land and sue them for every nickel they've got."

Hampton frowned, "Wow, seems a little harsh, but I can't say I blame you. What are you going to leave us to review after your dog and pony show?"

Clay Webb interrupted, "Nothing, everything is on my laptop; I'll be projecting onto your screen and you can take notes if you wish, but we're not leaving any exhibits. If we make a deal going forward, you'll receive information pertinent to specific projects on thumb drives. In return, you'll have to furnish us a list of all your current lease holdings so we can keep track of what you've got and where we'll be using our processes."

Hampton frowned again but slowly nodded in agreement. "Can't say as I like it, but if this works as well as you say, it's a game changer. Okay, we agree. Let's get started.

"One question first, if you don't mind?" He switched his gaze to me. "Why is Cort Scott here? Your card says, 'Business Development Consultant.' What the hell is that?"

Before I could answer, Mercy spoke. "Cort is an integral part of our team, Roger. This is his first meeting, but once he gets familiar with the presentation, he's going to be doing a lot of the presenting instead of me.

"As well as being a geologist, he has a strong background in corporate governance and industrial security. He's just one more level of protection for the company, our product, and me. Ultimately, he'll be liaison among our partners and us…that's protection for you too."

Roger Hampton stared at me while considering her statement. He smiled humorlessly, "No insult intended, Mercy, but that's the damndest bunch of gibberish I've ever heard…you'll notice I said 'gibberish' instead of bullshit…wouldn't want to offend anyone. Okay, whatever you say. There must be a good reason for him being here; I'll just have to trust you on that. Let's get started."

So much for being something more than hired muscle to sit around and look tough, I thought I'd better get up to speed technically as soon as I could so I'd be able to add something to the presentations. I also knew I'd been out of the game long enough that a lot of the current players wouldn't know who I was. In this role, I didn't know if that was good or bad.

*****

Two hours later, as we all stood to shake hands, I felt better about my ability to contribute. I'd actually been able to answer a couple of questions posed by Shale-Ex's VP of exploration. I hadn't needed Clay Webb's or Mercy's help. Frack 101 had served me well.

Roger Hampton was friendly as he said, "Sorry about questioning your role, Cort. I faintly remember hearing your name, but I thought it had something to do with the investigation into Wildcat Willie Davidson's murder. I didn't realize you were a technical guy."

I said, "Frack Focus's technology has application all over the world and I wanted to get in on the ground floor. When Mercy asked me to come aboard, I jumped at the chance."

Hampton said, "I can see why! Anyway, I'll look forward to working with you. From what I've seen here, I'm pretty sure we'll be joining up."

Back at the Hyatt, we freshened up and met in the restaurant for lunch. Mercy was ebullient in her praise of Clay Webb's presentation and then turned to me. "Cort, you were great too! When you jumped in to answer those questions on the application to exploration plays, all the tension went out of the room. I think Roger actually likes you now! And that's saying something because he's a real curmudgeon on most things. I think we'll make a deal with them and that'll be *big!* They've got leases in practically every shale oil play in the U.S. and are expanding all over the world." She raised her water glass to each of us and we toasted. "One hell of a start, I'd say! We'll have another toast when we get some drinks; where the hell is the waiter, anyway?

"And, by the way, I loved the way you danced around his question about Davidson's murder investigation. You didn't deny anything, but changed the direction into something positive about Frack Focus, Inc. Pretty cool!"

My memory flashed back to Wildcat Willie Davidson's murder. Unraveling that mess had damned near gotten me killed. I still suffer a twinge in my hip now and then where I'd been shot by a man I'd considered a friend. Discovering my "friend" had been involved with Davidson's daughter in a plot to kill him and take over his company had been a shock to my system. Remembering how Lindsey's DNA work had broken the case wide open made me think of her; made me wish we could solve the problem between us.

"Yeah, I guess I handled it okay. How do you know about the Davidson case?"

Mercy spoke quietly, "Tom Montgomery told me quite a bit about it; said you and your girlfriend were the ones who solved it. I'm looking forward to meeting Lindsey; she must be quite a gal."

I thought, yes, she is…I'd look forward to "meeting" her again, too.

# CHAPTER NINE

Meeting SUDPET the next day was "different." Their three-man contingent all held the title of "Minister of…" something or other. One was Minister of Science and Technology and one was Minister of Economic Development. The last one, Akabile, was the Minister of Defense.

I didn't know why the Minister of Defense was present, but as it turned out he was also South Sudan's "deputy" prime minister and would have the final okay on any deals we might make.

Akabile, who apparently went by just the one name, was an impressive looking and sounding man. Elegantly clothed in a well cut, probably Savile Row suit, he was a tall, athletic looking gent who spoke with a cultured English accent that had to have come from a U.K. boarding school. As we met and were introduced, he exhibited exquisite manners and acted the part of a gracious host, even though we were on "neutral ground" in the hotel's business conference room.

The other members of his delegation spoke reasonably good English, so we didn't need an interpreter. Unfortunately, almost immediately, it became painfully obvious none of them knew the slightest thing about oil and gas exploration or production. Fifteen minutes into Clay's presentation, Akabile interrupted and asked everyone but Mercy to leave the room. The other two ministers, Clay, and I spent ten uncomfortable minutes staring at one another in a hallway outside the conference room.

I tried to start a conversation by asking how much production South Sudan currently had and what their plans for expanding exploration were. I drew blank stares for a few moments before the Minister of Economic Development began trying to explain about how their inventory of producing properties was incomplete and he couldn't provide an accurate figure. I could understand that and tried to ease the tension by asking the "scientist" about their drilling plans. He, too, appeared perplexed by the relatively simple question. He finally attempted to answer by saying they were in the process of conducting a "worldwide" search for experienced oil people to assist them in their plans.

I should have kept my mouth shut but couldn't. "So, how many geo-scientists does your ministry currently employ?"

After several more seconds, he sadly shook his head and said, "We do not have any government scientists."

I was surprised at the answer. "Well, do you have a department of oil and gas? Who oversees your properties?"

Again, he shook his head. "No, we have no such department. Minister Akabile oversees everything."

Minister of Defense Akabile was the man talking to Mercy in private.

I decided I didn't need to know anything else. We lapsed into silence once more.

The door to the conference room burst open and Minister Akabile strode out, motioned to his lackeys to follow, and marched toward the lobby elevators without saying a word. Mercy followed, placed her finger across her lips, and shook her head. She remained standing in the doorway until the SUDPET representatives had entered an elevator and the arrows indicated they were on their way to the guest floors.

Clay said, "What was that all about? Did I say something wrong in there?"

Mercy shook her head, started to smile, thought better of it, and said, "Let's go to the coffee shop; maybe they'll put a shot of something in my coffee." She started walking and we followed in her wake.

At an outside table on the patio surrounding a central fountain, it turned out she wasn't kidding. She ordered three café amarettos with additional shots on the side. Turning to Clay, she said, "You need to run back in there and grab your laptop. We don't want it sitting around."

Webb jumped up and left. Turning to me, she said, "A goddamn *shakedown*! That impressive looking son of a bitch tried to shake me down!"

I wasn't too surprised considering the conversation I'd *tried* to have with the other representatives. "What'd he want?"

"Clay will be back in a moment and I'll fill you both in." She gulped down half a glass of water.

Webb returned with his laptop just as the coffees were delivered. Mercy sipped a small amount of the steaming brew and poured in the amaretto shot. It filled the cup to the brim; she leaned over and noisily slurped directly from the cup.

Webb stared in amazement, "Jesus, Mercy, what happened in there?"

Now, with color returning to her face, she angrily said, "Welcome to the big leagues, Clay. Welcome to the world of international business and finance. It was a goddamn kickback scheme. That fucking *minister* of defense, Akabile, is nothing more than a well-clothed, goddamn gangster! He was no more interested in looking at our presentation than flying to the moon!

"As soon as you left the room, he looked at me and said, 'For one million U.S. dollars, I will sign any agreements you want and we will be in business together. After you fracture oil wells in my country, I want one percent of your gross revenues paid every quarter.'" Mercy picked up her cup and took a huge drink. "I probably looked as shocked as I felt and I guess I started to stammer. I think he took that as a good sign because he actually reached across the table and tried to take my hand. I jerked it back and said, 'There's no way. There are laws against that sort of thing. The U.S. government would crucify me if I even considered something like that.'

"He just smiled and said, 'No one else, including your government, would ever know about it. It would be a private deal between us, Ms. Drexler.' I'm telling you guys, if I'd had this coffee, I'd have thrown it on him! Right in his goddamned face, I tell you!" There was no disguising Mercy's disgust and anger. "Did you learn anything from the other two?" She tried the coffee again.

I said, "No, not really. From what you said, I think they're probably just 'yes' men for Akabile. It turns out the country doesn't even have an oil and gas department; they don't know how much production they have; they don't have any geologists or engineers…nothing. Are you sure these guys even represent SUDPET…or, for that matter, South Sudan?"

Mercy shook her head, "I don't have a clue. About a year after their civil war ended, I contacted the prime minister's office because I saw an announcement in World Oil that all hostilities had ceased, there was a settlement in place, and South Sudan was 'open for business.' It took several weeks before I heard anything back--an email from Akabile saying he was in charge of all foreign relations having to do with business agreements. He talked about how important it was to *immediately* start developing the country's natural resources and he wanted to meet as soon as possible. *Shit!* I think I let dollar signs cloud my vision. I should have known better; we should have checked everything out before agreeing to meet.

"You know I had to clear this meeting with *our* damned State Department, but they said go ahead and wished me good luck! Lots of goddamn help, right?"

I sipped the fortified coffee, it was good. "You can't blame yourself. How could you have known? Plus, when was the last time the State Department ever did a good turn for a private company, especially an energy company? So what did you tell 'the minister'?"

"I told him *if* he was truly a representative of his country, they could forget *ever* having access to our technology and I would be sending a full account of his actions to our state department…as if they will care!

"And you know what…the bastard just sat there and smiled at me! Then, he said, 'There are many means to an end.'"

She finished the coffee, grabbed Clay's shot, and tossed it off, "I'm calling the pilot; let's get checked out and go to the airport. We can be back in Denver in two hours; maybe we can get some work done this afternoon."

## CHAPTER TEN

I struggled through an early morning run and was just letting myself in the patio door when I heard the phone. I gasped, "Cort Scott."

"'Morning, Cort, what's the matter, you sound terrible... sorry to bug you so early, but we've got a new problem." Mercy's voice sounded strained.

I faked a laugh and tried to control my breathing, "Well, good morning to you too. I was just coming back from a run; pretty rough. It was only the second time out since I got stomped; sure doesn't take long to get out of shape. What's the problem?"

"It's a new one on me. Some crazy-sounding outfit calling itself *Stop Fracking Us* has sent me a 'manifesto' full of all kinds of demands and threats. Some of it is pretty scary. Could you take a look at it and tell me what you think?"

I had regained some breath, "Sure. How'd you receive it?"

"Would you believe *snail mail*? It's been so long since I've actually received anything on paper I almost didn't open it. I figured it was just some kind of junk mail."

"Any return address? Where'd it come from? What kind of envelope?"

I could hear her rustling papers. "It's in a legal size, manila envelope and I'd guess the return is probably a fake. It says P.O. Box 666, you know...the sign of the devil...Devil's Lake, North Dakota, but the postmark is from Centennial, Colorado."

I thought about that for a moment and said, "Don't handle it any more than you have to, use latex gloves or tweezers or something, scan it, and email a copy to me. Get everything into a plastic bag like a big Ziploc. Does it have printed postage or stamps?"

"Stamps."

"Good. We might catch a break if somebody licked 'em."

"What should I do with it?"

"Centennial is in Arapahoe County, so I'm going to call my friend George Ivins in the Sheriff Department. He's a homicide investigator, but he directs the forensics lab. He'll send someone by to pick it up. In the meantime, I'll read the copy you email me and get back to you."

Mercy sounded more relaxed after hearing a plan of action. "Thanks, Cort. After the fiasco in Houston with that asshole, Akabile, I've kind of been on edge anyway, and now this! I hope this is all worth it!"

"I'm sure of it, Mercy. We'll get it sorted out and go on about our business."

My first self-serving thought was this is the opening I needed to get a conversation started with Linds. Since she handles the DNA work for the sheriff's office, she'd be involved and since it was my "case," we'd have to talk. My second thought was what a chicken shit I'd become. Why didn't I just man up and call her?

I decided to delay the inevitable a little longer and call George. He picked up on the third ring and I could picture him at his desk: he would be leaned back in his chair with his long legs crossed and draped over the corner. His black Justin Roper boots would be highly polished and the creases in his whipcord uniform pants would be sharp.

"Hey, George, been a while! How're you doing?"

"Howdy, Cort. I'm doing okay, I guess. Better'n you and Lindsey, I hear."

That dropped my spirits; Lindsey must have confided in him about our problems. "Yeah? What do you hear?"

"Well, that'd be talkin' outta school, wouldn't it? She told me you're having a rough patch and she was livin' in her own place for a while. She said you're back to acting like the Lone

Ranger, trying to get revenge on the guy who got you thumped. That right?"

"Pretty much I guess, although I'm kinda over that part of it. Something else has come up with my job for Mercy Drexler and I think some of it is landing in your bailiwick."

"Oh yeah; how's that?" I heard George's chair squeak and his boots hitting the floor.

"Mercy got a letter--she called it a 'manifesto'--and it's got some demands and threats along with a bunch of other bullshit about her fracking company. It's got her shook up and she wants me to take a look at it."

"So how does that involve me?"

"It was mailed from Centennial…Arapahoe County. You're still a sheriff there aren't you?"

George chuckled, "Wiseass! You know I am, but I'm also still working homicide. Tell me why I should have an interest?"

"Because you also run the forensics lab and I need to have this thing checked out for everything from prints to DNA. Since it's Arapahoe County, I know Linds will be handling that part of it, but I don't want to just cold call her about something like this; you know, like it's strictly business.

"Look, George, I need to tell her I've been wrong, and I will, but I'm looking for a way to ease into it. I was hoping you'd be willing to grease the slide a little."

George chuckled again but humorlessly, "No chance, bucko! You got yourself into this mess and you need to get yourself out. For Christ sake, just call her! She's been in a blue funk for two weeks. Tell her you're an asshole…which you are, by the way; tell her you're sorry…which you are, by the way; and get back to normal. You're both too damn proud for your own good! Now, where is this 'manifesto' thing?"

I slumped into one of the leather chairs in my rec room. He was right of course. I was looking for an easy way to get back with Lindsey without having to admit I'd been wrong about going after Rockson. "It's in Mercy Drexler's office, Frack Focus, Inc., downtown. It's the old Colorado National Bank building at Seventeenth and Champa."

I took a deep breath, "Okay, George, you got my attention. I probably needed a wake-up call and you've given me a good one. I'll call Linds soon as I'm done with you, in fact, you could just transfer the call. I'll get this taken care of."

George cleared his throat before saying, "Hang on…and good luck."

I took another breath and exhaled deeply as I heard the electronic beeps and clicks and then the buzz signifying a ringing phone.

"Hi Cort; George said you wanted to talk to me. I'm glad to hear from you."

That was a good beginning. "Hi Linds, it's great to hear your voice. Look, I'm not good at this; I haven't had a lot of practice at apologizing or trying to make things right. I'm just going to say I'm sorry for how things played out; how we got to this point. I *wasn't* thinking about you when I said what I said--you know, about going after Rockson. It sounded a lot worse than I intended and I've felt horrible since the moment you pulled out of the garage. I miss you, Linds. I hate not having you here. Like I said, I'm not very good at this…I don't know what else to say. Can we talk it through?"

I heard a catch in her voice when she whispered, "Oh, Cort, I've been miserable too! I shouldn't have flown off the handle like I did. I knew you were hurting and just wanted to lash out at whoever did that to you, but you seemed so intent on revenge or getting even it scared me to death. I probably overreacted too; I'm sorry."

"Linds, come straight home after work. I'll order a pizza and crack open a bottle of O'Reilly's pinot. We'll drink the whole damn bottle, hit the hot tub, and then settle our differences…if you know what I mean."

She gave a throaty laugh and I could see the lascivious grin spread across her face…the one that always got me stirred up. "I'll look forward to a reunion, sleuth; see you about six-thirty!"

If it hadn't still been morning, I would've opened a beer to celebrate; coffee would have to do. I went to the kitchen and poured a cup, added a dash of Bailey's French Vanilla creamer, and returned to my office. I opened my email and found the scanned "manifesto" from Mercy. The page count read ten pages; it seemed like a lot.

It took thirty-five minutes to read the rambling, at times incoherent, document masquerading as an indictment of the oil and gas business and companies like Frack Focus, Inc. For the most part it was "generic", covering every company and segment of the industry, including state and federal regulatory agencies. It didn't offer any solutions or compromises but apparently sought to "punish" the companies and everyone associated with them. The threats included sabotage and "worse", whatever that meant. It was poorly drafted and stupid, but I was afraid to not take it seriously; it was written in the same vein as the Unabomber's diatribes and I remembered how those had played out.

I called Mercy and asked if she'd had any incidents of sabotage on the frack jobs they'd performed. She thought about it for a while but told me she didn't think so. I said, "This looks more like a 'cease and desist' than a threat to go after you for past sins."

She replied, "That's not a lot of comfort; we're not going to stop operating."

I said, "I understand that, but you might want to think about adding some kind of security around your shops and yards. All it would take is some nut job getting inside and putting something bad in one of your pump trucks or sand hoppers. You sure as hell don't need an explosion or unexpected chemical reaction in the midst of a job."

"We already have secure installations. We've got security patrols twenty-four seven at our yards and storage facilities; everything is under lock and key. I don't think anyone could infiltrate those places."

I considered her answer. "That might be the good news *and* the bad news."

"What do you mean?"

"If they can't get to your material and equipment, they might go after people…like you."

"Cort, that's what you're supposed to be taking care of, it's why I hired you!"

"I can't be on guard all the time, Mercy. Has George picked up the envelope yet?"

I could "hear" a smile in her voice, "Well, *George* hasn't, but Lindsey has. She's lovely, Cort; I like her a lot! And, she surprised the hell out of me."

"How's that?"

"As soon as we were introduced, she started telling me she'd probably been wrong about me and what you are doing for me; she said you guys have been having a tough time over what happened in the garage. She said 'you'll get it together.' Is that right? Are you going to be all right?"

"I hope so. I'm a little surprised she said anything; she's not usually so forthcoming. But thanks for telling me."

"You're welcome. I know I'm not the one to be giving advice on such matters, but I sure hope you guys get everything straightened out. You're both too nice to be miserable apart and I can tell you are."

"Thanks again, Mercy. We'll work it out. I'll be in touch."

# CHAPTER ELEVEN

I slowly reread the manifesto looking for any hint as to who might be behind *Stop Fracking Us* but nothing jumped out at me. I had to hope whoever it was might have slipped up in the mailing and left some forensic evidence that would prove useful.

I decided to give Marty Gear a call about Mercy's suspicions that the merger with Rockson was a ruse to get at her trade secrets. After the mandatory five-minute conversation with Peggy Sue Crandall, Marty's administrative assistant of some twenty years and one of Gerri German's best friends, he came on the line. "Hey, Cort…good to hear from you. Don't hear boo for months and now twice in a week! What can I do for you?"

"Well, I wasn't a hundred percent forthcoming with you the last time we talked, Marty. When you told me about maybe merging with Rockson, I think I may have gone into shock. I think he may have hired the sluggers who worked me over."

Marty snorted, "That's ridiculous! Rockson is a lot of things, but he wouldn't be behind an assault! Why would you think something like that?"

I was trying to find a nice way to say it, but couldn't think of anything, "I'm consulting for Mercy Drexler and Frack Focus. She and Rockson are in a pissing match about her refusal to work for him and I was with her when they ran into each other at the Petroleum Club. He was being an ass and I laid hands on him…nothing rough, mind you, but enough to get him to back off. Later on, we saw him talking on his phone and immediately following that, I got jumped.

"Mercy thinks this proposed merger is Rockson making an end run to get at her technology so he can use it without paying the royalty she's demanding."

Marty Gear was silent for several moments before replying, "I'm not so sure you're wrong…at least about the merger. Rockson approached me about doing a deal; said he'd heard I was looking to get into oil and away from natural gas. One of the first things he wanted to know was whether I'd used Frack Focus on any of our horizontal gas wells. I told him we hadn't actually used them, but we'd signed contracts for several wells over on the Western Slope of Colorado. After that, he really started pushing a merger deal."

I digested his answer for a moment. "Marty, where are you on the merger? Will it go through before you frack your Colorado wells?"

"I don't know. It's a complicated deal, although there won't be any SEC problems because he's a private company. If I were to guess, I'd say 'Yes' there's a good chance it'll come together before we're ready to frack the wells."

I hated to say anything, but had to. "I don't think you should go through with the deal. I think Mercy is right about Rockson and he's using you and Mountain West as a stalking horse to get to her technology. If that proves to be true, everything is going to wind up in court and it could go on for years. Everybody loses."

Marty sighed, "It may be too late. There's a breakup fee if either company pulls out without a damn good reason; a *legal* reason. The fee is ten million dollars and, frankly, Mountain West can't afford a 'loss' like that right now. What's more, if I did it, my shareholders would sue me; probably get me kicked out as chairman in the process. I'm sorry, but I just can't do it, Cort."

It was time for Plan "B." I asked, "Would it be possible to delay fracking the wells for, say, six months or so? It might give Mercy time to tighten up her patents; make it impossible for someone to go around her?"

He was silent for a few moments. "I can try, but it's going to be a tough slog. Frankly, Western Gas needs the income from the production increases we'd get. It's the same reason we need a merger with a company who has some oil prospects. We need the income.

"Look, Cort, I'm willing to *try* and stall on both fronts: fracking the wells and the merger. But you need to understand if Rockson gets wise, I'll have to go ahead."

It was my turn to sigh, "I can't ask for more, Marty. Thanks. I'll be in touch and would appreciate it if you'd do the same."

I called Mercy and reported my conversation. She wasn't happy but agreed it was probably the best we could do. "I appreciate your effort, Cort. *Christ!* What a mess! But what do you think of the manifesto…God, I hate giving it a formal name like that! It feels like we're legitimizing it in some way."

"I hear you, but I don't know what to think. If we're lucky, maybe whoever wrote it was just blowing off steam and this is the last we'll hear from them. But somehow I doubt it. I don't want to tempt the lurking demons, but I believe they'll have to try and pull off some sort of 'action'; something to show they mean business."

Mercy's voice was low when she replied, "I hope you're wrong, but I've talked to our security people and told them to basically double up on everything: video surveillance, patrols at our facilities, access checks…the whole nine yards. We're even going to have security teams go out on the job sites with our trucks. I don't know what else to do."

Even though she couldn't see, I was nodding my head in agreement. "I think those are all good ideas. Say, do you have any jobs coming up right away?"

"Yes, we've got a job in North Dakota scheduled for next week. It's a big one, too! The well is a dual lateral: two horizontal boreholes, each extending over five thousand feet in opposite directions from the vertical section. The operator wants to frack four thousand feet on each side which will take over twenty separate operations. We'll be on the well for four or five days; it's a three million dollar job."

I whistled, "You aren't kidding about being big. I'd like to go see it; any chance of that?"

"You don't have to ask; you're part of the company. In fact, let's both go. I've been on several of them although never one this big, it'd be good for me to get out in the field again…get the stink blown off me, so to speak."

I said, "Great, what's the schedule?"

"The job is Tuesday. We can fly to Williston Monday afternoon and stay in our shop there. We built in some nice quarters because there're no hotel rooms in Williston."

"Sounds good; will we leave from Centennial again?"

"Yes, plan to leave about 1:00 p.m. And, Cort, if you figure out anything about who sent that damn manifesto, let me know, okay?"

"Of course, Mercy. Take care and I'll see you Monday."

*****

I felt like a teenager going to his first prom. I couldn't find enough things to keep me busy and my mind off Lindsey's arrival. I spent an hour spiffing up the house, putting clean towels in the bathrooms, and changing the sheets. I wanted everything to be perfect for the homecoming.

At 5:00 p.m., I called Paul's Pizzeria and ordered a large pie: half Canadian bacon and pineapple, Lindsey's favorite, and half "Kitchen Sink"…everything but anchovies for me. They promised to deliver it at 6:30 p.m. as I requested. I threw together a couple of small salads, and at 5:45 p.m. opened a bottle of the pinot noir.

The shave and shower felt good and by 6:20 p.m. I was dressed in golf shorts and one of my Hawaiian shirts. As I emerged from the bedroom, I looked out the dining room window and saw an old Honda Accord with a plastic sign on the roof pull into my driveway. I watched as a tall girl got out, opened the rear driver's side door, and then walked up the front steps with a pizza hot pack. Opening the door before she rang, I said, "Hi, you're right on time."

The girl was older than I'd thought, probably in her twenties, and very attractive. "Well, we try. Wow, nice house! I don't get out to this neighborhood very often. I saw about ten deer up around the corner!"

I smiled and said, "Yeah, they're thick around here. Be careful when you drive out. How much do I owe you?"

She looked at the receipt taped to the box, "$14.99 plus tax, so $15.81."

I gave her a twenty, "Keep it; I appreciate you being prompt."

She flashed a grin revealing a beautiful set of teeth, "That's over a twenty-five percent tip! Are you sure?"

"Absolutely. And if *you'll* be delivering every time, I'll be ordering a lot more from Paul's."

That must have been a little too flirtatious. "Well, you never know who you're going to get. Thanks." She bounced off the porch and went down the sidewalk to her car. Linds had to wait as the old Honda reversed into the street.

I carried the pizza to the kitchen and was pouring wine when she walked in. "Mmm, three of my favorite things: freshly baked pizza, pinot noir, and you…not necessarily in that order!" She set her purse down on the counter and walked directly into my arms.

The embrace and the kiss lingered forever…which was exactly the right amount of time. I didn't want to pull back. Finally, I straightened enough to whisper, "I'm glad you're here. I've missed you."

She sighed and replied, "Let's not do that again. I hated every hour we were apart." We moved to arms' length and stared in each other's eyes for several seconds. "Now, let's eat and drink that wine, I'm starving!"

We clinked glasses and sipped. I got the salads out of the refrigerator, slid slices of pizza onto the plates, and put everything on the table. We sat across from one another and tucked in, everything tasting better than it had in weeks. We didn't say much, just kept looking into each other's eyes. Finally, as we finished our second glass of wine, Linds said, "I met your new employer today. I went downtown and picked up that envelope. I'm sorry I said those mean things about her, she seems nice. I think she's scared."

I killed the bottle into our glasses, "I talked to her this morning and agree…she's worried and I think she should be. There are a bunch of people who are mad at her and she's got something they want. Some of 'em would probably do anything to get her technology. It's going to be up to me to keep her safe. She's got so many facilities and other businesses; that it's going to be a big job. She's a very public figure too; she's not going to want to just lay low."

Lindsey sipped her wine, "So it's going to be a real live 'bodyguard' job, huh? I suppose that means you're going to be traveling with her." She shot me a glance before grinning, "It's okay, sweetie. Now that I've met her, I feel better about everything. I *know* it's a job…and a damn well-paying one from what you said. All that before--it was just because I love you and worry about you; I know you're going to do what you have to. It won't keep me from worrying, but at least I understand. I may even have been a little jealous, if that's the right word, but I don't have the right. You are who you are--and were--long before we met."

I appreciated her words and air toasted her. "We'll make this work, Linds. We'll make it work for everyone. Do you think you'll be able to get any trace from the manifesto or the envelope?"

She wrinkled her brow, "I wouldn't get my hopes up. About all I've done so far is try to lift some prints. There's good news and bad news: there are tens of prints but most are smudged or just partials. We'd have to be lucky as hell to identify anyone; they'd have to be in the system already. And it doesn't look like the stamps will be much help either. They're the sticker kind, not the lick kind, so there's no DNA. We'll keep looking though; we'll go over every page in hopes whoever sent it screwed up at least once."

I shook my head in disappointment, “Crap! I got encouraged when Mercy said they’d used stamps; too much to hope for, I guess.”

She finished her glass, grinned, and said, “You’d better open another bottle of this; we’ll need it for the hot tub!”

## CHAPTER TWELVE

I hadn't been in Williston in several years…before the Bakken shale oil play had changed everything. The last time I'd been here the city had fewer than ten thousand residents; now it was pushing forty thousand. The new airport was unrecognizable from the old strip that had used a couple of Quonset huts for a terminal. The new metal and glass, swept wing design terminal looked as modern as the fifteen or twenty private jets parked on the expansive tarmac.

As soon as we stepped down from the Gulfstream, a silver eight-passenger Hummer with darkened windows pulled up and two men jumped out. The driver remained behind the wheel and the huge SUV idled as the men, obviously ex-military, did everything short of saluting before introducing themselves as employees of Gate Keeper Security, the firm Frack Focus had employed as their primary line of defense. The bulges of holstered guns under their matching dark gray blazers were hard to miss, as were their radio-telephone earpieces and dark glasses.

They'd been well schooled as to who was who; one grabbed Mercy's bag the instant the pilot sat it beside her while the other guard took her arm and hustled her toward the vehicle. I was left to my own devices, which was fine with me. I pulled the handle on my roller, followed to the back of the big truck, and hoisted it inside following Mercy's. She was already inside and buckled up when I climbed in beside her. One of the Gate Keeper guys jumped in the front passenger seat and the other piled into the third seat behind us. The whole operation, including the introduction, had taken less than a minute.

The truck surged forward and we exited through a rolling gate with a military checkpoint-style arm on the outside. The driver spoke into a mouthpiece telling someone we were departing the airport at 15:39 hours and would arrive at the Frack Focus facility at approximately 16:07 hours. I felt like I was back in Bosnia with the Rangers.

At 16:05 hours, according to the digital clock display on the dash, we pulled off the main road and approached another checkpoint gate, this one painted in Siren's aquamarine and white colors. The driver rolled to a stop next to a solid-looking guard shack, lowered his window, and said, "Unit 101, three Gate Keeper personnel, two passengers.  Passenger one is Ms. Drexler; passenger two is Mr. Cortlandt Scott."

The uniform stepped outside carrying a notepad computer which he handed to the driver who, in turn, passed it back to us. "Please place your index finger in the box next to your picture to verify your identities." We did as instructed, passed the notepad back, and waited as he watched the screen for a few seconds. He flashed a brief smile over his shoulder and said, "Thanks. It's nice to see you again, Ms. Drexler, welcome back! And nice to meet you, Mr. Scott."

Mercy said, "Good to be here. The place is certainly buttoned up tighter than last time.  Is everything going okay?"

"Yes, Ma'am. We've instituted several new things including this checkpoint procedure; we feel pretty good about the security."

She nodded her approval. "That's great. We'll be coming and going quite a lot for the next few days. Will we have to do this every time?"

"Yes, Ma'am, you will. Hope it's not too much of an inconvenience for you."

"Not at all!  I appreciate all you're doing."

The guard backed off, stepped inside, and appeared to swipe a card through a reader. The gate arm instantly rose and we pulled into the yard of Frack Focus Inc.'s Williston facility.

The main floor of the two-story, faux-stone trimmed building was a typical oilfield service company shop. Twelve huge pump trucks were parked in three-across, four-deep rows on the clean and polished stamped concrete floor. Large diameter hoses, six to eight inches, were coiled along the two side walls and a dozen racks across the back wall were filled with various metal valves and fittings. A row of offices extended across the front; an open stairway to the second level was centered in the entryway.

As we stepped inside, Clay Webb descended the stairs. "Hi, Mercy; Scott…How was your trip?" He extended his hand and I took it. "Quite the setup, isn't it? We've come a long way from just opening the gate at 5:00 a.m. and locking it at 8:00 p.m. haven't we?"

Mercy grinned and said, "You've got that right! Sign of the times, I guess, although I'd like to think we can get rid of a lot of this sometime."

The Gate Keeper guys came in with our bags and Webb said, "Put Ms. Drexler's in the owner's suite and Mr. Scott's in the Three Forks room. Thanks, fellas; we'll be eating here tonight so we won't need you until tomorrow morning. It's an early start so you need to be here at 5:30 a.m. and it'll take about forty-five minutes to get to the location. See you then." The security men acknowledged their orders, hauling the bags upstairs, and returning to wish us a nice evening as they left.

Webb waved toward the stairs, "Well, let's go on up. Everything's ready and you'll have time to freshen up before cocktails and dinner." I must have had a quizzical look as he grinned and said, "This probably won't be quite like your typical oilfield shop, Cort. The 'boom' has allowed us to do a few things differently."

Mercy Drexler smiled but didn't say anything.

He wasn't kidding. As I topped the stairs, I'm sure I audibly gasped. We entered on a type of balcony overlooking a room that could've easily been mistaken for a miniaturized lobby in a five-star Abu Dhabi hotel or an exclusive London gentlemen's club. It was three steps down to an intimate, oak-paneled room with ceilings easily fifteen feet high. One wall was all built-in bookcases with a sliding ladder for the upper levels. A solid-looking, granite-topped bar filled one corner. Horizontal, three bottle deep, wine racks lined the walls from each side and liquor bottles of every description were arrayed on diagonal glass shelves crossing the corner.

Two small tables, one square and one round, with leather barrel chairs were in front of the bar. The rest of the room had a variety of furniture, ranging from large club chairs with side tables and reading lamps to love seats and coffee tables. An octagonal gaming table and chairs occupied another corner.

The plush carpeting in Siren's distinctive aquamarine color was bisected by a marble center aisle leading to the bar then bifurcating to each side toward doorways apparently leading to the rear of the floor and building. Webb said, "Go through the door to the right of the bar; your room is the first door…the Three Forks room. I'll be next to you in the Lodge Pole room, then there's a vacant room before the Bakken room--it's the owner's suite. Mercy will be in there.

"At the end of the hall is a conference room which doubles as a dining room. The kitchen is behind it at the back of the building."

I said, "This is spectacular!  What a surprise!"

Mercy laughed sort of self-consciously, "Yeah, probably a little over-the-top, but it's something I felt like doing. The place has actually come in handy; we've had the VP's of production or the presidents of nearly all the major players here at one time or another." She waved her hand in shoo-ing motion. "Go ahead and check out your room, freshen up if you want; we'll meet back here in fifteen or twenty minutes."

I did as instructed, passed through the door to the right of the bar, and entered the first room on the left. Inside, the term "room" didn't do justice to the luxury suite I found. It was comprised of three separate areas: an office-like entry with a desk, small conference table, loveseat, and two visitors' chairs; a bedroom with a king-size bed, night stands, and a recliner with a reading lamp; a bathroom with separate toilet room, walk-in shower, dual sink vanity, plus a walk-in closet with a center dresser. The whole thing looked like something out of *Conde Nast* or *Travel & Leisure.* I could only imagine what the Bakken room, the owner's suite, must look like.

My bag was sitting on a luggage bench inside the closet. I pulled my DOP kit and went into the bathroom to brush my teeth. I put away my clothes and slipped out of the jeans and golf shirt I'd worn for the flight. I selected gray Dockers, a black short sleeve sports shirt, and a pair of loafers I'd thrown in at the last minute.

I walked down the hall to check out the conference/dining room. It, too, was impressive, with a twelve-place conference table, built-in wet bar and large windows at each end of the room…the first windows I'd seen on this floor. I assumed the door at the back lead to the kitchen. Three place settings were at one end of the table, one at the head with another on each side. I could see a bottle of Jordan Chardonnay chilling in an ice bucket, and two bottles of red standing open on the bar.

I returned the way I'd come and reentered the club room. Mercy and Clay Webb were standing at the bar and she smiled as I approached, "Ah, just in time for cocktails. What would you like? We've got most anything from beer to hard liquor plus several wines. I'm afraid it's 'serve yourself' in the bar. The chef is here, but he's busy in the kitchen at the moment and I usually only bring in servers or barmen if we're having eight or ten people."

I slapped my face in mock surprise, "Oh My God! You mean we'll have to take care of ourselves? What the hell's the world coming to? I assume you're having the Jordan chardonnay."

She shook her head, "Saving that for dinner; we're having a 2005 Far Niente. Will that do?"

I laughed; it was one of the finest California chardonnays ever made. "Oh, I guess so."

Webb walked behind the bar, opened a glass-front wine cooler, and extracted the Far Niente with its distinctive and elaborate label. He took a glass from an overhead rack and poured me a generous amount. I made a production out of swirling the light honey-colored wine, checking the nose, and finally hazarding a sip. It was outstanding. "Yep, that'll do!" I exclaimed.

We strolled to the round table and settled into the barrel chairs. Mercy took a sip, savored it, and said, "Well, what do you think of our security setup? At least what you've seen so far?"

"I'd have to say, 'So far; so good' at least as far as your personal protection and the yard and shop are concerned. It might be harder to control what goes on outside your gates though. Is there any way to control access to your materials and chemicals *before* you bring them here?"

She looked at Webb who shook his head and answered, "We haven't gone that far. The frack sand and beads and stuff come in by train. Most of it stays in rail cars in the Burlington Northern facility in the rail yard. BN's put in several additional sidings for that kind of thing, but I don't know how secure their yard is.

"Same thing for the chemicals; they're stored in their rail cars. When we need something, we have to drive our pump trucks and sand transports to the rail yard and offload it directly. I don't think we can do much about the chemicals, but we're looking into having the sand stored here. We've got enough room to build storage sheds and store enough for several jobs."

I nodded, "Sounds like a plan. What about personnel? Who has access to your yard and equipment?"

Webb studied me for a moment before replying, "Everybody has to check in through the main gate just like you did."

I nodded my approval. "Well, all this sounds good. I guess if anything happens on a job site, it would have to come from an external source of some kind. Let's hope for the best…and keep preparing for the worst."

The dinner was as fabulous as the surroundings: a small dinner salad followed by a North Dakota take on "surf and turf"-- an herb-crusted walleye filet beside a petite but thick beef tenderloin. Grilled asparagus and a dollop of au gratin potatoes filled out the plate. The Jordan complimented the fish and an

Oregon Domaine Drouhin pinot noir, followed by an excellent French Margaux Bordeaux, finished out the meal. We had blackberry cobbler and coffee at one of the side tables. Mercy exhaled and said, “I’m off to bed; 5:30 a.m. is going to come around extremely early tomorrow! See you gents then.” We both stood as she excused herself.

Clay Webb said, “I’m following her lead. Tomorrow will be a long day. Goodnight.”

I glanced at the wall clock and smiled, it was 10:37 p.m. Central Time…an hour earlier in Denver. I waited a couple minutes before going to my room. Inside, I kicked off my shoes, lay on the bed, and called Lindsey.

She answered on the third ring, “Hey, sleuth, what’s the haps in wonderful Williston?”

I thought I heard the gurgle of the hot tub and said, “You’re in the spa, aren’t you? You’d better not be drinking up all our premium wines!”

She laughed and said, “From the sound of *your* voice, I think you’re the one who’s been guzzling the grape! Tough duty, huh?”

Caught, I laughed. “You got me, babe. You wouldn’t believe this place out here in the middle of Nowhere, USA. Mercy’s got a damn castle inside a fortress, complete with gourmet food and fine wines. There were just three of us for dinner and the wine *did* flow. Everyone’s headed for the sack because we’re going out on a job at 5:30 a.m. Anything new on your end?”

She sighed and I could see her shaking her head. “No, it’s like I thought; we couldn’t get anything useful off the manifesto or the envelope. We got lots of partial prints but nothing we can match up; no DNA either. I think it’s a dead end unless we get something else from a specific source we can match. Sorry.”

“Yeah, me too; I had high hopes, but I guess it’s not going to lead us anywhere. Without something to go on I’ll have to keep my head on a swivel, looking in all directions.”

Another sigh, “Wish I could be more help.”

I meant it when I said, “You’re being a huge help by being back in our house, Linds.”

# CHAPTER THIRTEEN

The 4:45 a.m. alarm seemed even earlier since my body was still on Mountain Time. I dressed quickly in field clothes and stepped out in the hall to the smell of freshly brewed coffee. Mercy and Clay were already in the dining room when I entered. Several heated chafing dishes were arranged on the bar. Mercy pointed toward them and said, “Good Morning! Breakfast is served; grab a plate.”

I did as ordered and found sausages, bacon, omelets, potatoes, and French toast all perfectly done. I loaded a plate and joined them at the table in the same spots we’d occupied last night. Mercy stood as I arrived and asked, “Coffee? I’ll get it.” She walked to the sideboard and returned with a steaming cup on a saucer.

“Thanks. Pretty good service in this beanery.”

“We aim to please.” She smiled. “You ready to see all this theory put in action?”

I nodded between bites. “Yeah, I really am. It’s been a long time since I’ve actually been on a frack job. I suspect it looks a lot different than it used to.”

Clay Webb spoke up, “If it’s been longer than a year or two, it’s a whole different world! All the same components will be there: pump trucks, sand hoppers, water and chemical trucks, flowlines and such. But it’ll be ‘times ten’; everything is bigger and there’s a lot more of it. It’ll look like a military operation plus, like we said yesterday, this’ll take two or three days, twelve hours each, to get it done.”

“I can’t wait.”

Mercy jumped up and said, “Good…we’d better get going. The Gate Keeper guys are supposed to be downstairs at 5:30 a.m.”

I took a last bite of bacon, “Okay, I’ll grab my hard hat and meet you out front.”

The silver Hummer was idling outside the front doors as we exited the building. The front passenger door opened and the same guys from last night piled out, “Morning, Ms. Drexler; Mr. Webb; Mr. Scott! Ready to go? It looks like we’ve got good weather; we’ll be at the well site in about forty-five minutes.”

We reversed the security procedures and were on the highway five minutes later. In half an hour, the driver turned off the highway onto an unpaved farm road. I ducked low and peered out the windshield. I could see the derrick of a service rig just peeking above the rim of a valley. The trees on the far rim were just being illuminated by the sunrise. The security guard was good to his word and we pulled onto the location a few minutes later.

Clay Webb hadn’t exaggerated. There were nearly a hundred vehicles of every shape, size, and description, all arranged in a 270-degree semicircle around the derrick. The ground was covered with a jumble of hoses, pipes, and valves that appeared to be color coded for their functions or what they were going to carry to the wellhead. At the gap in the circle, a large semi and a trailer with several windows were pulled across the opening.

Webb strode to the end of the trailer where a set of metal-grate steps and a door were located. “Let’s go inside; this is the command center for everything that’s going to happen.”

Inside it looked like the cockpit of a 747. There were several consoles, each with a computer screen and keyboard, as well as dashboards covered with switches and gauges. Above the dashboards, the windows I’d seen provided a view of the wellhead and the equipment fleet ready to work. An operator wearing headphones and a microphone sat at each console. As soon as we entered, Webb signaled to the operators and said, “Okay, let’s get going; the boss is here so let’s do it right.” He grinned at Mercy who gave everyone a mock military salute.

Immediately, a dull roar from outside penetrated the trailer as the frack trucks sprang into action. Clay opened a closet and handed us earplug-style headsets saying, "Here, put these on. It can get pretty loud even in here, but it's absolutely deafening--enough to cause serious damage--if you step outside."

I put in the plugs and glanced out the windows as twenty or more workers, all with headsets, scrambled among the hoses and pipes to hammer the valves and connectors tight. Inside, the guy at the center console raised his hands like a musical conductor, paused, and gave the downbeat. Everyone began flipping switches and dialing gauges as the roar increased. Outside, the hoses were trembling and the pipes vibrating as water with some dissolved chemicals began coursing through them and down into the well. I watched the pressure readings on the screen closest to me; they were increasing rapidly as the frack fluids were forced into the well.

As I'd learned in "Frack 101", when the pressure behind the fluid exceeded the ambient pressure of the shale surrounding the drill hole, eventually the formation would breakdown and a fracture would be propagated into the rock. When this happened, the operators would see a sudden decrease on their gauges and would signal the other workers to begin adding sand and glass beads to the stream of fluid. These were designed to "prop" the fractures open after the operators quit pumping fluid into them. In theory, oil and gas trapped in the rock would then start to flow into the fractures and eventually up the casing to the surface. The "theory" had become fact in over ninety-five percent of the wells fracked to date.

Suddenly a loud klaxon alarm sounded and a red light began flashing at one of the consoles at the far end of the trailer. Clay Webb started toward the trouble spot, but before he was halfway there, another alarm and flashing light erupted at the console nearest me. I watched the pressure plunge precipitously, dropping several hundreds of pounds per square inch in less than a second. I looked out the windows at a scene of chaos.

At least three hoses had ruptured and were spraying streams of frack fluid wildly around the wellsite. Workers were running and leaping to dodge the sprays. The high pressure streams would rip clothes off and flay human flesh if it hit the crew.

As suddenly as it had begun, everything throttled down. The wild sprays subsided, the sound level decreased, and the alarms quieted, although the red lights continued to flash. The automated shutdown systems that sensed catastrophic system failure had deployed. The fracking operation had come to a stop.

I jerked open the door, stepped out on the tiny metal-grate landing, and started down the stairs. Mercy was directly behind me. But before I reached the ground, and even through my headset, I heard the sharp splat of a bullet hitting the metal door. I turned and pulled Mercy with me down the two remaining steps to the ground. Her ear protection slipped off as we landed. "*Roll under the trailer!"* I yelled. She stared at me for a second before I roughly pushed her to the ground. She immediately understood, rolled under the trailer, and crouched behind the tires. I pulled my Colt Army .45 automatic from my shoulder holster and ducked down beside her., ditching my headset.

Clay Webb's cowboy boots started down the stairs above us. I shouted, "*Go back! Stay in the fucking trailer!"* The boots kept coming and I realized he was still wearing his ear protection and probably hadn't heard me. The ground exploded in a burst of dust and pea gravel as another slug hit in front of the stairs. Webb jumped the rest of the way and rolled in beside me.

He jerked out the ear plugs and yelled, *"What the hell is happening? Were those bullets? Is someone shooting at us?"*

"Damn sure are! It must be coming from that grove of trees up on the hill." I pointed the .45 toward the valley rim. It was the only place I could see offering concealment and cover for a shooter. Whoever was firing must be a good marksman as the grove was at least five hundred yards away. "Stay here; I'm going to crawl out the other side and try to get to the Hummer. The Gate Keeper guys probably have a long gun of some kind. Maybe we can return some fire if we spot a target."

As I started crawling toward the outside, Mercy grabbed my arm and pleaded, "For Christ sake, Cort, be *careful*!"

I yelled at her, "Stay here until I come and get you! Understand?" She nodded and let go of my arm.

I rolled out from under the trailer toward the inside of the circle of frack equipment. There I was sheltered from the shooter, so jumped to my feet and ran to a pump truck opposite the Hummer. I estimated it was far enough around to be out of sight to whoever was shooting. I cut between the truck and a sand hopper and had guessed right--the Hummer was right in front of me. The guards had taken cover behind the vehicle and were sweeping the horizons with military-issue, sniper scope equipped rifles. I yelled, "Focus on the trees near the top of the hill!"

Both rifle barrels swung into position and the driver said, "What are we looking for?"

"Movement, any kind of movement or light flashes off scopes or sunglasses…anything! We're taking fire, probably from just one gun, and it pretty much has to be coming from those trees." I watched as they zeroed in and quickly but methodically scanned the area.

After a full minute which seemed like an eternity, they both lowered their rifles and one said, "Don't see anything, man! Anybody hurt?"

I slowly stood and replied, "I don't think anyone's shot, but I don't know whether someone might have caught some frags or maybe got hit by the high pressure fluids. You guys keep watching the trees while I grab Mercy and Webb. When I get 'em back, I want to load up and get the hell out of here. One of you call the sheriff and tell him what's happened and that we're on the way in to base. Clear?"

They both said, "Yes, sir!"

I ran back to the gap between the pump truck and the sand hopper, sprinted around the circle, and dove under the control trailer. Mercy and Clay Webb were huddled together behind the duals near the axle. I said, "C'mon, we've gotta go. Slide out this side and we'll run to the Hummer; when we get there, jump in, and we'll get the hell outta here. The Gate Keeper guys are watching the hill where the shots came from and also calling the sheriff's office. Okay, follow me!"

We rolled out and retraced my steps to the Hummer. The guards had the doors open and we piled in. The driver was already in place and hit the gas before the doors closed. The tires threw up a stream of sand and dirt as the big SUV accelerated out the rig road and onto the farm road. When we regained the highway, the driver punched it to the floor for the first quarter mile and we were doing eighty-five.

Mercy finally spoke. Her voice was low and strained. "What the hell happened back there?"

I looked at her intensely before saying, "Someone was trying to sabotage the frack job and maybe kill you." I wanted to see her reaction.

Her eyes widened slightly, "I get the sabotage part, but do you *really* think they were trying to kill me?"

"The slug that hit the trailer door was aimed at you, Mercy. They didn't shoot at me when I came out, and I don't think the one that hit the ground in front of Clay was aimed at him."

She shook her head in disbelief. "This has got to be stopped! But who is behind it? Who would seriously want to kill me?"

I said, "I wish I knew, but I don't." I turned to Clay Webb, "What do you think happened with the frack job?"

He considered his answer carefully, "I think they probably shot randomly toward the wellhead until they hit some hoses. It looked like at least three of them were hit. The hoses are under such extreme pressure they ruptured. We're lucky our systems are designed to shut down everything when they sense a pressure drop like that."

Mercy interjected, "Luck doesn't have anything to do with it. I designed it that way as a safety factor, although I hadn't planned on having to deal with a gun battle! Cort, until we…or really *you*…can get to the bottom of this, I'm going to change some things.

"First, we're not going to do any more 'road shows'; if somebody wants to see our presentation, they'll have to come to our offices. We can beef up our office security and control the environment.

"Second, I'm going to be a lot more selective on who sees our technology. Unless they pass the smell test, they won't see it. And by that, I mean the Guilford Rocksons and SUDPETs of the world aren't going to get through the door!

"And, lastly, I want you to concentrate on figuring out who's after me. You won't need to be worried about making technical presentations. All right with you?"

I nodded, although it meant I had just been demoted from "Business Development" to bodyguard. Exactly what I'd said I didn't want to be.

# CHAPTER FOURTEEN

Siren's jet touched down at Centennial at 6:05 p.m. and I was home just before seven. I spotted Lindsey standing on the deck gazing toward the open space and the hillside park behind the house. The outside speakers were playing some '80s rock…she changes channels when I'm not around…and she must not have heard the chime from the door. I didn't want to frighten her so I flicked the light switch for the deck lights and she turned around.

"Hey, sleuth! What are you doing home? I didn't expect you for a couple more days!" She slid the door open, stepped in, kissed me, and hugged me tightly. "This is a nice surprise; it's good to see you!"

"I should have called you, Linds, but things got a little hectic this morning and we had to abort the trip. I had a lot of things to think about and just spaced out giving you a call, sorry."

She backed off and held me at arms' length, "Sounds serious; what happened?" I told her about the attack on the well, our visit with the sheriff, and the hurried departure for Denver. She was silent until I finished. "This is the second time something bad has happened since you took this job. Are you having any second thoughts?"

"Plenty! Not about the job itself but about my role. Right now, I'm just hired muscle; not something I want."

"Why don't you quit?"

I shook my head, "Because I'm not a quitter and I owe it to Mercy Drexler to figure out who's behind it."

Lindsey stepped to the mini-bar between the kitchen and dining room, took out a bottle of "J" pinot grigio, and poured two glasses. "You know I didn't like this from the start, but I'm glad to hear you say what you did. Mercy deserves the best and that's you. And Lord knows you've never been a quitter! Now, what can I do to help?"

We went back to the deck and watched a couple of rabbits begin nibbling the back lawn. "I don't know, Linds. It doesn't sound like there's much going to come from that 'manifesto' or the envelope it came in. About all I've got so far is Rockson, a veiled threat from the crooked Minister of Defense from South Sudan, and now this Stop Fracking Us outfit, whoever that is. Not much to go on. Starting tomorrow, I'm going through everything we've got with a fine-toothed comb. Maybe I've overlooked something."

*****

The postmistress in Devil's Lake laughed when I asked if they had a P.O. Box number '666.' "Unfortunately, we don't. You'd be amazed at how many requests we've had for one, though. The thing is, we've got four hundred boxes starting at number 101; we don't even get to '666.' Come Halloween, I bet we average ten or twelve requests every year. Probably be a money-maker for us if we just designated a box and numbered it 666!"

I thanked her and hung up. The answer hadn't surprised me, but it was another "T" crossed. I gritted my teeth and called the offices of Rockson International. The receptionist informed me "Mr. Rockson is not expected in until after lunch. Would you care to leave a message?" I asked if there was any possibility he would return my call and laughed at her honesty: "Mr. Rockson doesn't even check his messages most of the time; I don't know why I bother."

"Well, why don't you print my name and number in great big letters on a piece of paper and put it right in the middle of his desk. The message is, 'Cort Scott says to call back or the police will call you!' and make sure you put an exclamation point at the end. Do you think that'll get his attention?"

She lowered her voice, "I'll make sure he at least sees it, Mr. Scott."

I called Tom Montgomery on his private cell number rather than the DPD switchboard. "Hey, Tom, what's the haps?"

He must have already had his four cups of morning coffee and seemed to be in an unusually good mood. "Well, well…if it ain't Cort Scott, the amazing human punching bag! You gettin' around any better since the last time I saw you? Been doing any more sparring?"

"No hand-to-hand stuff, but I've had to step kinda lively. This job with Mercy Drexler seems to have its dangers; maybe I should have let you have it, buddy."

That seemed to get his attention, "Oh yeah? How so?"

I told him about the incident in North Dakota and the threats Mercy had received.

Tom exhaled heavily, "So what are you going to do now? It doesn't sound like you've got much to go on. Anything I can do?"

"I'm not sure. Do you think your tech guys could get anything off her phone? Chances are the texts came from burners, but maybe we could get a tower location to give us a lead. I'm clutching at straws here, man. It's damn frustrating."

"I hear you. Get her cell and bring it in; I'll get the IT bunch started just in case. Any other ideas?"

"Well, I put in a call to Rockson and--

"GODDAMNIT, Cort! I told you *not* to contact him. We're still following up on your beat down. You're just going to piss him off or, at the very least, alert him that he's a suspect. What the hell were you thinking?"

I bristled, "Well, you guys haven't gotten very far, have you? I need some answers from him and not just about me. I've gotta try and figure out if he's involved in any of this shit swirling around Drexler. If I can talk to him directly, I think I've got a better chance to learn something than waiting on you."

"Look, I get it that you're frustrated, but you're gonna screw this up! I'd been waiting to tell you until we had a little more, but we may have a break on the hitters. You know they taped off the camera on the fourth floor, but the dumbasses either forgot about the ones on two and three or didn't figure they had time to get 'em all. Anyway, we've got some video of two guys climbing the stairs just before the camera on four went black and some more of the same two running down the ramps to the Champa street exit."

I yelled into the phone, "*JESUS CHRIST, TOM!* When were you going to tell me? Why didn't you--

"Hold on, damn it! Look, both guys were in hoodies when they climbed the stairs and we've, *maybe*, got some partials on their faces. The cameras on the ramps are designed to get license numbers and car makes so about all we've got are their backsides. The IT geeks are running everything through facial recognition frame by frame trying to get a match. Chances are it wasn't these guys' first rodeo so we might get lucky, but I wouldn't get your hopes up. That's why I was waiting to tell you."

My pulse rate slowed a little. "I get it. But I still plan on talking to Rockson. It isn't going to foul up anything; he's gotta know I already suspect him. I just want to see him face to face when I ask a couple of questions."

Tom had also cooled, "And I still think it's a bad idea, but do what you've got to do. One favor, though--don't start pounding on him. I'd have to run you in and that'd fuck up the whole case." He laughed at the thought of slapping the cuffs on me. "Let me know what you find out."

"Yeah, well--*you* let *me* know if you ID the bastards."

*****

I had a wild hair. A couple of years earlier, when I'd been investigating Denver oilman Wildcat Willie Davidson's murder, one of the initial persons of interest had been a committed environmental activist…a "professional" demonstrator and agitator by the name of James Builder. Although I disagreed with most of what he believed in and how he went about expressing himself, he at least had been committed to nonviolent, peaceful protests. The last I'd heard he was headed to Pennsylvania to join a movement opposed to fracking there. I knew it was a longshot, but I wondered if Builder might know someone in the Stop Fracking Us bunch.

It took a few minutes of searching, but I found James Builder. He'd been arrested during a protest in Harrisburg, Pennsylvania, for pouring oil on the steps of the Department of Natural Resources building. The newspaper article said he was a member of a group called NFW: "No Fracking Way." Cute.

A Google search turned up a website for NFW with an email address and telephone number. Hoping my luck would hold, I punched in the numbers and held my breath as the phone on the end began ringing. A sweet-voiced girl answered, "Make a difference today; support No Fracking Way! How may I help you?"

I was taken aback by actually getting through and speaking to a real person. "Good morning, may I speak to James Builder please?"

The girl responded immediately, "Who's calling please?"

Christ, it sounded like the main switchboard of an insurance company; not some left-wing, anti-everything protest group. "Uh, this is Cort Scott. I'm a friend of his from Colorado." I didn't know if the lie about being "a friend" would help; he would either take my call or not.

The connection clicked a couple times and I heard the buzz of an extension ringing. "You've got a lot of fucking nerve, Scott! You're no goddamn *friend* of mine! You're no better than a cop! What the hell do you want?"

"Thanks for taking the call, Builder; gotta admit you surprised me. Look, I know we're on opposite sides of the fence, but I was hoping you'd remember I treated you okay back when Wildcat Willie was murdered. You convinced me you really are committed to trying to change things peacefully; that you aren't into violence."

He interrupted, "Yeah, yeah, yeah…get on with it! Whadda you want?"

"There's some outfit out here calling itself Stop Fracking Us. They're into sending manifestos and making middle-of-the-night calls threatening all kinds of shit. I'm working for a woman who runs a fracking company and I think they're coming after her personally. Then, someone shot the hell out of a wellsite fracking operation up in North Dakota while I was there. Nobody got killed, but it *could* have been a disaster and I don't think whoever is responsible is done. I don't want anyone to get killed and if this Stop Fracking Us bunch is behind it, I need a name."

Builder exclaimed, "You've got the balls of a high diver, Scott! You're asking me to snitch on somebody who's working on the same things I am for chrissakes! What makes you--

I jumped in, "You're wrong, Builder! Whoever this is *doesn't* believe in the same things as you. They believe in violence and maybe even murder. Like I said, I don't think you're that way. You work on things I don't agree with, but you're not going to kill somebody to make them happen."

He sighed, "We agree on that much at least; hurting or killing people doesn't solve anything. Look, I'd never heard of Stop Fracking Us until last week when some guy called and said he'd started it. He wanted me to come back to Colorado; said he needed to learn how to hack into a company's computers. He kept talking about how important everything was and that he had access to some company's computers; about how this was a chance to really do some good. But then he started talking about what he was planning and I cut him off. I actually hung up on him.

"I'm telling you, Scott, this guy is bat-shit crazy! He wants to sabotage equipment and stuff like that. If he's serious, he's *definitely* going to get somebody killed."

I held my breath, "Got a name?"

"You never heard it from me, understand? And don't *ever* fucking call me again! Understand?"

"Okay, got it. Thanks, Buil--

"Trey Worth." The line went dead.

"Hi Mercy, it's me. You ever heard the name Trey Worth?"

She laughed. "Well, good morning to you too, Cort! No, can't say as I have; who is Trey Worth?"

"I think he's the guy behind Stop Fracking Us and, if so, possibly the one who's been sending you the threats."

The laughter stopped. "Where did you get the name? Who is this guy?"

"I ran some traps and came up with the name. He's here in Colorado. I'm going to start looking for him, but thought I'd check with you first…see if you knew him."

"No, I don't. What are you going to do if you find him?"

I had to think about that. "I'd like to talk to him; figure out if he's just another left wingnut or maybe something more dangerous. I don't take kindly to people who try to blow me up or shoot me."

Mercy laughed nervously, "I hear you. Keep me in the loop, okay?"

"Sure. What's happening on the frack job?"

"Clay just called to say we had all the equipment back on location first thing this morning and they are well underway. Gate Keeper brought four ATVs with them and put a guard on every high point around the rig. Which reminds me; the sheriff called and said he'd searched the grove of trees on the hill where you thought the shots must have come from. You were probably right, but all he found were some tire prints down in the gully on the far side of the hill. The soil's too sandy to get a plaster cast of the tracks though. He said they found a few crushed plants and maybe some marks where someone had set up a shooting stand. But he didn't find any shell casings or anything they can use."

I sighed, "Well, I guess I wouldn't have expected the shooter to leave a business card. Too bad, though, we need a break. I'll let you know what I find out about Worth."

I called Montgomery back and asked if DPD had anything on a Trey Worth; he said he'd run the name and get back to me. I had another disparate thought…there were lots of organized protest groups calling for the abolition of fracking, horizontal drilling, and practically any kind of oil or gas operation. Maybe some would have websites where they posted their objectives and, if I got lucky, even their officers and members.

I Googled "oil and gas protest groups" and got over twenty million hits in 0.61 seconds, so I refined it to "Colorado oil and gas protest groups." That was *much* better…only four hundred and seventy-four thousand in 0.46 seconds. This was going to take a while.

I continued to narrow my search parameters until the hits were reduced to about a thousand; still too many for an efficient search but a good starting point. Next, I plugged in "Trey Worth" on one of the sites Google had turned up. Bingo! The home page for something called No Fracking United, or NFU, popped up and I clicked the header for 'About Us.' There were sub headers for 'Officers', 'Funding,' and 'Staff.' I clicked on 'Staff' and sure enough, there he was: Trey Worth, Activities Manager. I gave myself a mental slap upside the head…why hadn't I just entered Trey Worth to start with?

Under 'Contact Us', I found a post office box, an email address, and a telephone number. The box was in Boulder; no surprise there. Since the 1960's, Boulder, Colorado, had been referred to as the "Peoples' Republic of Boulder" for a reason: literally hundreds of anti-government, anti-establishment, anti-anything-you-can-think-of groups had sprung from the fertile environment of the University of Colorado. CU's hard earned reputation as the nation's number one party school had been submerged by a flood tide of liberalism and social unrest. And now the state had legal recreational pot; maybe the protests would be a little more laid back.

I dialed the telephone number and got a recorded message, "Thank you for calling No Fracking United. Please be aware that fracking operations are a danger to you, your family, and the environment. No Fracking United is pledged to end all such operations within Colorado. For security reasons, we do not occupy a physical office. If you wish to contact us, please leave a detailed message and a telephone number where you can be reached. Someone from our staff will return your call. Thank you."

I said, "My name is Cort Scott. I'm a former geologist in the oil and gas business. I'm tired of what is happening in the business and with fracking operations in Colorado. I'd like to talk to someone about No Fracking United's operations and activity."

I left my cell phone number and hung up, pleased with my message. I *was* tired of what was happening in the business and with fracking operations, but mostly I was tired of outfits like No Fracking United and their ilk. I hoped I'd been clever enough to illicit a response from someone who thought I wanted to help.

Where had the day gone? Lindsey would be home in an hour. We needed to do something special for a change; get away from the house for an evening. I called Shanahan's, the ex-Denver Bronco coach's steakhouse, and made reservations for 7:15 p.m. We'd have plenty of time for a relaxed drink before dinner.

## CHAPTER FIFTEEN

"Good evening, Mr. Scott! Long time, no see! It's nice to see you!" Shanahan's maître d' had been a front-of-the-house man for nearly every top line steakhouse in Denver. I'd heard he was Shanahan's first hire after the executive chef.

"How ya doin', Topper? Yeah, I guess it has been a while. You remember my girlfriend, Lindsey, don't you?"

"Of course I do!" He shook hands with me and stepped into Lindsey for a hug; Topper was a hugger. "Ah, Miss Lindsey, as nice as it is to see Mr. Scott, it's an even greater pleasure seeing you!"

Linds disengaged herself and winked at me over his shoulder, "Now *that's* how to greet someone! Take a lesson, sleuth."

He laughed and turned to the attractive girl standing next to the reservations podium with an armful of menus and wine lists, "Misty, please seat Mr. Scott and the lady at table seventeen; it's their favorite." We shook again, followed 'Misty' outside, and were seated at a table for two at the southwest end of the patio.

Lindsey reached over and squeezed my hand. "This is special, sweetie. What's the occasion?"

"Oh, nothing super special, I guess. We haven't been out since I got my head kicked in, plus we needed a do-over on the tiff about me taking this job. Besides, I had a good day and might have turned up a lead on who's behind some of this. Mostly, I just wanted to spend some time with you."

"God, you don't know how great it is to hear that! I was so miserable after we fought. But, you know I'm just as hard headed as you; I couldn't make myself call you. I wanted--

"*Well, well*! Look who's here…Mercy Drexler's hired boy!" Guilford Rockson's grating voice interrupted Lindsey. "She's gonna be all pissed off about you slippin' around on her, Scott." He had approached from the bar and was standing next to Lindsey's chair. I started to get up but a heavy hand on my shoulder held me in place. The hand belonged to a man standing behind me. Rockson shoved his hands, palm forward, toward me, "Oh, no need to stand on my account. I just wanted to stop by and say 'hi.' Incidentally, I got your phone message, but I don't respond to threats, especially if they're meaningless. I don't have any idea what you're talking about."

I glared at Rockson and said, "You know damn good and well what I'm talking about. Now get away from us; you're interrupting our dinner."

Rockson laughed, "You just don't get it, do you, Scott. You're punching way above your weight class, buddy. And people who do that get hurt, know what I mean? Well, like I said, I just wanted to say 'hi.' You and your *date* have a nice meal now, ya hear. C'mon, Ross." He turned and walked away. The hand on my shoulder let up and "Ross" followed Rockson.

I started to jump up but Lindsey said, "Let it go, Cort. You can't do anything here. You don't know how many more goons he may have with him. This is exactly what we were talking about…your need for revenge. Now is not the time or place; it'll come. C'mon babe, we can still have a nice evening."

I slumped back into my chair. "This is hard for me, Linds. I feel like I need to do something; something like beating the shit outta that guy and everybody with him!"

She smiled, "I can see how you'd feel that way. What a prick! But let's have some good wine and a nice dinner and then go home and, you know…see what happens."

The waiter's timing was perfect. I ordered a bottle of 2012 D'Arenberg Love Grass Shiraz and asked him to open it as soon as he could and we'd let it breathe while we had a cocktail and ordered dinner. Like always, the service was terrific. He was back in two minutes, opened the wine, and took our drink orders: a Lemon Drop martini for Linds and a house margarita for me. She ordered a petite filet and I had the prime rib.

As soon as the drinks arrived, Linds reached across to clink glasses and asked, “So what’s the ‘lead’ you mentioned before ol’ shithead showed up?”

I filled her in on what I’d learned about Trey Worth and No Fracking United. She agreed it sounded promising but said, “Right now, though, your only tie-in is this guy Builder and what he said about Worth contacting him.  You think that’s enough?”

I sipped the margarita, “Yeah, I do. These outfits are like whack-a-mole…soon as you hit on one of ‘em, two more pop up. The names and ‘causes’ are too close not to make a connection.”

She turned serious, “This case is like a damn tarantula…lots of arms and legs. How are you going to sort everything out?’

“I’ve just got to keep following up until something comes clear. I hope I don’t get Mercy hurt or killed before I get to the bottom of things.”

The meals arrived and the presentations looked fantastic. The waiter poured the wine and I lifted my glass to Linds, “Here’s to us, babe.”  Her eyes misted as we touched glasses.

## CHAPTER SIXTEEN

"Is this Cortlandt Scott?" The caller ID said 'Private Line.'

"Speaking."

"This is Trey Worth returning your call. I'm very anxious to talk to you about getting a petroleum geologist involved our cause. Thank you *so* much for contacting us!"

"No, thank *you* for calling back; you're a little hard to find. I finally found a website for No Fracking United and it led me to you. Now I'd like to put a face with a name and a voice; could we meet someplace?"

Worth hesitated before replying, "Well, we don't usually meet anyone in person. There are a lot of pretty violent people out there who don't like what we're doing."

I said, "I can understand your apprehension, but before I'd be willing to get involved I need to get some things straight, and I don't want to do that over the phone."

I thought I heard a long sigh before he said, "All right, I'll meet with you, but it's got to be in a public place. Okay with you?"

I smiled to myself and said, "Sure, I understand and wouldn't have it any other way. I'll be coming from south of Denver so where's a good place to get together?"

"Well, I'll be coming from north of Denver so maybe somewhere downtown would work for both of us. Have you been to the new Union Station? There are several bars and restaurants there; how about the Terminal Bar; it's right off the lobby."

I wanted to sound enthusiastic and said, "Perfect! How about 1:30 p.m.? We'd miss the lunch crowd."

"That's fine. I'm fairly tall and thin; I'll be wearing jeans and a red and black checked flannel shirt."

"Okay, I'll be inside the bar. See you at 1:30." I silently laughed at the thought of him wearing jeans and a black and red checked shirt. It was almost a uniform for protesters--one I'd seen a hundred times in person or on TV.

Lindsey walked past my office and said, "Who in the world is calling at 7:15 in the morning?"

"A very anxious anti-fracker name of Trey Worth."

She stopped, "No kidding? He actually called you? What did he want?"

"Probably wants to sign me up for a protest; I'm going to meet him at Union Station."

She stared at me for a moment before saying, "At least it sounds like a safe place."

I grinned, "For him or for me?"

She shot me a middle finger and laughed. "Well, I *was* thinking of you, but now that you mention it, probably for both of you. What if you find out it was him and some buddy in the parking garage?"

I grabbed my coffee cup, gave her a kiss, and headed to the kitchen. "Then even Union Station isn't going to keep him safe! But I don't think it was him; he wouldn't be so dumb as to meet me. More than ever, I'm convinced Rockson was behind it. I just need to see if Worth is mixed up in threatening Mercy or the attack in North Dakota."

Linds stopped at the door to the garage and said, "I gotta go or I'll be late. You kept me up way too long, uh, 'apologizing' for being a jerk. I'm not complaining, mind you, but I don't want George giving me the evil eye all day. I gotta run. You be careful!" She dashed into the garage as I filled my cup.

Since I was meeting an environmental activist, I decided to be 'politically correct' and take the light rail downtown. As I was driving to the County Line train station, it dawned on me that Worth must not have taken the time to Google me or otherwise check me out. If he had, he probably wouldn't have agreed to meet; in fact, he would never have returned the call. I'd Googled myself a few weeks earlier and found several articles about my career in the oil and gas business; the murder of my girlfriend, Gerri German; my role in solving the murder of Wildcat Willie Davidson, and some other cases. He'd have seen right through my subterfuge message of wanting to be "involved." I hoped he wouldn't do it now; if he did, I felt sure he'd stand me up.

The light rail trains parallel the I-25 freeway and I found it amusing that we were doing the same speed as the auto traffic in an area I knew was posted at 65 MPH. The ride through the old industrial areas and new residential apartments and condos along Santa Fe Drive was interesting. I hadn't been through there in several months and some areas were almost unrecognizable. Most of the signs of the Great Recession…the boarded up factories, the abandoned storefronts, and the vacant warehouses…were gone. Today's *Denver Post* newspaper had outlined how the "legal" marijuana grow houses had taken up every square inch of warehouse space; Denver was definitely booming. The train pulled into the new Union Station stop forty-three minutes after I'd boarded.

Walking the two blocks to Union Station was also "entertaining." There were lots of panhandlers, several of whom were carrying "Homeless, please help!" signs. From the looks of their clothes, haircuts, and, in some cases, venti-sized Starbucks' cups; they may not have been too hard done by. I'd recently read some newspaper articles concerning the new "urban beggars" who, in fact, were residents of some of the high rise apartments that had sprung up around the revitalized downtown. The articles had said they were crowding out the truly poor and homeless who had been forced onto the mean streets around the Denver Rescue Mission at 23rd and Broadway. Apparently, many of these new arrivals "worked" an eight-to-five shift in the lower downtown and were banking as much or more than the office workers they were begging from. I gave two bucks to a longhaired, disheveled-looking dude whose sign read, "Help get me a drink. I ain't lying to you." At least he was honest.

Inside Union Station, I stopped and gazed at the beautifully restored Terminal Lobby, the polished staircases and balcony facades, and the bustling activity around the edges. Bookstores, florists, a hotel reception, and several bars and restaurants all looked busy. The actual Amtrak ticket windows were now an afterthought tucked away in a hallway leading to still another upscale restaurant. I walked through the potted plants and comfortable-looking couches to the Terminal Bar on the east side of the lobby.

The room was like an enlarged Pullman car with a lengthy bar down one side and a row of booths down the other. I took one of the booths where I could see the doorway to my right and look down the bar toward the entrance on the other end. A waitress sailed a paper drink cozy in front of me and asked what I'd like. When I ordered a Bud, she shook her head and pointed at the "timetable" hanging behind the bar. It advertised that the Terminal Bar offered thirty-three Colorado brews on tap…but no bottled beer. I like beer that tastes like beer, so I passed on the peach lagers and honey-wheat pilsners in favor of Railyard Red ale.

As she walked back to the service station near the center of the bar, a tall guy in jeans and a red and black checked shirt came in from the far end. It was Clay Webb. Funny though, his hair was longer than it had been only a few days ago.

He stopped a third of the way up the bar and looked around so I waved my hand. He acknowledged the wave with a head bob and started toward me, but I pointed at the waitress and gave him the sign for drinking. He stopped, said something to the girl, and continued on to the booth. It couldn't be Webb; no one's hair could grow that much in a week.

I slid out and said, "Hi, you must be Trey. I'm Cort Scott." I started to extend my hand, but he grabbed it in one of those 'brotherhood' hand and wrist clasps that had been popular twenty-five years ago…probably before he was born.

"Hey great, man! Like, I've really been waiting to meet you, man! This is too cool, I mean, having an oil driller wanting to help us out!" Obviously, he hadn't looked me up.

I extricated my hand and said, "Well, thanks for coming. Did you order something to drink?"

"Yeah, thanks; I told her to just bring me whatever you're having."

"Probably no need for us to stand here and wait, Trey. Let's have a seat." We slid into the booth on opposite sides of the table. The waitress arrived with two old English Pub style pints of ale with a half-inch head on each. I picked up mine and raised it in a toast which he clinked, "Here's to it." It was an innocuous enough start.

Worth was anxious to enlist me in the cause, "So, like what turned you off about this whole drilling and fracking scene, man? This'll be great having someone with your background on our side!"

I was also anxious and hoped to get some answers before having to confess I wasn't a supporter. "I'm not a hundred percent sure of just where I stand yet, Trey. I was hoping you could help me out with that; hoping you could give me some answers."

He paused for a moment before answering, "I can try, I guess. What do you want to know?" So far, so good…

"Well, first, what's the relationship between No Fracking United and Stop Fracking Us?"

Worth blinked a couple of times before slowly saying, "How do you know about Stop Fracking Us?"

"I read the manifesto you sent to Mercy Drexler."

"There's no way you could trace--

He realized as soon as he opened his mouth, he'd screwed up. It was the answer to one of my questions: Worth *was* the one behind the manifesto and therefore Stop Fracking Us. "Oopsy! You probably shouldn't have said that, Trey. I didn't know for sure 'til right now."

His face reddened and I could see a vein throbbing at his temple. "Who the hell are you? Like, where do you get off lying to me? I don't have to answer any fucking questions!" He started to slide out, but I clamped my right hand on top of his left forearm and pinned him to the table.

"Yeah you do, Worth! And I've got a bunch of 'em. But just to clear one thing up…I didn't lie to you about anything. You were just so anxious to recruit someone who actually knows something about drilling and fracking that you jumped off the cliff without looking."

He continued to strain against my grip, "You bastard! You did to lie! You said you were tired of what's going on in the drilling and fracking operations in Colorado. That was just a pretext to get me here."

"Nope, I'm just tired of dealing with a bunch of dumbasses like you who're going to fool around and kill somebody."

He wrenched his arm from beneath my grip and slid out. I quickly followed, grabbed him above the elbow, and kept him off balance as I steered him toward the exit. The waitress started at what was happening and opened her mouth to speak. I pulled a twenty from my pocket and handed it to her as we passed. I whispered, "Leave the glasses where they are; I'll be right back. Keep the change." Her mouth opened and closed a couple of times and her lips trembled but she nodded and didn't say anything.

I did an elbow perp-walk on Worth out the front of Union Station into the plaza fronting Wynkoop Street. He tried to pull away, but I increased the grip pressure until he winced in pain and quit trying to escape. "Let go of me, you bastard! I'll have the cops on you for assault; you ain't got no right to grab me like this!"

"Shut up! I'm not done asking questions yet." I pulled him onto a bench in the little greenbelt area. "How'd you get Drexler's private number?"

He sneered as he said, "I know people, asshole. It wasn't hard."

"What do you know about the attack on a frack job up in North Dakota?"

"I don't know what the hell you're talking about."

"I think you do and as soon as I can prove it, I'll be coming after you. You need to be looking over your shoulder every minute of every day. I'm not like the cops; I don't have to play by the rules. And one more thing, stay the hell away from Mercy

Drexler and her company. Anything happens to her…you're dead meat. Got it!"

I released my grip and stood up. He reached across his body and began massaging his arm where I'd grabbed him. He looked up and quietly issued a cold threat, "Like I said, Scott, I know people. I know people who can put you in the ground anytime they want; people who won't think twice about shutting you and Drexler down for good."

Trey Worth's words stunned me. I had just threatened this asshole and he'd hardly blinked; he was threatening *me!* There was something wrong with this picture, but I couldn't put my finger on it. The answer must be in his words of 'I know people.'

*****

Mercy rose, walked around her desk, and took a seat beside me on her office couch. "Cort, you look worried. What's going on?"

"I'm not sure. How much do you know about Clay's background?"

She looked startled, "What do you mean…background? He worked at Halliburton, but he told you that. What else do you want to know?"

"Do you know where he went to school; where he was born; who his folks are? Anything other than his work history?"

She shook her head, "Not much, other than he went to Colorado School of Mines; we checked his transcripts. Why? What does it matter?"

I said, "Because he's a twin; his twin brother is Trey Worth."

Mercy reacted as if she'd been slapped. "You've got to be kidding! The enviro-nut you told me about? That's impossible! What makes you think such a thing?"

"Because I just met Trey and he's identical to Clay. Even the names sound like twins when you think about it…Clay and Trey. Can you pull up his personnel file? We need to get some answers."

Mercy strode to her desk, lifted the phone, and punched in three digits. "Janelle, would you pull Clay's personnel file and bring it in please." She continued on around the desk and sat in her chair, "Everything is, of course, in password protected files on the computer, but we keep paper copies in a file behind Janelle's desk. Everything is locked up and only Janelle and I have the combination."

Janelle entered, gave us both an inquisitive look, and laid a file in front of Mercy. Mercy opened it and slid forward in her chair to study the contents. After a few seconds, she looked up and said, "Interesting. Clay's history only goes back to the School of Mines; no high school and it lists his hometown only as 'Denver'; no addresses. We've never required employees to provide information about their parents."

I considered this for a moment and asked, "What about emergency contacts?"

She nodded and thumbed another page from the file. "Again interesting. He gave a professor from Mines."

"I'm guessing he's not married."

She nodded again.

"Where does he live?"

She said, "I don't have to look that up; he lives in a condo over The Wynkoop Brewery at 18th and Wynkoop."

Right across the street from where I'd questioned Trey; I said, "That's a high rent locale. Does he make that kind of money?"

"Absolutely, he's got a piece of the action just like I offered you…only more."

I wagged my finger at her but grinned. "Is there any chance you'd have his fingerprints anywhere?"

"Yes, I'm sure they're in his digital file. We use radioactive elements as tracers in some of our work, all our operators and managers have to be registered with the Atomic Energy Commission and that requires fingerprints."

I stood and walked to the door. "Well, I managed to get a beer glass with Trey Worth's prints. I'll take it to Tom Montgomery and get his CSI guys to lift a set. We can request

Clay's from the AEC and Tom will run both through NCIC and see what we can come up with."

Mercy stood also, "This is super strange and very disturbing, but I don't believe Clay could possibly be involved with any of the threats. And, he was being shot at just like us in North Dakota."

I said, "At least we *think* he was being targeted."

I started to leave when Mercy said, "Well, here's something else for you to think about: I just got an email from South Sudan---from that bastard, Akabile. He asked if I would reconsider my position on working with South Sudan 'after what has happened' with my operations in the US. What do you think that means? If he's referring to North Dakota, how the hell would he know about what happened?"

Her news startled me. "I don't know. Tell me again what he said when you walked out on the meeting in Houston."

She furrowed her brow in thought for a second before replying, "He said 'there are more than one means to an end'."

I said, "It doesn't sound like someone giving up on an idea, does it?"

"Oh, Cort, this is getting way too complicated for me! We've got Rockson, maybe Marty Gear, this Trey Worth guy, and now, Akabile all after me and my technology. How do they all fit together; I can't fight them all, can I? It might not be worth it; no matter how much money it could bring in."

I stepped back and put my hand on her shoulder. "That's for you to decide. Your technology is revolutionizing the oil industry. The U.S. has damned neared doubled daily production in the last three or four years…that's no small deal and it's all due to you. It's not just about you, or Siren, or making money anymore; it's about the future of the oil business."

## CHAPTER SEVENTEEN

It was a warm Friday evening and Linds and I were enjoying a glass of 2010 Eberle California cabernet as we watched the sunset from the deck. I was annoyed when my cell quacked; it broke an idyllic mood. "Hello."

"Mr. Scott, *Cort,* this is Janelle." Her voice was trembling. "You've got to come immediately; Mercy's been hurt!"

"What do you mean, *hurt?* Where are you?"

"In the emergency room at Denver Health."

"How was she hurt? What's happened?"

I heard Janelle stifle a sob, "Somebody set off a bomb in her car. They tried to kill her!"

"A *bomb!* I'll be there as soon as I can. Have you called the cops?"

"Yes, Tom Montgomery is here."

"Okay, I'm on my way."

Lindsey had followed me inside and heard my side of the conversation. "That didn't sound good; were you talking about Mercy?"

"Yeah, that was her assistant; somebody bombed Mercy's car. I've gotta go."

She put her hand on my shoulder. "A *bomb*! For Christ sake, Cort, who sets off a bomb? I know you've got to go, but be careful; keep your eyes open."

"I will; I've gotta run."

I ducked into the closet for some shoes and ran to the garage. The top was down on the 'Vette as we had taken a drive over to the little farm town of Elizabeth earlier. I powered out of the garage and sped up the street. My new neighbor, who I hadn't met, was standing in his driveway and shot me a dirty look. Most of the others in the neighborhood had, unfortunately, grown used to my hasty comings and goings.

Breaking most of the speed limits through the subdivision, Parker Road, and the E-470 expressway, I was stymied by slow moving northbound traffic on I-25. The drive downtown took almost forty minutes, about the same as when I'd ridden the light rail; I was pissed off when I finally pulled into the visitors' lot at Denver Health; the dashboard clock read 7:48 p.m. I ran to the emergency entrance, dashed inside, and approached the admitting desk.

"Cort--over here!" I spun around and saw Tom and Janelle emerging from the waiting area. They both looked worried. Tom took my arm and said, "Let's go outside where we can talk." He looked at Janelle, "Probably be best if you stay here; if there's any word, come and get us."

Outside, I asked Tom, "How is she?  How bad is it?"

Tom answered, "Bad. I don't know if she'll make it. The car's torn to shit; everything is covered with blood. The emergency guys had to cut her out of the car."

I asked, "What happened?"

He said, "Looks like somebody tucked a bomb between the transmission and the firewall on the driver's side.  When it went off, it collapsed the firewall and leg compartment and shot a bunch of shrapnel into her. Toughest thing was getting her out before she bled to death…I'm not sure they did."

I felt sick; thought I might vomit. "I know it's probably way too soon, but you got any idea of who did it?"

Tom grimaced, "You've already answered your own question--it's way too early. What about you? You're the one who was hired as security.  Got any ideas?"

I didn't appreciate the low shot but ignored it for the moment.  "Not really.  When I met Trey Worth and tricked him into admitting he sent the manifesto, I threatened him, but he didn't seem to scare and actually threatened me right back. Said he 'knew people' who could put me in the ground."

Tom was silent for a few moments. "I'll ask the forensics guys to expedite those prints you got off him and I'll put a couple detectives on it; we'll find out everything we can about him--and his brother too. Let's get back inside in case she comes around enough to talk."

Janelle was standing next to the intake desk watching us approach. Her face was lined with worry, "She's going to be in surgery for another hour or more. The doctors say it could be touch and go. They've already put over a hundred stitches in just her right leg and thigh and are getting started on everything else. They're worried about the wounds to her abdomen and side; they need more X-rays to see if she's got any penetration wounds or internal bleeding."

I couldn't think of anything to say so I patted her shoulder.

Tom checked his watch before saying, "Ms. Simmons, I know how much you want to see her, but if she's able to talk at all I'm going to need to talk to her alone. Cort can be there, but I would like you to wait until we're through before you see her."

Janelle bristled, "Why in the world is that necessary? I'm her best friend and closest associate at work. If she sees anyone when she awakens, it should be me!"

Tom looked at her intently, "It's because you *are* close at work that I want to question her first. I need her full concentration on the bombing and *not* on you or something related to work."

Janelle backed off, "I understand, I'll wait until you've finished…but I don't like it."

Tom stepped to the desk, badged the admitting nurse, told her we'd be in the waiting area, and to let us know immediately if there was any change in Mercy Drexler's condition. The three of us made the short walk to the emergency waiting room which was about half filled with anxious looking relatives and friends.

We found seats and I asked if they wanted anything to drink. Tom said he could definitely use a coffee; Janelle opted for tea. I walked up a flight of stairs to the main lobby area of the hospital where I knew there was a small independent coffee shop with better coffee than the cafeteria. I'd learned about it when I'd been here; it was where Lindsey bought coffee for us. I got a large brewed, non-flavored black coffee for Tom, an Earl Grey tea for Janelle and a small cappuccino for myself.

Three hours and more coffee later, it was twelve minutes past midnight when a male nurse's aide found us and said Mercy was out of surgery and in ICU. Tom and I jumped up and followed the nurse; Janelle frowned at us but remained seated. Two men in surgical gowns and hats stood just outside the door to ICU. One stuck out his hand to Tom and said, "Hello, Lieutenant, good to see you again although it could be better circumstances."

Tom shook his hand, "Doctor, this is Cort Scott. He's working this case with me. Cort, this is Dr. Bob Warren. He's patched up more cops than I want to count." I was amused at Tom's introduction but reasoned it saved time over trying to explain who I was.

The doctor extended his hand to me while saying, "And this is Dr. Miguel Arias, he's our chief of neurosurgery. He's had a long evening." More handshakes.

Tom asked, "What's her condition?"

Arias spoke up, "She'll be classified as 'extremely critical,' but that's not as bad as it sounds. She's going to make it. She'll have a lengthy recovery and some of it is going to be fairly painful. She had quite a bit of nerve damage and it'll be slow to heal. Frankly, she's a very lucky woman; she nearly bled to death before we got her into surgery."

Mercy was slightly elevated in the bed with IVs attached to the back of both hands which were anchored to arm boards. Several small bandages were scattered along her right arm and a large dressing covered the right side of her jaw. Under the bedcovers, the large mounds indicated her legs and feet were heavily wrapped and bandaged. Her normal complexion, which was always tanned and healthy, was wan and her eyes were closed. She looked like hell.

An ICU nurse was standing at the foot of the bed looking at a chart. As we approached on opposite sides of the bed, Mercy's eyelids fluttered, closed momentarily, and then opened to slits. It seemed like a smile flickered across her face, but it might have just been wishful thinking. I looked across the bed at Tom who slowly shook his head. After a minute or more, Tom said softly, "Mercy, can you hear me? It's Tom Montgomery and Cort Scott."

Her eyes opened wider and she slowly rolled them from side to side lingering on each of us for a moment. Finally, she seemed to focus on me and an actual smile did form. She ran her tongue across her lips then whispered, "Water please." I looked at the nurse who shook her head, 'no', but moved to the bedside table, took an ice chip from a cup, and placed it on Mercy's lips. She touched it with her tongue and pulled it into her mouth. After a moment, she pushed her tongue back across her lips and nodded slightly.

The nurse fixed us with a stare and said, "No liquids; she can have an ice chip every minute or so. Got it? And you have five minutes, that's all, understood?" We agreed.

When we looked back, Mercy's eyes were fully open. She spoke again, slightly stronger now, but still in a whisper, "What happened?"

Tom stepped forward and her gaze shifted to him. "Somebody tried to kill you, Mercy. Somebody set off a bomb in your car."

A look of surprise and then shock passed over her face, "A *bomb!* My God, *why*?" Her whisper was slightly louder.

Tom answered, "We'd rather know *who?* I think we know the why. I need to know if you saw anyone in or around the parking garage before you got in your car?"

"I don't remember seeing anyone before I got in and tried to start the car."

Tom raised his eyebrows, "Did you say you 'tried' to start your car? Do you mean the engine turned over and didn't start?"

She closed her eyes for several moments; I thought for a moment she had lost consciousness. But, at last, she murmured, "Yes, that's right. I got in, fastened my seat belt, pushed on the brake pedal, and hit the start button. The engine turned over but didn't catch. All I remember after that was pain and smoke and my ears ringing. My leg and foot hurt like hell and I couldn't pull free; I think I was kind of in and out of consciousness, because the next thing I knew, somebody crawled in through the passenger door and started working on me. I remember them using some kind of saw and cutting around my leg. Every time they jostled me, I had a lot of pain. I just told them to hurry."

Tom said, "You're a brave woman, Mercy. I'd have been screaming my head off."

A stronger smile. "I doubt it, Tom, but thanks for the thought." She turned her head to look at me, "So, what have you got to say for yourself, Cort? I thought I was paying you to keep this kind of thing from happening."

Her words hurt. "I'm sorry, Mercy. I've been trying to figure out who's after you, but I guess I'm not doing much of a job."

As I reached over and touched her fingers, she said, "It's all right, Cort. I never would have expected something like this--and neither would you. Maybe we should have thought everything through more carefully…it's more dangerous than we thought."

Tom broke in abruptly, "Cut the lovefest! This is goddamn serious and we need to get out in front of what's happening. Our time's up and I need to get to work. Mercy, I'll be back to see you when you're up to it. C'mon, Cort." He turned and walked toward the door.

I touched her hand again, "I *am* sorry, Mercy. I'll do everything I can to run down whoever is responsible. If you're up to it, Janelle is waiting to see you."

She seemed to be fading but nodded once and said, "Give me an ice chip please." I got the ice and turned to leave. "Cort, figure it out quickly. I can't take any more of this."

As I exited into the hall, I saw Janelle Simmons accompanied by the ICU nurse walking toward me. I heard the nurse tell her she had three minutes.

Tom was waiting near the exit to parking. “Did you pick up on the deal about the car not starting?”

I hadn’t. “I guess not. Why is it important?”

We walked outside, he stopped and looked at me, “I think the bomb was remotely controlled and not wired to the car’s ignition. If it hadda been wired, it would have gone off as soon as she pushed the starter button. I think whoever set it wanted to watch his handiwork. I think he was inside the garage. Her car’s already been towed and the techs have gone to work on it. With a bombing, we’ll be able to get the feds to help. If there’s anything left to give us a clue, we’ll find it. It’s too late tonight, but we’ll get the video tapes from the garage cameras first thing tomorrow. Maybe we’ll get lucky.”

I said, “If it’s like everything else with this case, you might as well shit in one hand and wish in the other and see which one fills up fastest!” Tom didn’t smile.

# CHAPTER EIGHTEEN

Twenty-one days later, Mercy Drexler was released from Denver Health at her insistence and after signing her own release. Janelle Simmons arranged for an ambu-cab limo to drive her the two miles to her high rise condo in the newly fashionable "RiNo" or River North neighborhood. Janelle called at 6:30 p.m. and asked me to come by at 2:00 p.m. the following day.

The thirty story, all glass building looked strangely appropriate in the rapidly expanding artsy-crafty neighborhood. The front entrance was dominated by a porte-cochere, complete with a parking attendant who grinned as he eyed my 'Vette. "Good afternoon, sir; visiting one of our residents?"

"That's right.  You know how to drive a stick?"

"Yes sir, actually several of our residents have sports cars; most are stick shifts."

That made me feel better; I hated the sound of people grinding the gears and slipping the clutch. "Okay then, I'll catch you later." I got out and walked to the entry where a uniformed doorman ushered me in as he tipped his billed hat. There was so much gold braid on his cover and uniform, he would have been at least an admiral if he'd been in the navy.

Inside, the place was pure luxury…understated but luxurious none the less. The multi-level atrium featured a huge polished metal and mother-of-pearl mobile. Plush couches and chairs were arranged in what appeared to be a haphazard fashion, but somehow, it worked. The reception and security desk was discretely placed near a wall-mounted stairway extending at least three levels that I could see. A tall, athletic-looking woman sat next to an equally athletic--and tough-looking--rent-a-cop in a paramilitary uniform.

The woman smiled and said, “Welcome to Urban Scape; are you expected?”

“Yep, my name is Cort Scott and Mercedes Drexler is expecting me.”

The woman glanced at a discreetly hidden computer screen, tapped a couple of keys, and smiled, “Yes, Mr. Scott. You’re on the visitors’ list. I’ll ring Ms. Drexler you’re on your way and Mr. Rushing will take you up.”

“Well, it’s good to know I’m on somebody’s list.” I shot her my best smile. “I’m probably fine on my own.”

She frowned and said, “I’m sorry, but Urban Scape requires *all* visitors be accompanied by security to and from their host’s door.”

I was impressed and told her so. It was one less thing I needed to worry about regarding Mercy’s security. The uniform stepped from behind the desk and motioned toward the back of the atrium where I could see an elevator lobby. As we approached the six doors, three on each side, he pointed to the last one on the left and said, “That’s the penthouse elevator; it only serves the top floor.” He led the way, pushed the call button, the door silently slid open, and we stepped inside. There was only one button, marked “PH”, which he pushed and I felt the car smoothly begin its ascent.

Apparently, Urban Scape’s security forces were the strong, silent types as “Mr. Rushing” never spoke during the thirty second ride. As we glided to a nearly imperceptible stop, the doors parted, he motioned me out, and pointed left. A hallway extended all the way through the building and I could see exterior windows at the far end. Another hall stretched left and right from the elevators and I followed my guide’s directions to the left.

I counted thirty paces until we reached a doorway that must have been nearly twenty feet high. A polished brass plate at eye level read “M. Drexler.” He pushed the bell and we waited several seconds before the door opened and Janelle Simmons smiled at us.

"Good afternoon, Cort. Right on time as usual! Thank you, Mr. Rushing. We'll call when Mr. Scott is ready to leave." He gave a brisk nod, turned on his heel, and retreated down the hall. "Come in, come in! Mercy is in the living room."

So this is how the other half--or more likely--"the one-percent" lives. The penthouse exuded big money and good taste. The front entry was probably ten feet wide and double that in length. The floor was a light-hued wood and travertine parquet with each square being sixteen or eighteen inches. On each side, matching Turkish carpets with intricate geometric designs in an array of browns and tans extended to the walls. The room was like a mini-gallery; the walls were hung with paintings of all sizes and frame designs. Most appeared to be impressionists and I would have placed a sizeable bet on them being originals. "Wow, this is striking! Any names I'd recognize?"

Janelle smiled, "Well, you just might! Monet, Gauguin, Van Gogh…any of those ring a bell?" I must have looked stunned as she continued, "Mercy is a *very* eclectic collector; every room in the house contains paintings of a distinct style. This is her 'French Impressionist' room, but she also has modern, American *plen air*, the Hudson Valley School, and *lots* of western art.

"I'll give you the full tour later if you'd like, but come on, she's expecting you."

We walked down a short hall opening into the living room and I came to a complete stop. The condo was located on the southeast side of the building, but because the structure was aligned northeast-southwest, the "corner" pointed due south. From this room, the vista extended from Denver International Airport to Cherry Creek Reservoir to Pikes Peak and the entire Front Range mountains. In the immediate foreground, Coors Field, home to the Colorado Rockies baseball team, and Sports Authority Field, home of the Broncos stood out. A third sports venue, owned by another Denver billionaire, Stan Kroenke's Pepsi Center was where the Avalanche and Nuggets played. It was in the middle of everything.

Mercy was propped up in a double wide, white leather recliner where she could take in the whole panorama. A burgundy-colored throw was pulled to her waist and a matching pillow was behind her head. I had visited her several times in the hospital and had worried about her slow recovery. She had seemed discouraged every day by her progress and complained about the physical therapy. Although I knew she had been anxious to be released, I hadn't thought she was well enough to be discharged. It didn't surprise me to hear she had checked herself out, but it *was* a surprise that she looked far better here, in her own home, than she had ever looked at Denver Health.

She waved and said, "Hi Cort; thanks for coming. How do you like the view?" Her voice sounded almost normal.

Stumped for an adequate answer, I stammered, "Incredible! I had no idea a place like this existed. This is far better than the Petroleum Club. How'd you find it?"

"Find it? I built it! Or at least one of my companies did. We quietly put together almost forty acres of land probably ten years before anyone thought about Denver expanding in this direction. As soon as I got a piece of the Rockies baseball team, I started putting ground together. With that much surface, I was able to situate the building like this: parallel to the river instead of a traditional east-west and north-south. As you can see, my place takes advantage of everything."

I walked across to her chair and stood next to her enjoying the view. "It sure as hell does!"

"You want a drink? I can't have anything because of the pain meds, but you don't need to hold back."

"Well, maybe just a beer. Geez, it must be quite a sacrifice not to have your Jordan Chardonnay!"

She shot me a dirty look, "I can think of a couple of words for you, wiseass…one's a verb and the other's a pronoun! Janelle would you get this jerk a beer, please?" Janelle turned and rounded a curved wall toward what I assumed was a bar…or maybe the kitchen.

I took a seat on a small couch. "So what do you want to talk about, Mercy? Did you remember something else about the bombing?"

She shook her head, “No, in fact it’s almost fuzzier now than right after it happened if that makes any sense. But I need you to check out something that’s bothering me; something I don’t even want to consider, but have to.”

“Okay, what is it?” Janelle returned with a bottle of Bud…no glass…which she handed to me. I glanced at Janelle, then Mercy, and raised a questioning eyebrow.

She said, “Janelle needs to be here for this. I’m really getting worried there may be someone inside my company involved in the bad things that’ve been happening. I hate to say this, but I want you to take a hard look at Clay Webb. I need to know what the deal is with his twin.” She glanced at Janelle, “Tell him what you told me.”

Janelle spoke softly, “Ever since Clay started, he’s asked lots of questions and some of them don’t have anything to do with the business. He’s asked about Mercy’s charities, her politics, who she knows, even her art. It got so bad, I finally told him flat out that her personal life was none of his business.

“After that, he started asking if the company had a corporate ‘manual’ covering our environmental policies. When I asked him what he was after, he said he just wanted to be sure we were being good stewards.”

Mercy interjected, “But the most disconcerting thing of all happened recently; we found out he’s been requesting information on all our patents and copyright material concerning our frack treatments.

“The patent information and copyright stuff is a matter of public record, but without our proprietary operational manuals it’s so much mumbo-jumbo. With the manuals, which of course he has, someone could conduct a thorough search for ‘loopholes.’ Unfortunately, there will be lots of areas where; if somebody wanted to, they could come very close to duplicating our techniques and wouldn’t violate the patents.”

I sipped my beer before asking, “Why would he want to find the loopholes? What’s in it for him?”

“I assume money, lots of money!”

I considered that for a moment before replying "Doesn't he already make 'lots of money'?

"Yes, of course, but not as much as I do--I think that's what he wants!"

I scoffed, "Yeah, but Siren was already a going concern when you came up with the idea of Frack Focus. How could he ever come up with the capital to start a whole new outfit?"

Mercy replied quickly, "My first thought is from somebody like Rockson."

I said, "Webb hasn't impressed me as a guy consumed with thinking about money. But I'll start pulling everything we've found together and get you a report. Tom decided to let Arapahoe County handle the DNA research since that's what Lindsey does for a living. She told me this morning it'll be at least tomorrow before she'll start getting results.

"In the meantime, I assume you'll be here, right? It'll be a lot easier on Tom and me if we know you're safe and sound."

She grimaced before replying, "I'll stay here for the rest of the week, but I plan on going in next Monday. I'll be stir-crazy by then."

I drained the rest of the beer as I stood and walked to her recliner. I put my hand on her shoulder and said, "I hear what you're saying and I understand. At least I'll have a few days when I won't worry about you."

She put her hand over mine, "Don't worry about me; I'll be right here and I'll be fine. In fact, I think I'm going to put this chair back and have a nap. All this talk was more tiring than I expected. Janelle can show you out. Thanks for coming and keep me informed."

Janelle rose from the other couch and asked, "Cort, do you like western art?"

"It's actually my favorite. Who do you have?"

She smiled and said, "Come with me; we've got a special room to display it." She walked across the room around another curved wall toward a door hidden from the living room.

We entered what was obviously Mercy's home office; it was at least twice the size of the one downtown. It was carpeted with a plush tan and dark brown Berber, bordered by a dark hardwood of some kind. The back wall was floor-to-ceiling bookshelves, except for a large cutout where an expansive landscape was hanging. I thought it was probably a Bierstadt and I was right: the brass plate on the bottom of the frame said "Storm in the Rockies". I glanced around and spotted one wall of nothing but Russell's and Remington's; another wall was covered with modern masters: Turpening, Stevens, Bama, and some others.

Each corner of the room was occupied by tall statuary-display tables with arguably the most famous western art sculptures ever crafted. There were two Remington's and two Russell's. I looked at Janelle, "Are those originals?"

She nodded and pointed, "All except that one by Remington. It's from his second run of castings: number seventeen of twenty." I looked at the sculpture's name plate "The Broncho Buster." Although I was familiar with the piece, I'd never known the artist's original spelling of the work contained an "h."

I shook my head, "How in the world--

She whispered, "Mercy simply overwhelmed the owners of most of the pieces. When she located a piece in a private collection, she would offer as much as twice the appraised value, agree to let the owner 'keep it' for up to eighteen months, and then give them a contract specifying she would loan each work to the Denver Art Museum for inclusion in their rotating displays.

"She is the largest private collector of Western art in the world in addition to being the largest source of display objects for the art museum. The pieces in this room alone are worth something north of fifty million dollars."

I gave a low whistle, "I had no idea."

Janelle smiled, "Very few people do, but like I said earlier, she's got lots more from several different 'schools' of art. She likes to share it by underwriting the city's museum and gallery exhibits."

I slowly did a full 360 degree turn before saying, "I'm going to get whoever's after her; losing someone like Mercy would be a tragedy in so many ways. But, I've got to ask you something,

Janelle…is she all right? She seems different some way; not as enthusiastic; not as energized. She almost seems like she's lost interest. This question about Clay Webb is the first thing I've seen her have an interest in since the bombing."

Janelle glanced over her shoulder to reassure herself Mercy wasn't standing there or could hear. "She's changed, Cort. I went to see her every day in the hospital and you're absolutely right, she's not the same. At first I thought it was just the shock of the bombing, or the pain meds, or maybe the whole situation, but now it seems like she's resigned to her fate if that's the right expression. She seems, I don't know, uh, *fatalistic*. And you're right about Clay, too; it's literally the first question she's asked about *anything.* I'm worried about her because I can't decipher what's going on in her head."

I glanced at The Broncho Buster as more questions came to mind. "Did she, uh, 'talk' to anybody while she was in the hospital?"

"You mean like a shrink?"

I nodded.

Janelle thought for a moment before replying, "Yes. But, it was early on, like maybe in the first week. I thought at the time it was too soon. She was still in a lot of pain and taking a bunch of meds. And afterwards, she wouldn't talk to me about it, so I don't know what was said."

"Do you think she'd see someone now?"

Janelle shook her head, "No, she won't stand for it. She's never believed in that sort of thing."

We didn't say anything else until we were back at the entry. I said, "I think we've got a big problem. I'm wondering if she's looking for someone to go after? I know she said you were the one who brought up Clay Webb, but she seems to be seizing on it. Keep an eye on her, Janelle, and call me if anything seems wrong."

She didn't speak, just took my hand in both of hers and looked into my eyes. There were tears in hers.

## CHAPTER NINETEEN

Tom was excited, "The tech guys just called and they've got something wild."

"So spit it out! This case is driving me nuts."

"The explosive was Semtek, which is the Czech version of C-4. By international law, it has to contain an identifying taggant with a vapor signature. They vary the taggant slightly for each production run so it's possible to pinpoint when a batch was made. Soon as we get it, we'll get a list of all original purchasers of that batch."

I was stunned, "Holy shit, Tom! You mean we'll have a list containing the name of the bomber?"

"No, it's not *that* easy. I said we'll have 'original purchasers'; this stuff gets resold…legally and illegally…all the time. It gets stolen and there are, literally, tons of it 'gone missing.' We'll be looking for some kind of tie-in on the list."

I was still impressed. "It's a hell of lot more than we've had up to now. Anything on the fingerprints?"

"Some…not much. Clay Webb checks out: registered with the AEC like Mercy told you; no criminal record; School of Mines, etc. Trey Worth, though, has several arrests, all for minor stuff related to civil disobedience busts and the like. They were both in a Catholic Charities orphanage but adopted by some people by the name of 'Webb.' It looks like 'Worth' was a name given to them by the orphanage; it probably wasn't their 'birth name.' Trey changed his back to 'Worth' when he was twenty-one. We're still working on the rest of the background for both of 'em."

"That's all progress. I guess the next step is to talk to Clay Webb and ask him about his brother. I know this is a criminal investigation because of the bomb, but do you have a big objection to me talking to him first? He might open up to me more since I'm not a cop."

Tom was silent for a few moments. "It's probably not the best thing legally speaking and it might scare him into running if he's guilty of anything, but I think you're right about him maybe talking to you in preference to us. Go ahead, but try not to scare him into taking off."

"Got ya, Tom. I'll talk to him tomorrow."

I was waiting in Siren's reception area the next morning when Clay Webb walked in at 7:45 a.m. "Clay, if you've got a few minutes, I'd like to talk to you."

I hadn't seen him since the bombing and he looked surprised to see me. "Sure, come on back. You want coffee?"

"No thanks."

We walked down the hall towards Mercy's office, took a left at her door which was closed, and went into the next office. Clay switched on the lights and said, "Well, *I* need some coffee. Sit down, I'll be right back."

Thinking back to Tom's warning, I didn't want to let Clay out of my sight, "If you're having some, I guess I will too." I followed him to the coffee bar.

When we returned, he motioned to his visitor's chair, shut the door, and went behind his desk. "So what's so important?" He sipped at his cup.

"Why didn't you tell Mercy or me about Trey Worth?"

Webb choked on his coffee but managed to swallow what he had in his mouth and carefully set the cup on his desk. "I didn't see where it was anybody else's business."

I stared at him for a moment before saying, "That's bullshit! With all the crap going on around Mercy and Frack Focus, you *had* to know Trey was involved in some way. Did the two of you try to kill Mercy?"

He looked like I'd slapped him. His face drained of color and he slumped in his chair before saying, "*NO!* Jesus Christ, I would never hurt Mercy…and Trey wouldn't either! Look, I know he's deep into the anti-fracking stuff, the anti-drilling movement, all of it, but he wouldn't try to kill anyone."

I jumped to my feet, "Goddamn it, there's a disconnect of some kind here. You work for a frack company, you work for Mercy Drexler, you work in the oil business and yet you sit here telling me your twin brother, who is anti-everything, wouldn't do something violent. What am I missing? In the last month, ever since I walked in the door, there's been nothing *BUT* violence! I get the shit kicked out of me, we get shot at, and now Mercy gets bombed! What the hell am I supposed to think?"

He took a deep breath, picked up his coffee, and slugged down a gulp. "Okay, okay, I'll tell you what I know." I sat down prepared to listen. "Trey and I turned eighteen in the spring of our senior year in high school. We'd both been accepted to colleges, School of Mines for me and Colorado for Trey. We both landed jobs for the summer: I was going to work on a drilling rig and Trey for the US Forest Service.

"Before we left for the jobs, we started kidding about how we were going to be on opposite sides of the fence when it came to environmental issues. That got our parents stirred up and involved: our dad was one of the first hires when the EPA was formed; he started out in Oregon doing water quality surveys and worked his way up until he became the regional administrator here in Denver. He was pretty much a pragmatist, but leaned toward the anti-development side of the equation. Our mom, on the other hand, was from an old time Colorado farming family up by Greeley. She and her brothers and sisters inherited mineral rights under several hundred acres in Weld County. They've had various amounts of oil and gas royalty income for as long as I can remember. She was really pleased I was going to Mines and was interested in the oil and gas business. My dad…not so much; he liked the idea of Trey working for the Forest Service.

"Anyway, we overlapped at home for about a week at the end of the summer before we left for college. What started out as, uh, 'spirited discussions' about our disparate views of the energy business and the environment ended up in a bunch of yelling and, finally, a fist fight.

"From then on, we drifted farther and farther apart. I loved working and studying in the oil and gas business while Trey got deeper into the radical environmental movement. It got so bad we had to schedule our visits with the folks so we wouldn't be there at the same time. The final straw for me was when Trey changed his name when we turned twenty-one; he said he didn't want the same name as me…or them…anymore. That hurt Dad, but it almost killed Mom.

"When Trey changed his name the folks wrote him out of their will, and six months later they were both killed in an auto accident. Everything was so bitter by that time; he didn't even attend their funerals."

"After I found out about the will, I tried to contact him because I wanted to give him half of everything. He wouldn't answer my calls and when I tried to send him a letter, it was returned. After a year, I gave up. I finished school and went to work for Halliburton and then came to Siren and Frack Focus. I hadn't seen or heard from Trey until about six weeks ago."

I sat up straight at that. "Did you make contact or did he get ahold of you?"

"He called me. Like I said, I gave up even trying years ago."

"What did he want?"

"He said he was getting a lot of conflicting information about fracking and its possible effects on the environment and wanted to know if I could give him some straight answers. But the big surprise was when he told me he'd been feeling bad about what happened to the folks and the way he had acted. He hoped we could reconcile, although he said he understood we'd probably still have our differences."

I asked, "Did you believe him? Did you think he was being sincere?"

Clay studied my question for several seconds, "For the most part, yes. He seemed sincere."

"So, did you meet?"

"Yes, we had dinner downtown."

"How'd that go?"

"Good! He seemed like his old self…funny, telling jokes, making fun of himself and me. He got very serious and emotional when we talked about mom and dad. I made my offer to share the inheritance, but he turned it down. He said he couldn't keep credibility in the anti-fracking and drilling movement if he was collecting oil and gas royalties."

I nodded. "Makes sense to me; so what did he want?"

"Well, mostly just to talk about the fracking process; he was really focused on the potential for ground water contamination and triggering earthquakes. I told him the truth…that most ground water contamination comes from surface spills not from fracking operations. It took a little more explaining about earthquakes. I tried to explain about quakes being the result of deep disposal of frack water and *not* the actual fracking operation."

"Did he buy into your explanations?"

"I don't know, but I don't think I changed his mind about opposing the operations. He was pretty adamant about it."

"Where'd you leave it?"

"We agreed to disagree but to be more civil about it. He said he'd make an effort to talk to me before he mounted some kind of crazy protest."

I asked, "How did you arrange to keep in touch?"

"We exchanged email addresses and cell phone numbers."

My heart skipped a beat. "Did you keep it personal or did you include Frack Focus, the office, contact information?"

"I gave him all my contact stuff. I didn't want to miss him if he wanted to get in touch."

Now I knew how whoever was threatening Mercy had obtained her private numbers. "Did you find out where Trey lives?"

Clay looked at me strangely, but nodded, "Yeah, he's crashing with some friends in Boulder. He said they've got a house on Mapleton Street between 5th and 6th. Why?"

“I may need to talk to him and I doubt he’d agree to meet me.”

“*Jesus Christ,* Scott! Don’t hurt him; he’s my brother.”

“I said ‘talk.’”

# CHAPTER TWENTY

"Cort? Marty Gear."

"Hey, Marty, how ya doin'? What can I do for you?"

"I thought I'd give you a call about the merger deal with Rockson. Or more properly, 'lack of a deal.'"

My ears perked up. "What do you mean?"

"The merger is off. I've spent the last two days huddled up with our attorneys and we figured a way to call it off without triggering the breakup fee. I just got off the phone with Rockson and gave him the bad news."

"Wow, that's good news for me…and for Mercy Drexler, Marty! How'd Rockson take it?"

"Just like you'd expect; he went ballistic. He started screaming and yelling about how he would sue, take me to court, break me, etc. I got him calmed down long enough to explain that regardless of any deal we'd ever make, my contracts with Frack Focus stipulate there can be no transfer of 'intellectual' property and/or disclosure of any proprietary information or processes. It's all bullshit, of course, a bunch of legal mumbo-jumbo, but my attorneys assure me it'll stand up in court if it comes down to it. I don't think it will go to court; Rockson is more bluster than ballast. He was mad as hell and he pretty much admitted the whole reason for the merger was to get around Frack Focus' patents and copyrights."

"Jesus, this is *big*, Marty! It's one hell of a load off our minds. We owe you one and I'll make sure Mercy understands."

"You don't owe me anything; it would never have worked out with that bastard and I'm glad to be out of it. I'll figure out another deal for Mountain West Gas and move on."

"Thanks for letting me know, Marty. I'll keep my ears open for you."

I closed the call, leaned back in my deck chair, and heaved a huge sigh of relief. The deal breakup meant one less player in the mix of who was after Mercy. I had never suspected Marty Gear was involved but now I didn't have to worry about Rockson running a concealed operation to steal her secrets. I still worried about the bastard though; the more I'd thought about it, the more convinced I had become that he'd been behind my beat down.

I called Mercy and delivered the news. She was pleased about Marty, but immediately asked about Clay Webb. I had replayed my conversation with him several times and didn't know what to think. On one hand, he'd seemed highly offended I'd even asked him about being involved in the bombing or that Trey might have been. On the other, he'd been quick to tell the whole background story on Trey. Could he have subtly been trying to sic me onto Trey? I was kicking myself for not digging deeper into Clay's finances and his motivation for sticking with the oil and gas business. I resolved to make those questions a high priority.

I decided to stall Mercy. "I'm still thinking about him. I haven't found anything incriminating, but there's a good chance your contact numbers were compromised through his email and cell phone. I think you need to change out all your private numbers and make sure they don't get back on Frack Focus' contact list."

"Oh God, Cort! Just what I need now, right? I hope there's no connection to Clay. I've trusted him with a lot."

There were still lots of loose ends to this case, although a few things seemed to be coming together. Marty Gear was out of the picture and I believed I had solved the mystery of whoever was threatening Mercy had gotten her numbers. But I was still in the dark about the relationship, if any, between my beating, Rockson, shooting at the rig, the bombing, the threats, and Akabile, the Sudanese thug.

When Tom Montgomery called, a few things began to clear. “Hey, Cort, hang onto your hat! This thing is going ballistic.”

“What the hell you talking about?”

“The feds just called and the analyst nearly jumped through the phone with the information on the bomb…on the Semtek. The residue analysis indicates the batch was manufactured and sold in May of 2010. It was sold originally to the Egyptian military but when the ‘Arab Spring’ uprisings began in late 2010 and early 2011, all hell broke loose and the Egyptians lost track of practically everything in their arsenal, including this stuff. It’s possible some of it was smuggled across the border into Sudan where their civil war was going on at the time.

“And I think it’s way too big a coincidence after what you told me about that hinky ‘minister.’ My question, though, would be how the hell it could have ended up in Denver, Colorado, all the way from fucking Africa?”

I wondered too, but had an idea. “Is there enough to get the FBI or maybe the State department involved?”

“Well, the ATF and FBI are already involved because a bomb was used. I don’t know about State; what do you have in mind?”

“I’d like to know if Rockson International has done any business in Sudan either before or after their civil war. I’d like to know if any of their employees have traveled there or if they’ve done any import/export work.”

Tom was silent for a few seconds before saying, “I see where you’re going. It shouldn’t be too hard to find out. I’ll contact the FBI office here in Denver and get the ball rolling. What are you going to do now?”

I wasn’t sure myself. “I’m going to sit here in my office and try to figure out how everything fits together. Get back to me as soon as you have anything, okay?”

*****

Clay Webb hadn't given me a street address for Trey, but he'd said it was on Mapleton between 5th and 6th. I thought a little stakeout might be worthwhile and besides, I hadn't been to Boulder in a long time. I called Lindsey and told her I was going to Boulder and wouldn't be home until late. She gave me the usual admonishment about being careful and I reminded her about how "mellow" Boulder had become. She laughed and said, "Mellow guys can hit just as hard as laid-back types, sleuth. Be careful!"

There is no "easy" route to get to Boulder from Parker; I had to grit my teeth and prepare to face ninety minutes worth of urban freeways. At a little past twelve noon, it was hotter than hell. I put the top down on the 'Vette and grabbed an old CU hat from the closet; hoping it would keep me from fricasseeing my scalp and help me fit in around Boulder.

I took Parker Road to the E-470 toll road and then I-25 all the way to the NW Expressway and into the southeastern edge of Boulder.

I decided to cut through the CU campus and checkout the coeds. With the sunshine and warm temperatures, it was always a revelation to see just how far they'd go with their attire. It wasn't disappointing and I got an eyeful. I thought about Lindsey and felt guilty. Either she meant more to me than I'd admitted to myself or I was getting old; things like that had never occurred to me before.

I cruised Mapleton Street from 4th to 7th to get a good look at the five-hundred block. It was typical old Boulder: mature elms and oaks; Craftsman-style houses set well back from the street on big lots. There were only six houses on each side of the street; not a lot to keep track of but the trees made it difficult. I lucked into a parking spot in front of a van a couple of spaces from 5th. I could see both sides of the street for most of the block. I put the top up hoping Worth wouldn't spot me if he came strolling along. It was cooler in Boulder than Parker but still hot; I hoped he would show up soon.

My wish was granted after half an hour. I spotted Worth walking west, toward me, along the south side of the street. Although I was sweating inside the 'Vette, he was wearing the same long sleeve, red and black checked flannel shirt as he had in

Denver; he must have been ripe by now. Near the middle of the block, he took a residential sidewalk to the front porch of a dark green, shingled house set well back from the street. He checked the old-fashioned, top hinged mailbox on the porch column before entering. He didn't have to unlock the door.

I waited several minutes before unwinding from the 'Vette and sticking my .38 Walther PPK in my middle-of-the-back holster. The loose Hawaiian shirt hung outside my pants covering the little automatic. I strolled the fifty yards up the street and sidewalk onto the porch. The door had three rectangular windows at eye level, but they were green water glass and impossible to see through. I could hear melodic, instrumental music playing.

I knocked on the door and immediately heard footsteps approaching. The door opened to reveal a youngish black woman dressed in a free flowing, shapeless, ankle-length dress in a flowered print nearly identical to my shirt. Between her dress and Trey Worth's shirt, it felt like I'd been transported back to Boulder circa 1968. "Hi, may I help you?" She had a high-pitched voice with a rather pleasing, non-specific, slightly British accent. I couldn't place it--might have been Jamaican or maybe South African. Something about her was vaguely familiar, but I couldn't place that either.

"Hi, is Trey Worth here?" I knew he was, but wanted to hear the answer.

"Yes, he's here; just came in actually. Who're you?"

"Name's Cortlandt Scott; I met with him last week." Her eyes went to slits; I could see she was trying to remember where she'd heard my name. Suddenly, it registered. She tried to slam the door, but I had the tip of my shoe on the jam near the hinge side and she couldn't get any leverage. She yelled, "Trey, it's the guy you went to see in Denver! Help me!"

I wasn't trying to force myself in; I was just keeping her from closing the door. From down the hall, I saw Worth race into view from a room on the right. He ran to the front and screamed, "What the hell are you doing here, Scott? I told you to leave me alone! Get out of here or I'll call the cops!" He replaced the girl on the other side of the door and continued to try to squeeze it shut. "Bre, call 911; tell them there's a break-in in progress!"

I said, "Hold on, *Bre*. I'm not breaking in, I just wanta have a short conversation with Trey. But if you get the cops here, I'm gonna tell 'em he was involved in a bombing in Denver. If I do, he's going to be arrested and end up sitting in jail for a few days." She hesitated and looked toward Worth whose face was obscured behind the door from me.

He yelled, "That's bullshit! I don't know anything about any bombing!"

I said, "I want to believe you, Trey, but if you don't talk to me *right now*, I'll get you arrested and it'll get sorted out at the jail." I felt the pressure on the door decrease slightly.

Slowly, he stepped back and opened the door until I could see him. Bre stayed at his side with a shocked look on her face. "I'll talk to you, Scott, but I won't do it alone. Bre gets to stay in the room and listen. She'll be a witness to anything you say or do. That's the only way this is going to happen."

"Fair enough." He opened the door and stepped back; Bre moved to the side and I walked into the entryway. "I appreciate it. This shouldn't take long." I'd been right about his need for a change of shirts and a shower.

He closed the door and led the way down the hall to the room I'd seen him exit. "This is the best place."

The room looked like it had once been a dining room, but had been converted into an office. It was jam-packed with furniture and equipment. Folding tables covered with neatly stacked piles of documents that looked like flyers and leaflets lined three walls; a small round table with four folding chairs occupied the center of the floor; a student-type desk with a computer monitor faced the wall to the left of the doorway. A rolling cart held a printer and a copier. One side wall was nearly covered with a banner depicting a drilling rig being devoured by fire and the words "STOP FRACKING US" running across the top.

Worth and Bre took two chairs from the table leaving me standing, so I grabbed the desk chair and turned it to face them. I pointed at the banner and said, "That's not right. Drilling rigs don't have anything to do with fracking operations. If you're going to protest something you ought to get the right images. You should have a completion rig."

Trey Worth's face reddened with a pained expression. "You're an asshole, Scott. Now, what the hell do you want?"

"I *want* to know the truth about what you're up to and how you go about it. I *want* to keep from having you and your brother, Clay Webb, arrested for attempted murder. And, most of all, I *want* to put an end to the shitstorm around Mercy Drexler and her company."

Bre looked at Worth and said, "How does he know about your brother? And what's this all about anyway?"

Before he could answer, I asked her, "Do you know who Mercy Drexler is? Do you know what Frack Focus is? Are you involved in this Stop Fracking Us operation?"

Worth jumped in quickly. "Leave her out of this, Scott. She hasn't done anything wrong; she--

Bre interrupted, "You don't need to protect me, Trey. I haven't done anything wrong." She turned to me and answered my questions. "Yes, I know who Drexler and Frack Focus are; that's her fracking company…the one trying to totally destroy the environment." She waved her arm as if encompassing the whole planet. "She's the one we're trying to shut down. But what's this rubbish about bombings and murder? We don't believe in violence." The term "rubbish" reinforced my first impression of Bre as having a British connection.

I shifted my gaze from one to the other until settling back on Bre. "Somebody tried to blow Mercy Drexler away with a bomb planted in her car. Your boyfriend and his brother, whom I suspect you know works for her, are currently at the top of the list of suspects. The cops, with my help, have traced the faxed threats and your manifesto back to you. Unless you can prove otherwise, you're all going to go down for the bombing and an attack on a fracking operation in North Dakota."

Worth quickly said, "Look, Scott, didn't you hear me? We don't do violence…I don't know anything about this bomb you're talking about, and I don't know anything about North Dakota either. And why are you dragging my brother into this?"

I stared at him. "I think you got Mercy's contact information from him. I don't think he knows you did, but that won't make any difference if it comes to making an arrest. He'll still be an accessory; he'll still be charged with conspiracy to commit murder. You'll both--

Worth leaped to his feet, "*THAT'S NOT TRUE!* Clay hasn't done anything! Look, I admit I got Drexler's phone numbers and email addresses by hacking his phone and computer, but he didn't know. He gave me *his* contacts so we could keep in touch and I used them as a backdoor into his work computers and phones. But I swear I didn't have anything to do with any attempts to kill Drexler or any attack in North Dakota or anyplace else. All we did was hack into his phone and computer to get to Drexler. Sure, we faxed our demands and some meaningless threats and mailed the manifesto to her, but we didn't threaten to *kill* anybody! We--

Now, it was my turn to be loud, "*GODDAMN IT*, you threatened to sabotage her operations and destroy her equipment! What did you think would happen if you tried? People work around that equipment and your stupid tricks could have been catastrophic. Someone *COULD* have been killed and you would have been the killers! Did you think Frack Focus would just close up shop and go away? Oh, wait a minute; let me rephrase…*DID YOU FUCKING THINK?"*

Bre jumped at my shouting; Worth sank back into the chair. She put her hand on his shoulder for a moment and then looked at me. "We're desperate to stop these insane drilling and fracking operations; they are slowly killing *us*! We want to make a difference…but, but, oh my God! This can't be happening; we don't want to hurt *people!*"

I softened my voice, "Okay, just a few more questions and I'll leave you alone. I can't promise the cops won't talk to you or you won't face some kind of charges for hacking computers, but, for now, I'm going to take your word you weren't involved in the bombing or North Dakota."

Worth took Bre's hand before looking at me and nodding. "What are your questions?"

I asked, "First, how many people are involved in Stop Fracking Us?"

Bre answered, "Six of us; we all live and work here."

"Okay, whose house is it?"

She answered again, "It's a rental; I signed the lease."

"Have you or anybody you, uh, *work* with actually sabotaged anything? Ruined any equipment? Tried to stop an operation?"

Trey finally said something. "Not really; we scattered some tacks and nails on a rig road once and we painted graffiti on some frack tanks over by Greeley. One of the other guys and I were going to break into a Halliburton facility in Brighton but got scared off by all the lighting and the signs about guard dogs and electric fences."

I wanted to laugh and say something about what a brave bunch of terrorists they were but thought better of it. They were cooperating and I needed it to continue. "When I saw you downtown, you said you knew 'people who could put me in the ground'; who were you talking about?'

Worth hung his head before answering, "I just said it to get you off my back. I don't know anybody like that."

I was glad to hear it, although he'd been very convincing at the time. "Do you know anything about a guy named Guilford Rockson or a company named Rockson International?"

They looked at each other for a moment and shook their heads. Bre said, "We've never heard of either one before."

He continued to shake his head. "Who are they?"

"Never mind, just an outfit we're looking at. Has anybody in your group ever been to Africa, specifically to Egypt or Sudan?"

Bre glanced at me but shook her head again. Worth said, "I was in South Africa about four years ago; Cape Town."

"How long were you there? What were you doing? Who'd you meet?"

"I was there for four days for an environmental conference on forestry."

"Were there any delegates from the Sudan or Southern Sudan?"

"I don't remember, but I doubt it. The conference was about rain forests and tropical environments. I think most of Sudan is arid; desert actually."

I thought about one more thing. "How well do you know James Builder?"

Both faces were blank until Worth snapped his fingers. "I don't *know* him at all, but I talked to him on the phone once. I tried to recruit him to join us and help with our protests."

I sharpened my gaze, "How come he didn't? This should have been right up his alley."

Worth dropped his eyes, "I think I scared him off. I told him we were thinking about going operational with a plan to blow up some equipment; to drive the fracking companies out of business."

"Did you have a plan in place? Were you planning to up the ante?"

Worth didn't say anything. He just shook his head. Bre stared straight ahead and showed no reaction.

# CHAPTER TWENTY ONE

When I returned to the car, I put the .38 in the console; it didn't fit with the contoured bucket seats. I took Mapleton to 9th, 9th to Boulder Canyon Drive and then Broadway south. Just after merging onto Broadway, my cell buzzed through the hands-free feature of the sound system. The screen read Tom Montgomery.

"Hey, Tom, what's the haps?"

"Bad news…where are you?"

"I'm in Boulder headed south. What's the bad news?"

"Your buddy, Martin Gear, and his secretary have been assaulted. I'm at Denver Health emergency right now. They'll both recover, although he's in bad shape…concussion, maybe a skull fracture, lots of cuts and bruises; she's not so bad except probably a fractured jaw."

"*JESUS CHRIST!* Marty's seventy-two years old and Peggy Sue Crandall has got to be sixty; maybe more! Who the hell would go after them?"

"Well, there's some good news with the bad…we've got two mutts in lockup for the assault and, get this, I think they may be the same guys who got you."

It suddenly all came together. "I'm on my way, Tom. I can probably be at Denver Health in forty or forty-five minutes. Will you still be there?"

"Yeah, I need to talk to her and maybe him if he's able. I'll wait here for you."

I took Broadway to Baseline and merged onto U.S. 36, the old Denver-Boulder Turnpike. I broke most of the speed limits all the way to the intersection with I-25 where I hit traffic and had to slow. The assault on Marty cemented my thinking about Rockson being behind all the rough stuff. He was getting his "revenge" on anyone who was getting in his way. He'd come after me for the incident in the elevator at the Petroleum Club and now Marty for backing out of the merger deal. I was betting the bomb in Mercy's car and the North Dakota well site attack was also his doing. I probably would need a lot of help to tie it all together, but I was focused now. I was going to take his ass down.

*****

I spotted Tom standing outside the emergency entrance and thought about the fact it was the third time in a month I'd been here…not a good thing. As we walked inside, I immediately spotted Nurse Mickey, Miss Blonde and Purple hair, who gave me a look of recognition. She'd been my first emergency nurse when I'd been here the first time. I asked Tom, "How are they?"

"Better than I would have expected from when I first saw them. Gear does have a concussion but no skull fracture. His face is beat to shit, though; lots of stitches and bruises. The woman is bruised up badly too; she does have a fractured jaw but won't need to get wired up. The doc says that other than being sore as hell, she won't have to be eating through a straw or anything. She's waiting around until Gear's out of ICU and in a room. We can talk to her if you want."

"Of course I want! What have you figured out so far?"

"Well, I'll tell you one thing, she's one tough woman…and smart too!"

"How's that?"

"For starters, as soon as the hitters walked in the office door, she *knew* they didn't belong. They were like you'd described them, a rough looking salt and pepper team in hoodies. Turns out, almost every office in the building has a panic button right on the reception desk to alert building security. When the two creeps walked in, Crandall pushed the button immediately.

"She said they didn't say a word and the white guy slapped her in the face with a sap knocking her off her chair onto the floor.

She had sense enough to play like she was knocked cold. They charged down the hall into Gear's office and she heard him yell a couple times and then some banging. Her purse was on the floor under her desk and she grabbed a canister of pepper spray out of it, scrambled back up, and stood to the side of the entrance to the hall.

"When they started to run out, she got both of 'em with the spray and then raced out into the corridor. By then, the rent-a-cop security team, two of 'em, were stepping out of the elevator. The hitters spilled out of the office right in front of them, cussing and yellin' and rubbing their eyes, so it wasn't much of a trick to get them on the floor and slap the cuffs on."

Even with the gravity of the situation, I had to smile. "I've known Peggy Sue forever and she's a pistol. She worked with Gerri and was one of her best friends. Ever since Gerri's murder, she's been extra careful about her own security. I'm not surprised by any of this. And, you're right; she's tougher than a boot."

Tom continued, "The security guys called 911 before they even went into the office and a patrol unit and EMTs were there in four minutes. I guess Gear's office looked like a goddamned slaughter house; they probably used the sap on him too. He wore wire-framed glasses which were broken and shattered and cut the shit outta his face. There was blood spatter everywhere.

"He was unconscious on the floor when the help arrived. They didn't try to move him or anything; just checked his pulse to make sure he was still alive and waited for the EMTs. Like I said, they were there almost immediately. He was here twelve minutes later."

I said, "Damn good work by everyone; now, tell me about the perps. A black guy and white guy in hoodies, huh? It's a lead pipe cinch they're the ones who stomped me. Has anyone started questioning them yet?"

Tom shook his head. "You know, I'm kinda pulling rank here; officially, I'm assigned to homicide and there haven't been any killings…yet. But I asked the detectives who caught the case to throw 'em in holding and wait until I could sit in. You can listen in if you want."

I hadn't thought about that. "Damn right and I appreciate being included. If we're lucky, maybe there won't be any bodies."

"Yeah, if we're lucky. C'mon, Crandall's waiting for us."

We walked down the hall to ICU where Peggy Sue Crandall was sitting in the waiting room along with two couples and three singles. She stood as we walked in and gave me a long hug. The left side of her face was swollen and bruised, her eyes were bloodshot, and her hair was a mess. After we separated, I held her at arms' length and said, "So, how's the other guy look, sweetie?"

She started to grin, winced and thought better of it. It was obvious it hurt to talk when she said, "Funny, you asshole!" She barely moved her lips or teeth when she spoke. "The nurse just told me Marty is coming around and they'll be moving him to a room in the next half-hour. They said he's doing well."

I said, "That's good news! Look, I think Tom's told me everything you told him so I won't make you repeat it. I just have a couple things…you can just nod or shake your head if you want, okay?"

She nodded.

"Good, you get it. Marty told me he'd pulled out of the merger with Rockson. Were you familiar with the deal?"

She nodded again.

"Did he tell you about Rockson's reaction?"

She nodded vigorously and spoke through clenched teeth, "Said Rockson went nuts; swore he'd get even. He do this?"

"I'd bet on it. Tom thinks it's the same guys who stomped me after I had a run-in with Rockson; that'd be too big a coincidence to think it was anyone else."

Peggy Sue stared at me for a moment. "Not as bad as when Gerri was murdered, but bad enough. Get the son-of-a-bitch, will you?"

"I'll try, sweetie. Get well!"

*****

I rode with Tom to police headquarters and we walked up to the second floor interrogation rooms located near the crossover bridge to the holding cells and jail. Tom put me in small observation room equipped with one way glass. He said, "I'll have one of the assholes brought over in a couple of minutes. Take a good look and see if you recognize him when I bring him in; the room is miked so you can hear everything in here. The detectives will do the questioning, but I'll be in there. I told the dicks to try the old 'first guy to talk gets the deal' ploy; see if one of these dummies goes for it. You and I will talk after we're done with the first guy and before we bring in the other one."

I took a seat and looked at the interrogation room. It was smaller than I would've thought; maybe ten by twelve. The bare walls were painted "institutional green." The floor was twelve-inch square gray and green tiles. A table with a ring hasp for handcuffs was bolted to the floor; one chair on the far side of the table faced me where I assumed the wall looked like a mirror. There were two chairs with their backs to me.

I heard the door open and watched as a medium size white guy in black pants and a green hoodie shuffled inside. The hoodie was off his head exposing short-cropped but shaggy dark brown hair with a little gray at the temples and in his sideburns. His face was pockmarked, he needed a shave and I suspected a shower too.

One cop was wearing a dark blue suit; the other was in a white shirt and dark gray slacks. Both were wearing ties; I felt sorry for them. Tom followed, carrying a paper coffee container. He closed the door and leaned against it.

The suited cop told the guy to sit in the single chair, unlocked one of the cuffs, and clamped it through the hasp on the table. The detectives took the two chairs with their backs to me. The other cop said, "Okay, asshole…what's your name?"

The guy looked up and I could see his eyes were still bloodshot and runny. Peggy Sue Crandall must have sprayed him squarely in the face because it had happened over two hours earlier. I was pissed--I didn't recognize him. He blinked a few times and said, "Name's Doug Mitchell, but I ain't tellin' you shit, man. I want a fuckin' lawyer!"

The detective slammed a pen down on a yellow legal pad. "You just said the magic word, shithead…lawyer. Just one thing first…you know damn good and well we've got you dead to rights on assault and battery, elder abuse, and if I write it up just right, attempted murder. We've got everything we need, including a witness statement and…you're gonna love this part, *Dougie*…video. You're dead meat, jerkoff.

"But now comes the fun part for us…since the same charges are going to come down on your partner, we're going to play 'let's make a deal.' The first one of you slimeballs who drops a dime on whoever set this up is gonna get a break; the other one ain't going to get shit. We'll come with everything we've got. You're looking at twenty-five to life, dumb-ass. And our deal is gonna be on the table about fifteen minutes starting now, so you'd better make a decision and I mean *RIGHT NOW!"*

The slugger muttered sourly, "You ain't gonna charge nobody with attempted murder. And I ain't rattin' on anybody. Now, get me the goddamned lawyer!"

The cop glanced at Tom as his partner stood up and unlocked the cuff from the table. "Have it your way, tough guy. I think we'll go ahead and sweeten the deal for your buddy; maybe offer him a get out of jail free card. Whadda ya think of that, dummy? Shoulda took our offer." He turned to his partner and said, "Get this stupid son-of-a-bitch outta here; we'll do better with the other one." Mitchell's expression didn't change. I figured he'd heard this song before and wasn't interested in dancing.

After he was taken out, the detective turned to Tom and said, "God *damn* it! I thought sure he'd be the one to take a deal; the other one looks too dumb."

Tom shrugged his shoulders looked toward the mirror and said, "You never know. Let's tell the next one this guy is cooperating, but let him know he's still got a chance if he rolls right now."

The door opened and the cop brought a black guy in. He was also wearing a hoodie, but it was not covering his head. The first thing I noticed was his right hand…it was covered with white spots: vitiligo. My heart rate speeded up. I flashed back to my stomping. He'd been the second guy in the garage.

I tapped the window and walked into the hall. Tom immediately stepped out to meet me. "I'd forgotten about it until right now, Tom, but that's one of the guys from the garage. I recognize the white skin discoloration on his hand."

"*SHIT!* You didn't put that in your statement, did you? It doesn't mean a goddamned thing now. We can't go back."

I knew he was right and felt stupid about it. "I'm sorry, man. I just didn't remember that at the time, but I'm damn sure it's the same guy. Isn't there some way we can use the skin thing?"

Tom studied his coffee for a few seconds before saying, "Maybe…I've got an idea. It's worth a try. Go back in the observation room; when I point at the mirror, rap on your side."

I went back and Tom reentered the interrogation. The cop in the suit was just asking the prisoner, who was now cuffed to the table, his name.

"Dobbs." The guy had a deep voice.

The cop said, "You got a first name, *Dobbs?*"

"Marcellus." It didn't appear the guy was much of a conversationalist.

Tom stepped away from the door, set his coffee on the end of the table, and reached down to pull up Dobbs' sleeve. Most of his exposed hand and wrist were splotched with the pinkish-white discolorations. Tom looked toward the mirrored window and said in a loud voice, "Is this the man?"

That was my cue and I didn't miss it. I rapped loudly. Dobbs' raised his gaze to the mirror and both detectives turned to stare in the same direction. Tom laughed, again maybe a bit too loudly, and said, "You're fucked, Dobbs. That knock was the guy you hammered in the parking garage and he just positively ID'd your ass, or I should say, your hands. Now, with what we got today, you're on the hook for big-time felonies: at least two assaults with deadly weapons, attempted murder, battery, elder abuse, breaking and entering, trespassing, and I'm sure we'll find a few more."

I had to smile behind the mirror as Tom listed the possible charges. He was making them up as fast as he could, trying to make it sound even worse than it was. He continued, "You're going in for a long, long time, asshole."

Dobbs slumped slightly in his chair. It was the sign Tom was looking for and he winked at the detectives. They didn't miss their cue either. "You know, Dobbs, there might be a tiny window of hope for you if you're smart enough to recognize it."

Dobbs jerked upright and looked at the detective. "What you be talkin' 'bout, what windah?"

The detective said, "Look, we know somebody else hired you two dummies. Somebody else set these beatings up; you two don't have a motive to just beat up on a bunch of total strangers. You didn't try to rob them; you just stomped 'em. We basically don't give a shit about you; we want whoever hired you.

"I don't know how well you know your buddy, Mitchell, but he's got a rap sheet long as your arm and right now he's sitting in another room getting ready to write everything up because we told him the same thing we're telling you; the first guy to give us some names gets a break. We can reduce the list of charges *way* down; down to practically nothing. I'm not going to lie to you and tell you we'll give you a walk, that ain't going to happen, but we might reduce everything to, maybe, just simple assault or something like that. If you don't have too bad a sheet, you might not do too much time. But here's the deal, you need to give us a name *RIGHT NOW!* Mitchell is thinking hard about it, but he hasn't started writing yet. You could beat him to the punch. What do you say, Dobbs? Wanta make a deal?" Once again, I was amused at how far the cops would stretch the truth to get some dummy to roll over.

"You ain't read me no rights yet; I ain't seen no lawyer either. What's up wid dat?"

I saw a cloud pass over Tom's face, but the other detective quickly answered, "You haven't been arrested yet, man. We don't read you the Miranda stuff until you're arrested. We couldn't be offering you this deal if you'd been arrested, and we can't offer you shit if you lawyer up. Now quit fucking around and tell us what you want to do…either take the deal or we'll arrest you, read the card, and get a fucking lawyer. You got one minute!"

I knew most of what he'd said was bullshit and definitely not in the proper sequence of events. I had to hope my sparring partner, Marcellus Dobbs, just wasn't bright enough to know the difference. It was a narrow and risky path, particularly if he'd been down it before. I was almost holding my breath.

"Ah 'ight, I wants the deal. I wants it 'fore dat damn Mitchell can get it. W'at you wan' to know?"

I was able to exhale.

The detective pulled the yellow legal pad in front of him, raised the pen, and said, "Who hired you?"

Dobbs furrowed his brow before saying, "Mitchell knowed dat guy from before. I doan know his last name but his first name be 'Ross.' Mitchell say he work for some rich dude. Is dat 'nough to get my deal?"

The detective replied, "I don't know. It's thin, man. We might need some more; what else you got?"

Dobbs got a startled look. I figured he knew he'd stepped across a line but wasn't sure it would get him the break he felt he needed. "Shee-it, man! Wha' you' all want from me? I ain't got no more! C'mon, man, you gotta cut me some slack here."

Tom spoke up, "We don't have to do *shit* for you, Dobbs. Get that through your thick skull! But there's more you can do for us; like telling us where you met this 'Ross' guy for starters."

The thug looked slightly relieved. He couldn't wait to answer. "Me and Mitchell was standin' in line at da Denver Rescue Mission and some guy called up Mitchell on his cell phone. Dey talked for a minute an' Mitchell said, 'I got somebody right here.' Den we humped it over to da loadin' dock for dat big hotel over dere on Welton Street…the Hyatt. 'Dis Ross guy was in a big hurry, whipped out $500, an' tole us to go thump some dude." Tom couldn't resist glancing at the mirror. "He tole us to get over to the parkin' g'rage 'tween 14th and 15th on Champa Street and go up to da fourt' floor and wait for a guy; said guy'd be wearin' tan pants and a dark blue coat. He give us a roll of tape and tole us to put it on da cameras in da stairwells and to bust our ass outta dere soon as we did da job."

One of the detectives said, "You saying he *sent* you to that specific garage and the fourth floor?"

Dobbs nodded, "Dat's right. He tole us right where to go."

"How come he called Mitchell? You and Mitchell ever do this before?"

"I ain't never done nothin' like dat, but Mitchell, he been busted for 'ssault before; done time too."

The detective asked, "How do you know Mitchell?"

"Met him at da Mission las' winter. Social Services put us up in a motel together in January. Me and some other nigger got in a fight 'bout a bottle Mitchell and me had and Mitchell kep' dat bastard from cuttin' me. I owed him."

"Musta been a hell of a fight and a big debt; I mean, why in the hell would you agree to get involved in beating a man you've never met? And what about those two old folks today…why the hell did you go after them?"

Dobbs hung his head and didn't answer. Tom said, "Take him back to holding and then come back here and let's talk this out." He signaled to me to come to the interrogation room. As I entered the hallway, the detectives were escorting Marcellus Dobbs out. He looked at me without the slightest bit of acknowledgement. The son-of-a-bitch had no idea who I was.

But I knew for sure who had set up the beating.

"Well, shit, we didn't learn a whole hell of a lot from that dumb-ass." Tom sounded discouraged. "I'm not sure we got enough from him for the ADA to even write him a deal."

I shook my head, "Maybe not…yet, but he gave us more than you might know."

"How do you figure?"

"Dobbs might not have had a last name, but he said the guy who set everything up was named 'Ross.' That's Rockson's muscle; he was with Rockson at Shanahan's when they braced Lindsey and me. I've got enough to go after those low-life bastards starting right now!"

# CHAPTER TWENTY-TWO

Lindsey had just left for work when my home office phone rang; caller ID read Tom Montgomery. "Hey, is DPD opening early these days? You probably haven't had your coffee yet."

Tom growled, "You want what I've got or not, wise-ass?"

It had to be important for him call at this time of day, "Sorry, buddy, of course I want whatever you've got."

"That's better. We had a fax from the feds when I got in this morning. That was a good idea to check out Rockson International for a South Sudan connection. Turns out they have one, and what's more, we lucked into a name for 'Ross' with it."

"Holy shit! What'd they send you?" I couldn't believe our good luck.

"Rockson International notified the State Department they were negotiating a petroleum exploration and production concession…whatever that is…with South Sudan back in 2011. That had to be within six months of them even becoming a country. Anyway, State gave 'em the go-ahead, subject to a review of the final document plus a list of all the Rockson employees and the names of whoever was signing for the Sudanese.

"There's a guy listed as an 'independent security analyst' by the name of Ross Dailov. I figured he's gotta be our guy so I had the FBI run him. Turns out he doesn't have a criminal record; never been convicted of anything, *BUT* he's been investigated several times for everything from racketeering, to fraud, to operating a criminal enterprise. Apparently he has a long juvie rap sheet from Illinois, but that'll take some time to get 'officially', so

I talked to a friend of mine in the state attorney's office in Springfield. She read Dailov's sheet and then called me. He was a teenage strong-arm man out of Chicago; lots of arrests for assaults and related shit. How in the hell he's kept his record clean since turning eighteen, I have no idea."

I was elated with Tom's findings. "Did Rockson get the concession?"

"Yes. They've been sending people and equipment over there for the last three or four years. It doesn't look like they've tried drilling anything yet, though."

"Who signed for the Sudanese?"

"Hang on for a minute--this fax is four pages long--I think I saw that some place." I heard pages rustling. "Here it is: some guy with a one word name…Akabile. That mean anything to you?"

"Bet your ass, it does! He's the thug masquerading as a defense minister who tried to work a kickback deal with Mercy Drexler to use her company's frack technology in South Sudan. Jesus, this cesspool is getting deeper and stinkier all the time."

Tom exhaled loudly and said, "You got that right! You have any bright ideas about how everything fits together?"

"Yeah, matter of fact, I do. First of all, I'm pretty sure there are at least two separate, uh, *conspiracies* going on. There's no question this Ross Dailov asshole, and therefore, Rockson, is responsible for the assaults on me, as well as Marty Gear and Peggy Sue Crandall. Second, I'm betting Dailov and Rockson…and Akabile too…are mixed up in the bombing of Mercy's car…the Semtek 'connection' is just too strong for any other explanation.

"As for Trey Webb and his Stop Fracking Us crowd, I think they're just a bunch of do-gooders who are in over their head with their protest movement. They might be guilty of something for hacking Mercy's phones and computers or maybe for those faxed threats, but I doubt they're into violence."

Tom interrupted me, "What about the shitstorm you guys ran into up in North Dakota; who did that?"

"Well, I gotta admit that one has me guessing. It doesn't seem to fit either outfit's patterns."

"What are you going to do now?"

I wanted to think about that for a moment, so I decided to stall. "I'll be waiting on you, I guess. Do you have enough to arrest Dailov?"

"Probably not; I'm going to meet with the DA this afternoon and lay it all out. Next, I'm meeting with the feds to see how they want to handle the bombing investigation. To tell you the truth, I think we may be stuck in neutral for a while, except for the assaults…the DA filed charges yesterday on both those cases."

I perked up at that news. "What'd he file?"

Tom chuckled drily, "Threw the book at Mitchell and went easy on Dobbs: two counts of attempted murder, aggravated assault, battery, and elder abuse for Mitchell. Just one count of misdemeanor assault for *Marcellus;* guess you don't count for much, buddy…a misdemeanor assault." He laughed out loud. "Of course, Mitchell turned out to have a heavy-duty record of shit like that…bunch of assaults, robbery, menacing. He'll do a stiff jolt. Dobbs' record was petty stuff…larceny, trespass. He shouldn't have picked Mitchell to hang with--this'll serve him right."

"Thanks for the information, Tom. I'll be in touch."

At 10:05 a.m., I called Rockson International and asked for "Mr. Dailov." The receptionist asked who was calling and I thought about making up a name but instantly reconsidered. Dailov was the type of egotistical jerk who figured he was either smarter or tougher than everyone else--he'd take the call. I said, "Cortlandt Scott. Tell him this is concerning the South Sudanese concession."

"Yes sir, please hold."

Apparently South Sudan was the magic word. "You gotta lot of fuckin' nerve, Scott. You don't have anything to do with South Sudan! What the hell do you want callin' me?" I'd figured right about his ego.

"That's where you're wrong, asshole; I have a *lot* to do with South Sudan *and* your buddy, Akabile."

Dailov was silent for several seconds. "What do you want?"

"I want to sit down with you for a little heart-to-heart. And, I don't want Rockson around."

"Why should I talk to you? We ain't got nothing to talk about."

I laughed, "You're wrong again, Dailov. I'm actually cutting you a break here; I'm giving you a big heads up."

He interrupted. "What the fuck you talkin' about?"

"About the fact the cops know you're the one who setup the beatings on me and Marty Gear and his secretary. I'm talking about the *fact* the feds can tie you to the bombing of Mercy Drexler's car--

"*You're full of shit!* You don't have dick!"

"You're wrong on all counts; which makes you three for three. Obviously, your hired hitters haven't been able to get in touch. Hell, you probably don't even know they fouled up the hit on Gear yesterday, do you? The dumb asses didn't count on getting pepper sprayed or grabbed up before they could run. They're both in central lockup and one of 'em is singing like Lady Gaga. They dropped a dime on you, dummy. Plus, I can ID 'em from the parking garage. You're going down big time, shithead."

I heard him take a deep breath. "If you've got all that, why the hell are you calling me?"

"Because I'm not focused on you. I want Rockson. You're just a means to an end. If you cooperate on him, I can probably get the cops to cut you a break on the assaults."

I heard him breathing heavily. "I'll talk to you, Scott. No wires; no cops; nobody else around. Got it?"

"Yeah, works for me; no wires on you either, okay?"

"What the fuck? Who am I going to talk to?"

"I don't know and I don't care…but no wires! How about meeting me at the Blue Bonnet? It's neutral turf for both of us, it's loud, and nobody who goes there would recognize either one of us."

"That the Mexican food dump down on South Broadway?"

"Yep, four hundred block south. Meet me there at 11:15 a.m.; that'll beat the crowd and we can get a booth."

"Don't try to fuck me around, Scott."

There were maybe twenty-five customers scattered around the cavernous interior of the Blue Bonnet, along with two tables of four under the umbrellas on the patio. When the girl at the entrance asked, "Inside or patio seating?" I asked for a back corner booth on the far side of the kitchen. She gave me a wondering glance like 'who the heck would want to be inside on a day like this' but didn't say anything other than "follow me." I gave her my name and said a guy would be joining me and she said she'd bring him right over.

Five minutes later, the girl brought Ross Dailov by and he slid in the opposite side of the booth. He was not as big as I remembered, although I'd been sitting down at Shanahan's when he and Rockson had braced me. I didn't want to shake hands with him so didn't extend mine, which seemed to suit him. A waitress had followed him to the table and asked if we wanted anything to drink, suggesting house margaritas. Dailov said he wanted a Coors Light and I ordered a Bud.

When the waitress left, Dailov said, "You've got the balls of a high diver, Scott. You don't have one shred of evidence about anything."

I fixed him with a stare before saying, "If you really believed that, you wouldn't be here. I don't need to prove anything, but if the cops bust you, you're going to spend years and probably millions fighting it out in court. I hope you have one hell of a deal with Rockson because you're going to need it. But, like I said, I think you're just so much cannon fodder; I want Rockson and I think you can get him for me."

The beers arrived and Dailov drained half of his in one long swallow. "Let's say I might know something that'll help you; what's in it for me?"

"I'm not the cops or the DA so I can't cut you a deal. What I *can* do is tell them you were instrumental in getting to Rockson; tell 'em you cooperated and are willing to continue to do so. I'm not going to blow smoke up your ass, Dailov; you're going to have to testify against Rockson in court to get any kind of deal and I think you're in deep enough that you'll have to do some time.

"*But,* I think they'll do something for you like they're doing for your hired slugger, Dobbs, because he's cooperating. They offered Mitchell and Dobbs the same deal but Mitchell clammed up so the DA is charging him with everything from trespass to attempted murder and he's probably going to do fifteen to thirty. But Dobbs is a different story; he's looking at one count of simple assault. The chances are good he'll walk away with a suspended sentence or maybe a few weeks in county lockup. You won't do that well, but you could help yourself…a lot."

Dailov peeled the beer label as he slowly twirled his bottle. "That's cold comfort. I don't fancy doing hard time. Maybe I should just take my chances that you and the cops can't prove anything."

"Your call, but you don't know what we have already."

He ripped the remaining piece of label free, seemed to make a decision, and looked straight at me. "Ask your questions; I'll answer if I know."

I silently breathed a sigh of relief. "How'd you know where I'd be when you sicced Mitchell and Dobbs on me?"

"Wasn't hard; Rockson called me and said he was sitting in the Petroleum Club looking at you and Drexler and needed to 'send a message.' He gave me your name, and described what you were wearing. I looked you up in the Geologist Association index and got your office address. I called the management company with a cock and bull story about being an auto glass replacement guy and was supposed to work on your car, but you hadn't told me where to find it. I asked if they also handled your parking and if they could tell me where it was.

Dailov smirked, "Amazing what some pencil pusher will tell you if you ask nicely; girl gave me your cell number, home phone number, *and* your parking slot. Took me less than three minutes. I called Mitchell and told him to bring another strong-arm guy and meet me in the Hyatt parking lot. When they showed up, I gave them some tape for the cameras and $500."

I needed to have a "talk" with my office leasing people. "Tell me about Akabile and South Sudan. How the hell did you get mixed up with him and what's happening on that front?"

"That's Rockson's deal. He's trying to get control of the whole damned country's oil and gas operation, but Akabile is as big a crook as Rockson and maybe a lot smarter, so they had to cut a deal."

I perked up, "What kind of deal?"

Dailov thought for a moment before replying, "It's got lots of arms and legs, but, basically, if Rockson can get Drexler's frack techniques, Akabile will grant him exclusive rights to explore in South Sudan; on the other hand, if Akabile can get the secrets and pass them on to Rockson, Rockson will give him an overriding royalty that's not in the official concession contract."

"That's totally illegal in the U.S.; it's a form of bribery."

Dailov laughed, "Rockson doesn't give a shit about any of that! He's got more 'illegal' contracts and concessions than legal ones."

It was time for the $64,000 question: "Did Rockson and Akabile bomb Drexler's car? And how are you involved?"

He hung his head and shook it from side to side before answering, "I'm in over my fucking head, that's how. Rockson insisted early on that I become the go-between with Akabile, so he gave me some kind of title with the company and I actually signed some contracts and shit. That got my name on the flight manifests and kind of gave me, I don't know, 'courier' status or something; anyway, the U.S. State Department knew I was coming and going.

"Right after Drexler and Rockson had the big blowout and she said she wasn't going to let him use her company, he sent me to Juba, the capital of South Sudan. He told me he'd been negotiating with Akabile who needed to get some ultra-secret papers and documents to us, but Akabile didn't trust their airlines or any of his own people, so he wanted me to fly there on Rockson's plane, pick up a sealed 'diplomatic pouch', and deliver it back here.

"I thought it was strange as hell but did what they asked. It was sealed all right…zippered and locked with a combination lock.

Akabile told me Rockson already had the combination; he'd telephoned it to him. I thought it was heavy for just papers, but I never thought much about it until I plopped it on Rockson's desk, he opened it up, and pulled out some sheets of C-4! I about jumped through the window!"

I didn't know if Dailov would answer the rest of my question, but he continued. "Rockson asked if I knew anyone who could do a little job for him; someone with experience with plastic explosives."

At that point I couldn't control my anger. "*Jesus Christ!*

So you *did* arrange for the bomb!

"Screw it! I've changed my mind about going to bat for you, you asshole! You need to go down hard!"

Dailov raised his hands as in self-protection. "No, no…you don't get it. Listen, I told Rockson I didn't want anything to do with something like that, you know…a bomb or maybe a murder. I told him I wanted out. But he said he didn't want to kill Drexler, he just wanted to scare the living shit out of her; make her willing to listen. But I told him again I didn't want any more to do with it. He got mad as hell, started cussing and yelling and finally ordered me out; said he'd take care of it himself. And that's the last I heard about it until the news reports that somebody had blown her up."

I was seething. "I don't know whether to believe you or not. But, regardless, you're up to your ass in it; you smuggled the fucking explosives for chrissakes!" I had to settle down if I hoped to ask him anything else. I took the proverbial deep breath, "What do you know about Clay Webb? Is he involved in any of this?"

Dailov momentarily got a blank look on his face. "I don't know anybody by that name."

I tried a different tack, "What do you know about the Frack Focus operation?"

"I don't know shit about anything technical, but Rockson told me he was working another angle and might have somebody on the inside at Frack Focus. He thought he could get the information that way and it would lead to a big payday."

*Shit!* It wasn't what I wanted to hear. It had to be Clay Webb. He had lied to me as well as Mercy…and maybe even to his own brother. "What about a guy named Trey Worth?"

Dailov shook his head, "Never heard of him; who is he?"

"If you don't know him, he doesn't concern you. You got anything else?"

"No, but if you're going after Rockson, you need to know the son-of-a-bitch is crazy! When anything--and I mean *anything*--pisses him off, he goes off the high board into the deep end. Nothing will stop him when he's after revenge or getting even. That's what happened when he wanted you beat up; same thing with Gear. I honestly don't know who he found to do the bombing, but it's just another example. I don't think he cared one way or the other whether Drexler got killed; I'm betting he thought he could do a deal with whoever he had inside if she wasn't in the way. I *do* think he wanted to hurt her real bad."

I signaled the waitress, gave her twenty bucks, and told her to keep the change. She smiled broadly: she had a large tip in hand and would be able to turn the table again. She thanked me and left.

I stood and Dailov did the same. Again, no handshake which suited me just fine. I said, "I'm going to have a talk with the cops and the DA; I'll keep my part of the bargain and tell them you're cooperating and will continue to do so. If I were you, I'd get shut of Rockson as soon as you can. Give me a number where I can reach you at any time and make yourself scarce; don't even go back to the office. You said yourself Rockson's crazy…imagine what he'll do if he finds out you're talking to me."

Dailov pulled two cell phones from his pockets, asked for my number and "sent" me his. He looked beaten when he said, "This is a phone Rockson doesn't know anything about. I gotta go back and pick up some stuff, but he's out of town today. I won't be there after today. Get this wrapped up, Scott; nobody is safe as long as that fucker is walking around." I nodded and we walked out in opposite directions.

More than anything, I wanted to get my hands on Rockson and stomp the bastard into dust, but Dailov had said he was out of town, so I decided to start building the case against him with Tom and the DA. I called to make sure Tom was in, told him I had a shitload of information, and we needed the DA to sit in. Driving the twenty or so blocks from the Blue Bonnet to police headquarters gave me time to think about Clay Webb. I didn't know if he'd done anything illegal at this point; doing a deal with Rockson was immoral and unethical but probably not illegal unless he had given him some of Frack Focus' proprietary information. I decided I'd leave him out of the discussion with the cops and the DA.

ADA Skyler McMillan was staring at Tom and fidgeting in one of his visitor's chair when I walked in. She stood, offered her hand which I took, and stepped in close to hug me. "Long time, no see, Cort. How've you been?"

"Oh, can't complain, Skyler; wouldn't do any good anyway, nobody much cares, right?"

She laughed, "That's a fact! Hey, Tom says you've got some dope on one of our preeminent Denver businessmen, one Guilford Rockson…the prick! I hope you've got something good; we've been trying to get to the S.O.B. for years"

I was glad to hear it. "I didn't know the DA's office had a hard-on for Rockson. What have you been looking at him for?"

McMillan resumed her seat before answering, "We think he's involved in all sorts of shit: extortion, bribery, and maybe even some federal stuff like racketeering and corrupt practices. We've never been able to come up with enough evidence to arrest him, let alone get it to court. You gonna be able to help us?"

"I hope so. How'd you like to add conspiracy to commit murder, attempted murder, conspiracy to commit assault, theft of proprietary information; and that's just locally. You might be able to bring the feds in too…bribery, importing explosives, and I don't know what all."

McMillan started smiling, "If you've got proof of *anything*, I'm going to kiss you on all four cheeks! C'mon, spill…what have you got?"

It took nearly half an hour to tell her everything I'd learned from Dailov. I left out anything about Clay Webb; I wanted to deal with him myself. She took copious notes and double underlined the last page when I said that's all I had. "First thing is you've got to get this Dailov to come in and give a statement and we'll get him in protective custody; get him the hell out of Denver and Rockson's reach. Without his official statement, we can't prove shit! As much as I hate it, we'll cut him a deal if it leads to Rockson. Can you get a hold of him? Tell him we'll put him up in a luxury resort in the mountains or send him out of state; anywhere he wants. And we'll give him a bodyguard."

Tom scowled but didn't say anything as I pulled out my cell and hit the speed dial for the number Dailov had given me. It rang three times and went to voice message. I waited for the beep and told him things were speeding up, the DA's office needed to talk to him a.s.a.p., and they'd agreed to cut him a break *if* he'd turn himself in and make a statement. It bothered me he hadn't answered at the number which he'd assured me was safe. I told Tom and McMillan I'd keep trying.

# CHAPTER TWENTY-THREE

It was a quick ten-minute walk to my office in the Equitable Building. I was amazed at the amount of mail in my box downstairs; at least some of it was the good kind: mailbox money…royalty checks from production I'd found years before. It served to remind me I still had a toe in the oil and gas exploration business, although it seemed a world removed from international bomb plots and industrial espionage.

I called Janelle and asked how Mercy was healing. I hadn't seen her since the day I'd visited her condo. Janelle sounded depressed and told me she *seemed* to be doing fine physically, but mentally, it was going slowly. "What do you mean?" I asked.

"It's kind of hard to explain. She apparently gets up early like always and her PT guy comes to her condo at 7:00 a.m. She works with him for an hour and a half, showers, and is in her home office by 10:00 a.m. According to the therapist, she's coming along really well…has regained most of her strength and nearly a full range of movement in her right leg.

"The problem is, she just sits at her desk sort of staring at the walls until mid-afternoon, goes into the living room, gets a glass of wine, and then stares out the windows until early evening. I have all the morning reports emailed to her by 10:30 a.m., but I don't think she even looks at them. When I've called her with something needing her attention or an answer, she obviously hasn't been reading the reports. She always says she'll get right on it, but then doesn't call back. It's like she's got something heavy on her mind and can't be distracted, but the trouble is, uh…there doesn't appear to be *anything* on her mind."

I was stumped for something to say. Finally, I asked, "How long have you been noticing this, Janelle? She's been home, what…almost a month now, isn't it?"

"It'll be a month on Monday and seven weeks since the bombing."

"Has she said when she will be coming into the office?"

"No, and that's another strange thing. When she first got home, it's all she could talk about, you know, getting to the office and back to work. Remember when you visited and she said she was coming in 'next Monday'? It never happened."

"What's been happening with Clay while she's been out?"

"Funny you should ask; he's been *really* quiet, almost secretive or something. He spends most of the time with his office door closed and he's gone a lot; he says he's in outside meetings or else he goes to the field."

I let that sink in. "Has he been making any presentations of the frack techniques?"

She was quick to answer, "Oh no! That's *one* thing Mercy was definite about before she, you know, 'withdrew'; she said no more presentations until she got back."

"So how often do you see her?" I asked.

"At first, I was stopping by every day after work. But for the past couple of weeks, I've only gone maybe every third day or so. It just seemed like she was impatient for me to leave five minutes after I'd gotten there. I still call every morning, though."

I made a decision, "I'll go see her. What's her normal schedule like?"

"Well, like I said, she gets up early and the PT guy comes from7:00 to 8:30 a.m. She's in her office by 10 o'clock and her nurse comes at 11:30. After that, I'm not entirely sure…except for the wine in the afternoon."

I pondered the information before saying, "Okay, thanks. If you set it up with her security, I'll go Monday and check it out for myself. Thanks again, Janelle, I'll touch base with you after I've seen her."

I tried Dailov's cell again; still no answer, so I left another message to call me as soon as he could.

On Monday, I repeated my earlier routine at Mercy's condo. Personnel turnover in the condo security business seemed to be low…the same people were at their posts as on my previous visit. This time, Mr. Rushing, the rent-a-cop, served double duty by dropping me off at the door as he picked up Mercy's nurse on her way out. Mercy was at the door and was surprised to see me.

I was shocked by the change in her appearance. Her face was thin and drawn and she had developed crow's foot wrinkles around her eyes. Her color was off, changed from her normal "Mediterranean olive" to a much paler version. She was wearing a Rockies' purple velour warmup suit that hung off her as though she'd lost a lot of weight. Although enthusiastic in her greeting, her voice seemed a little reedy and the handshake wasn't as firm as previously. "Oh, Cort, it's so good to see you! I've been meaning to call you or have you drop by. I'm so glad you took the initiative! I know it's not as convenient as coming to the office so I really appreciate it."

We walked down the art-lined hallway to the living room and its incredible views. I said, "Well, it's good to see you too; and speaking of the office, I thought you were going to start coming in. Are you planning on doing that soon?"

She took a seat and motioned for me to do the same before replying. "Oh yes, I need to start going in. It just seems so hard to get motivated."

I caught her eye, but she wouldn't hold my gaze, "What's the matter, Mercy? You've changed. You've even changed since you came home."

She dropped her eyes, sighed deeply, and leaned back in the chair. "I know you're right, but I don't have an answer. At first, right after the bombing when I was still in the hospital, I was just shocked. I was shocked someone would seriously try to kill me, especially over business. Then, after I came home, I was mad: mad at whomever did it, mad at myself for not being more careful, maybe mad at the world!

"But then my thoughts seemed to change; I guess I became more introspective and began to question *my* motives for doing things. Why do I want all these *things*?" She swept her arm in an encompassing wave of the impressive room and its contents. "What kind of statement am I making other than it's good to have a lot of money? What good am I?

"After I started wondering about those kinds of things, I lost interest in going downtown just to do more of the same. What's *really* changed is wanting to know who's responsible for everything: wanting to find out who set off the bomb, or shot at us, or sent the threats. I mean, what difference does it make? What does it all mean?"

I was taken aback by Mercy's soliloquy. This was the woman whose drive and ambition, not to mention talent, had made her the richest woman in Denver. She had turned much of her success into philanthropic ventures benefitting the city, the state, and probably even the country. I tried to summon an empathetic voice, take a tone that would change the direction of her thoughts. "Mercy, your words worry me. You're the most vital, life affirming person I've ever met. Your personal efforts, drive, and spirit have literally changed the face of downtown, hell, maybe the whole Rocky Mountain region! You're an inspiration to everyone who comes in contact with you…male or female. Young women who aspire to careers in science hold you up as an example; petroleum professionals idolize your achievements. Talk like this will let down an awful lot of people; people who *need* positive role models. And I'm not just talking about your financial successes. You've taught people how to give back; how to be better citizens; how to share. Don't let those kinds of influences slip away!"

I didn't know where that had all come from. I had given plenty of "how to" speeches over the years, but never a "why" speech. I believed what I'd said, but had surprised myself with how it had come out.

Mercy stood and walked to the bar where she took a bottle of Bud and a half full bottle of Jordan chardonnay out of the refrigerator/cooler. She poured a generous glass of the wine, twisted the top off the beer, and walked back. "Other than my physical therapist, my nurse, and Janelle, you're the only *real* person I've talked to in seven weeks. I think I needed it. I guess when it comes down to brass tacks, I've been feeling sorry for myself; wondering why I was being targeted; wondering if I had some personal flaw making me a bad person.

"I *am* going to make some changes...like not worrying about cutting the toughest deal I can just to make more money, but 'I hear you,' Cort. I understand what you've said; I *have* been a positive force and I can continue to be one. I *do* have something to offer; I *do* make a difference. And you know what, I like the image." She sipped her wine, seemed to savor it, and raised her glass toward me in an air toast. "You're a good guy, Cortlandt Scott. Lindsey is lucky to have you!"

I didn't know how to respond, so I didn't; returning the toast without speaking.

Mercy stood again and took a seat beside me setting her glass on the table. "Now, first things first...it's too late today, but I'll be in the office first thing tomorrow and--

I interrupted, "Who says it's too late; it's only 2:00 p.m. for chrissakes! C'mon, put on some 'office' clothes and I'll take you downtown. I know everyone will be glad to see you...especially Janelle. She's the one who's been most worried about you. It'll be a big lift for everyone. You can resume 'normal' operations tomorrow."

She grinned, jumped to her feet, and said, "I'll just throw on some jeans and a shirt. I'll be ten minutes max. Oh Cort, thank you so much for this; it'll be fun!"

As she danced out of the room, I thought about the best way to bring her up to date on the various investigations. Her change in attitude was going to negate all those introspective thoughts about not caring who was after her.

# CHAPTER TWENTY- FOUR

As I coasted into the garage, the door on Lindsey's side rumbled up and she pulled in alongside. We walked into the kitchen where I pulled her to me and engaged her lips in a long lingering kiss. When we pulled back, she flashed "the" grin and said, "Whew! What brought that on? Not that I'm complaining!"

"I don't know; I guess it was a particularly good day. I think Mercy had a big breakthrough today and things are looking up for her. We had a heart-to-heart and I honestly feel like it made a difference. She even got dressed and I took her downtown to her office. I feel like celebrating. Let's crack a bottle of something good and sit on the deck for a while. That work for you?"

She continued to smile and said in a low, husky voice, "You sure know how to turn a girl's head, sweetie. You go select 'something good' while I change clothes. I'll meet you on the deck in five minutes." She stepped back in for another kiss; it was a good one.

I raced downstairs to the wine closet and studied the racks. The really good reds were on the left in floor to ceiling horizontal, three deep bottle racks; our everyday 'drinking wines' in the middle two racks; the whites were on the right. I concentrated on the best reds and finally pulled a 2004 Caymus cabernet sauvignon. The neck tag had a 97 rating from the *Wine Enthusiast.*

I used a rabbit opener to ease out the cork, and took a tasting glass from the little rack above the cabinet. Pouring about half an ounce, I held the glass against the light from the tiny ceiling spots and vigorously swirled. God, it was beautiful! Deep garnet-purple with numerous well-formed "legs". I plunged my beak into the glass and checked the nose…again, it was beautiful: full, very "berry" with deep, dark notes of fruit, tobacco and leather.

I started laughing to myself at my description. Who was I kidding? Like I've always said, "My favorite wine is any kind that runs downhill and makes me dizzy!" I tasted what I'd poured, curled my tongue, and brought it back as far as I could without swallowing. I let it sit there for a moment then sloshed it around before letting it slide down my throat. It was incredible for having been open less than a minute.

I hurried upstairs, grabbed two of the long stemmed crystal wine goblets designed for "big" reds and went out to the deck. I poured two glasses, set them on the table between the lounge chairs, and went back toward the bedroom. Linds was coming the other way and we met in the hall outside the bedroom. She had made herself more comfortable…in spades! She had donned loose shorts, an undershirt top and obviously nothing else. I said, "Your glass awaits, young lady. I'll be right back."

She smiled and said, "Don't tarry; I'll be tempted to start without you."

I tried my hand at a lecherous smirk and said, "You mean the wine?" She slugged me on the shoulder.

I threw on some shorts and a tee shirt and headed back outside. Linds was stretched out on a chaise but hadn't touched her wine. I sat beside her, picked up my glass, and reached across the space between us. She did the same and we clinked. Taking small sips, we savored the Caymus and both sighed in unison. "Wow, where have you been hiding this stuff?" She took another drink and exhaled in pure pleasure.

"It's been right there in plain sight…admittedly on the very top rack and out of your reach." I laughed. "What do you think?"

"It's fantastic! Ranks right up there with Far Niente and some of the Heitz rarer vintages, I'd say. So, what are we celebrating? You said you had a good meeting with Mercy; what happened?" I thought back to the first bottle of wine I'd ever shared with Lindsey…an Oregon pinot noir, an Erath. Back then, she hadn't known a pinot noir from a jug of Finger Lakes "red." We'd both come a long way.

"Well, remember what I told you Janelle said? That Mercy was acting very strangely; not her old self and hadn't even been in the office since the bombing? I went to see her and, you know what…at first, I couldn't believe it was even her! She's lost a lot of weight, which isn't a good thing, looked all drawn, and her color was off, too. We started talking and it was like she was giving me a verbal suicide note or something: life had lost meaning; what good was she; making money didn't bring happiness…I mean, it was *depressing*! She said she didn't even want to know who tried to kill her."

Lindsey brought the back of her chair up. "Geez, I thought you said it was a *good* day! Where does the good news come in?"

I acknowledged her observation and said, "I didn't know what to say, so just listened until she kind of ran out of steam and then I started talking about all the great things she's done, what a difference she's made for Denver, for young women, for oil business professionals. I tried to explain about her being a role model and a mentor; basically, anything I could think of to raise her spirits. It must have struck a chord. It was like the clouds parted and she could see the sunshine. You know what I think: I think she was just isolated and lonely. The only people she's been seeing are her PT guy and a nurse. Hell, she's even been turning Janelle away.

"It seemed like just talking to her, propping her up a little, was a lifeline. All at once, she was the old Mercy Drexler, Denver's richest woman, the city's most generous philanthropist, the company builder and entrepreneur. Fifteen minutes later, we were on our way downtown…she even wanted the top down on the 'Vette."

"Sounds like you did some good, all right; did you go into the office with her?"

"No, I thought about it, but decided it would temper the effect too much. I wanted her staff to think it was all her idea; that she was ready."

Lindsey nodded, "Probably right. So what happens now?"

I savored another sip. "I figure she'll have it out with Clay Webb and sort out what the hell is going on with him. Then, I'm betting on 'business as usual.' I'm not kidding you, Linds; she was the old Mercy when she climbed out of the car."

"How about with you? Where are you going with everything?"

"I'm pushing the DA to set up a meet with Dailov and get his deal worked out. The sooner we can go after Rockson, the sooner I'm going to start sleeping better.

I picked up the bottle, "Speaking of things like that, what would you say to finishing this off in the hot tub and then heading for the bedroom?"

She looked at me with mock horror, "Good grief, buddy, it's only five 'til seven! It won't even be dark for another hour and a half! But…Okay!"

# CHAPTER TWENTY-FIVE

I was luxuriating in the shower after a hard run; I hadn't done three miles in a while and could feel it. I cursed when the phone in the bedroom rang, scrambled out of the shower, and caught it on the fourth ring. Caller ID read Ivins@Arapahoe County, "Hey George, what's up? Lindsey left fifteen minutes ago; she should be in any minute."

George Ivins' voice was terse, "We've got a homicide…maybe a murder; maybe a suicide, I don't know which yet, but I need to talk to you. Dead guy's got your number in his phone."

"Who is it, George? Lots of people have my number."

"Name's Dailov. Know him?"

*"Shit!"*

"I'll take that as a 'yes.' What's the story?"

I walked back into the bathroom and took a towel from the bar. "He is, or *was* a real badass; worked for Rockson so this all ties into the Mercy Drexler case. I talked with him last week and was working a deal with Skyler McMillan in the Denver DA's office for him to drop a dime on Rockson. Without him, I don't know if Tom Montgomery and the DA can make a case against the bastard. Dailov pretty much confirmed Rockson set up the bombing of Mercy's car. What do you mean you don't know if it's a murder or suicide?"

George exhaled loudly, "Lindsey should be here in a few minutes and can probably help with an answer. Dailov is sitting in a big leather easy chair with the whole top and back of his head gone. Place is a real mess and there's a big-ass pistol in his lap…a Smith & Wesson Model 500. At first glance it looks like he ate it, but to my eye, the gun isn't where it should be if he'd been holding it in his mouth. It's still in his hand and his index finger is inside the trigger guard. I don't know if you've seen this particular gun, but the barrel is over eight inches long and it's damned near impossible to put it in your mouth and pull the trigger with your index finger. The reports I've read about suicides with long-barreled pistols usually say the shooter used his thumb."

"How come you caught the case, George? Where's the scene?"

"Just my lucky day, I guess. It's in the Vellagio townhome development at Inverness golf course, south of Dry Creek Road, north of County Line. You know where I'm talking about?"

"Yeah, it's not too far from Lindsey's place. So, do I need to come by?"

George laughed drily, "Not unless you want to see all the blood and brains; why don't you come by the Justice Center this afternoon. I should be back by 1:30 p.m. or so."

"Okay. Have you talked to Tom yet?"

"No, I didn't know he was involved until you just said it. I'll give him a call; maybe he'll want to come at the same time."

I closed the call, finished toweling off and pulled on some jeans and a golf shirt. I could smell the freshly brewed coffee when I walked out to the living room and mentally blew Lindsey a kiss for starting the pot when she'd left for work. I poured a cup and retreated to my office to call Mercy.

"Morning, Janelle; is Mercy in yet?"

"Boy…is she ever! What in the world did you say to her yesterday? She blew in here about 2:30 p.m. yesterday, apparently stayed until after I left at six o'clock, and it was like she had never been gone. Same thing this morning; she was already in when I arrived at 7:35 a.m. and from the looks of her desk and *my* files, she may have been here for a while. If she hadn't been wearing different clothes, I'd have thought she had spent the night! Whatever you did or said, Cort…*THANKS!* It's like old times. You want to speak to her?"

"Yes. I'm glad she's better. Let's keep her that way, okay?"

"I'll vote for that! Hang on, I'll connect you."

"Hey, good morning, Cort! How are you today?" Mercy Drexler didn't sound like the same person I'd seen yesterday. Janelle was right; she sounded like old times.

"Morning, Mercy; you sound good. I don't want to ruin your day, but we've got to talk about something."

She answered, "Ooh, this sounds serious, but I feel so good I don't think anything can ruin my day. What is it?"

I charged ahead, "We didn't talk about what I've found out about Rockson and everything that's been going on. Some things have happened; things that have me worried."

"What kind of things?"

"First of all, several different strings are getting tied together. The biggest thing of all is that your suspicions about Rockson having someone inside your organization are probably correct."

I heard a loud bang and assumed she had slapped her desk. "*Goddamnit!* I knew it! It's Clay, isn't it?"

"I haven't confirmed that and it's part of the problem; I had turned one of Rockson's muscle men, a guy named Dailov, and he told me you had a mole. The trouble is Dailov is dead; he either shot himself or somebody 'helped' him. He hadn't talked to the cops yet so what he told me is the only thing we have tying Rockson to Akabile, the bombing, and having someone inside Frack Focus. Without a sworn statement, it's just going to be hearsay; not admissible in court."

"*OH MY GOD!* A murder! How are we going to stop this madness? I can't stand this, Cort! Maybe I *AM* going crazy; my *GOD,* what else has happened?"

"Like I said, I'm probably going to ruin your day, but this Dailov guy arranged to have Marty Gear beaten up after he dropped out of the merger deal with Rockson. As it turns out, he was also the one who hired the sluggers who got me. At least those guys are in the jug and with Dailov dead that kind of stuff should come to an end."

I heard Mercy stifle a sob and her voice caught, "I can't believe what you're telling me. Marty Gear was beaten? And Rockson was behind it? Did this dead guy you're talking about blow up my car?"

"I don't think so. He told me he'd had enough; had enough of Rockson. But Akabile is in it up to his eyeballs; he sent the explosives used…all the way from South Sudan."

She sighed, "What about the attack on the job site in North Dakota?"

It was something I hadn't considered. "Good question…it didn't come up with Dailov. And I'm pretty sure Trey Worth didn't have anything to do with it. It seems strange Clay would have been involved since whoever it was shot at him too; unless that was cover."

"Cort, I want you to concentrate on Clay. I've got to know if he's the spy or if I can still trust him. If we can resolve that question, I think I can move forward."

I thought it a good idea. "Okay, I'll do what I can. And, Mercy, be careful."

At the Arapahoe County Justice Center, I drove to the back visitors' lot. I could see Lindsey's Ford Edge parked inside the gated compound where the cops parked. Heat waves were rolling off the rows of vehicles left by the on duty officers. Walking across the concrete to the side entrance was like being in a toaster oven. A woman deputy sat at the small desk placed crosswise in the narrow hallway. The rest of the hall was taken up with a metal detector arch and x-ray tunnel. Another deputy was standing at the end of the conveyor belt. I recognized both of them but couldn't put names to the faces.

I spied the woman's name plate, L. Thomas, and remembered meeting her at a party Lindsey and I had attended. She'd been with George Ivins and I'd sensed they might have been more than just good friends. "Hi, Laurie…How're you doing? I'm Cort Scott; I'm here to see Sheriff Ivins and Lindsey Collins."

Laurie Thomas stood, smiled, and said, "Hi, Cort, nice to see you again. George, uh, I mean, *Sheriff* Ivins left word you'd be coming in. You packing? You'll need to turn it in while you're here." I'd caught the slight slip; it confirmed my suspicions.

I nodded, pulled up my Hawaiian shirt, and removed my brand new Heckler & Koch VP9 9mm from its back holster. I dropped the clip and jacked it open to show the empty chamber before I handed it to Laurie. She replaced the clip, slid an orange plastic trigger lock on, dropped everything in a heavy-duty, clear, evidence baggie, and placed it in a cubby hole on the wall behind her. "Okay, walk on through the metal detector. Sheriff Ivins said to meet him in his office, number 142, on up the hall."

"Thanks, I've been here before; I know where it is." I cleared the detector, picked up my wallet, nodded to the other deputy, and walked to George's office. The door was open and George was standing behind his desk. His face had aged in the years since we'd chased Gerri German's killers from Denver to LA, on to New Orleans and ended up in a shootout in the back of a mob hangout. He still looked like he had stepped out of a central casting office for the part of a modern-day western sheriff: tall and slim, he was wearing sharply-creased uniform pants and a short sleeved uniform shirt with epaulet shoulders. His old west style, five point star badge was pinned over his heart. A short-brimmed dove-gray Stetson sat on its crown on the right front of the desk. When he walked around to shake hands, I had to smile at the shine and buff on his black Roper boots.

"Hey George, how ya doin'? It's been a while, huh?"

Like always, his grip was crushing. "Yeah, it *has* been a spell. You doing okay? I guess you and Lindsey made up all right. She's sure as hell been in a better mood lately!" He laughed and pointed at the small, round table with four chairs occupying the corner of his office. "Grab a chair; she'll be here a minute."

I did as ordered and said, "I saw Laurie Thomas working the security desk out front. You seeing her? You guys an 'item' these days?"

He grinned sheepishly and bobbed his head. "Well, I guess that's what you call it these days…an *item.* We've been hanging around together for a few months now; first woman I've had much interest in since those scumbag bastards murdered Mary and your friend, Gerri."

It seemed like a lifetime ago since my first client as a private investigator, Mary Linfield, had been killed. I'd met Lindsey and George during the subsequent investigation and when the same hired killers murdered Gerri, George and I had run them to ground. During the chase, he'd admitted to being in love with Mary Linfield, although nothing had ever come of it. That knowledge had created a special bond between us. "Well, she's a great-looking gal, buddy, although I'd never figured you for a redhead fancier." I laughed as he took a seat across from me.

"Always a first time for everything…jerk!" He was laughing as Lindsey walked in with a file folder under her arm.

She asked, "What's so funny, guys? Dirty jokes?"

I stood and pulled out a chair for her. "Geez, that's a little rude. Can't two old friends share a laugh?"

"Not you two bandits! Anything that causes you two to laugh can only mean bad news for someone!"

George harrumphed, "So, what've you got from the crime scene?"

I asked, "Is Tom coming?"

George said, "No, he called and said he's too tied up with the ADA, McMillan, trying to figure a way to get everything you told them into some kind of evidence. He said he'd catch up with me later."

All the smiles were erased when Lindsey opened the folder. "Well, our interpretation of the crime scene evidence seems to confirm your first impression, George. It would have been extremely difficult for the victim to have held that long-barreled pistol in one hand, put the muzzle in his mouth, and pulled the trigger with an index finger. He might have been able to get it positioned correctly but would've *had* to engage the trigger with his thumb.

"I suppose he could have used his thumb and still ended up with his index finger through the guard when it fell, but I doubt it. We tried to get a print off the trigger to match with either his index finger or thumb but the trigger is crosshatched, so no prints.

Another thing: there's blood spatter on the underside of his fingers *AND* his thumb. That would be hard to do if either or both were used to pull the trigger."

George was listening and slowly nodding his head as Lindsey spoke. He asked, "Anything else?"

"We also looked at the angle from the entry point in his mouth and throat to the exit in the back of the head to the impact point of the slug in the wall behind the chair. It's not consistent with someone putting the muzzle in their mouth and pulling the trigger. It's too low an angle.

"And one more thing, the blood spatter on his sleeves and the chair arms; it looks like someone was holding his arms down on the chair. There are areas on both sleeves where there's no blood and there's no blood on the arms of the chair."

George said, "I think that ties a knot around it, Lindsey. The guy was murdered. And from what you've said, there were at least two people doing the killing: somebody holding his arms and another pulling the trigger. They tried to doctor the scene to make it look like a suicide.

"Did you find anything to help identify the killers?"

Lindsey shook her head. "No. We dusted every surface in the place for prints, vacuumed the chair and carpet for fibers and hairs; everything, so far, belongs to Dailov. There's so damned much blood, it's going to take more time to run samples from every drop to make sure it's all his."

George turned to me, "When you talked to him, did he seem like a guy who'd commit suicide? Did he mention anybody who might be gunning for him?"

"No to both; seemed like a tough guy, although he was drawing the line at bombing Mercy Drexler. He mentioned Rockson was big on revenge and getting even and we've heard that before."

George appeared to be deep in thought, finally saying, "Okay, I'm going to treat it as a murder investigation. When I talked to Tom, I suggested we have a joint team for the whole investigation. We'd be coming at it from the murder side; he and his guys would come from the Drexler side…you know, the threats and the bombing.

“Cort, if you’ll agree, you’d be our liaison. I know it’s asking a lot since you’re not connected to either department, but Tom and I thought it would work. We could start with you bringing me up to speed with what you’ve already found out. Lindsey thanks; good work today.”

We all stood, Lindsey picked up her folder and said, “I’ll see you at home later, okay?” I nodded and gave her a quick hug as she headed out the door.

I stayed for half an hour and ran George through everything I’d done, who I’d talked to, and all that had happened since taking the job from Mercy. He took some notes, asked a few questions, and then said, “The one common theme seems to be this guy Rockson and his reputation for getting back at people who piss him off. Would you agree?”

“Yeah, I do. I also keep wondering about the possibility of him having a mole in Drexler’s office. It seems likely, but if it’s Clay Webb, why would he take the chance of getting hurt in the shooting up in North Dakota?”

George studied the question for a few moments. “Think it could have been some kind of cover story for him? You know…make it look like he was a target just like Drexler and you?”

“It has certainly occurred to me. I think I’ll go have another talk with him; I’ll bring up Dailov and check his reaction. If he’s involved, it might scare him into rethinking any relationship with Rockson, assuming Rockson had Dailov murdered.”

George stood and walked around his desk which meant our talk was over. At the door, I said, “Why don’t you bring Laura out to the house on Saturday afternoon? I’ll mix up some margaritas and we can sit around and chat. I’d like to get to know her if you two are going to be hanging out.”

He looked at me with a quizzical expression before saying, “I’ll ask her. We’ve kinda kept everything under wraps around here for all the obvious reasons. Maybe it’s time to let a few others in on the secret.”

I "shot" him with my thumb and forefinger.

# CHAPTER TWENTY-SIX

As we arranged the deck chairs, I asked Lindsey, "So how well do you know Laurie Thomas? How long have she and George been seeing each other?"

"Good questions; too bad I don't have good answers. I guess I've seen her around for a couple of years, but she's been in patrol division while I've been in the lab. I think she just moved into administration and office security. We probably haven't spoken more than two or three times. And as for whatever she's doing with George, the only time I'd ever seen them together was the party you and I went to. If it's a big deal, they've managed to keep it one hell of a secret. I'm anxious to see what they say today."

I glanced at the Aztec sun-face clock over the door, "Well, shouldn't be long now; they're due in five minutes." The words weren't even out when the front bell chimed. I grinned at Linds and said, "They must be anxious." She swatted me across the butt with the towel she'd been using to wipe down the tables.

"Come in; come in! Hey, it's good to see you. Laurie, welcome to our place; George, welcome back. You haven't been here in a while." True to form, George was wearing Wrangler jeans and a short sleeve, checked western shirt. He had a broad-brimmed, straw cowboy hat and highly-polished brown boots. Laurie, by contrast, looked like she had stepped off the cover of a ladies' golf fashion magazine. She had on knee length skinny golf shorts in a turquoise color, with a sleeveless silver top. The fit and form of the shorts showed off her long legs, not to mention a trim and shapely caboose. She looked a lot younger in the sport togs than her sheriff's uniform.

George doffed his hat as he stepped in. "Thanks for having us, Cort. We haven't been out and about much; it'll be nice to sit and talk without looking over our shoulders. Hi, Lindsey, long time, no see." They both laughed at that as they hugged.

Laurie awkwardly stuck out her hand, "Yes, thanks so much for inviting us." I stepped inside her proffered handshake and gave her a chaste hug.

Lindsey did the same. "You're very welcome. We both felt like we needed to get to know you. George and Cort have been friends for a few years and I've worked for George for almost eight years now. I actually feel bad about not ever saying anything at work, but you know how it goes."

We led the way out to the deck and took seats under the covered section. I asked, "Margaritas for everyone? Salted rim or no?"

Laurie answered for both, "Margaritas would be great! And definitely salt for me; how about you, George?" He nodded.

"Okay, coming up; I've already got 'em mixed so just have to fix the glasses and pour. Linds, why don't you give me a hand with the fetching and carrying? We'll be right back."

Inside at the kitchen island counter, I raised my eyebrows and gave a silent whistle toward Lindsey. She feigned slapping me and whispered, "Watch yourself, sleuth. Your face is getting red and your tongue is hanging out."

I mouthed a big 'WOW' and poured. We carried the drinks outside, put down drink coasters, and placed one in front of our guests. When we'd all taken seats, I raised my glass and proposed a toast, "Well, here's to many more times like this…good times and good friends." Everyone reached and we clinked. A few grains of the rim salt fell. "So, Laurie, tell us about yourself...what brought you to the sheriff's department and, more importantly, how in the world did you hook up with this cowboy?"

She sipped delicately at the margarita before answering. "Wow, that's good! There's not much of a story; I came out to Colorado from Pennsylvania about three years ago, applied for jobs at every cop shop from Fort Collins to Pueblo, and cooled my heels tending bar for three months until Arapahoe finally called and I went to work. I've been there a little more than two years."

Lindsey asked, "Were you in law enforcement before? You must have been, I mean, to go directly to patrol."

Laurie nodded, "Yes, I was at the Erie PD for five years before moving here. Most of it was in the patrol division. Way back when, I was a flight attendant for U.S. Airways; I worked there for five years until I got married."

Lindsey wondered, "Where's Erie? Is it a big department?"

Another sip of the margarita, "It's right on Lake Erie about a hundred miles east of Cleveland, Ohio. The population is about a hundred thousand so, no, it wasn't a very big department, maybe 150 officers."

I said, "If you don't mind my asking, what brought you to Colorado?"

She lowered her gaze and hesitated a moment before replying, "Divorce and escaping an abusive relationship."

I stammered a little at her forthright answer, "Oh, sorry, I didn't mean to be so personal. Geez, you must feel like you're getting an official interrogation here. We'll lighten up!"

Laurie smiled, "It's okay. I'm over most of it. It happened while I was still working for U.S. Airways; it was the main reason I left and became a police officer." She reached across the chair arms and took George's hand. "This guy has helped a lot. And I've told him everything; no secrets. Don't apologize, it's okay; I've gotten used to it."

George looked slightly embarrassed, "We've had some good talks. Laurie had a pretty rough go of it back there, but she's doing great now."

I could see her squeeze his hand tightly now. She said softly, "I was scared about coming here today, but George said you two were his best friends. He was anxious to let you know about us." I was surprised to hear George considered me his 'best friend.' In thinking about it, it probably meant he didn't have that many friends. Still, I was honored.

I made another pass with the drink pitcher and said, "Well, we're glad to have you here, Laurie. We're looking forward to lots of good times together."

We spent another hour on the deck talking about everything under the sun and watching the deer scamper through the oak brush behind the house. At 4:45 p.m., I fired up the grill and asked how they wanted their steaks done. Laurie said she could help and went inside with Lindsey. George and I picked up our drinks and walked to the far end of the deck where it jutted out near the walking path. As we leaned on the railing, George said, "She's pretty special, Cort. First one I've felt anything for since Mary and that's saying something. It's strange how we came together; I mean I saw her around the office of course, she's kinda hard to miss if you catch my meaning, but other than a few 'good mornings' or 'howdy', we hardly spoke. Then we had a drug-related murder out by Byers and she was first on the scene, so we ended up working it together for a couple of weeks. She's a damn good cop and made the investigation easy for me. When we wrapped it up and got an arrest, everybody went to Bud's Bar down in Sedalia and had a few celebratory drinks.

"I ended up talking to Laurie most of the evening; everyone else left and it was just the two of us. That's when she told me a little about what had been going on back in Pennsylvania. She wasn't divorced yet…took a few more months until it came through…but it was easy to see she was hurting. I guess it finally hit me I was still hurting too…or at least I was damn lonely. Anyway, we started seeing each other outside of work; we've been careful on the job, making sure there's no impropriety or favoritism. We haven't exactly 'hid' anything, but we don't advertise it either.

"I've talked to the Sheriff and he's made sure we haven't worked any more cases together or that her rotation doesn't put her reporting to me. Her assignment at the security entrance is as close as we've come, but sooner or later, we'll have to cross that bridge." George drained his drink, turned to look at me directly, and said, "I can see a future for us, Cort. In fact, tomorrow she's moving her stuff to my house; we're going to see how living together for a while works. It's another step in the process."

I tilted my drink toward him and said, "I'm happy for you, buddy. It's been a long time since I've seen a real smile on your face…since Mary Linfield. C'mon, can you tend to the steaks while I go pick a good wine? I feel a proper toast is required."

After we'd cleared the dishes and were putting the finishing touches on our second bottle of a Barossa Valley, Australian shiraz, we all swiveled our chairs to face west and caught a magnificent Colorado sunset as the sun slipped behind Mt. Evans. Laurie sighed deeply and said, "I want to thank you for this day. Everything has been absolutely perfect! You've made me feel so welcome. And now, with this perfect sunset, I can see why everyone loves Colorado!"

George finished his wine, stood, and said, "We'd best be getting back, Laurie. Lots to do tomorrow! Cort, Lindsey, thanks for everything; it was great."

# CHAPTER TWENTY-SEVEN

"This is getting to be a regular occurrence, Scott; twice in a week you've been in my office." Clay Webb didn't look happy to see me.

I went for the shock effect. "Ross Dailov is dead; murdered. I talked to him before he was killed and he said Rockson claims to have someone inside the operation here at Frack Focus. I think that 'someone' is you. If it is, now's the time to tell me and *maybe* get yourself removed from Dailov's murder investigation."

Webb looked like he was going to pass out. His face turned red, he began to sweat, and he was batting his eyes like a toad in a hailstorm. He opened and closed his mouth several times before he could form any words. "That's, uh, that's fucking crazy! Is it what Mercy thinks too? It's just crazy! Jesus Christ, Scott…I was with *you* when the shit storm in North Dakota came down; I got shot at too! I'm not a goddamn spy; I don't work for Rockson!"

"Have you ever talked to him?"

He stared at me for several seconds before slowly nodding his head. "Yes, I've talked to him, but it didn't mean anything. I'm telling you, I *don't* work for him!"

"What did he want from you? What did he offer? I know he wouldn't have talked to you just to pass the time of day."

Webb's face began to recover its normal color. "You're right about that. He did try to hire me to work for him; he was offering to set up a whole new fracking company and I'd be the head guy. He offered me a lot of money. *BUT,* I didn't do it! You've got to believe me, Scott; I turned him down."

"How did he take it?"

"Went ballistic; started screaming and yelling about how he'd find a way to get to me *and* to get inside the company."

I wanted to believe Clay Webb, but there were still some loose ends. "You know when you gave your contact information to your brother it was the back door into Mercy's private numbers *and* the company's computers, don't you?"

He looked sad. "Yeah, after you told me, I knew what had happened. I feel bad about it, too. But, like I said, I'm not a mole; I wouldn't do anything to hurt Mercy. I'm sick about what's happened to her; I know it's my fault."

I wanted to try something else. "You seemed to be sure your brother wouldn't be involved with any of the violence, but what about his friends and other people in the Stop Fracking Us crowd?"

"I don't know any of them. I've never met anybody else."

"Okay, one last thing: had you ever met Akabile before Houston? And, have you had any contact with him since the meeting?'

He shook his head sharply. "No, I'd never met him before and haven't seen or heard from him since." Webb looked like he was whipped. "Where do we go from here? What's next?"

I wasn't sure. "You need to talk to Mercy as soon as she comes in today. Tell her about talking to Rockson and reassure her of your loyalty. You need to make her believe you. I think this is going to come to a head quickly and the shit's going to hit the fan. I just hope there aren't any more murders…but I wouldn't count on it. Watch your back, Clay."

For the second time I believed him, although I wished he would have told me about his contact with Rockson from the beginning. I thought Rockson must have told Dailov he had someone inside Frack Focus to get him to go along with his scheme to "scare" Mercy into cooperating. The hack of the phones and computers still bothered me. I wondered how much information may have been compromised and what was being done with it. I also wondered how Stop Fracking Us fit into the puzzle. Regardless of what Tom or George thought, I wanted a face to face with Guilford Rockson.

I took a page out of Dailov's operational manual: did a little research, told a few lies, and figured out Rockson's parking space. His office was in the Lincoln Center building at 17th and Lincoln in downtown Denver; a building with its own parking structure. Rockson International reserved a quarter of the entire third floor parking. Lucky for me, the rest of the floor was open public parking.

By 7:20 a.m. the next morning, I was sitting in my tricked out Ford Bronco in a spot on the northeast wall of the third floor. Rockson International's area was along the northwest wall and from my spot I could see most of their reserved spaces. At this hour, there were only four cars in their area and none were the Mercedes or Cadillac limos Rockson was known to favor. I was taking a chance he would be coming in, or for that matter, was even in Denver.

I hated doing stakeouts. It usually meant hours of sitting, trying to stay awake, drinking Thermos coffee, eating crap food, and figuring out ways to relieve myself. I hoped the empty plastic milk jug wouldn't be needed too often. I'd backed into a space next to a column so the driver's seat was obscured from entering cars. The tinted side windows of the Bronco were barely legal in broad daylight which made them completely opaque in the dark interior of the garage. I'd brought a couple *Oil and Gas Journal* magazines and a new James Lee Burke novel featuring Dave Robicheaux, my favorite flawed fictional detective.

By 10:30 a.m. I was bored, restless, and had to pee. Another five cars had parked in Rockson's area but there'd been no sign of him. I decided to run another trap and phoned his office. I got the same secretary or receptionist who'd helped me before. I asked if "Mr. Rockson" was expected in today. She surprised me by volunteering he'd phoned to say he would be in immediately after lunch; probably around 1:30 p.m. When she asked if there was any message, I said, "No, I understand he doesn't return calls anyway."

She giggled and said, "I think I've spoken to you before…it's Mr. Scott, isn't it? Last time you called, I took him a message from you and learned some new swear words."

I said, "Well, protect your tender ears…don't tell him I called this time, okay?"

"No problem, Mr. Scott. Nice talking to you. Goodbye." She was laughing as she clicked off.

I left the Bronco and took the elevator to the lobby. Someone was just unlocking the door to the lobby bar, so I ducked in and used the restroom. Walking the six blocks to my friend Andy Thibodeaux's restaurant and bar, Sounds of the South, cleared my head some and I began to question what I hoped to accomplish by confronting Rockson.

Inside, the early lunch hour drinkers were already assembled along the bar and several of my old friends were in their customary spots. I took the end stool at the hinged section and waved greetings to the assembly. Andy saw me, walked down to the beer cooler at my end and started to take out a Budweiser, but I showed him a palm forward stop sign and said, "Too early and I've got things to do later; give me an Arnold Palmer."

Andy put his hand to his brow, faked a stagger as if he was fainting, and said, "Who-ee, who dat man sittin' dere on dat stool? Dat shore ain' my ol' fren, Cort Scott! My ol' fren *always* have him a Bud!"

I grinned, gave him a middle finger, and replied, "Like I said, I've got things to do later, you coon-ass. Make me the AP and I want to ask you something when you've got a minute."

Andy put the bottle back in the cooler, picked up an iced tea glass, filled it with cubes, and then poured it to the brim with lemonade and iced tea. When he set it in front of me, he glanced down the bar to see who might be listening and quietly asked, "So, Mon ami, how you been? You been recovered from dat beatin' you got? Your fren, dat Tom Montgomery cop, tell me you was in bad shape."

"Oh, I'm okay, Andy; took a little while, but I'm back."

"Dat's good to hear. What you want to ask, Andy me?"

"Do you know Guilford Rockson and does he ever come in here?"

Andy opened his eyes wide and exclaimed, "Hoo mon, dat Rockson am one asshole, sumbitch! I t'rowed him out back two-t'ree mont's ago 'cause he was loud and was giving shit to some gud customers." He waved his arm down the length of the bar to indicate who Rockson must have insulted. "He start yellin' dat he would shut me down; said 'no one t'rew him outta some place and got away wid it.' He had some udder guy wid him who start up wid me too, so I yell for my son, Marcel, from outta da kitchen to come. Marcel, he put da clamps on dat Rockson's man and we t'rew bot a 'dem out. He ain' been back since den.

"Why you wanna know 'bout shithead lak dat?" Andy's Cajun accent became more pronounced when he was agitated or excited. He was both. I could barely understand him.

I was amused by the mental picture of Andy, who was about five-ten and maybe two-twenty, and Marcel, who was more like six-four and two-fifty, giving the bum's rush to Rockson and, probably, Dailov. "I think it might have been Rockson who had me stomped and I'm trying to catch up with him to ask him." I felt a little pang of conscience about not telling Andy everything I was after Rockson for, but thought it better to leave him thinking I was just looking for revenge. "I assume you aren't letting him back in, so I don't have to keep watch here, do I?"

"You be right 'bout dat, my fren'. He ain' comin' in here no more!"

"Okay, thanks; I've gotta hit the bricks; what do I owe you?"

"Ol' Andy doan charge for no Arnold Palmer drinks! You go find dat asshole and stomp him good. When you done, tell him Andy say 'hey'."

I made a four block roundtrip circuit of the 16th Street mall to kill a little time. I marveled at the seedy aspect of the once thriving pedestrian walkway. Where my oil business friends and I used to ogle the secretaries and attractive women professionals of

Denver's downtown, I spotted at least twenty beggars and a couple of alleyway conversations I suspected were drug deals.

The upscale jewelry, clothing, shoe stores, and independent restaurants had been replaced by low-end knickknack and souvenir shops, interspersed with a few fast food joints. The step-on/step-off mall busses were still full, but I figured they were probably transporting people from the business offices and high rises at opposite ends of the mall and not dropping off shoppers. Several times I caught the distinctive smell of pot being smoked out in the open, although that was illegal even with Colorado's legalization of recreational marijuana laws. It made me think about giving up my office lease in the Equitable Building which, even though on 17th Street, was only a block removed from this cesspool.

Back in the Bronco, I checked the clock: 1:05 p.m. I thought I'd give it until two o'clock although I still didn't know what I planned to do.

At 1:21 p.m., a long silver-gray Cadillac limo slowly passed in front of my spot and pulled up in front of the elevators. A big guy in a dark blue suit climbed out of the driver's seat, stepped to the back door, and opened it. Guilford Rockson emerged and followed the driver around the back of the car to the other passenger door where the driver stopped and opened the door as Rockson waited.

The Minister of Defense for South Sudan, Akabile, appeared above the roof line of the Cadillac and followed Rockson into the elevator.

# CHAPTER TWENTY-EIGHT

I called Tom Montgomery and excitedly gave him the report that Rockson and Akabile were together in Rockson's office. I was disappointed but understood when Tom said, "So what? We can't do a damn thing about it; neither one of them is wanted for anything…yet. We don't have any reason to bust into the office and roust them. Until McMillan figures a way to get what you heard from Dailov admissible in a court, we don't have anything to charge either one of them with. Best thing I can tell you is try to keep an eye on them; see where they go and if they meet up with anybody else."

The limo driver backed the car diagonally across four spaces in the reserved area and hurried to the elevators to follow his boss and Akabile. As soon as the doors closed, I jumped out of the Bronco, ran to the limo, and attached a tiny, magnetic transmitter to the metal cross brace under the rear bumper. It was a pain in the ass car manufacturers had gone to fiberglass "bumpers"; magnets wouldn't stick to them.

Barely back at the Bronco, I heard the elevator chime. Ducking below the fender, I watched as Rockson's driver stepped out, heading back to the limo. Knowing that was my cue, I jumped in, started the Bronco, and pulled into the down lane. The limo driver glanced up as I drove past, but showed no sign of recognition. I had never seen him before.

When I reached the exit and stopped at the pay booth, the limo pulled up alongside in the monthly parker lane, hesitating only long enough for the driver to swipe a card through a reader.

He turned right on 17th and I followed until we reached Washington where he turned right again, heading south. I continued east to City Park, parked in the lot for the lake and paddle boats, and turned on the GPS tracker on my iPad.

Everything was working. The red dot indicated the limo was still southbound on Washington, approaching Speer Boulevard. At Speer he turned southeast and continued to University, where he turned north and then back west on 4th. He drove four blocks to High Street, turned south, entered a driveway, and stopped.

I brought up the location information: 360 High. I connected to Google and went to street view, followed by satellite. The place looked like old Denver money…a huge lot, L-shaped house with tennis courts. What appeared to be servants' quarters over a five car garage formed the short leg of the "L." Large mature elms and oaks dotted the lot making the house nearly invisible from the street.

I called Tom to get the ownership information for 360 High and wasn't surprised to learn it was owned by Rockson International. It had been purchased four years previously and everything was up-to-date and in compliance: taxes and utilities were paid; there were no liens or judgements outstanding.

Either Rockson and Akabile were going to dinner someplace within walking distance of downtown or they would summon the car when they were ready to leave. Either way, the main floor bar in the Lincoln Center building would be a perfect observation point. If I could get an inside table on the mezzanine level near the point of the bar, I could watch the parking elevator lobby as well as the street exits. The GPS app would allow me to keep tabs on Rockson's driver as well. My only problem would be if Rockson and Akabile split up; I'd have to make a decision on who to shadow.

I called George to give him a report and he had a solution for me. He offered to send Laurie Thomas, in plain clothes, to join me at the bar. Not only could she provide additional cover but could pick up a trail if our suspects left separately. I agreed and George said she could be there within an hour.

Fifty minutes later, Laurie walked through the revolving door of the Lincoln Center. She was dressed in dark rust-colored slacks, a long sleeve butterscotch-colored top, and brown flat shoes. The shoes would be a wise choice if she had to follow someone on foot. I raised my hand as inconspicuously as possible; she acknowledged with a quick bob of her head and headed straight to my table.

"Hi Laurie; thanks for doing this. I'm glad you're available and could get here so quickly."

I had stood when she arrived at the table and she leaned in for a quick kiss on the cheek. "I'm glad too! It's pretty exciting actually; I've never done plain clothes. I thought you had to be detective grade for that."

I pulled out the chair beside me so we could both observe the lobby. With a mocked look of surprise, I asked, "What? You mean you've never dressed up as a hooker for a honey trap sting? That *always* falls on patrol officers; the women detectives think it's degrading and beneath their station."

She laughed and said, "We only ever ran one 'John sting' back in Erie. I was still on rookie probation so it was just a ride along for me." Her face turned serious, "So what's the play? All George said was you're sitting on two possible bad guys who might be involved in this whole mess related to your beating, the death threats to the female tycoon, and the murder George's investigating."

I had to smile, "That's pretty much it in a nutshell. You're a quick study. What I thought was a simple case of intimidation by a bunch of enviro-nuts turns out to be a lot more complicated and, like you said, now involves a murder. I'm basically trying to protect my client and help George solve the murder.

"But, here's the kicker…there's an international conspiracy threaded through everything. One of the guys I'm trying to watch is the so called 'defense minister' of South Sudan, but he's actually just a thug who's trying to get rich through extortion and bribery. He's tied in with a Denver guy who runs an international oil company, but in reality, he's as bad as--or even worse--than the

African. He's a part of the bribery and maybe a lot more. I think he's the one ultimately behind getting me stomped.

"There are just so many loose ends and false leads that I'm having a hell of a time trying to tie everything together."

The cocktail waitress came by and gave us a disdainful look when we ordered an Arnold Palmer in a tall cocktail glass and a Perrier served in a martini glass. I felt like telling her we were cops on duty but thought better of it. I'd let her think we were just a couple of weird teetotalers. I explained the set up for Laurie: who we were looking for and the iPad display which continued to show the limo parked at 360 High.

We filled the time with small talk about Pennsylvania and Colorado until I gutted up and asked about her relationship with George. A broad smile erupted and she gushed, "I can't believe it myself, Cort. I honestly feel like I'm about twenty years old and have the biggest crush of my life on some guy! I probably sound like a teenager, but it's how I feel. I've never met anyone like him: he's kind, considerate, treats me like a lady, and respects my opinion. I mean, he's *everything* I've ever imagined a man could be. And, more importantly, he's all the things I've never had."

I was glad to hear all her compliments about my friend. It had been a long lonely road for George since Mary Linfield. "I'm glad to hear you say it, Laurie. I can tell from talking to George that he feels the same about you. It's been forever since he's been truly happy and I feel like he is with you. He's a good man…about the best I know…and I would hate to see him get hurt."

She reached for my hand, squeezed it tightly, and said, "You're a good friend; I'll never do anything to hurt him." I believed her.

At 4:17 p.m., my iPad chimed; the limo was on the move. It had just turned south on University and west on Speer. It seemed to be retracing its route to downtown. With afternoon rush hour traffic, it would probably take half an hour or more, so I told Laurie I thought Rockson must have called to be picked up at 5:00 p.m. I signaled the waitress and paid our tab, leaving her a generous tip for taking up one of her tables for almost three hours.

At five to five, Rockson and Akabile appeared in the elevator lobby, walked around the corner to the elevators for the parking garage, and exchanged a handshake. Akabile turned toward the building's street exit, and Rockson pushed the elevator call button for parking.

"Okay Laurie, we can keep tabs on Rockson with the GPS app. Let's follow Akabile; if he catches a taxi, we'll do the same. Hopefully, though, he's got a downtown hotel or is headed for a restaurant or something."

She asked, "How careful do we have to be? Does he know you on sight?

"I don't think he'd recognize me. I only saw him for about fifteen minutes almost a month ago. I was wearing a sport coat and tie then; not khakis and a Hawaiian shirt like today."

We waited until he had passed through the revolving door before following. He crossed Lincoln Street, strolled to Broadway, and crossed diagonally at the five street intersection to the Brown Palace Hotel. We jumped the walk sign to the opposite side of 17th and were able to stay close as he entered the Brown.

Skirting the ornate lobby, we spotted him in front of the elevators near the Ship's Tavern. I didn't see anyone else enter the car so we watched the floor indicator. It stopped on eight.

"Do you have your badge with you?"

Laurie nodded, "Of course; why?"

"Go to the front desk, identify yourself as a police officer, flash the badge, and ask for the room number where Akabile is registered. Hopefully, they'll tell you…otherwise we'll have to sit here until he leaves."

She turned on her heel and walked swiftly to the reception desk which was located around the corner. I took up a position near the Tremont Place entrance where I could see the elevators and the front desk. I saw Laurie talking to the registration person, taking the badge from her purse, and holding it in front of her chest. Smart, I thought…she's holding it close enough he can tell it's real but too far away to actually read it. She nodded a couple times and returned the badge to the purse, turned back, and spotted me near the door.

She smiled as she approached, "No problem; he's in 818."

I said, "Good job! Reception give you any problem?"

"Nope, asked to see a badge, but didn't inspect it. Hotel management would probably jump all over him if they knew how easily he was giving up room numbers, but it's good for us. What do we do now?"

"Have a *real* drink in the lobby bar work for you?"

The Brown Palace's famous high tea was just wrapping up and we were able to score a couple of formal upright chairs with a small table in a corner spot where we could see the elevators. Laurie ordered a Lemon Drop martini and I asked for Balvenie neat. The drinks had just been delivered when I caught sight of a bright African-print kaftan entering from the Tremont Place entrance. It was Trey Worth's friend, Bre.

Risking her recognizing me, I jumped to my feet and walked quickly to where I could see the floor indicator again. Before the doors closed, I was able to see Bre's arm as she pushed a floor button. I watched intently, although I felt sure I knew her destination; I also knew why Bre had seemed strangely familiar. She was obviously related to Akabile.

When I returned, Laurie asked, "What in the world was that about?" Her expression was one big question mark.

"I don't know whether the plot is thickening or thinning. I recognized someone who is a part of all this, but I don't know how all the parts fit together." I explained as much as I could about who the players were and the entanglements I could see. We had finished our drinks and declined another round by the time I'd completed my story.

"Good grief, Cort, this case has more arms than an octopus! Do you think this puts the twin brothers back in the frame for trying to sabotage Mercy Drexler's company…or blow her up? Is *everybody* on Rockson's payroll?"

"I honestly don't know. Somehow, I just don't think the brothers are the kind to get involved in a murder; I can't help but think they are being used. But I'd bet my bottom dollar Rockson is behind everything."

Laurie said, "Like I asked before, what now?"

"We're going to need more help to keep an eye on everybody. Let's call it good for today; I'll contact George, Tom, and maybe McMillan, the ADA, about having a task force meeting tomorrow. Hopefully, we can come up with a better plan than just running around tailing people. How did you get here; need a ride?"

She gave me a wry smile and said, "Believe it or not, George said that considering the time of day, the fastest way downtown was to take the light rail train. He drove me to the Arapahoe Crossing station and said I should give him a call when I was headed back."

"I'm parked in the Lincoln Center building; same floor as Rockson's company parking. C'mon with me; I'll give you a ride home. Am I right in assuming 'home' is George's place?"

She ducked her head and I thought I saw a blush spreading up her neck, "Yes, I moved in last week."

# CHAPTER TWENTY-NINE

When I got home, Linds was downstairs in the exercise room on the elliptical machine. I flicked the lights so I wouldn't startle her, stuck my head around the corner, and asked about doing a hot tub with a glass of wine when she finished. She grinned and said, "Great minds think alike! I'll be done in about thirty minutes."

Back upstairs in my office, I called Mercy and ran an idea past her. It took some convincing, but after telling her we might be able to put an end to the attacks and threats *plus* put Rockson in prison, she agreed. I had sealed the deal by saying if everything came together, we'd also be consummating the biggest business deal she'd ever done.

Next, I called Skyler McMillan at home, explained part of what I had in mind, and told her I needed some help from her office and everything had to be ready by tomorrow morning. She was extremely curious and quizzed me as only a good ADA can, but finally, although reluctantly, agreed to make the arrangements.

*****

We met in a conference room at Denver police headquarters: George, Tom, Skyler McMillan, Laurie, and Lindsey. I'd been surprised when George said he wanted Lindsey and Laurie to attend.

I got everyone on the same page by reviewing everything from the time I'd received the first call from Mercy Drexler through last night when Bre had walked into the Brown Palace. There was an electric pause when I said I was sure Bre was related to Akabile. When I finished, I said we probably needed some eyes on each of the main players: certainly Rockson, Akabile, and Bre, if not Clay Webb and Trey Worth.

It was disconcerting to watch Tom slowly shake his head. "Without a lot more to go on, DPD can't spare the manpower for twenty-four/seven surveillance. We need to tie some of these people directly to one of the crimes: your assault or the bombing or Dailov's murder. I--

"Hold on, Tom, I think I might be able to help." Skyler had interrupted and raised her hand like a kid in class. "Even though most of the stuff Dailov told Cort is hearsay and probably not admissible in court, Dailov *did* work for Rockson and the two hitters sitting in lockup are tied to Dailov…it's enough to name Rockson a person of interest. With that, the DA's office can employ an investigator to tail him…and since Cort has worked for us before, he's the natural one to follow up.

"The rest of this is 'off the record' if you catch my drift…but *if* while following Rockson, Cort just happens to encounter some suspicious activity involving anyone else, well, he'd be obligated to let our office know and we can request that DPD assist us in the investigation. The final thread is that Dailov was killed in Arapahoe County; we'll 'officially' ask for the sheriff's office assistance. That gets everybody involved. It should give us all the manpower we need."

Tom gave a wry smile and said, "Been thinking about this a little, have you? You're getting creative in the DA's office these days! But I like it! How about you, George? Arapahoe County willing to go along?"

"Absolutely, the Sheriff doesn't like to have open murder cases on the books. We can dedicate both Lindsey and Officer Thomas to this." I ducked my head to smirk at George's reference to Laurie as "Officer Thomas."

Tom turned to me and said, "Okay…you should have enough bodies to keep an eye on all these scum bags. Where are *you* gonna start or are you just going to sit on your ass and watch?" Everyone, including me, laughed at that.

"I want to solidify the connection between Akabile and Rockson and maybe to Bre and Trey Worth. If there's nothing there, we can move both Worth and Clay Webb to the back burners. My best guess is they'll turn out to just be tools."

McMillan and Tom nodded their agreement, so I continued, "Since Bre has seen me up close and personal, I think *Officer* Thomas should pick up the tail on Bre; Lindsey can take Rockson. I'd like to stick with Akabile for a while; I've got an idea to maybe break this whole thing wide open.

"Let's plan on a conference call every morning, starting tomorrow, to coordinate what we find out. And each of you can call me anytime something breaks? Any questions?"

Tom shot me a look and asked, "You going to share this 'idea' about Akabile?"

I shook my head and answered, "Not yet, I've still gotta flesh it out a little; do some heavy thinking."

Everybody looked at me like I was nuts.

Before we left, Laurie got the address for the Boulder house where Trey Worth and Bre were living and I gave Lindsey my iPad with the GPS app for Rockson's limo. Laurie had driven her own car downtown and said she'd leave for Boulder immediately; Linds had parked in the same spot I'd used in the Lincoln Center parking. As everyone was leaving, Tom grabbed my arm and said he'd like a word.

"I don't know what the hell you're up to, buddy, but there are some things about this I don't like. First of all, what's the deal with having Lindsey working surveillance? She's a crime scene tech for Christ sake! And what do we know about this *Officer* Thomas…come to think of it, what the hell was all the smirking and smiling going on between you guys anyway? And last, what's this *idea* of yours?"

"Ah, c'mon Tom…you know Lindsey is no stranger to surveillance or arrest operations. She saved my ass when we were in California and the Chinese spies had us dead to rights; she kicked the crap out of one of them and saved the day during that gunfight down near Sedalia when she T-boned an armored personnel carrier with a patrol car. She can handle herself; no problem.

"As for Laurie Thomas, she's from Erie, Pennsylvania PD, been in patrol for Arapahoe County for a couple years, and more importantly, she's George's main squeeze and *he* trusts her. She's a new face and you know George wouldn't put her in a bad situation.

"As for my idea, you need to trust me on that one. Frankly, you wouldn't like it if I told you the details. But, like I said, if it works, I think we can get a running start on breaking this thing. Okay?"

Tom sagged his shoulders in acceptance, but said, "Good points, I guess, at least on the women, but you know I don't trust your judgement as far as I can throw you. It sounds like you're fixing to put yourself in a pickle of some kind. If you don't let me in on what you're doing, I can't bail your ass out if you need it."

I put my hand on his shoulder, "I get it, buddy, but I've got to do this my way. I can handle it."

I hadn't meant to sound so mysterious to Tom, but I knew he wouldn't approve of what I had in mind. I'd told Lindsey about my conversation with Mercy last night. Linds didn't like my idea either but was willing to let it play out.

I called Mercy and said, "Well, it's all in motion. We're going to have eyes on Rockson, Akabile, and Bre. As soon as we're off the phone, I'm going to the Brown and see Akabile."

She spoke softly, "Do you really think this is going to put an end to everything? Just knowing Akabile and Rockson are in cahoots has given me a bad feeling. I couldn't sleep at all last night thinking about it. I'm still worrying about Clay being part of it…and his brother too."

I probably sounded more convinced than I was. "Like I said last night, I don't know about his brother, but I want to believe Clay. On the other hand, I'm convinced this Bre is in it up to her neck. The bigger question, though, is who she's working for: Akabile or Rockson…or maybe both of 'em.

"Regardless, it's going to be the end for Rockson. We can tie him to Dailov and the explosives. Our biggest problem is figuring out who murdered Dailov; if it was Rockson, or at least if he ordered it, he'll go to prison for the rest of his life."

Mercy murmured her agreement and said, "Okay. So, as I understand it, you just want me to be 'available' to take a call from Akabile in case he questions what you tell him…is that right?"

"Yep, that's the extent of it. Can you do it?"

She didn't answer for a few seconds. "I'll try, but that's all I'm going to promise. The thought of agreeing to *anything* concerning him nearly sickens me. I'm hoping you won't need me!"

"I hope the same thing, Mercy."

I used the lobby phone in the Brown Palace to dial Akabile's room. At 9:45 a.m., I had to hope he was still in his room. The phone rang five times and I thought he must have left. I was relieved when he picked up. "Good morning, Akabile here." His soft tone and cultured British accent belied the person I knew as a self-serving thug and profiteer…and maybe a murderer.

"Good morning, Minister, I'm glad I caught you. This is Cortlandt Scott, I met you in Houston along with Mercy Drexler and Clay Webb. We were presenting the fracking technology program."

There was a momentary pause; I didn't know if it was him trying to place me or if he knew me as Rockson's enemy. "Ah yes, Mr. Scott! I *do* remember you although our previous meeting was uncomfortably short. And to what do I owe the pleasure of your call?"

*Pleasure of your call…* This guy was unbelievable! "I think there are some things we could discuss which may be mutually beneficial."

"My, what an intriguing opening, Mr. Scott. And what type of *things* do you have in mind?"

"Not the kind to be discussed over a hotel phone line, Minister. I'm in the lobby; could I come to your room? Are you up and around?"

"I'm an early riser and a bit jet lagged, but I would certainly enjoy some additional tea or coffee. Yes, please come to my room, it's number eight-eighteen. Should I order up something for you?"

"Coffee would be great; I'll be up in a couple of minutes." At least I was making progress; I would be able to talk to him without confronting Rockson at the same time.

I knocked on 818 and Akabile answered immediately. "Ah, Mr. Scott…Yes, your face is as I remembered. Come in, please." He stepped back from the narrow entrance hall, waved toward the interior of the room, and closed the door. "Room service will be here momentarily."

His room was actually one of the "Top of the Brown" suites on the top floor of the hotel. Rooms on this level had been occupied by the likes of U.S. presidents, foreign dignitaries, and even the Beatles. The hall opened into a spacious sitting room with a mix of couches, tables, club chairs, and lamps. The couches and chairs were an eclectic mash-up of dark leather and bold cloth patterns. I suspected the armoires on three walls contained widescreen TVs. The rust-colored, plush patterned carpet felt like walking on the eighteenth green at Cherry Hills Country Club. Doors leading off the sitting room apparently led to the bathroom and bedrooms.

"Nice accommodations; I assume you know lots of famous people have stayed in the hotel; some probably in this room."

Akabile studied me carefully before replying, "Yes, certainly; I read several historical articles about the world-famous Brown Palace Hotel before booking here. Of course what you Americans consider old or historic pales in comparison to virtually anything in Europe or the Middle East." He laughed at his own observation. "When I visit London or Paris or Zurich or Cairo, I often stay in hotels that have been in continuous operation for five hundred years or more." He laughed again.

The door chime sounded discretely and Akabile raised his index finger as if to signal "one moment." He went to the door and admitted a female room service runner carrying a tray covered with silver coffee service, porcelain teapots, cups and saucers. She placed the tray on a large coffee table in front of a couch and across from one of the leather club chairs. She arranged everything and turned to leave; Akabile tipped her a $20 bill. The girl did a double take and stuttered an embarrassed thank you.

When he returned, Akabile motioned toward the couch while he took the chair. Gesturing at the table, he asked, "Which would you prefer…tea or coffee?"

"Coffee for me, thanks." I started to reach for one of the pots, but he deftly beat me to it, lifted a saucer and cup, and poured.

When he had filled my cup, he poured tea for himself, leaned back in the chair, and asked, "Now, Mr. Scott, what are these mysterious, mutually beneficial *things* you'd like to discuss?"

"You might call it a mutually beneficial *trade*, actually. I propose you give me enough information to put Guilford Rockson in prison and, in turn, I'll help you return to South Sudan without being arrested. In addition, I have a way for you to get the frack technology to develop your country's oil and gas reserves. I suspect you can find a way to profit from that knowledge."

Akabile's only reaction was to raise one eyebrow as he politely sipped tea. "Your point eludes me, Mr. Scott. What makes you think I have information pertaining to this Mr. Rockson or, more importantly, have a need to flee your country?"

I set my cup and saucer down with a bang and stared daggers at him. In the most disdainful tone I could muster, I said, "Drop the fucking charade, Akabile! Before Rockson, or maybe *you,* had Dailov murdered, I had a long talk with him. He told me about the deals you've cut with Rockson…deals that are illegal here in the U.S. and probably in South Sudan too. More importantly, he told me how you sent Rockson the Semtek explosive used to bomb Mercy Drexler's car; how he…Dailov…carried it in. The local police and the FBI have already identified it and traced it to Egypt and South Sudan.

"In case you haven't been paying attention, sending that shit here is an act of terrorism. If the cops or the feds grab you, you're headed for a federal pen.  I'm telling you this because I work for Mercy…not the cops or the feds. I'm willing to cut you a break in order to get Rockson and put a stop to the threats and attacks on her."

He gently lowered his cup to the saucer and placed both on the table, steepled his fingers, and gazed intently across at me. "When we parted in Houston, Ms. Drexler made it abundantly clear she didn't wish to conduct business with me…or, I should say, with South Sudan. Has she had a change of heart? Are you here as her representative?"

"I'm here as part of Mercy's security; nothing else has changed. In fact, that stupid, clumsy bombing attempt only served to harden her resolve. Hopefully, it wasn't your idea; I suspect your buddy, Guilford Rockson, was the brains, or lack thereof, for that stupidity."

Again, there was very little reaction; a hint of a knowing smile softened Akabile's features. "Ah, so you know Guilford and I formed a, let's see…what should I call it…hmm, ah yes, a *strategic alliance* with regard to Ms. Drexler's precious secrets. An alliance that, to date hasn't born any fruit, I might add." Akabile remained composed as he continued, "Does Ms. Drexler agree to this, ah, *arrangement*? And, what about your local police? Or the FBI?  Or your State Department?  How do I know I won't be arrested the moment I give you a statement…assuming I'm willing to do it in the first place?"

"Mercy is a businesswoman; she'll go along, although she'd rather see you sitting in a cell next to Rockson. If you don't believe me, you can give her a call right now. As for everything else, you're going to have to take my word for it. That may seem like one hell of a risk, but the way I see it, you don't have a lot of choices. As soon as you give me a videotaped and notarized statement, you can leave for the airport. There are several late afternoon flights leaving for east coast hubs from Boston to

Atlanta. From any of them, you can catch a flight to Europe or even Africa. After that you're on your own, but if I were you, I'd head back to South Sudan as soon as possible. The U.S. extradites from most of Europe."

Akabile said, "A rather tenuous plan at best; but what about this possibility of acquiring the fracturing technology? What will I have to do to achieve that?"

"Basically, you'll have to go straight, if you follow my meaning. You need to abrogate the concession agreement with Rockford International, which shouldn't be difficult since it's illegal anyway, and then sign a new one with Frack Focus, Siren Exploration and Production, and a company named Mountain West Gas. There won't be any kickbacks or 'side agreements' in your favor from this end, but you're a smart fellow…you'll figure a way to turn a profit."

For the first time I saw a look of concern pass across Akabile's face. "You paint a rather dire picture, Mr. Scott. In fact, my first inclination, in the colorful language of many of your countrymen, is to say 'Fuck OFF!' However, I am a realist. I'm not sure of the depth or accuracy of any evidence against me at this point, but I *am* sure that a dogged pursuit of Guilford Rockson could yield enough to get me charged under your anti-terrorism laws. I don't fancy spending the rest of my life at the notorious Guantanamo or in your local 'Super Max' federal prison.

"Therefore, although not ideal and certainly no guarantee of freedom, your offer of a head start, as you call it, appeals to me. As a sometime student of your laws, I believe any assistance you render me results in you having, as another colloquialism puts it, 'skin in the game.' It would seem you are bearing some risk in helping me which gives me at least a modicum of reassurance you'll do your best.

"With that being said, I will do as you ask and I will not require an affirmation from Ms. Drexler. How will we accomplish the statement part?"

Relieved that he wouldn't be calling Mercy, although she had agreed to play along, I gritted my teeth and said, "I'll trust you to live up to the parts of the bargain concerning the concessions.

But keep this in mind, *minister,* since I'm *not* a cop or any kind of government official, I don't have to play by the rules. If you renege on *any* of this, I'll come after you myself…and I'm good at what I do if you follow my meaning."

I thought THANK YOU, Skyler as I said, "I've arranged for an official videographer from the District Attorney's office. She's waiting downstairs with her equipment; as an employee of the DA's office, she's an officer of the court and can certify your identity and notarize your statement.

"One more thing…this is off the record and doesn't have to be in your statement, but I want to know your relationship to 'Bre' and how she fits into this puzzle."

Akabile's eyes snapped open with surprise. "You seem to be very well informed, Mr. Scott, very well informed indeed! And, I might add, your timing is also excellent…if you had brought this up as a condition prior to my agreeing to cooperate, it would have been, as you might say, 'a deal breaker.' As it now stands, I feel a sense of urgency to complete this odious arrangement and return to my country."

I was impressed with his command of the language and his vocabulary. "Yeah, well, good for me. So, who the hell is she?"

He sighed in resignation and spoke in a softer tone, "Her full name is Zebrezicka and she is my niece, my older sister's child."

I had been right about them being family. "So what's she doing here? Working for you?"

Akabile shook his head, "No, Zebrezicka, or as you know her, *Bre*, is what you might call a 'free agent.' She sells her services to the highest bidder; she is truly a mercenary who insinuates herself into any situation where she can command large sums of money. She serves no flag other than a dollar sign."

It took me a moment to contemplate his answer. "You aren't asking me to believe she is here entirely independent of you, are you? That stretches your credibility to the breaking point."

He shrugged. "Seems to be your problem, not mine, Mr. Scott. All I can do is state the facts."

"So who is she working for if not for you?"

"I do not know, I--

"*BULLSHIT!*" I was ready to forget everything I'd promised this lying turd and beat the truth out of him. "I saw her coming here to meet you last night. What was that…just a little family get together; a quiet talk about home? C'mon, asshole, you must think me stupid!"

Akabile spread his hands and shrugged again. "My, my…such language, Mr. Scott. Regardless of what you may believe, 'a little family get together' is exactly what occurred. The only linkage in this case is the fact Bre was the one who sent Guilford Rockson to me. When he contacted me, it was with a letter of introduction from her. She asked me, as my niece, to extend him every courtesy with the caveat that it could prove extremely lucrative for all concerned."

"So is she working for Rockson?"

Again, a shrug; he didn't answer.

"Did she talk about a protest outfit called Stop Fracking Us? It's where she's hanging out."

He nodded, "She spoke of them and of a young man named Trey Worth. I believe she may be romantically involved with him."

This was sounding more and more like a fairy tale. "Surely, you can't believe she's here for love? You just told me she follows the money; that money is her only motivation."

"Perhaps you can explain women to me, Mr. Scott."

# CHAPTER THIRTY

Akabile's video statement, complete with the videographer's verification, took nearly an hour. As I watched him, I was reminded of a final dress rehearsal for a stage presentation of a courtroom drama…he was that good. He gave complete details of the illegal oil and gas concession to Rockson International; his under-the-table agreement for cash payments or overriding royalty interests; and, most important of all, the delivery of the Semtek explosives to Rockson via Dailov. He vehemently denied any knowledge of the actual bombing but acknowledged Rockson had "requested" the explosives.

He made no mention of Bre. I was still suspicious about his explanation of her presence in Denver and I wondered how someone nominally associated with a protest group would have made contact with Guilford Rockson. Their interests should have been diametrically opposed.

As soon as the videographer had finished, Akabile called the travel agency located in the lobby of the Brown Palace to check his options for returning to South Sudan. I was surprised when he chose a 9:45 p.m. British Airways direct flight from Denver to London. He would have nearly a twelve hour layover in London before his Emirates Airlines flight to Doha, Qatar. When I asked, he said that schedule would put him in Doha in the mid-morning hours and he wanted to meet with some people there. He said there were several daily flights to Entebbe, Uganda, which would be the closest international airport to South Sudan.

I knew of several earlier departures from Denver to the major airports on the U.S. east coast which would offer flights to London and probably better connections to the Middle East. I asked why he wanted to risk spending several hours in Denver and then again in London. He said he needed time in both places to get his affairs in order and set up some meetings.

I worried about why he needed that much time in Denver and told him so. He gave me the shrug that was becoming extremely annoying. When I reminded him the local authorities would be looking for him as soon as I delivered his statement, he pointedly told me he had done everything I'd asked and he "expected" me to provide the head start I'd promised. I reluctantly agreed to delay as long as I could.

Finally, he had the concierge arrange for a limo to Denver International Airport and hurriedly packed. When the porter arrived for his bags, I walked to the elevator with him and we rode in silence to the lobby. I stood to the side as he settled his bill and we walked out the Tremont Place exit where a limo from First Class Denver Rides was waiting. Before getting in, he stopped and gazed intently across the street toward the Navarre building which housed an impressive western art museum. At the turn of the twentieth century, the Navarre had been an upscale brothel connected to the Brown Palace through a tunnel beneath Tremont Place.

Akabile smiled ironically, "Too bad your local authorities adopted such a provincial attitude towards prostitution. As I said, I read a bit of the history of the famous Brown Palace Hotel and I would like to have had the opportunity to sample *all* the pleasures of historic Denver. The European hotels I mentioned maintain a much more 'enlightened' stance." He didn't offer to shake hands which suited me; I wanted to be shut of the bastard.

As the limo pulled away from the curb, I saw him put his cell phone to his ear. My first thought was he was calling Rockson and all this would be for naught, but strangely enough, I wanted to believe he would catch the British Airways flight and make good on his "escape."

I started walking west on Tremont Place toward DPD headquarters at Colfax. I called Skyler McMillan, told her what transpired, and asked her to meet me there. I kept a brisk pace and entered the cop shop twelve minutes later. Skyler was standing in the lobby, badged us through security, and we hurried up the three flights of stairs to Tom's office.

When we barged in, Tom looked up from his desk in surprise. "What the hell are you two up to? You're grinning like Cheshire cats; what's up?"

I tossed a flash drive on his desk and said, "Plug this into your computer."

We gathered around his monitor watching as the videographer identified herself and described the conditions under which the following statement was being made. Soon, Akabile's cultured voice began. After eight minutes, Tom hit the pause key, leaned back, and glared at both of us. "How the hell did you get this? Where is this son-of-a-bitch *right now?* He's admitting to a whole laundry list of crimes including terrorism; I want his ass arrested!"

Skyler looked at me and "shot" me with her thumb and index finger indicating she wanted me to talk. "Well, this will show you how much you can trust me, buddy. I gave him a gilt-edged promise I would give him a head start and 'let' him return to South Sudan. I--

"You *what?* You stupid bastard! You don't have the authority to do something like that! I'll have your balls not to mention your license for this!" He turned to McMillan, "Are you part of this bullshit? I'm going directly to the DA; he's going to can your ass on the spot!"

I put my hand on Tom's shoulder, "You said you didn't trust me any farther than you could throw me. Well, I'm just proving your point; Akabile shouldn't have put trust in me either. He's on his way to DIA even as we speak. He's booked on a British Airways flight for London scheduled for 9:45 p.m. You've got eight hours to grab him.

"I'm breaking every promise I made to the shithead; let's just say I had my fingers crossed…and you know what? I don't give a damn. Even though I believe every word he says on this tape, and it's all we need to put Rockson away for a long damn time, I don't believe for a New York minute he's going straight *or* that he's running scared, headed for home."

Tom began to laugh, "Well, you've certainly restored my faith that you're a lying, cheating, SOB who will say anything." He held up a finger for us to wait, picked up his desk phone, punched in an extension, and said, "Hey Lee Anne, it's me!" Lee Anne LeBlanc was Tom's wife of two years and a newly-minted lieutenant at DPD's substation in Denver International Airport. They had become an item when she worked for Tom in Homicide and investigated the Wildcat Willie Davidson murder…the murder that damned near got me killed. After that case wrapped, they'd gone to Denver's police chief, explained their situation, and he'd made the arrangements for her transfer to the airport. Six months later they'd been married on my deck in front of a small group of family and friends.

Tom's demeanor had changed to serious when he said, "Hey, *lieutenant,* I've got a hot one for you. Cort has managed to get the goods on a real bad guy who's headed your way. Guy's name is Akabile, that's spelled A-K-A-B-I-L-E, and he goes with just the one name. He's traveling on a South Sudan diplomatic passport and is supposed to catch a BA flight to London departing at 9:45 p.m.

"We want this a-hole for everything from extortion to terrorism and the feds may end up with jurisdiction, but it'd be big feather in DPD's cap if we make the arrest. According to Cort, you can't miss him: he's black and looks like he just stepped off the front page of GQ; he's wearing a bluish-gray, tailored suit. We don't expect him to be packing, but you should be damn careful anyway; put a four man detail on him. He left downtown about half an hour ago and should be there by 2:00 p.m., maybe 2:30 at the latest. Give me a call when you've grabbed him. Okay?" He listened for a few moments before saying, "Yeah, it might be a problem for most things, but he's going to get tagged with terrorism so all that diplomatic immunity BS is out the window.

Just put the cuffs on him and we'll sort the paper out later. Yeah, okay; thanks, hon."

After hanging up, he said, "Lee Anne wondered about him traveling on a diplomatic passport; wondered if we can arrest him. You heard what I said--you in particular, Skyler--so you better have my back on this."

Skyler said she'd already contacted the U.S. attorney's office and they'd told her that terrorism trumped everything.

We watched the rest of Akabile's statement and at the end, Tom slowly shook his head and sourly said, "I guess this's the *idea* you were talking about, huh? You're right about one thing; if you'd have told me, I'd have put the kibosh to it. Christ, you've broken practically every rule ever made for entrapment: consorting with a criminal, impersonating a police officer, and I don't know what else!" He looked at Skyler, "How big a part did you play in this? Are you sure you're in the clear?"

Skyler replied in a serious tone, "I don't know, Tom. I'm hoping the results justify the means. Officially, *I* didn't make any promises or compromise the DA's office. Cort only briefly described to me what he had planned and I agreed to arrange for the videographer to be available. From a legal point of view, none of Cort's 'promises' are on the tape and it is what it is…a sworn statement that will become the basis for an indictment of Rockson, a person we've been pursuing for a long time."

I said softly, "For the record, I told Akabile I am *not* a police officer or a government official."

Tom scowled and sighed, "For both your sakes, I hope you're right."

I asked, "Tom is there anyone you can contact about this Bre or Zebrezicka? From what Akabile told me before we recorded his statement, she is some sort of mercenary who sells her services--whatever that means-- to the highest bidder. I'd think someone like that must have a record of some kind."

He nodded in agreement, "Yeah, you'd think so. I'll contact the feds about it."

The fax from the JTTF, the Joint Terrorism Task Force, ran almost nine pages and was chilling. As soon as it arrived, Tom made two copies, handed one to me, and we went to his office to read. At least once per page, one of us would curse or simply raise our gaze and stare at the other.

Bre, or Zebrezicka, had apparently adopted her uncle's affectation of using one name at an early age and it was the only one in her lengthy criminal record. The only daughter of Akabile's older sister and a Lebanese commodities trader, Akabile's description of her as a free agent mercenary was apt. She was wanted for a myriad of criminal acts by several Mideast and North African governments and, in some cases, was being hunted by both sides in the civil wars being waged in the region. One side's patriot was another side's traitor.

A onetime student at the American University in Beirut studying chemistry, she had been recruited by Hezbollah radicals and was suspected as being the bomb builder for several violent car bombs around that city. She had been tracked to Damascus where she worked for the Mukhabarat, the Assad regime's secretive intelligence and police apparatus. According to a slim dossier from Israeli intelligence, she had probably become an "operative." She killed people.

Following the Lebanese civil war, she reappeared as an intelligence officer for the Fatah movement in the West Bank. Two years later she was found in the same capacity for Hamas in Gaza. Her "services" apparently took her to the faction with the biggest bank account regardless of philosophy.

Her trail vanished for a year until she reappeared during the Sudanese civil war, again as an intelligence officer, but on the side of the secular rebels of South Sudan. All of her previous "employers" had been Shiite-influenced radical Islamists but now she was fighting against them. The JTTF report speculated her family ties to Akabile and South Sudan had won out over the strictly mercenary nature of working in the Muslim jihadist campaigns.

The political and familial altruism apparently hadn't lasted long however. Zebrezicka disappeared from everyone's radar within six months of the shaky truce to end the war. How the hell she'd managed to enter the U.S. was a scary question of its own.

I thought being an environmental activist in Boulder, Colorado was completely out of character. Trey Worth's "girlfriend" and apparent fellow protester had *never* worked for free, and since she had introduced Rockson to Akabile, she probably wasn't doing so now. My bet was she was on her uncle's *and* Rockson's payrolls and had been "placed" in the Stop Fracking Us group for one reason only: she'd been instructed to develop a relationship with Trey Worth as a back door into Frack Focus' technology by using Clay Webb.

Tom exclaimed, "Jesus, Cort, what have we stumbled into with this? That woman is a goddamned, dedicated revolutionary! What the hell is she doing in Boulder running around with a bunch of hippy-dippy greenies?"

I shared with Tom what I'd been thinking. "She's working for her uncle and probably Rockson too; she's trying to steal the frack technology by going through Worth to get to Clay Webb. If she gets it, she'll cash in by being in the middle of Akabile's and Rockson's deal.

"But what really gets my attention is her involvement in those car bombings in Beirut. What are the odds she blew up Mercy's car? Pretty damn high, I'd bet. And there's one more thing…Dailov's murder. Her file says she was an 'operative' in Syria; that's just a politically correct way of saying she's an assassin. Assassins know how to make murders look like suicides; my money is on her for killing Dailov."

Tom listened attentively before saying, "I wish we had someone other than George's girlfriend watching her. Did you see anything suspicious in the Boulder house?"

"I didn't look around; I was just in one room they were using as an office. If you're asking if I saw guns or dynamite, the answer is 'no.'"

Tom said, "I don't know what I'm asking. I'm just worried this whole thing is going to blow up in our faces…no pun intended."

# CHAPTER THIRTY-ONE

Lindsey, with excitement in her voice, said, "Something's happening; Rockson just raced outta the elevator with his chauffer. They piled into the limo and tore off. I followed them going north on Lincoln, crossing over to Broadway, and turning onto Park Central. I'm guessing they're heading for I-25. I've got 'em with the GPS locator so we won't lose them."

I'd been hanging out in Tom's office and wasn't surprised by the call…disappointed maybe, but not surprised. "Akabile has called Rockson. I told you my idea would bring this to a head. It looks like lots of pieces and players are being put in play.

Tom cursed, "Goddamn it! Why can't anything ever go smoothly? Why couldn't that asshole just go to the airport and try to catch the fucking plane? Lee Anne and her squad could grab him and it would be a lot easier for all concerned. Now, I guess, we'll have to deal with him…and Rockson too. What do you think is up?"

"Akabile still has lots of time to catch that flight, but I'm betting they're planning to meet someplace. I don't know why Akabile didn't just go to Rockson's office. He was probably trying to throw me off by catching the limo to the airport."

Tom leaned back in his chair, closed his eyes, and said, "With the GPS locator on Rockson's car we should be able to keep track of him; if he's meeting up with your buddy, we'll know where. I'm going to call McMillan and see if they've got the arrest warrant for Rockson yet. If they do, maybe we can nab both of them at one time. You want to be in on it?"

I gave him the most withering look I could manage, "What do you think? *Of Course* I want to be in on it!"

Tom posed his question to Skyler, listened as she answered, nodded several times, and ended the call. "Yep, we're good to go; arrest warrant is signed. Now we'll sit back and wait for them to meet. If Akabile is trying to run too, maybe they'll end up in the same place."

Lindsey called back. I put her on speaker and told her Tom was listening. She said, "Okay, Rockson's car just turned onto U.S. 36, the Boulder Expressway; he's definitely headed to Boulder."

Tom and I exchanged glances. I said, "Linds, stay well behind and rely on the GPS. He's headed for Mapleton Street; it's where Trey Worth and Akabile's niece live. It's the house Laurie Thomas is watching right now. We'll alert her and head that way."

"Okay, will do."

We raced out of Tom's office, took the elevator to the underground parking, and piled into his Ford Crown Victoria Police Interceptor. Tom spiraled out of the garage, exited on Colfax, and switched on the lights and siren. At Speer Boulevard, he turned northwest and sped to the freeway interchange where we blasted onto northbound I-25. Four minutes later, we were on U.S. 36 and Boulder bound.

I called Laurie to tell her what was happening and asked her to stay put…just watch and wait. She said Bre and some guy she figured was Trey Worth had left the house just before noon and returned at 2:15 p.m. No other activity had taken place. I asked her to call immediately if either Rockson or Akabile showed up.

Next, I called George to bring him up to speed. He wasn't happy about Laurie being in the center of things, but I assured him Tom and I would be there quickly and we'd keep him informed.

Just as we entered Boulder, my cell quacked and Laurie said, "Cort, the limo just pulled up and Rockson and the chauffer ran inside…and I do mean *ran.*"

We were a good ten minutes from Mapleton Street. "Okay, sit tight; we'll be there in--

"Wait a minute; they're coming out. Oh shit! This doesn't look good!"

"What's happening? What doesn't look good?"

"The chauffer is walking ahead, Rockson is following and has Worth by the arm; Bre is behind them. The driver is opening the back door, passenger side…Rockson is sliding in and kinda dragging Worth…Bre is getting in behind him so all three are in the back seat. The driver just ran around to the front and got in; they're pulling away. What do you want me to do?"

I'd had my phone on speaker and Tom had heard the report. He leaned toward me and yelled, "Can you follow them without being spotted?"

Laurie, sounding breathless, said, "I'm facing the wrong way, but I'll pull out and watch which way they turn then race to the parallel street and head the same way. If I'm lucky, I can cut back on the next cross street and fall in behind them."

Tom nodded even though she couldn't see him. "Okay, sounds good; give it a try. Stay on the phone and keep giving us directions. We'll try to catch up as soon as we can."

"Ten-four, will do."

I interjected, "Laurie, have you seen another limo? Has Akabile shown up?"

"No. I haven't seen anybody else."

I said, "Okay, good luck…and be careful!"

My caller alert was pinging; it was Lindsey. "Laurie, listen…stay on the line. I'm taking a call from Lindsey and we'll make it a conference call so we'll all be on. Okay?"

"Yep, got it. They turned south on Fourth; I'll try Fifth to Pine and try to catch 'em there."

I took the incoming call. "Linds, hang on, we're going to conference; Laurie is in pursuit southbound on either Fourth or Fifth. Do you still have the limo on the GPS?"

I was glad to hear her voice, "Yeah, I was calling to say I tracked them to Mapleton just like you said. But, I never got on Mapleton; stayed parked on Fourth when their signal stopped moving. They just turned in front of me and I'm following with two cars in between us…a red Prius and a blue Volkswagen Beetle."

Tom said, "Good work, Lindsey. We're at Thirty-Six and Baseline Road; we'll wait here until you and Laurie have a solid heading for these assholes. Stay back and try not to be spotted.

"Laurie, are you on? You following this?"

"I am; I'm at Fourth and Pine and they're just passing in front of me. I can see Lindsey and the two cars she described. I'll pull in behind her and maybe we can tag team the limo for a while?"

Again, Tom nodded his approval, "Sounds like you might have done this before, Laurie. Have you?"

"Yes, I was on the patrol detail back in Erie and we did some unmarked car surveillance jobs. Hang on, it looks like they're turning east on Boulder Canyon Drive. Lindsey, you got 'em?"

Lindsey said, "Got 'em; you're right, they're eastbound on Boulder Canyon. What do you guys think? I'm thinking they're headed back to Denver."

I said, "Tom, let's get turned around so we can go southbound if they go back the way they came."

Tom maneuvered across the interchange, killed the lights and siren, and pulled to a stop on the shoulder of the southbound access road. "Looks like we'll have a damned parade if we all head for Denver. I wonder what's happened to Akabile?"

"I don't know; maybe they've set up a meeting place. It seems to answer the question about whether Bre is working for Rockson though, doesn't it?"

Lindsey broke in, "Okay, they're turning onto 28th; that'll take 'em to U.S. 36; they should be passing by you in three or four minutes."

Laurie said, "I'm right behind you. Do you want to switch places?"

"Sure, let's do it. You stay in the inside lane and I'll switch to the outside." She laughed as she said, "Hey, do you *professionals* figure you can do as well?"

Tom grimaced at me and mouthed the words, "Wise-ass!" But he said, "We'll try. Let us know when they're about a block from Baseline and we'll ease into traffic."

When Laurie alerted us that she was approaching Baseline, Tom drove into the access lane, checked over his shoulder for oncoming traffic, and slowly accelerated. The Lincoln limo passed us and Tom merged into the freeway traffic with one vehicle, a tan Ford F-150 pickup, between us.

Our little caravan maintained telephone contact on the forty minute drive back to Denver, occasionally switching positions, although the girls stayed closest. Even though Tom's car wasn't marked, it was still obviously a cop car. From U.S. 36, the limo, as expected, turned onto I-25 southbound.

We were surprised when they failed to take any of the exits to downtown Denver, instead continuing south. Once we passed the Broadway exit, I called George to alert him again. The change in direction from where we'd assumed they were heading seemed to grab his attention. "Any chance they might be headed for Centennial Airport?" He asked.

Tom and I exchanged glances; for some reason, it hadn't occurred to either of us. We nodded simultaneously. Tom said, "Good thought, George. Can you get someone over there?"

"I'll go myself; it's about three minutes from here. Got any ideas on what to do?"

Tom said, "If that's where they're going, I hate to think about letting them take off, but it'll be tough to stop them without a shootout. We sure as hell don't want that!"

I said, "George, can you call airport operations and ask if Rockson International has a plane there? If they do, ask the tower if they've filed a flight plan today."

Sounding a little breathless, George replied, "Yeah, I'm running out the door at the moment. I'll call as soon as I get in my car. I'll let you know."

Two minutes later, the police radio crackled and George came on. "Right on all counts, Cort; Rockson International actually has three corporate jets at Centennial; they called at noon to have one rolled out for a departure to Houston…George Bush International."

Tom said, "We need to stop that takeoff. If they get in the air, there's no telling where they might actually go and we'd be playing catchup as well as depending on some other cop shop to grab 'em. We're right on their tail with visual contact; I don't want them to get into the terminal at Centennial, so we'll light 'em up as soon as they turn south on Peoria."

George said, "I'll get a patrol car to head north on Peoria from E-470. If they don't stop for you, we can force them east onto Broncos Parkway and into the industrial park. Where are you right now? How much time do I have?"

I jumped in, "We've just turned off I-25 on Arapahoe Road. There's lots of traffic so it'll be slow going. I'm guessing ten minutes or more before we get to Peoria."

George was silent for a moment, "Should be enough time; I'll get that patrol car to block Peoria just south of the airport entrance and I'll park in the entrance itself with my flashers going. As soon as they see you behind them, they won't have a lot of choices other than to pull over or turn east like I said."

Tom spoke into my phone, "Did you guys hear all that? Do you have the plan?"

Lindsey spoke first, "Yes, I got it. I'll be right behind you. Laurie, did you hear?"

"Yes, and I've got you both in sight. What are we going to do about Trey Worth? He looked like a hostage when they came out of the house."

Tom said, "Right now he's a bargaining chip; he's not worth anything to them dead. In fact, it would be sealing their death warrant if they killed him right in front of us. If we can get them corralled, we can promise them anything to get him. I learned a lot from Cort's dealing with Akabile…promise 'em anything but don't deliver shit!"

Traffic had thinned on east Arapahoe Road and nine minutes later we watched the limo turn south on Peoria. As soon as we followed suit, Tom lit the flashers and pulled within a few feet of their bumper. At the first sign of the flashers, the limo's brake lights blinked and Tom, who was driving with his left foot on the brake pedal, reacted immediately. Suddenly the limo sped up and we did the same; by the time we crested the hill approaching the airport, we were going nearly sixty mph. Their brake lights flashed again the same instant we spotted George parked across the terminal access road with headlights and flashers blazing. Two hundred yards farther down Peoria, an Arapahoe County sheriff's patrol car blocked the road.

The limo careened left onto Broncos Parkway, but suddenly, at the entrance to the Broncos' new practice facility, the Lincoln skidded to a stop and the driver's door flew open. The chauffeur dove from the vehicle, rolled twice, and ended up in a heap near the back of the car.

Tom nosed his car in front of the limo as Lindsey and Laurie bracketed the driver's side and rear. I pulled my .45 and piled out, walking down the passenger side as the others surrounded the car. I got as far as the front passenger side door when the rear window on that side slid down and I heard Bre say, "Everybody go slow; I've got a gun in Trey's ribs and I'll blow him away. You arseholes need to listen to me." Her British accent was much more noticeable than I'd heard in Boulder. "Scott, what the hell are you doing here? Tell that copper to get over here where I can see him!" Lindsey had emerged from her Edge and I could see her securing the chauffeur with twist-tie cuffs.

I looked across the hood at Tom who nodded, started around the front toward me, and, using his best defuse-the-situation voice, said, "Look, Bre, or whatever your name is, you've got no place to run. Give it up; throw the gun out and we'll all be able to calm down." Tom's voice *was* calm, but he sounded determined. "Don't make this any worse than it is; give it up."

Just then George pulled up beside Laurie's car, unwound himself from behind the wheel, and walked behind his car to her door. I could see him talking and then reach inside to put his hand to her face. As he resumed walking toward the rear of the limo, Laurie slowly backed her car away, did a three point turn, and sped off toward Centennial Airport. George was now standing at the back quarter panel in Bre's blind spot.

Bre said, "Let's make this real easy. You buggers need to let us go back to the airport and get on a plane. I'll let Trey go as soon as I'm on board and--

"*Ain't gonna happen!*" Tom's voice was louder now. "What *you* need to do is toss the gun out. Right now all you're looking at is, maybe, a kidnapping charge; if you shoot Worth right in front of us, you're going to be dead. Think about that, Bre…on a kidnapping beef, you'll eventually get out of prison…but you don't get over being dead."

Bre laughed, "That's a good line, copper; you must've read it somewhere. Maybe I'll use it someday." She stopped laughing and hissed, "Now here's what's *really* going to happen: first, you two are going to back off and go back to your car; next, my friend Guilford is going to climb out of the back and get in the driver's seat; then, you're going to move your car so he can make a turn and drive back to the airport. When we get there, we're going to drive right out to our plane and get on. The pilots are on board and the engines are started. Five seconds after the door closes, I want to be taxiing."

I asked, "What about Trey?"

Bre snarled, "I've changed my mind about him; he's going with us. I might need him again. Now, get moving!"

George moved his hand to get our attention and gave a barely perceptible nod followed by a shake. I was puzzled but assumed he wanted us to agree to her demands because he had something up his sleeve. Tom reluctantly acquiesced to her demands, "All right, Bre; we'll do it your way...for now. You're only making things worse for yourself though…now you'll have hijacking to go with the kidnapping."

She laughed again as the window slid up. Rockson slowly opened the rear door and climbed out. He was blinking his eyes rapidly as if trying to adjust to the light or maybe to comprehend what was happening.

When he closed the rear door, I spoke quietly, "You're screwing up, Rockson. It's just like with Bre, at the moment you're facing some charges all right, but nothing you won't be able to bargain down. If you go through with this, and particularly if

Worth gets hurt, you're either going to die today or rot in prison for the rest of your life. Give it up; you can just walk over to the police car and this part of it will be over."

He stopped blinking and focused a malevolent stare at me. "You're fucking crazy, Scott. It ain't ever going to be 'over.' Why didn't you just mind your own business; none of this shit would have happened if you hadn't taken a hand."

His words stunned me for a moment. Could what he was saying be true? Was I to blame for any of this? "No, you're the one who's crazy, Rockson. If you weren't so greedy, you'd have cut a deal with Mercy, she'd have fracked your wells, and both of you would have made a mint. Even if you'd had to pay off Akabile, you'd still have had more money than God."

He stepped to the driver's door, jerked it open, and started yelling, "Get the hell out of the way! If you try anything else…any of you…Worth is going to die! Got it?"

Tom said, "Back off, Cort. Somebody is going to get hurt." He edged back to his car, got in and moved it away, giving Rockson room to pull out.

I watched in frustration as Rockson maneuvered the limo through a laborious U-turn and accelerated toward Centennial Airport. I ran to Tom's car, but halted as George yelled. "Cort…I've got something happening at the plane. Jump in with Tom and follow me."

## CHAPTER THIRTY-TWO

Lee Anne's voice came through Tom's police radio, "Tom? I've got some bad news…I fucked up! Akabile fooled all of us and he's in the wind."

I was shocked. I had never heard Lee Anne utter a profanity worse than a "damn" or "hell" let alone an F-bomb--and over the radio to boot. Tom worriedly asked, "What do you mean?"

"Just what I said!" She sounded exasperated. "When he didn't show up at the Denver International terminal around the time we expected, we contacted the limo company and talked to the driver. He told us Akabile started making calls from the limo and booked first class tickets on several different commercial flights…at least six…leaving anywhere from right now to the 9:45 p.m. British Airways flight. They're all going to different airport cities on the East coast that offer connections to Europe or Africa.

"That was bad enough, but then he booked a private jet out of Front Range Airport and told the driver to take him there as fast as possible. He was dropped at Your Jet and when I called them, they said their charter took off over an hour ago with a flight plan for New Orleans. But get this…its already changed destinations twice: once for Kansas City and then to Jacksonville. We're assuming he's making them change the flight plans to confuse us, but we don't know if he intends to go to *any* of those places. He might be holding a gun on the pilots or something."

Tom grimaced as he answered Lee Anne. "Who the hell is 'Your Jet'; I've never heard of them?"

"Me either; I'm running a check right now with the fixed base operator and the FAA. I'll get back to you as soon as I have something. What do you want us to do?"

"There's not much you *can* do; just relay what you find out as soon as you get it. Hey, there is one thing…what kind of jet is it? What's the range?"

Lee Anne exhaled into the radio, "Cessna Citation Six; according to the person at their counter, it can go about 2800 miles."

"Okay, thanks; that might help."

Back at Centennial, we sprinted inside the departure terminal and looked out the windows as Rockson's limo rolled onto the tarmac beside a Falcon 2000S. The stairs were extended and three people, two men and a woman, were standing at the base. The men had on dark blue uniforms; the woman was wearing matching color pants with a white, short sleeve shirt and dark blue scarf. The woman was Laurie Thomas.

Rockson jumped out of the driver's seat and ran around to the far side, rear passenger door. The car blocked our view of what was happening, although we could see Bre's and Trey Worth's heads and shoulders emerge.

All three started toward the jet with Rockson in the lead. Worth, in the center, was walking stiffly with Bre following closely. She had a jacket draped over her hand, wrist, and lower arm which I assumed was covering a gun. After they entered the plane, the uniformed "crew" quickly followed. Laurie was the last to climb the stairs. At the top, we saw her turn, reach up, and engage the door closing mechanism. The steps retracted and the door closed behind them.

Tom exclaimed, "Was that *Laurie Thomas* closing the door? What the hell is going on?"

Lindsey and George walked up behind us and George answered, "When I checked on Rockson International's planes, I asked about crew staffing and found out they always have a flight attendant on board…they call them a 'hostess.' That's pretty unusual; usually it's just a pilot and copilot. Anyway, when I saw what was happening out there on the road, I guessed they might try to bargain their way back here and use their hostage to get on the plane.

"I took a hell of a risk betting Rockson wouldn't know each and every crew member for three different planes…especially the flight attendants. When I pulled up and talked to Laurie, I asked her to hurry back here and try to change uniforms with the regular girl, meet the pilots, and then act like she belonged. So far; so good, I guess…Rockson didn't seem to tumble to who she really is. I'm not sure what she can do, but at least we'll have eyes and ears on the scene."

Tom clapped George on the back and exclaimed, "Jesus, George, you've got the balls of a high diver! I hope it wasn't an *order* to Laurie; this could turn out to be dangerous."

George glared at him and said, "I told you, I *asked*. I wouldn't have done it if I hadn't known she used to be a real flight attendant. She's going to have her service weapon in her flight bag too. At some point she may have an opportunity to get the drop on that Bre woman and take her gun. It's what I'm hoping anyway."

Lindsey spoke up, "Guess I'm glad I've never been a flight attendant; I sure wouldn't have liked you to *ask* me to do something like that!"

George gave her a questioning look, then grinned and said, "I wouldn't. Besides, you always manage to get in enough trouble on your own."

We watched as the Falcon slowly started forward, turned down the apron taxiway, and headed toward the south end of the takeoff strip. George said, "Let's go to the tower; we can hear what they say." We hurried up the stairs to the flight operations tower where an armed security guard stood outside the door.

The guard raised his eyebrows and said, "Hey, Sheriff--interesting operation you've got going! I suppose you need to get inside, right? All these folks with you?"

George replied, "Hi, Morg; yeah…they're with me and we do need to listen in on the Falcon that's taxiing. Open up, okay?"

"Morg" looked at us for a moment before turning and punching in a combination on the door locking mechanism. "Go ahead, but I hope you don't make a habit of this, Sheriff. If I didn't know you, I'd have to have a bunch of ID's; as it is; this is not strictly according to Hoyle."

George bobbed his head and said, "I know; and I appreciate it."

We hurried inside, walked across the surprisingly spacious room and gathered behind the two air traffic controllers seated at their consoles. The guy on the right looked up as George approached, gave a thumbs-up sign, and flipped a switch. The controller said, "Falcon G 357RJ, taxi to runway three-five right; cleared for takeoff. Turn for heading one-seven-oh."

The pilot immediately responded, "Falcon G 357RJ acknowledging."

We watched as the sleek jet started its rollout from the south end of the runway, gathered speed, and rushed past the tower located near the midpoint of the 10,000 foot runway. In another blink of the eye, the plane lifted smoothly into the air headed north. We watched as it continued to climb and then start a wide turn.

The controller turned to us and said, "As soon as he leaves my airport control zone, I'll turn him loose."

"Tower, G 357RJ turning to heading one-seven-oh."

"Falcon: tango Romeo Juliet cleared; VFR; have a good flight."

Tom exhaled deeply, "Well, they're off. Do all those heading numbers say they're going to Houston?"

The controller turned his chair and said, "For now, at least; one-seven-oh is the correct heading. Doesn't mean they won't change it somewhere."

"So, can we track them…see where they're *really* going? Will we know where they land?"

The controller paused for a moment before extending his hand and waggling it. "Yes and no; Rockson International is a BARR company. They--

"What the hell is BARR?" Tom demanded.

"It stands for Block Aircraft Registration Request. A company can request it and if the FAA grants it, which they always do, we don't track their aircraft."

"Jesus Christ! That's fucking ridiculous! Why the hell not? What qualifies them for that kind of secrecy?"

The controller held up his hands as if surrendering, "Hey, man, I just work here, okay? Anybody can qualify: some companies don't want their competitors to know where they're flying. They might be working on a merger or something. Some big-time college sports programs get it because they don't want other schools to know where they might be recruiting. Lots of outfits, even super churches, have BARR protection."

Tom looked as if he might explode. "So where is the 'yes' part of the answer?"

"Well, we can keep them on radar until they pass out of our coverage…we're not supposed too, but we can do it. But if they turn off their transponder and don't talk to anybody on the ground, they'll be blind to us. If they fly at low altitude, it's next to impossible to spot 'em on radar."

Tom said, "Sorry I yelled at you; but what about knowing where they land?"

"If they go to an airport with a control tower, they'll have to make contact to get landing instructions and we'll know almost immediately. But if they go to VFR--

"God *damn* it!" Tom was yelling again, "Now what the hell's that…VFR? Jesus! You guys have more damn abbreviations than cops!"

"Visual Flight Rules. It means the pilots can see where they're going and weather conditions and visibility will allow for landing without instruments. They might fly to some private airport someplace; an airport without a tower or air traffic control. They could set it down without ever talking to anybody. We wouldn't know anything about it."

Tom was growing increasingly perplexed. "Even at night?" He asked.

The controller nodded, "Yep, if the strip has lights and the pilot can see, he can land anywhere long enough to accommodate him."

"So you're telling me that as soon as he's off your radar and if he turns off the, what did you call it, transponder…he's essentially lost to us?"

The controller nodded. Tom smashed his fist into his other hand.

I suggested we all have a cup of coffee or better yet, a drink, and discuss our options. We crossed over the second floor bridge walkway to the Perfect Landing restaurant and lounge. There were two people sitting at the bar, but the rest of the place was empty. It had just opened for happy hour.

We took a table near the panoramic windows overlooking the parking apron and the runway. I hadn't noticed it before, but Siren's Gulfstream G280 was parked at the end of a row of five business jets. It had been six spots from Rockson's plane. "Bit early for cocktails, but I guess we deserve one…on duty or not," George said humorlessly. "I wonder if Laurie is mixing drinks for those assholes?"

The waitress approached, wished us a good afternoon, and took the orders: a sauvignon blanc for Lindsey; Glen Livet on the rocks for Tom; Jack Daniels and water tall for George; a Bud for me.

"Well, shit! This whole day pretty much turned out to be a bust." Tom's voice expressed the frustration we were all feeling. "Only positive thing I can think of is flushing out all the bad guys; at least now we know who we're looking for. Unfortunately, they're all in the wind at the moment."

Lindsey said, "Let me see if I've got this right…obviously Akabile and Rockson are in bed together and Bre's the connection, but I can't get my arms around them being willing to commit murder." She turned to me, "Is the money really that big?"

The waitress delivered the drinks and we stayed silent while she unloaded her tray. "Happy Hour" turned out to be two-fers…everyone grimaced. After she left, I said, "Yes, the money *is* that big. It can be in the billions for a producer like Rockson *if* he gets the technology and in the hundreds of millions for the fracking company, in this case Mercy Drexler. One percent of a billion dollars is ten million…and that's the kind of cut Akabile was looking for. Those kinds of numbers constitute a lot of motive."

George ran his fingers through his hair and whistled. "I had no idea. But that's the big picture; I've got a smaller focus…like who killed Dailov and why? What's your theory on that, Cort?"

"I figure Akabile and Rockson are the only ones who had a motive, but in this case it wasn't money…Dailov could tie both of them to the car bomb. Because he provided the explosives, Akabile can be charged with terrorism, which is a federal rap and trumps his diplomatic immunity. If we get him on terrorism, we can also nail him with attempted murder and bribery. Rockson is on the hook for all of that plus the assaults on me and Marty Gear.

"From what we know about Bre's background, she's an obvious suspect for both the car bomb and for Dailov. I'm betting after Dailov bailed on arranging for the bomb and said he wanted out, Rockson talked to Akabile who suggested Bre. She was already working for Rockson trying to get the frack technology; all he would have to do is up the ante and she'd be all in for setting a bomb *and* taking care of Dailov."

Tom and George nodded their heads in agreement, but Lindsey had a perplexed look on her face. I watched her for a few moments before asking, "What is it, Linds? You don't look like you're buying in on everything."

She had some wine before replying, "There's one more piece of the crime scene evidence bothering me. Remember what I told you about Dailov's sleeves and the arms on the chair? The underside of his sleeves and the arms didn't have any blood spatter so I concluded someone else probably held his arms while the killer put the muzzle in his mouth and killed him. If Bre was the shooter, I think there's a second person involved in Dailov's murder."

Tom's cell, which had a ringtone even more obnoxious than my duck quack…a police siren…interrupted the conversation. He glanced at the screen and answered, "Hey, Lee Anne, what've you got?" He listened intently for a few seconds and I could see a flush rise from his neck to his face. “Shit! That’s exactly what I didn’t want to hear. We might have the same thing going on here. Would you get back to the FAA and see if they’ve got any ideas? Let me know, okay?” He looked as if he would like to push the “end call” sign through the touch screen.

He slugged down most of his first drink. “Akabile’s charter disappeared from radar and isn’t answering any calls from air traffic control. They’ve apparently turned off the transponder. Sound familiar?”

Lindsey asked, “Do you think they had a plan to hook up somewhere?”

Everyone was silent for a moment before Tom exclaimed, “I’d bet on it! There are just too many coincidences to think otherwise…and I don’t believe in coincidences anyway.”

I asked George, “Does Laurie have her smart phone with her?”

“As far as I know. Why?”

“Assuming she put it in ‘airplane mode’ to keep it from ringing, I think her service provider can ping it or track it on GPS. Which provider does she use?”

“Verizon. And I think you’re right!”

Tom joined in, “*Finally!* Something might work for us.”

A look of concern passed over Lindsey’s face. “I hope she hid it someplace. And not with her gun. If Rockson or Bre find either one, she could be in big trouble.”

George said, “The phone wouldn’t be a problem, everybody has one. You’d be right about her gun though.”

I said, “There’re lots of places to hide either one on a plane: seat backs, storage holds, in the cabin, under seats, even in the refrigerator or trash bins. She’ll know them all.

“Does anyone know whether we can track them in real time or will we be playing catchup?” Everybody shook their head; nobody had an answer.

George pulled his phone, opened the screen, scanned across, and touched an icon. He looked up and said, “We’ll know in a minute, I’m calling Verizon.” We could all hear the ringing and then the connection but couldn’t make out the conversation. I wished George would put it on speaker but he didn't. He identified himself and asked to speak to a supervisor; he was on hold for only a few seconds, re-identified himself, and gave his badge number before making his request. He nodded and said, "Okay, I'll have it there within five minutes. Thanks for your help."

He ended the call and announced, "First, they need a search warrant which I'll have Judge Sammoury fax over immediately; second, we can track them in real time assuming Verizon has good coverage. She said there are a few blind spots mostly here in the Rocky Mountains and Midwest. Hopefully, the bastards don't fly through many of those, or what's worse, fly into one and then change direction." He held up an index finger, scanned his directory, connected with the judge, and made his request. He ended the call and grinned at us. "Nice to have a cooperative judge like Sammoury; he's on it and said the fax will be there in minutes. Soon as Verizon has it, they'll start feeding us the data."

# CHAPTER THIRTY-THREE

It seemed like everyone sat back in their chairs and took a deep breath. Although this was far from over, we were at least doing something proactive, something that might bring this to an end. I had another idea and needed to make a call.

"Hi, Mercy, it's Cort. Is your plane getting ready to take off from Centennial?"

Mercy was silent for a moment before saying, "Clay is going to North Dakota tonight. Why?"

"I'm sitting in Centennial Airport looking directly at it and watching the pilots doing a ground inspection.

"Listen, Mercy, Rockson is running--actually flying--and he's managed to take a hostage. He's got a woman with him who we think bombed your car and probably killed one of Rockson's thugs. They've taken Clay's brother with them.

"He's just taken off for parts unknown, but we may be able to track him. There's a cell phone hidden onboard. If we can figure out where he's going, we'll need to go after him and try to stop him before he skips the country. Your plane would be perfect if you'll allow us to use it."

"Oh my God! He's got Clay's brother?! Of course you can use my plane! I'll call the pilots and tell them to get ready for an immediate take off.

"Do you have *any* idea where Rockson is headed?"

"They mentioned Houston and left on that heading, but air traffic control just told us the transponder has been turned off. They could be headed anywhere: anywhere they can catch an international flight. But we think there's a good chance he's trying to hook up with Akabile who's also in the wind in a hijacked jet.

"But we don't think either of them will fly directly into a major airport because of air traffic control. We'd find them in time to stop them."

"Cort, do you remember me telling you Rockson has a ranch near Dallas? The place I'd heard he was turning into a damn military base or something? Well, it's near Garland *and* he's got an airstrip there. From Denver, it's literally on the same heading as Houston and it can't be more than fifty miles from DFW."

It made sense. "Holy Shit, Mercy! That's gotta be it! Rockson is definitely looking to flee the U.S.; it's over for him here. DFW is a gateway to the world; he can get almost anywhere from there…including South Sudan where Akabile can protect him. I'm sure he's already set up there…money, people, whatever he needs to pick up where he leaves off here."

"Cort, get off the phone and get on my plane! You can be in Garland in two hours. You've got to stop Rockson, the son-of-a-bitch!"

I ended the call and pointed at Siren's plane, "Let's go, Mercy is giving us her plane, plus she told me Rockson has a private airstrip maybe an hour's drive from DFW. That's gotta be where they're headed and I'd put money on them meeting Akabile there too.

"Lindsey, we'll need you to coordinate things from this end; we need Skyler's input and make sure Tom's and George's offices are brought up to sp--

Lindsey interrupted loudly, "That's bullshit, Cort! I deserve to go; I've been involved in this from the first day--the day you were beaten." She turned to George and said, "You know I'm right, George. *You're* my boss, not him! *YOU* tell me I can't go!"

George said quietly, "We don't have time to argue. You can come."

I wanted to protest but knew it would be futile. "C'mon then, let's move! We can contact the offices from the plane."

Tom and George ran to their cars and grabbed their shotguns and attack rifles as well as several Kevlar vests. The pilots were already at the plane and clambered inside when they saw us racing toward them. At the top of the stairs, I turned to see Tom and George hurrying while struggling with the long guns and vests. Inside, the pilot was already in the left seat; the copilot pointed toward the cabin, and yelled, "Grab a seat and buckle up! We'll start the rollout as soon as the others are in and I secure the door."

Tom led George through the door as the copilot eyed the weapons warily. "Put those in the netted cargo area behind the last row of seats; there're some bungee cords to tie them down…and hurry, we're ready to roll!

"Ms. Drexler said to set a heading for Garland, Texas, and see if we can locate an airstrip registered for Rockson; she said you guys will notify us any changes."

With the weapons secured, we selected the "business conference" seats: Lindsey and I sat facing aft with George and Tom facing forward. Lindsey and George had the window seats. The instant the last buckle clicked, the plane began taxiing; three minutes later we were airborne and making the same wide turn as Rockson's plane coming to heading one-seven-oh.

We needed a game plan and had less than two hours to come up with one. I suggested we find out if there were any direct flights leaving DFW tonight for Africa or Mideast destinations. If there were, I thought we could assume Rockson and Bre would try to make one. The others agreed, so I pulled my cell and dialed a travel agent I'd used for years. On this flight, there were no silly rules about shutting down all phones and electronic devices during takeoff and landing.

When the agent answered, I posed my question and she said it would take a couple minutes to pull up a flight matrix; I said it was important and I'd hold. It seemed like an eternity with no one speaking until she said, "Well, there's not much. It looks like the best bet is an Emirates flight leaving DFW at 8:57 p.m. It's a numb-bum special direct to Dubai: 14 hours and 45 minutes."

I remembered Akabile saying there were several flights from Dubai to Entebbe, Uganda, with a short hop to Juba. I told the others that *had* to be Rockson's plan.  But Tom said, "Wow, we're making some pretty big assumptions: one, they're headed to Rockson's strip in Garland, and, two, they'll try to make the flight to Dubai. If we're wrong on either, we stand a chance of losing them."

Lindsey said, "I know I'm not the leader here, but for what it's worth, I think Cort's right."

George remained silent for a moment then said, "I agree. We need to bottle 'em up at that ranch or close to it. We can't take a chance on them getting into the airport; if they do and it ends up being a fire fight with thousands of people around…"

He sighed deeply and continued, "The more I think about it, the more I wish I hadn't asked Laurie to sneak on board. If they figure her out, she's in trouble; if we manage to catch up with 'em, they may want more hostages, and she'll be in bigger trouble; sneaking her on was a bad decision." Worry was etched on my friend's face.

Tom made a decision. "Okay, I agree, they're probably going to the ranch and then try to make that flight. And George is right; we need to run them to ground outside DFW. Let's see if the pilots have located Rockson's ranch and airstrip; maybe they can find some kind of maps or aerial photos of the Garland area."

I had another thought, "Hey, I've got a friend who also has a place somewhere around Garland. I've never been there, but I think he's got an airstrip too. I know for a fact he has a plane…a Lear 45. His name is Redmond; his company is Red Mountain Resources."

Tom unbuckled and walked to the cockpit door, "Hey guys, any luck on finding Rockson's airstrip?"

We couldn't hear the reply, but Tom returned with an iPad and said, "Good news…they've got it nailed! Egotistical bastard even calls it "Rockson International" just like his company; what's better, we can see it in satellite view. Here, take a look." He turned the iPad so we could all see as he continued and began pointing at the screen, "Here's the strip, the outbuildings, and the main house. It looks like his whole air force was on the ground when this was taken and you can see where there's a parking apron behind the main house and next to the strip. But take a gander at the roads and access…there's only one road in and out from the two-lane highway, Farm Road 371 S. It looks like a long driveway; must be damned near a mile. If we could put a stopper in place on that, we'd have them in a trap.

"George, you think the Texas Rangers could help us out; get some cars and men out there?"

George looked relieved to be doing something even if it meant possibly putting Laurie into more danger. "You bet! This ought to be right up their alley; from the looks of the aerial there are two or three places along the highway with enough trees where Rangers could hide until the plane almost touches down. They wouldn't be spotted from the air. As soon as it passes over, they can seal off the driveway to keep everybody at the ranch." He pulled his phone, spun through the directory, and started to punch in a number.

Tom held up his hand and said, "Hang on a sec, George. There's more good news; they found Cort's buddy's place too. It's about five miles north of Rockson's and he *does* have a strip. The pilot says we need about three thousand feet to land and about double that to takeoff; the strip is almost eight thousand, so we'd be in good shape if we want to go in there. He said if we hit top speed, there's a good chance we could be on the ground ten minutes before Rockson. If we get some Rangers to meet us and haul ass to Rockson's, we might even beat those bastards!"

I studied the iPad photo. "Look at this, guys. The outbuilding probably serves as a hangar but it looks like it's been recently expanded. See all the lighter colored dirt around the outside and the different colors on the roof…that looks new. Mercy said she'd heard rumors Rockson's been stockpiling military equipment like he's preparing for a war or something. What do you bet this place is his fort?"

Although George hadn't put his phone on speaker, it was obvious he spoke the same language as whoever his counterpart was on the Texas Rangers. It took about two minutes for the arrangements to be made and George smiled as he ended the call, "Those guys ate it up! They'll send six Rangers in four units to Cort's friend's place. The captain I talked to said they know exactly where Rockson's ranch is and where to hide. They can have the driveway blocked two minutes after the jet touches down.

"He also said they'll be careful with Worth--or anybody else who might end up as a hostage." He looked relieved.

I said, "Here's another assumption--a big one: I think Laurie will have told Rockson's pilots what's going on; she might have even slipped them her gun or her phone. There's a good chance when Rockson, Bre, and Worth get out of the plane, we'll have some backup. We *should* have them outgunned.

"Does anybody know if our pilots can talk to theirs' without the bad guys knowing?" That drew blank looks from everybody. "Okay, me neither, I'll ask." I unbuckled and went to the cockpit door. "Hey guys, can you talk to the Falcon pilots without their passengers knowing?"

The pilot spoke over his right shoulder. "Well, yeah, we can probably reach them on 123.45 VHF but *any* pilot who's listening can hear what's going on, including the charter you said the other bogey is on. As long as none of the bad guys have headsets on, it might not be a big risk, and if the charter pilots have been hijacked, they're not going to say anything."

I said, "Thanks, I'll discuss it with the others and be back in a minute."

Returning to my seat, I said, "Okay, apparently there's kind of an open or universal channel any pilot can monitor or talk to another plane. Obviously, there's a risk that Rockson's pilots are in on this, but I doubt it. And, of course, either Rockson or Bre *could* be wearing a headset. Truthfully though, I don't think there's much chance of that; I think it's a risk worth taking to let Rockson's pilots know what we're planning."

Everyone was silent for a moment as they considered the problem. Tom spoke first, "I think we've got to risk it; have our pilot try and make contact, tell them what we're doing."

George nodded and added, "If Akabile is trying to rendezvous with them, he's had a big head start and could already be on the ground or close to it. If his hijacked charter pilot is listening, it'd put him in the loop too."

Lindsey asked, "Should we risk it? We're still putting all the eggs in one basket."

One by one, we all raised a hand like we were voting in a school election. Tom said, "I don't think we have much choice."

I returned to the cockpit door and told the pilots, "Okay, here's the deal: first, you need to kick this thing in the ass and head to the Redmond strip--we *absolutely* have to beat the Falcon! The Texas Rangers will meet us there with transportation and we're planning to intercept Rockson's bunch somewhere along the driveway into his ranch and bottle 'em up.

"When we get close, say fifty miles out, we want you to get on that VHF channel and hail 'Falcon tango Romeo Juliet' but tell them not to acknowledge. I know we're running the risk of one of the assholes listening in, but, if you're right, it's a remote chance. If they don't acknowledge your call, nobody can see them talking. Tell 'em to do whatever Rockson asks and not to put up a fight. Don't say anything else; I don't want to put them or Laurie into a worse fix than they already are." The pilot nodded and leaned forward to his controls. I heard the engine whine increase and felt acceleration.

"She'll be topped out in a few seconds, Mr. Scott. We'll do our best to get there ahead of 'em. We should be starting our descent in about twenty minutes and be on the ground fifteen minutes later.

"Tell everyone to buckle in as tightly as possible. When we land, we'll be coming in hot, and I plan to shorten the rollout as much as possible to save you some time. When those reverse thrusters cut in it's going to create one hell of a braking effect, and as soon as I can, I'll hit the wheel brakes too. It'll be kinda, uh, *stressful,* and louder then hell. Tell everyone to be prepared."

Back in my seat, I relayed everything about the landing. In the exchange of glances that followed, everyone rolled their eyes. Even though we had the better part of twenty-five minutes to go, everyone cinched up on the seat belts.

Tom said, "Okay, we need to work as a team from the instant the wheels touch down right through saddling up with the

Rangers. As soon as it's safe to stand, George and I will get the weapons and pass them forward. There are two shotguns and two tactical assault rifles…one long gun for each of us. I suggest George and Cort take the shotguns; Lindsey and I will take the rifles. The shotguns are riot guns so they have quick drop magazine clips; two of 'em. The rifles are thirty-round clips with an extra for each. Everyone has a handgun. Obviously, the Rangers are going to have their own weapons. We should have a firepower advantage, although from what Mercy Drexler told Cort, the place might be an arsenal. I hope like hell it doesn't come down to a shootout.

"As soon as the door is opened, jump out, and run for the Rangers' vehicles. Cort, you and Lindsey are a team so stick together; George and I will do the same.

"We'll have time to talk to the Rangers during the drive to Rockson's. Hopefully, since it's their turf, they'll already have a plan for what's going to happen.

"And one more thing, remember Laurie is involved. She may or may not be a hostage when we stop them; we won't know whether they've brought her along. We have to assume they'll continue to haul Worth around; they definitely need at least one hostage to have any bargaining power. We'll just have to see how everything plays out. Anybody have anything to add?"

We exchanged glances but no one said anything. Everyone heard the pitch of the engines change and felt a deceleration. The pilot came over the intercom, "Okay, we're starting down. Get prepared."

Even with the forewarning, this was unlike any jet landing anyone had ever experienced. It felt at first as if we were in free fall…the kind where your ass kind of sucks up into your guts, your guts suck up into your stomach, and your stomach sucks up into your throat. The pressure on our ears changed so rapidly, that they couldn't adjust and we were almost deaf for a few seconds. Everyone's hands were gripping the armrests; there were lots of white knuckles. I glanced out the window and could see the ground approaching way too fast, but before I could think about it again, we slammed down. It felt like we might have bounced once and the roar of the reverse thrusters started immediately. It was frightening and reassuring at the same time. That was followed by more deceleration from the wheel brakes. Since Lindsey and I were facing the rear of the aircraft, it threw us against the seat backs while pitching Tom and George forward. I could see Tom's eyes bulging as he strained against his seat belt and we lurched to a stop.

"*GO, GO, GO!*" The pilot yelled. "The Rangers' vehicles are right there, straight out the door." The copilot was already opening the door and dropping the stairs.

Tom jumped for the guns and the rest of us formed a line with George next to Tom, then me, then Lindsey. An assault rifle and ammo belt came forward which I passed to Lindsey; she turned and started down the stairs. Next came a shotgun and extra clips for me and I followed her.

I spotted the Rangers' fleet about fifty yards away: a Ford Taurus Police Interceptor, two club cab pickups, and a Chevy Suburban. Although all were obviously police vehicles with the Rangers' circle star insignia emblazoned on the doors, they had different color variations on a gray, black, and white theme. I don't know why that seemed strange, but it did.

I heard George, then Tom, hit the ground and we all ran toward the Rangers. The rear doors of the Suburban and one of the pickups were open and attended by Rangers who were waving us forward. Again, the funny little things that register…the uniforms differed from man to man although they were all in western-cut pants, boots, and long sleeve white shirts. One guy had a baseball cap with a circle star; another wore a narrow-brim cowboy hat like Lyndon Johnson used to wear. I didn't see any ten-gallon Stetsons.

Lindsey and I raced to the pickup as George and Tom piled into the Suburban. The guy waving at us jumped into the passenger seat and the truck began moving before we buckled in.

"Hey, good timing, guys! Ah'm Junior Bigelow and the ol' boy drivin' us is Ben Franks." Our host was a tall, lean cut, but powerful looking man who resembled George Ivins in his build and demeanor. His Texas accent was thick, but not objectionable.

"As far as we know, y'all beat the other plane so we should be in good shape. You mind tellin' us what the hell is going on?"

I nodded a greeting, "Good to meet you fellows; I'm Cort Scott and this is Lindsey Collins. She's with the Arapahoe County Sheriff's department in Colorado and I'm a PI. The other two guys are cops: Tom Montgomery from the Denver Police Department and George Ivins from Arapahoe County; both work homicide. We've got a murder case and reasons to believe everything from terrorism to international bribery is mixed in. One of the fugitives we're after is a government official from South Sudan so there are some delicate issues with diplomatic immunity, but we think we've got all the bases covered.

"Everything came to a head this morning and the suspects are apparently trying to flee the country. In a nutshell, we think two business jets are converging here on Rockson's airstrip. One was hijacked and is carrying the South Sudanese official who is up to his eyeballs in everything I mentioned; the other plane is actually owned by one of the passengers, Guilford Rockson…it's his ranch and airstrip. He's got a woman with him who *may* be a terrorist…or a mercenary…or a murderer--probably all three--we're not sure. She's the niece of the crooked South Sudanese official on the other plane.

"And along with everything else, we've got a hostage situation. When they took off, Rockson and the woman were holding a gun on a guy we think is, or was, the woman's boyfriend and the leader of an environmental protest group. To complicate things even more, we were able to sneak a woman police officer on board their plane. We don't think they've tumbled to it yet, but we've got to be careful."

Junior Bigelow blew his breath out in a long whistle. "Christ, y'all shore believe in complicated mess ups, don'cha? Actually, our captain musta got most of it on the phone call from your sheriff back there. We understand the plan is to get to Rockson's place as soon as we can; let their plane land and then block off the exit. You're plannin' to catch 'em there and keep 'em from getting' to DFW, which would be bad deal. That about right?"

I nodded, "Yep, you've got it."

The pickup slewed around a corner onto a paved farm road and accelerated rapidly. Bigelow said, "We're pretty sure the first plane you mentioned has arrived; we had a chopper up and they called about fifteen minutes ago to say a small jet had landed. It's a half mile to the main road and then about four miles to the driveway for Rockson's place. There's a stand of live oaks a couple hundred yards from the gate where we can park 'til they land."

We were to the trees in ten minutes, pulling in behind the Taurus and the other pickup. I glanced back and saw the Suburban right behind us. Our driver lowered his window and shut off the engine; I lowered mine too. Within seconds, we heard the high-pitched scream of a descending jet. Craning my neck to look northeast, I caught a glimpse of the low-flying Falcon streaking toward the strip I knew was only a mile away. After the plane passed overhead, we watched the lead car throw up dirt and gravel as it sped toward the gate entry. The rest of us followed.

The driveway was marked by a wrought-iron arch which spelled out "ROCKSON" in letters a foot high. There was no gate, only a cattle guard. The drive had wide gravel and dirt shoulders bounded on each side by thick mesquite. Ahead, I could see a low hill that blocked any view of the house and strip. The Rangers deployed quickly, with the Taurus parking at a forty-five degree angle across the road, the two pickups pulled into a "V" facing the Taurus, and the Suburban blocked the road behind us.

The six Rangers and the four of us piled out and gathered on the road between the pickups. A short, stout Ranger wearing a baseball cap was leaning against the fender of the truck on the right and watched everyone approach. "Howdy, I'm Captain Reynoso. Shee-it! Y'all look like you're prepared for a goddamn war! Hope you know how to use all those weapons!"

Tom and George stepped forward, shook hands with Reynoso, and introduced themselves. Tom said, "We don't have any idea of the weaponry they might have, but there's a chance they're well-armed. We'd love to show an overwhelming force to make 'em think twice about a fire fight."

Reynoso nodded, "Better to show too much than not have enough. You figure they'll be inclined to fight?" I stepped into their circle and the captain eyed me curiously before asking Tom, "Who's this? Plain clothes?"

"No. This is Cort Scott; he's a PI who's been working this case since the start and knows more about the big picture than anybody else."

Captain Reynoso extended his hand, "Howdy, Jaime Reynoso; got some bad asses, do you?"

I returned the grip. "Glad to meet you, Captain; we really don't know what we've got. The hijacker on the first plane that landed is a cabinet minister for the new government of South Sudan and crooked as a dog's hind leg. He's so deep in this mess that his diplomatic immunity isn't going to get him a pass. His niece is on the other plane and she is a mercenary terrorist…guns, chemical weapons, bombs…you name it and she's done it if the money's there.

"If I were a betting man, I'd say they're the kind who might choose to fight it out. The 'wildcards' are Rockson and the hostage, Trey Worth. Rockson is an irascible son-of-a-bitch and prone to physical violence, although I don't know about his appetite for guns or personal involvement. We know he ordered a car bombing and probably the murder of guy who was involved but ready to cooperate with us.

"The hostage, Trey Worth, is a complete unknown. Supposedly he's a non-violent environmentalist involved in protests and demonstrations, but we don't think he's mixed up in the bombing or the murder. He and the girl have been in a romantic relationship, but now she's holding a gun on him.

"We honestly don't know if he's a hostage or not, but we've got to assume he is until we find out differently."

Reynoso seem to consider all I'd said for a moment. "What about this woman police officer onboard? Is she going to be able to help or is she just going to be in the way?"

George volunteered, "She works for me, Captain. She's a veteran officer and has shown pretty good instincts so far, so unless she's been discovered, I think she'll be an asset."

Reynoso nodded, "But apparently all she's got is a service pistol, right?"

George answered, "Yes."

Reynoso said, "I hope she doesn't have to use it. Okay, here's the deal as far as blocking them in. They can't see this location from the house; they'll have to top the hill before they see us." He pointed toward the crest of the low hill. "We've arranged our vehicles in a classic roadblock array so it's impossible to run the block with anything less than a tank.

"I'd love to cut 'em off from returning to the house and isolate 'em out here in the open, but without a vehicle behind them, I don't think we can.

"Worst case, I guess, is if they get turned around and try to get back on the plane. That's where your gal might come in handy. Another option will be to park a vehicle across the strip to keep 'em from taking off. Hope it doesn't come to that. Well, best get ready; light 'em up, boys."

A man ran to each rig, reached inside, and immediately the overheads blazed into a carnival show of red, blue, and white. Reynoso yelled to his men to get out their long guns and take up positions on the inside of the "V" formed by the pickups. The Rangers produced an assortment of guns ranging from a rather ancient looking lever action Winchester to an AR-15 sporting a large capacity banana clip.

I looked at Lindsey who rolled her eyes. As I leaned in close, she whispered, "I don't like the looks of this, Cort. I'm afraid we're about to witness a massacre."

"I hope you're wrong, babe, but it's scary as hell."

# CHAPTER THIRTY-FOUR

A vehicle topped the hill five hundred yards away. It was closely followed by another; both appeared to be oversized SUVs like Hummers or Ford Expeditions. They skidded to a stop just over the crest; the driver of the lead truck threw open his door and used it as cover as he ran back to the second rig. One of the Rangers, watching through a spotting scope said, "I can see somebody in the passenger seat and at least two people in the second truck. I can't tell anything about the rear seats."

The lead driver ran back to his truck, made a hard left onto the dirt shoulder, and completed a three point turn to head back the way he'd come. The second vehicle copied the first and both disappeared over the hill.

Captain Reynoso looked at me and asked, "You guys want to follow them?"

I glanced at Tom and George, nodded at Reynoso, and said, "Yes. We've already achieved one of the objectives…we've got 'em bottled up and didn't let them get to DFW. Now, we need to grab 'em up and put an end to this before they can fly back out of here." I watched Lindsey bob her head in agreement.

Reynoso called his Rangers in and said, "Okay, boys, you heard the man. Let's go get these guys. I reckon we'd best be a little careful after we clear the hill; no telling what kind of surprise they might have for us or what kind of weaponry they might have; we don't know how many others are back at the house and might be interested in a fight. Anyway, be careful going in and stay under cover until we get everything sorted out.

"Okay, let's saddle up. I'll take the lead; soon as we're over the top, everyone stop and we'll check it out." He walked to the Taurus as the other Rangers returned to their vehicles. Reynoso pulled forward and waited while the others maneuvered into single file then drove up the road toward the ranch and airstrip on the other side.

At the top of the hill, we had a good view of the ranch and airstrip. The two SUVs we were chasing were already pulling to a stop in front of a low building next to the strip. The doors on both trucks flew open and several people jumped out and ran inside.

Three of them were wearing uniforms and, unfortunately, I recognized the flight attendant's outfit Laurie had borrowed; the bastards *had* decided on additional hostages. George was standing next to me and sucked in a deep breath. "Shit! They grabbed her! Hope they haven't figured out she's a cop."

Rockson's plane was parked on the apron next to the building with the cabin door open and the stairs down. Another smaller jet was parked beside the Falcon: the charter Akabile had hijacked.

Reynoso walked up and asked, "How do you want to handle it?"

I answered, "I think they're going back to the plane to try and take off. If they do, there is no telling where they'll land. We need to keep them from doing that."

Reynoso said, "They'll need to taxi all the way to the far end of the strip, turn around, and head back this way to take off. I can get down there before they get turned around; I'll block the runway far enough down they can't take off." Before anyone answered, he ran to the Ford and peeled rubber toward the ranch. A hundred yards away, he hit the siren to go with the flashers.

Tom yelled, "Let's go! Follow him in, spread out when we're inside the yard, surround the low building, and park the Suburban in front of the ranch house. That'll isolate them in the plane or in the building if they make it back that far." Everyone ran for the vehicles and raced down the road.

Junior Bigelow's voice was tense when he said, "Looks like you called it, Mr. Scott; they're walking outta' the building toward the plane; they've got the pilots."

We were closing fast and I leaned low in the back seat to see out the windshield. I confirmed Bigelow's view: three figures in blue were walking single file toward the Falcon, followed by a single, followed by three more walking abreast. I assumed the single was Worth. The pilots and Laurie were within a few yards of the plane. We were close enough to see everyone suddenly turn toward Reynoso's fast approaching black and white. I recognized Akabile, Bre, and Rockson as the three trailers.

It didn't take them long to recognize Reynoso's plan. Bre and Akabile began waving their arms; both were carrying Uzis or similar machine pistols. Rockson didn't appear to be armed. It was obvious that Akabile and Bre were screaming at the others to turn back and return to the building. Worth sprinted between Akabile and Rockson toward the hangar. But as they turned to watch him, Laurie and the pilots broke the other way toward the Falcon. I watched in horror as Bre spotted the break, turned, and started to raise her gun.

We skidded to a stop but before we could unload, I heard the sharp crack of a high-powered rifle. I jerked my head toward the sound of the shot and saw our other pickup had stopped a hundred yards back. Both Rangers were using the truck's doors as shields and aiming long guns at people on the tarmac. One of them had fired the shot that distracted Bre from slaughtering Laurie and the pilots.

Bre swung her weapon in our direction and opened up. Slugs were splattering dust and gravel and walking a trail toward the Rangers' truck, but they were beyond Bre's effective aiming range. She loosed one more short burst in apparent frustration before racing after Rockson and Akabile who were at the door of the building. Worth had disappeared inside.

Lindsey yelled, "Cort, look! Laurie and the pilots made it to the plane!" I switched my gaze in time to see the Falcon's door closing. "*Holy Shit!* That was close! If a Ranger hadn't taken that shot, Bre would've cut them in half! She couldn't have been more than ten or fifteen yards away!"

Reynoso's car sped down the runway and slewed to a stop three quarters of the way to the end. Our Suburban took up a position between the airstrip building and the ranch house. Two men walked out onto the wide porch of the house and we heard shouts coming from the Suburban. The men disappeared back into the house. Meanwhile, using each vehicle as a shield, the Rangers, Tom, and George dashed from one to the next until everyone was assembled behind our pickup.

Junior Bigelow's radio crackled and Reynoso's voice came over loud and clear. "Good work, you 'all! Looks like you managed to split the good guys from the assholes! Now, we've got to figure a way to smoke 'em out. What's the hostage situation?"

Bigelow handed me the handset, "The female hostage, our officer, got away and she's in the plane with the pilots. Unless there's somebody else in the building, they've got one male hostage."

George looked at his cell with amazement as it rang. "*Jesus, it's Laurie!*" He exclaimed. "She must be calling from inside the plane."

"Are you all right? Is everyone all right?" His voice was tense.

He opened the speaker and Laurie's voice poured out, "Oh, George; *OH MY GOD!* YES, I'm inside the plane with the pilots. We made it! I can see you standing behind the truck. Listen, *you need to pull back!* THEY'VE GOT AN ARSENAL IN THERE!

George's face looked stricken. "What do you mean? What's in there?"

"It's like a National Guard armory! They've got heavy machine guns, assault rifles, shotguns! I think I even saw an RPG launcher! *You guys need to pull back!*"

Tom grabbed the police radio and yelled, "Captain Reynoso? Did you copy that?"

"Yeah, this is deep shit! Are my men monitoring this?"

"Yes."

"Okay, listen Rangers, I want you to get in your rigs and pull back at least two hundred and fifty yards. Try to get at an angle to the doors of the building so they'd have to step outside to fire something big at you.

"You guys in the Suburban, stay put for the moment. You're already at a bad angle for them; train your rifles on both doors and if you see *any* movement, open up on 'em. After the others are clear, move your truck around to the side of the house. Soon as I see you behind the house, I'll come back and join the rest of 'em at the pickups. Got it?

The guys in the Suburban acknowledged and Reynoso yelled, "GO, GO, GO!"

Everyone jumped in the pickups; George and Tom climbed in with us, making four in the back seat. Ben Franks gunned the engine in reverse kicking up a cloud of dust and gravel as he weaved backwards. We traveled the two hundred yards in a few seconds and then swerved hard to the left putting us at an acute angle to the front door of the building. The other truck veered the opposite way leaving over a hundred yards between us.

As the dust cleared, we saw the Suburban lurch into reverse and swing around the ranch house. The driver leaped out and aimed an assault rifle across the hood of the truck at the side door of the building. Reynoso was already in motion and coming toward us like a bat out of hell. He cut between the planes and the ranch house, swerved out, and skidded to stop behind our pickup. When he'd joined our group, Tom surveyed the scene and said, "Now what the hell do we do?"

George spoke into his cell, "Laurie, are you still there?"

"Yes, I'm here."

"What's the situation with Worth? Have they harmed him; are they threatening him? And are the pilots involved in any of this? Do they know what's going on?"

"The pilots are clean. I had about three minutes before Rockson got to the airport, but I managed to tell them I was a cop and we had a bad situation. I explained I was going to act like a flight attendant, but they needed to hide my gun in case I was discovered. They didn't ask a single question; just told me they'd been expecting something like this to happen. When Rockson boarded, he ordered them to shut down the transponder as soon as we took off--and to stay off the radio.

"As for Worth, I don't think Bre or Rockson said three words to him the whole time; they left him alone.

"When we got here, Akabile was sitting inside. They put me and the pilots in an office; Rockson and Worth stood outside the door while Akabile talked to Bre in another office.

"Then, they marched everyone outside to those SUVs. They put me, Rockson, Bre and one pilot in the lead truck with Rockson driving. They told Worth to drive the other rig with Akabile and the pilot.

"Soon as we crossed that hill, Rockson saw all your vehicles and flashers and slammed on the brakes. He ran back and told Akabile we had to turn around.

"As soon as we got back here and started through the building, Akabile yelled for everyone to go to the plane. That's when the black and white cruiser came roaring down the hill and, well…you saw what happened then."

George exhaled deeply, "I'm glad you guys made the plane, but it may not have been the best move. If that Ranger hadn't fired, Bre would have cut you down. We'll talk about it later. Do you still have your gun on board?"

"Yes, I just got it back; we never had a chance to use it. Bre sat there with a gun in her lap watching us the whole way. And, as soon as we landed, she grabbed one of those machine pistols."

Reynoso, who'd been listening asked, "What happened to the pilots from the other plane?"

Laurie answered, "I don't know; we didn't see anyone else. They must be in the ranch house."

"Do you have any idea how many more may be in there?"

"No, but there are at least two because somebody brought the SUVs to the building."

Reynoso quietly said, "I think you need to move the plane away from the building."

Laurie sounded strained when she answered, "What's to keep them from blowing us to hell when we try to move? They're only about fifty yards away. We'd be sitting ducks!"

Reynoso calmly said, "I'll have my guys in the Suburban cover you. If the perps open that door toward the jet, we'll hit 'em with everything we've got. They'll have to take cover while you move the plane."

George and Tom exchanged skeptical looks and both slowly shook their heads. George said, "Sounds awful risky to me."

Reynoso sounded exasperated as he exclaimed, "More risky than just sitting there fifty yards away? If they've really got RPG armament, they can blow that plane to shit any time they want!"

George stared at the Ranger for a moment. "It's your call, Captain, but I don't like it. I think as soon as they try to move the plane, those bastards will blow it up."

Reynoso returned the stare. "It's Rockson's plane for chrissakes! What the hell is in it for them to blow it up? They've got to know we aren't going to let them get back on board and just fly away. That'd just be stupid--

*"ANYBODY LISTENIN' OUT THERE?"*

Rockson's

amplified voice over a loud hailer interrupted Reynoso. "*Put somebody who can make decisions on the PA! We've got some things to tell you.*"

Tom looked at George before turning to Reynoso, "Like George said, Captain, it's your call. You need to do the talking. I know you don't have a dog in this fight, but those shitheads in there are dangerous and getting desperate. Unless we're all careful, somebody…or a lot of somebodies…are going to get killed."

Reynoso studied the faces of everyone gathered around him, leaned into his car, and pulled out the handset. He pushed a button, looked toward the building, and his voice ballooned out of the cruiser's PA speakers, "This is Captain Jaime Reynoso of the Texas Rangers. You inside the building need to lay down your weapons and walk out. If you do tha--

"*SHUT THE FUCK UP!*" Rockson's voice cut through the air like a knife. "*We're the ones doing the talking here! Now, shut up and listen*--we've got a hostage in here and unless you pull back and let us leave, he's going to die. Pull all your rigs back while we walk outta here and get on my plane. Try and stop us and Worth is dead! You dumb asses got that?"

Reynoso didn't hesitate. "You're talking through your ass, Rockson. You kill your hostage; you ain't got shit! We'll open up on you with everything we've got. We'll keep you inside until we can get a chopper here to drop a goddamn bomb on you. We'll pick you up with a fucking spatula! Now drop those guns and walk out with your hands up!"

Reynoso's belligerent reply must have confused Rockson. He was silent for a few seconds and something occurred to me. I motioned to George to hand me his phone, took it off speaker, and asked, "Laurie, you still there?"

She answered immediately. "Is this Cort? Yeah, I'm here and listening. What do you need?"

"When George asked you if they were threatening Worth, you said 'No' and that they were leaving him alone. I noticed when you started to get back on the plane that Worth was walking by himself, not with you and the pilots. Has he ever been alone with just you and the pilots?"

Laurie paused before replying, "No, he was with Rockson and Bre in the plane and with Akabile for a short time in the SUV. He's never been with us. Why?"

I said, "I'm wondering if he's really a hostage. Do you have any thoughts about that?"

She didn't answer for several seconds, "I don't know. What difference does it make?"

I explained, "If he's actually a part of this whole deal, it changes everything. It takes away their leverage of threatening to kill him. It gives us some options."

Tom and George, who'd been listening, looked at me like I had lost my mind. Tom said, "I think we've *got* to assume he's a real hostage at least until we get indisputable evidence he's not."

My cell sounded and I dug it out of my Kevlar vest pocket. The screen read 'Mercy.' "Hey, Mercy…listen, we're kinda busy right now. I'll have to call you ba--

She interrupted and delivered a terse message. I ended the call, turned to the others, and said, "I think we just got that indisputable evidence!"

## CHAPTER THIRTY-FIVE

"Clay Webb, Worth's twin brother, is sitting in Mercy's office and has just told her everything he knows or suspects about Worth and the depth of his involvement. Turns out, he's afraid Worth is going to be killed--either by us or by Akabile and Bre."

Tom looked confused. "I thought you said Webb wasn't a part of this; that he wasn't involved with Worth. And how the hell does he know what's going on?"

"Mercy's pilots called her as soon as we jumped in with the Rangers to head here. They told her we had a small army and intended to capture or kill Rockson and Akabile. Webb was in her office at the time and when she told him what was going on, he started talking."

Tom puffed his cheeks and slowly exhaled, "That still doesn't explain why you told us Webb was in the clear. We might have nipped everything in the bud if you'd gone after Webb harder."

I didn't have time for this right now. I exploded, "I just *FUCKED UP*, all right, Tom? We'll have to sort it out later, okay? Right now, we need to get this situation resolved. Worth is definitely a part of it; he's not a hostage. But, the most important thing is to get Laurie and those pilots out of harm's way. I believe Captain Reynoso is right; I think the pilots need to fire up the plane and taxi it away."

George frowned, "It's still dangerous. How do we keep them from blasting it; blowing it sky high?"

I turned to Reynoso, "Rather than waiting for those assholes to try something, let's be aggressive. Can you have your Rangers lay down some suppression fire? Have them open up on that windowless door facing the plane. According to Laurie, the building is like a fort with reinforced doors and a cement block interior. If we use two or three fully auto assault rifles all targeting the door, it'll be so loud they'll probably never hear the engines. Plus, even if they hear something, they won't dare open the door to see."

Reynoso was nodding before I finished, but George and Tom looked doubtful. George sighed, "But what if doesn't work, Cort? What if they stay back from the door and fire an RPG from back in the building where we can't see them? We'll get three people killed!"

Reynoso spoke up, "There's nothing to keep them from doing that right now. They can blast the plane any time they want, but it's their last hope of escape, so I don't think they will. There's even less of a chance if we're pounding them."

Tom put his hand on George's shoulder and softly said, "I hate this, George, but I think he's right. As long as the plane sits there with Laurie and the pilots inside, there's a chance those bastards can somehow convert them into hostages. If they do, there's no light at the end of the tunnel."

George seemed to shrink within himself as he took off his Stetson and ran his hand through his hair. "Captain, what's the heaviest caliber assault rifle you've got?"

"We've got a belt-feed, Saco-Lowell 7.62 with select fire for full auto. Why?"

"I was an MP in Desert Storm. I'm checked out on everything up to .50 caliber Brownings. I want to be the gunner on the door facing the plane."

"You've got it!" Reynoso actually snapped George a salute. "I was there too; infantry ground pounder. There's an AR-15 5.56 with a drum in the other truck. I'll circle over there and get set up to use that one. I'll signal you when I'm ready." He turned to Ben Franks, our driver, and said, "Get that spray-and-pray out and help him get it mounted."

Franks one-handed the hard cover on his pickup and hoisted out the deadly-looking weapon. George hefted the gun, snapped out the bipod legs, and walked slowly to the front corner of the pickup where he anchored the legs and arranged the ammo belts.

He retrieved his cell phone and said, "Laurie? You still there? Listen, all hell is going to break loose out here. Tell the pilots to get ready to start your engines. We're going to open fire on both doors of the building and as soon as we do, taxi down the apron and get the hell away from the door. And stay on your phone--GOT IT?"

Laurie, her voice sounding tight and strained, said, "Got it; I'll tell the pilots. Be careful, George."

While Ben Franks and George were getting the heavy gun ready, Reynoso had jumped in his car and circled out several hundred yards before returning to the other Ranger pickup. We watched him lift a sandbag from the bed, place it across the hood, and rest the assault rifle on it.

Just as he started to raise his arm, Rockson's loud hailer roared out. "*What the fuck you guys doing out there? You got thirty seconds to pull back or we're going to kill Worth! We want to--*

Reynoso dropped his arm and opened fire on the front door. George followed suit immediately with a deep throated hammering from the heavy gun. George's bullets were slamming into the side door and pock marking the cement exterior of the building.

The jet lurched and slowly began rolling forward. Suddenly, the door opened inward and we watched in horror as a missile, a rocket-propelled grenade, streaked toward the jet. George yelled, "*NO!*"

## CHAPTER THIRTY-SIX

The RPG smashed into Akabile's hijacked charter and the jet exploded in a ball of smoke and fire. The missile had passed barely inches below and behind the tail section of Rockson's plane and, for an instant, it had been impossible to tell which plane had been hit. The Falcon was rolling faster now and had reached a sufficient angle to prevent whoever had fired the missile from firing another round without exposing themselves at the doorway.

Tom yelled "*HOLY SHIT!*"

George stopped firing and I saw his shoulders sag. He motioned to Junior Bigelow to take over the machine gun and again grabbed his cell. "Laurie, Laurie, are you there?" He was yelling into the phone at the top of his lungs.

Her trembling voice came over the speaker, "Yes, yes--I'm here! My God, what the hell happened? We saw a flash and heard an explosion, but we couldn't see what happened."

George looked drained, "The sons-a-bitches got the door open somehow and fired an RPG at you, but you'd started to roll and it missed you by inches. It hit the other jet parked beside you. *JESUS!* That was *way* too close! Keep rolling; go all the way to the end of the runway; we'll come get you in a few minutes."

"What are you guys going to do now?" Laurie asked.

"I don't know. Cort got word that Worth is involved…he's *not* a hostage. That's going to change everything, but I doubt if we'll just unleash hellfire on them. We'll probably try to talk 'em out some way. Do they have supplies inside? Food and water?"

Laurie hesitated a moment before answering, "I think they do. They've definitely got water and I think I saw an entire pallet of military MREs, you know, those 'meals ready to eat' packages."

"*Crap!* Okay, well that's good intel anyway; I'll pass it on. I'm glad you're safe, babe. I don't know if I've ever been that scared." George looked at me as he made his admission.

I gave him thumbs up and said, "Me neither, buddy. I'm glad for both of you." He looked played out and tired. He just nodded.

Reynoso had stopped firing a second after George and it seemed unnaturally quiet as the smell of cordite began to dissipate. Reynoso turned his gun position over to another Ranger, climbed back into his big Ford, and again took a "great circle" route to return to our position. He gave an exaggerated brow wipe and exclaimed, "What a deal! We couldn't see the planes or the door from our position, but we sure as hell saw and heard that goddamn explosion! I feared the worst until I finally saw the jet roll out from behind the building.

"Now I can see what happened. The dumb bastards blew up the other plane, huh? Musta been a close call; glad it worked! But how the hell did they get a shot off?"

George said, "They must've had a way to get the door open without being right behind it…maybe a pull bar or something…so they could stand way back inside to fire the RPG. I about fainted when I saw it come out. The jet was barely moving, just enough to make 'em miss, but when the other plane went up, we didn't know for a second they *had* missed."

Reynoso stepped up to George and extended his hand. "I'm sorry you had to go through that, man. I'm sorry it was so close." The two men shared a long handshake before Reynoso turned to us and said, "So, you guys got any good ideas on how to get those *cabrones pendejos* out of there?"

"*WHAT THE FUCK? YOU DUMBASSES JUST GOT WORTH KILLED! WE WANT THAT--*

Tom grabbed the car PA mic and interrupted Rockson's manic rant. "NO, YOU LISTEN, ROCKSON: We know Worth isn't a hostage; his brother just told us the truth. Drop your weapons and walk out of there!"

After about a minute that seemed like an hour, Akabile's cultured voice came over the loud hailer. "Outside…Mr. Scott are you there? I have something I'd like to discuss." We could hear the sounds of yelling in the background but couldn't make out any words.

I took the mic from Tom. "I'm here. What do you want?"

"I 'want' to discuss the situation we seem to find ourselves in--along with a possible resolution."

I glanced at the group surrounding me and raised my eyebrows in a question. Reynoso, Tom, and George all shrugged. Lindsey said, "Talking seems better than shooting."

I keyed the mic, "So how do you propose having this discussion? I assume you're not dropping your weapon and coming out, are you?"

His laugh echoed across the space. "No, that would be imprudent on my part; if you have your cell phone, give me the number which I will call. We can proceed on what I believe you call 'FaceTime'. There are some interior scenes I'd like to transmit to you."

Again, I surveyed our group and received a chorus of "Why not?"

"We're running pretty short on patience out here, Akabile. This had better be worth our time." I gave him my number and handed the mic back to Tom.

My phone quacked which seemed to surprise and amuse Reynoso and the Rangers; my friends…not so much. I answered, "Okay, it's me. Hit the FaceTime app and I'll do the same." I put it on speaker just as Akabile's face filled the screen. Everyone crowded around to see.

"Oh, my…you have assembled quite a force, Mr. Scott! Good evening, everyone…for those of you who don't know me, I'm Minister of Defense and associate Prime Minister Akabile of the independent nation of South Sudan. I--

"Get on with it! What the hell do you want?" Tom shouted over my shoulder.

"Ah yes, the typical American reaction to proposed negotiations, I assume. Well, since there is a deadline of sorts, I suppose we need to press forward. I'm going to swing the camera lens around. There's a scene you need to see before we talk further."

The motion of the camera was disconcerting, but it quickly refocused on three people standing and facing a wall. Akabile said, "As you can see, I have accomplished much of what your task force set out to do…I have taken these criminals into custody for you." He zoomed in and we could see his "prisoners" were wearing twist tie handcuffs and were connected by a rope or cord looped through their arms.

"What the hell are you trying to prove?" I was confused by the scene.

"Ah, come now, Mr. Scott; surely you must see where this is heading? I am prepared to make a trade of sorts. I am offering to end this standoff by turning over these three in exchange for being transported to the international airport and placed on the evening flight to Dubai. It will--

Again, Tom shouted at the phone, "*You gotta be out of your fucking mind!* We aren't about to let you leave! You've got a shitload of charges to face."

Akabile's tone didn't change, "That sounds like the voice of a policeman, but if I may make my argument, I think you'll see the logic of what I'm proposing."

I put my hand on Tom's arm and spoke to Akabile, "I'm getting a glimmer, but fill in the details."

"Anything I might be charged with in America is minor. I have *not* committed murder or acts of terrorism. Technically, I *may* have consorted with people who *have* participated in some of those heinous deeds, but *I* have not. In any case, I claim diplomatic immunity, and since your country is so anxious to forge a relationship with South Sudan, I'm sure they will overlook any possible indiscretions.

"In return, you can get your pound of flesh by prosecuting Mr. Rockson, Mr. Worth, and, unfortunately, my niece, Zebrezicka. Plus, unless you've once again lied with your comment concerning Mr. Webb, you'll have him to prosecute also."

I scoffed, "What's to keep us from just outwaiting you or, if we get impatient, blowing you and your buddies up? Like Captain Reynoso said, we can just drop a bomb on you!"

He answered immediately, "That's just not the American way, Mr. Scott. You know that. A siege of this facility could be months long, as I'm sure you've discovered we are well supplied and particularly well-armed. A direct frontal assault with anything less than heavy armor or artillery would be futile and would result in casualties on your side. And even though my associates are infuriated at me, they recognize they will at least be alive. If you choose, however, to attack, they will have no other choice than to fight you. If they try to escape or shirk the battle, I will kill them myself before taking as many of your people with me as possible.

"It would be a disaster for all concerned, Mr. Scott. And all of it can be avoided by simply guaranteeing my passage out of your country.

"The deadline I mentioned is fast approaching. The flight is scheduled for 8:57 p.m. and it is currently almost 5:25. It is about one hour to the airport by car so you must make your decision quickly. I will need to be transported directly to the plane and would board through the stairs directly from the tarmac. I am giving you until six o'clock, Mr. Scott. Make your decision wisely." The screen went blank as Akabile ended the call.

Everyone began cursing at once. Reynoso yelled, "Who the *hell* is that guy? Is he kidding? There ain't no way we're lettin' him skate!"

Lindsey motioned to me to step to the side. As the cussing and yelling continued, she said softly, "I know I don't have much influence at this level, hell…who does? It just seems to me, as much as I hate saying it, Akabile makes some sense.

"Either we'll kill them all--and probably get somebody out here killed too, or we'll sit around for God knows how long and take a beating in the media for not resolving the situation. Either way, we're going to come out of this looking bad.

"If we do like he says, we get three or four big-time convictions. Sure, Akabile gets away with everything but he'll probably be forgotten in a year. Some other two-bit tyrant will take his place, probably murder him in doing it, and life goes on."

I wondered when she'd gotten so smart; I'd been thinking along the same lines. I just hadn't solidified it enough to make a good argument. I said, "You're right, you know. But I don't know if I, or *we,* can convince the others. They're pretty jacked up."

Linds was silent for a moment or so before saying, "I'll see if Reynoso will let me take his car to get Laurie and the pilots. I know I can convince her to put a word in with George. If the two of us work on him while you talk to Tom, we might be able to get them to see it our way. Of course, that leaves Reynoso; got any ideas about him?"

"Not any good ones, but if we get Tom and George on board, he might listen to reason. After all, we were the ones who asked for his help in the first place. If we tell him we'd like to avoid a bloodbath and still end up with a bunch of convictions--that he'll get a lot of credit for…it might do the trick. It's worth a try.

But, Linds, *I'm* the one with no influence; I'm not a cop. It's going to be up to you, hopefully with Laurie's help, to carry the ball. I've got faith in you, babe."

She shot me a look before saying, "We don't have time to debate the 'influence' thing, but I think you're full of it!" We walked back to the cops who were still vehemently cursing Akabile and his proposal. Linds spoke to Reynoso, "Captain, we'd like to get our officer and the pilots back here with us. May I take your cruiser around the perimeter and pick them up?"

Reynoso looked surprised at her request, thought about it for a moment before replying, "Yeah, okay--go ahead." Lindsey immediately jumped in his car and backed away from the crowd. Obviously, she didn't want to give him time to reconsider. Reynoso watched her swing wide around the house and head down the far side of the runway. "I guess it's a good idea to go get the others, but she sure seemed determined. I could've sent one of my Rangers."

I said, "She was pretty anxious about Officer Thomas and wanted to get it done. They'll both be very appreciative." Reynoso bobbed his head in acknowledgement.

I turned to Tom, "Hey, bud, can I have a word?" He gave me a questioning look but nodded and followed as I walked a few feet away.

"What's up? What'd you and Lindsey cook up? I have the feeling you've got something up your sleeve; something I might not like."

I decided not to try and finesse it. "Tom, just listen for a minute, okay? Linds and I think Akabile's proposition makes some sense. We'd be trading three or four arrests with high probabilities of convictions and lengthy sentences for letting a guy go who can probably put up an argument that will take years to clear the courts. The other side of the coin is we'll probably get somebody killed if we try to take him down right now. I don't give a shit about anybody in the building, but I damn sure care about any of us and the Rangers.

"Linds said she can get George to go along and if you'll support us, I think we've got a chance of convincing Reynoso. It would sure beat the hell out of having a damn firefight and probable massacre."

Tom puffed up and looked like he would explode but to my surprise, he emptied his lungs in one long exhale before saying, "I hate this, Cort, but it makes sense. If George agrees, I'm good with it." I extended my hand and shook with my friend.

We walked back to join the others as Lindsey pulled up with Laurie riding shotgun and the two pilots in the back seat. Typical of police cruisers, she had to open the rear doors from the outside to let them out. Linds shot me thumbs up and grinned. Laurie strode quickly to George and they hugged for several seconds. I could see her whispering in his ear and they turned and walked away. Reynoso looked askance and started to speak, but I beat him to it. "They're an item, Captain. Give 'em a minute, okay?" He nodded and closed his mouth.

I checked my watch: 5:45 p.m. Fifteen minutes until decision time.

From a few steps away, it looked like Laurie and George were having a "spirited" discussion with her facing him, a hand on each shoulder. George kept shaking his head and trying to step back, but she was holding him in place. Finally, he stopped objecting and I saw him take a deep breath before taking her in his arms. I wished they would hurry.

"Captain Reynoso, we've got a big problem here and we might have a way out of it." George's voice sounded resigned. I could tell his heart wasn't in what he was about to say, but he was willing to go along. "Although it's definitely your turf and you've committed most of the resources in this operation, those assholes inside are *our* problem. We're extremely grateful for your assistance, but since we were the ones who asked for your help, now we'd like to ask you to back off; to let us handle it."

For the third time in the last three minutes, I was surprised. Reynoso spoke quietly, "I figured that was the way this was headed. Can't say I'm totally on board but it makes sense; what can I do to help?"

Although silently, it seemed everyone heaved a sigh of relief before Tom said, "Let's find out how the son-of-a-bitch wants to pull it off and go from there. Cort, you're his 'go to' guy; get him on the phone and let's get going."

I touched the redial function and Akabile answered immediately. "Ah, Mr. Scott; good, you're calling rather than opening fire! Surely, that's a good sign. How should we proceed?"

"Well, that would be up to you. We need the details. How do we transport you to DFW and how do we take control of the others?"

"My requirements are simple. I want an unmarked car for the trip, but one equipped with grille flashers, siren, and a functioning radio. The Texas Ranger captain will make all the necessary arrangements to clear the highways and allow the car access to the tarmac. He will also obtain the concourse and gate number and deliver the information to us.

I want you to be my driver and the woman flight attendant will accompany us. The woman will, of course, be my 'hostage' during the trip; I will not hesitate to kill her if we encounter the slightest resistance or any attempt to stop me. I will release you both when I safely enter the plane."

I heard George suck in his breath and start to say something but saw Laurie put her hand on his arm. I said, "How do we get Rockson and the others."

Akabile said, "When we're safely away, your little army can just walk in and take them. Is that simple enough for you?"

"I'll be back to you in five minutes."

"Don't delay, Mr. Scott! That's all the time you have left."

Five minutes wasn't much time to formulate a plan but it was all we had. Lindsey, Laurie, George, Tom, Reynoso, and I gathered in a tight circle behind the big pickup.

Tom asked, "Anybody got any good ideas?"

Reynoso said, "We don't have an unmarked car here, but we can have one set up at the freeway interchange. We can probably buy a couple of minutes' time and maybe create an opportunity. I don't know what that might be but, like I say, it could buy some time."

Laurie spoke up, "Does anyone have a mini-pistol? I could conceal it and get the drop on him at some point; maybe when we change cars or even when we get to the airport."

George said, "No, no, no! That's too dangerous. If he finds it, he'll kill you both."

Tom spoke quietly, "George, it may be our only chance. He knows without hostages every cop in Texas would open up on him; he'd never get to the airport, let alone on the plane."

George started to reply but stopped when Reynoso pulled up the cuff of his right pant leg and produced a tiny blue-steel automatic with black grips. The entire gun was about two and a half inches long; the grip extended about the same. "What's that?" Tom asked.

Reynoso palmed the evil looking little pistol and extended his hand into the middle of our circle. "It's a Taurus 25 pocket pistol: .25 caliber; the clip holds nine rounds plus one in the chamber; whole thing weighs about eleven ounces. It isn't very accurate at anything much farther than about twenty-five feet but close in, it's deadly." He handed it to Laurie. "If he's wearing body armor, you'd need to be almost touching him. Your only shot will be to the head or neck, or maybe under the arm. Do you think you could do that? Do you think you could basically execute someone in cold blood?"

I thought Reynoso was being too graphic until I realized he needed to make an instant judgement on Laurie's ability to take Akabile out.

Laurie shifted the .25 from hand to hand, held it at waist level, and then with her arm extended. "This will work. It has a good feel." She glanced at Reynoso and then focused on George, "That bastard is responsible for a gruesome murder, a bombing intended to kill an innocent woman, and probably a lot more. He's a goddamn terrorist by anybody's definition. I won't have a problem with shutting off his light."

George sucked in his breath. Lindsey put her arm around Laurie's shoulders and hugged her tightly. Tom nodded his approval.

I said, "Chances are he's going to pat us down at some point, probably when we change cars; where can you hide it, Laurie?"

Reynoso answered for her, "Don't try to put it on your person; he's already described where everyone will be seated, so let's put it in the car. There's room between the side of the seat and where the floor comes up to form the door sill. Somebody would have to get down and look closely to find it if no one's sitting there, but when you're seated, there's room to get it out. C'mere, I'll show you."

He hurried to his cruiser and opened the rear door. As we peered in, he pointed out the slight gap he'd mentioned and told Laurie to sit down. When she did, the crack widened and she slid the little pistol in. When she got out, the spot was virtually invisible.

"Okay, now sit down and see if you can get it out quickly. Remember, you'll have to do it without him seeing and probably before you make the car exchange. This patrol car's rear doors can only be opened from outside and I'm guessing when Cort comes around to open the door on your side will be the best chance. I don't know if that'll be when you take him down, but remember there will be a couple of Rangers there with the unmarked. At least, you'll have numbers on your side for a minute or two."

Laurie got back in the car, put her left hand on the back of the front seat like someone leveraging their way out, and reached down to her right. She was able to smoothly extract the Taurus and exit the car all in one motion. She smiled at Reynoso.

"Are you sure you're still up for this, Laurie? It's going to be dangerous." Reynoso studied her face carefully.

Laurie opened the front passenger door and sat down. "We're wasting time, everybody. Let's get this over with."

# CHAPTER THIRTY-SEVEN

I called Akabile and said, "Okay, it's all set with one change. We--

"*There will be no changes!* It must be *exactly* as I directed!"

"Listen, goddamn it, we don't have an unmarked car here. We'll have to take the Ranger cruiser as far as the intersection with the southbound interstate where they'll meet us with an unmarked. It's about seven miles; it's on the way and won't take more than a couple minutes to make the transfer. That's the only thing different. You'll make your flight."

He didn't answer for a moment finally replying, "I am highly suspicious but am willing to proceed. I want you to drive with the woman in the front passenger seat; drive as close to the door of the hangar as you can, have the woman get out and open the back passenger side door for me. When I come out, I'll be fully clad in Kevlar. I will have my gun on the woman. If you are so stupid as to try to shoot me, I will kill her, but you will still be my hostage.

"When I'm in the car, the woman will get in the back seat with me and pull the door closed after her. Are you ready?"

"We're on our way, but remember this, if something goes wrong before we get to DFW, you're a dead man, Akabile."

"Don't be disingenuous, Mr. Scott. You're in no position to threaten me."

I slid behind the wheel of the cruiser, drove around the burned-out jet, and pulled to a stop about twenty feet from the side door of the hangar. Laurie got out and opened the rear door as instructed. A couple seconds later, Akabile, fully clad in body armor, including a helmet, sprinted from the door of the hangar toward the car. He was carrying a machine pistol in his right hand. He ducked into the car, slid across the back seat, and yelled at Laurie to get in.

"Drive, Mr. Scott!"

I hit the gas and accelerated across the apron to the exit road and headed toward the highway. Just before we topped the hill, I glanced in the side mirror and could see the Ranger vehicles approaching the hangar. Akabile said, "I assume your friends are taking mine into custody. I must admit to a bit of remorse for betraying them…a bit, but not a lot. I'm most sorry about not being able to complete my dealings. It would have been worth millions. You could have been part of that, Mr. Scott. You could have been rich beyond your wildest dreams. Did you think about that?"

I glanced at the mirror, caught Akabile's eye and said, "It wouldn't have been worth it, not for any amount of money, to be associated with you and Rockson. You're nothing but a thug or worse and I'm betting you'll be gone and forgotten within a year. If your government doesn't handle you, someone else will come for you. Who knows, it might be me."

Akabile smiled. "Best keep your eyes on the road, Mr. Scott. We wouldn't want to miss the location for our new car." As he spoke, he removed the combat helmet and lowered the zipper on the vest a couple inches. "Although I am used to a hot climate, your Texas heat is living up to its billing." Sweat ran down his face.

I turned onto the farm road and we rode in silence for the six miles to the interchange. A dark brown Ford Crown Victoria was parked fifty yards short of the on ramp. Two Rangers were standing at the back of the car.

I could feel sweat down my sides and on my hands gripping the wheel. I wondered if Laurie's hands were sweating and how she must be feeling.

As I slowed to park behind the unmarked, Akabile said, "Stop twenty-five feet behind them and tell those policemen to walk to the other side of the road. When we're stopped, get out, walk around, and open the passenger side rear door.

"Young woman, when the door is opened, get out and go to the driver's seat of the other car. Mr. Scott, you will be in the back with me from here to the airport."

I quickly glanced at Laurie. Her eyes were wide; I hoped it wasn't fear. I slid the window down and delivered Akabile's instructions. The Rangers looked momentarily confused, but began walking to the far side of the on-ramp. When they were across, I pulled up to the twenty-five feet Akabile had specified, got out, and walked around to Laurie's door. I opened the door and started to step to the back but Akabile said, "No, go stand between the cars. I don't want you behind me at any time. Now, it's your turn, young lady; get out and go to the other car."

The open door blocked any view I might have had of Laurie getting the hidden pistol. Through the windshield, I saw her put her left hand on the back of the front seat as she'd done before. She seemed to hesitate slightly as she slid out. She looked at me and winked as Akabile was exiting the cruiser. She walked past me but stopped near the back corner of the unmarked.

Akabile motioned with his machine pistol. "Move, woman--get in the car! Now your turn, Mr. Scott…get in the back behind our 'chauffeur.'"

As he stepped forward, the barrel of his machine pistol was aimed slightly to the right and away from Laurie and me. His carelessness cost him.

The sharp crack of the Taurus 25 came from my left. Akabile screamed, dropped his gun, and grabbed at his right collar bone. I charged him and executed an NFL-worthy tackle, carrying both of us over the shallow bank of the road shoulder and into the ditch.

He screamed again as he landed on his right shoulder with me on top. I jumped to my feet as he rolled onto his back. His neck was a bloody mess where he had lowered the zipper on the vest. He blinked several times trying to focus and started to reach for his shoulder again. I yelled, *"STAY STILL! Don't move!"* When he continued to move his arm, I kicked him in the ribs. He grunted and moved his lips but stayed still.

I looked up to see Laurie standing two feet above us, the mini-pistol still in her hand and aimed at Akabile. Suddenly the two Rangers appeared beside her. Both had handguns out. I looked back at Akabile and saw the fight go out of his eyes and the tenseness go out of his body.

"You all right, Cort?" Laurie's voice seemed strangely calm.

"Yeah, I'm fine. You did super, Laurie!" I stepped up to her level, turned to the Rangers, and said, "Do us a favor, will you boys? Hook this bastard up and take him to the nearest hospital. I don't think he's hurt too badly…broken collarbone, I'm guessing…but don't take any chances with him. Keep his good arm handcuffed at all times and keep an eye on him even in the ER." The Rangers hopped down beside Akabile and roughly lifted him to his feet, handcuffing his left arm behind his back and securing it to his belt. He carried his right arm across his body, bent at the elbow.

At the top of the ditch, Akabile looked at me and said, "All is not over, Mr. Scott. We anticipated some treachery." One of the Rangers grabbed his good arm, jerked him toward the cruiser they'd brought, and rudely deposited him in the back seat.

"What the hell was that about?" Laurie looked concerned.

"I don't know, but it sounded like a threat. I wouldn't think he's in a position to be making threats, but we need to get back to Rockson's ranch and see what's happening with the others; let's go."

Back in Reynoso's cruiser, I keyed the mic and said, "Cort Scott to Captain Reynoso--we've got Akabile in custody. He's wounded and your troopers are taking him to the ER in Garland. No casualties on our side. What's your situation?"

# CHAPTER THIRTY-EIGHT

"Scott? *Jesus Christ!* We've got a fucking disaster here! Get back here quick as you can make it! Hurry!" Reynoso's voice sounded frantic.

With flashers lit, sirens wailing, and hitting 100 mph, we were back at the entrance to Rockson's ranch in five minutes. As we topped the hill, I saw an array of police and emergency vehicles gathered around the hangar and burnt-out hulk of the charter jet. The number of flashing lights looked like a 4th of July fireworks show.

I accelerated down the hill, weaved through some of the emergency vehicles, and skidded to a stop a hundred feet from the hangar. We hit the ground running and sprinted toward the hangar.

Cops and EMTs were gathered around several gurneys, but I bulled my way through and burst into a semi-circle. IVs hung from hooks and portable vital sign monitors were beeping and flashing. The first thing I could focus on was Lindsey's ashen face on the white pillow of the closest gurney. As I started to rush to her side, Reynoso hooked my arm and swung me to the side. "You can't help. They're doing all they can; they just put her out to stabilize everything."

I jerked my arm away, "Get the fuck off me! I'm going to her! I don't give a shit if she's out!" I ran to the gurney and the four EMTs tending to her. "What's happened to her? How bad is she hurt?" From close up, I could see blood on the lower half of the gurney…lots of blood.

A huge guy in dark green scrubs stopped me with a forearm shiver to my chest. "Hold it, pardner! Stay back! We're working on her."

I yelled, "Get out of my way! I--

This time he grabbed me in a bear hug and motioned to a couple of uniforms standing nearby. "Hey, guys, hold this lunatic, okay?" When the cops had me, the guy said, "Look, man, we've got multiple casualties here. This lady is just one of 'em. She's hurt pretty bad, but it's *not* going to be fatal! You got that? *It's not going to be fatal!*"

Reynoso walked in front of me and leaned into my face; I hadn't noticed the bandage covering his right ear and cheek when he'd grabbed me. "Don't fight, Scott; You ain't helping!"

I forced myself to back off, took a deep breath, and slowly nodded my head. "What happened?"

Reynoso signaled the troopers to let me go and said, "It was a goddamn setup--a trap! That bitch, Bre, had explosives strung around the door and a satchel charge sitting in front of a desk inside and to our right. I was in the lead, Tom and George were right behind me and when we were a few steps inside, she set 'em off. Lindsey hadn't started through the door when everything went up.

"It looks like the desk kinda deflected the bomb towards the doorway. I was a step or two past it, so missed most of the force, but Tom and George took a hell of a blast, and Lindsey was hit with a bunch of shrapnel from the door and frame."

I blinked back tears and fought back the bile rising in my throat. "What about Tom and George? Are they alive?"

He touched the bandage on his ear and was silent for several seconds before clearing his throat, "It looks bad…multiple fractures and severe concussions. I gotta tell you the truth, it could go either way. At least one is on life support; the ambulances are leaving right now." As he spoke, two emergency vans began pulling out. The drivers hit the sirens and we watched as they accelerated up the drive and over the hill.

The Ranger captain rubbed his hand over his face and continued, "I think the only thing that saved any of us is that the bombs weren't armored. I'm betting it was a plastic explosive, you know, like Semtek or something. I think that's what was in the satchel and around the door frame. She wired it up and set it off with a radio detonator. The shrapnel that hit Lindsey came from the door frame."

I looked at Lindsey's gurney and said, "How bad is it?"

"Bad enough, but like the EMT said, it isn't fatal. The worst thing is a deep laceration on the inside of her left leg, up high on her thigh. It just nicked the femoral artery; enough to cause an ungodly amount of blood but, Thank God, not enough to where she would bleed out. She may have some other leg or knee injuries too. That's why she's still out here and they haven't tried to transport her. They needed room for three or four of the EMTs to get around her and get the blood flow stopped. They were getting ready to move her when you got here."

I looked around and asked, "Where's Laurie? She was right behind me."

"When you busted loose from me, I grabbed her and pointed out which rig they'd put George in. She turned and ran for it; she's inside."

The EMTs began rolling Lindsey's gurney and the crowd started to make way. I said, "I gotta go, Captain. I want to ride with her."

"I understand. Go ahead; I'll get somebody to drive me and be right behind you. They're going to Baylor Scott and White Hospital in Garland. It's the best emergency care facility north of Dallas. I'm pretty sure Lindsey will be in surgery for a time; we'll have a chance to get caught up."

I fell in behind Lindsey's gurney and winced each time the wheels hit a bump. At the back of the ambulance I stood beside the big EMT who had stopped me. I said, "I'm sorry about what happened back there. She's very special to me."

"Don't worry about it, man; I see it all the time. She's fairly stable now but won't wake up before we get to the ER. The trip should take about fifteen minutes; I guess you're riding with her, right?"

"Yeah, that okay?"

"It'll be crowded, but, yeah. Go ahead, climb in." I looked in as they were locking the gurney in place, climbed the step, and sat on a side bench near the back. The doors were shut and I heard the bang on the back to signal we were ready to move.

The trip took fourteen minutes. It was hard to tell in the artificial light of the entryway to the ER, but I thought Lindsey's color looked a little better. As we raced inside, I saw a clock: 7:49 p.m. It had been less than seven hours since we'd left Denver--it seemed like seven lifetimes.

The ER team took her from the EMTs and headed directly toward double doors marked "Trauma Center." I started to follow but was stopped by a formidable looking black nurse who was nearly as tall as me. "Hold on, suh! No civilians go in there; you with this lady?"

"Yes. She's badly hurt and needs some help!"

The nurse gave me a disdainful look, but spoke softly, "That's why she's here, suh. We'll take good care of her and we'll let you know what's going on as soon as we can. What's the name?"

I told her Lindsey's name and mine which she entered on the tablet computer she was carrying. Before she could ask, I said, "We're with the police and we're 'significant others', okay?"

She smiled and raised her hands in a mock surrender gesture. "Works for me--take a seat over there." She pointed to a small waiting area to the left of the entrance. "We'll get back to you when we know something."

When I looked in the direction she pointed, I saw Laurie slumped in an armchair with her face in her hands; I walked over to her. Reynoso came through the doors, strode directly to the admitting desk, and badged the attendant. After a few words, she spoke into her headset and another nurse came out the double doors, took Reynoso by the arm, and led him in. He hadn't seen us.

Laurie slowly lifted her head and stared at me for a few seconds. Her face was tearstained and haggard. I sat beside her and asked, "How's George?"

"Not good, he's already in surgery; so's Tom Montgomery."

"What're the diagnoses?"

"George has a severe concussion--he hasn't been conscious since the blast, but he's in surgery for his right arm and right leg. Oh God, Cort! It's horrible! It looked like his whole right side was just hanging by threads. There was so much blood!

"I don't think it's as bad for Tom, although he's been in and out of consciousness." Her eyes welled and overflowed. "What happened, Cort? I thought they were tied up; I thought they were prisoners. But what about Lindsey? How's she?"

The tears hit my eyes too. "Not much better, I'd say. Definitely a concussion, but the real problem is her left leg; shrapnel nicked an artery and she's lost a lot of blood. They're taking her into surgery too.

"I just saw Reynoso come in; he wasn't hurt too badly and they're patching him up. He should be out in a few minutes. He was able to tell me it was an ambush; Bre had rigged a bomb near the door and set it off after they started in. Reynoso was past it and Lindsey was still outside when it went off. The door frame got her, but George and Tom took most of the blast. Oh, wait, here comes Reynoso."

The Ranger captain had a new, smaller and cleaner bandage over his ear; he approached us slowly. I said, "While we're waiting, can you tell us more about what happened? Laurie doesn't know anything."

He pulled a chair close so he could face us. His voice was hoarse, probably from the smoke of the explosion. "Like I told you, it was a setup; a goddamn ambush! As soon as you guys left with Akabile, we started in the door expecting to see the other three tied up like the picture he'd sent us. They were standing there all right, but they'd moved a ways back in the room. I didn't think too much about it 'cause I could see the rope looped through their arms and it looked like they had cuffs on.

"I led the way in with Tom and George right behind me; Lindsey had stopped just outside the door. I was a few steps in when I saw Bre slide something out of her sleeve. It must've been a detonator because instantly, everything was all smoke and dust and noise.

I blurted out, "How the hell did *anybody* survive?"

He slowly shook his head before answering, "I'm not real sure, but I think that desk must have deflected the blast toward the door. I was almost past it when it went off, but George was right in front of it and Tom was to his side. Lindsey was either still outside or just starting in the door."

I thought for a moment before asking, "What happened to Bre and the others?"

Reynoso raised his gaze and locked eyes with me. "I shot her right in the fucking head. She's dead."

Laurie gasped; I held his gaze and said, "Good."

Reynoso told us his men had rushed in after he shot Bre and grabbed Worth and Rockson. "Both of them were dazed by the explosion but had been standing back far enough not to catch the blast. My guys had already hauled them off when you arrived. They should be in the Garland jail by now.

"But what about you? What went down with Akabile? You radioed you'd wounded him; how bad is it?"

I had to focus my thoughts before answering. It seemed like it had been days. "It went off just liked we'd hoped. When we were making the transfer between cars, he took his eyes off Laurie for a fraction of a second and she shot him. She made a hell of a shot; got him in the right collarbone through a gap of about an inch where he'd unzipped his Kevlar a little. When he dropped his gun, I got him down until your other guys could grab him. I think he's probably here too."

It had dawned on me the Rangers had probably brought him to this hospital. Reynoso seemed to be having trouble sorting all the information. "There are too many stories flying around. Hang on; I'll go check with the desk."

We watched as the attendant made numerous calls and relayed information to him. Finally, he returned and said, "I got several reports while I was there. First things first: George was the most seriously injured and he's still in surgery--

Laurie sobbed once and started to stand. I put my hand on her shoulder as Reynoso continued, "But he's holding his own; his vitals are good. They've already finished with his leg…set a fracture of the femur and put his knee back in place. Right now, they're working on his right arm and shoulder. There's a lot of damage; he's going to be in surgery for quite a while.

"Laurie, he's going to live. Hang on to that--it's the most important thing right now. It's going to be a long haul in recovery and rehab, but he's going to live!"

She dropped her face to her hands and heavy sobs shook her shoulders. I turned to Reynoso and started to ask, but he beat me to it. "Lindsey is out of surgery and in intensive care. Honestly, it wasn't as bad as it looked. The shrapnel wound was pretty bad, but the surgeons got the femoral artery stitched up, gave her three units of blood, and so far everything is holding. She's probably got some torn cartilage or ligaments in her knee and a bunch of other cuts and bad bruises but, all in all, she's going to be fine; probably a full recovery."

I felt a load lift and thanked Reynoso. "What about Tom?"

"Tough bastard, I'd say." He grinned. "Apparently no fractures or breaks, although they want to take some more X-rays of his pelvis. He's got a pretty bad concussion and it's going to take some time to recover from that. He's not going to be investigating any murders for a while. He's heavily sedated and will be out for several hours."

Finally, I asked, "What about Akabile?"

"You weren't shittin' about Laurie making a good shot. Slug broke his collarbone and lodged in the shoulder blade. It did a lot of damage on the way and it's no wonder he dropped his gun. It's going to be a while before he can raise his right arm at all." He gave me a close look, "And, you must have crashed into him pretty hard when you knocked him in the ditch. He's got a broken rib on the right side.

"At the moment, he's chained to a prison bed in a guarded room up on the third floor. They treated his wound and stitched him up. He's asking for a phone, but we're not giving him a damn thing until we've had a chance to sort some things out and that's going to take a while. I'm going to have to talk to the Texas attorney general, maybe the federal attorney, and probably the Colorado AG too.

I wish to hell there hadn't been all the shooting and the bomb and such. Without that, I could probably have just silently turned everybody over to you guys, you could have jumped on that jet and flown their asses back to Denver." He smiled ruefully, "But now I've got a shitload of paperwork; I expect you to help with that!"

## CHAPTER THIRTY-NINE

I watched carefully as Lindsey's eyelids began to flutter and, finally, to blink. When they remained open for a few seconds and she turned her head in my direction, I said as softly as I could, "Welcome back, babe. You've had quite a nap."

She rolled her head from side to side, let her eyes roam the room, and said, "Where are we? Looks like a hospital; what happened?"

I took her hand, "You got blown up, babe. I mean, literally *blown up*…there was a bomb blast. You've got a bunch of cuts and bruises and maybe a concussion, but the most serious thing was a cut on your leg…some shrapnel nicked an artery and you lost a lot of blood. Your knee is bunged up too. We're in the hospital in Garland, Texas."

She started to shift position in the bed but gasped with pain and her eyes welled. "*Ouch!* Damn, my legs hurt like hell! What's what with them?"

"The deep cut is on the inside of your left thigh; the bad knee is your right. How's your head?"

She closed her eyes for a moment and seemed to be considering her answer. "I've got a low-grade headache and my vision is a little blurred." Suddenly her eyes grew wide, "Oh God, Cort, what happened to Tom and George? And Captain Reynoso? I remember the explosion and they were inside!"

I was encouraged she remembered. If she did have a concussion, it wasn't as bad as Tom's and George's. "Everyone's alive, Linds. That's the good news, but they're all hurt. George is worse off than Tom. George was in surgery for almost five hours, mostly on his right arm and shoulder, although his right leg is banged up too. The surgeons think they were able to save his arm, but it's going to be a while before he's out of the woods. He's still in recovery, in intensive care. He's going to have some disability; no one knows if he'll be able to go back to work or not.

"Tom has a very serious concussion and is covered with scrapes and bruises.

"Reynoso was lucky. He's got a cut ear but, other than that, he's okay."

Tears began rolling down her cheeks and she struggled to get her words out. "Oh, Cort, that's so terrible! Poor George…what will he do if he can't return to the sheriff's office? It's all he lives for; all he knows. And what about Laurie? Is she here? Does she know everything?"

"She's sitting right outside intensive care. The doctors were straight with her and she's up to speed. She's a tough cookie, that one. I think she's handling it as well as can be expected."

Again, Lindsey blinked several times before asking, "Tell me about Tom, okay?"

"Big-time concussion; they put him under while they monitored his brain, but brought him out a couple hours ago. I talked to him for a few minutes but it's not too rewarding. He doesn't remember anything and I mean *anything!* Last thing he can recall was touching down in Mercy's jet. He doesn't remember the gunfire or the plane explosion. The neurologist says it might be weeks or months…maybe never, for the memory. Physically, they expect him to recover okay."

Lindsey took it all in and lay with her eyes closed for several seconds. I thought she might have gone back to sleep until she whispered fiercely, "What happened to those bastards who did this to us?"

I didn't know how much she could comprehend but thought I'd just tell her everything, and if I had to repeat later, so be it. "Bre's dead; Captain Reynoso killed her after the bomb went off…like I said, he wasn't hurt too badly. He actually saw Bre detonate the bomb.

"Akabile is here, in the hospital, in chains and under guard; Laurie shot him in the shoulder with that little popgun pistol when we were making the car exchange. He's not wounded too badly…more's the pity.

"Rockson and Worth are in the Garland jail; they're a little bruised up but nothing serious."

She nodded and asked, "What's going to happen now? And what time is it?"

"It's almost five in the morning. As to what's going to happen, I'm not too sure. You're going to be here for at least three or four days; probably the same for Tom. George is going to be longer…maybe a lot longer. Laurie and I are going back to Denver on Mercy's plane; we're leaving around noon. I want to question the living hell out of Clay Webb to find out just how much he knew…and when he knew it.

"We'll talk with Skyler McMillan and the US Attorney to sort out what charges will be filed against Rockson and all the others. We need to figure out the jurisdictions…Dailov was murdered in Arapahoe County, the bombing was in Denver, plus, all the federal charges."

Her eyes teared and she took my hand. "Do you really have to go today? I need you here."

"And I want to be here, sweetheart, but I need to help with getting this stuff sorted. I'll come back tomorrow evening and stay until we can go home together. Mercy is offering her plane for as much as we need it. I'm hoping I can take you and Tom back at the same time.

"Laurie is going to get George's house situated, so he can go directly there when he's able. Like I said, that might be a while."

Lindsey focused her eyes on mine, "Make sure those lousy bastards get everything they deserve--just like Bre!"

I nodded, bent down, and hugged her shoulders as tightly as I could without hurting her.

Laurie and I sat back with our drinks as Mercy's jet accelerated smoothly from Redmond's strip. We were facing each other at the conference table and as soon as we leveled off, we produced yellow legal pads and pens and began outlining what we knew about where and when everything had taken place. Two hours later as we started our descent into Centennial Airport, we had each filled several pages, beginning with my beat down and ending with the Akabile takedown. We didn't deal with the bomb because we hadn't witnessed it, but we made some comments on the aftermath.

"When we get in, I'm driving Lindsey's car downtown and have a sit down with Clay Webb. Skyler has it set up for him to turn himself in as soon as I'm done. I'm not sure how deep his involvement was or what he might be charged with, but I think he'll be willing to spill his guts.

"You should go home and try to get some rest. At 8:30 a.m. tomorrow, we meet with Skyler, the Arapahoe County DA, and a federal prosecutor to sort through everything.

"Laurie, you're going to be a big part of this all the way through the eventual trials, so you need to be ready. Nothing is going to be easy and you'll probably be caring for George through a lot of this. That's going to be tough for both of you. I'll do anything and everything I can for you…just ask."

# CHAPTER FORTY

Clay Webb was sitting with his back to his totally clean desktop staring into space when I entered his office. He slowly turned, looked at me as he would a stranger, and motioned toward the visitor's chair. "Mercy said you were on your way; can't say I'm looking forward to this."

I wasn't in a charitable mood. "I don't like it any better than you, but then, I don't appreciate being lied to, beat up, shot at, and damned near killed. What's worse is several people…friends of mine…*were* hurt. People *did* get killed and you were right in the middle of it.

"I'm trying to determine if you got caught up in something way over your head, or if you're a just a goddamn scum-sucking pig who was trying to kill your boss and anybody else who got in the way."

He looked like I'd slapped him. His face reddened and his eyes watered, but he didn't speak. I asked, "So, which is it? Are you a murdering asshole or are you just stupid?"

Words caught in his throat and he had to swallow before softly saying, "I never intended for anyone to get hurt, especially Mercy. I was just trying to reconnect with my brother. He lied to me. He lied and convinced me he was only interested in stopping the frack jobs because of the environmental concerns. But he used my email addresses and cell phone directory to infiltrate the company. When I figured it out, he told me he could make it look like *I* was behind everything: the attacks on Mercy and you and even the crooked deal between Rockson and Akabile.

"At first, I think he really was into the environment factors…they were certainly the 'in' Bre used to get to him…but then Rockson started talking about the millions--the *tens of millions*--of dollars he could get if he helped them. It turned his head.

"But Rockson and Akabile lied to him too. They told him they could make sure the frack technology would only be used overseas, starting in South Sudan. They told him he could get rich but keep on being an environmentalist activist here. He figured out their lies, but they started threatening him and Bre. It wasn't 'til the last minute that he found out she was part of everything; that she'd been using him from the start."

I got out of the chair and paced to the window taking in the view of the Front Range. "Are you telling me he's innocent of everything but being lovesick or dumb?"

"No, that's not what I'm saying. They were using the same argument on him he used on me…that they could put him in the frame for everything unless he continued to help them, so why not take the money and keep his mouth shut."

Webb leaned across the desk to ask, "Where is he? Has he been hurt? All Mercy told me was you were coming back and everyone had been arrested. What can you tell me?"

"I can tell you that bitch, Bre, is dead; Akabile is shot, and Rockson and your brother are in the jail in Garland, Texas. I can tell you my friend, Sheriff George Ivins, may lose his right arm; another friend, DPD Lieutenant Tom Montgomery, has a severe concussion; and my girlfriend, Lindsey, is still in ICU. Those bastards exploded a bomb on them!

"A lot of that is on you, Webb. You should have told me what you knew right off the bat. Now, you're going to face up to it; you're going to have to tell the cops everything and hope like hell they believe you. If you're lucky and cooperate every inch of the way, you might get off easy. If you hold back or, worse yet, lie, you're going to go down for a long damn time."

He sat back in the chair, steepled his fingers over his chest, sighed deeply, and said, "I'll do whatever I can. What happens now?"

"I've got one more question and then we're going to walk out to the reception area where Denver ADA Skyler McMillan, an FBI agent, and a DPD detective are waiting. You're going to tell them you're turning yourself in and are willing to cooperate. They'll take you to central lockup and book you in; if you've got a lawyer, call as soon as you can.

"After that, you're looking at several days of nonstop questioning from all kinds of prosecutors. If you tell the truth, cooperate, and don't complain, you'll probably make bail. Good luck, Webb, you're going to need it."

He inhaled deeply. "What's the question?"

"When did you know about Trey?"

He looked away before answering, "He called me and we met a week after Mercy made the presentation in Rockson's office. That's when we traded addresses and numbers, but I *swear* I didn't know what he was doing. He told me after our Houston meeting with Akabile that I was making a mistake by not taking the deal. I tried to tell him it wasn't my decision and that's when he threatened to tell Mercy…and you…I was involved."

I stared at him for several seconds. "You could have stopped everything if you'd have told us that."

I motioned him up, escorted him to the reception area, and turned him over to Skyler. He looked stricken when the detective produced handcuffs and snapped them around his wrists. As they exited, I heard Skyler reciting him his Miranda rights.

Mercy and Janelle were watching me from the hall leading to the offices. "It's not as bad as it looks. I asked Skyler to scare the living shit out of him while they haul him over to DPD headquarters. I told her I didn't think he was guilty of anything other than worrying about his brother, but if they scare him enough and work him hard, they might learn a lot.

"I'm guessing he'll spend the night in jail, get several hours of questioning tomorrow, but be out by evening. He probably won't even have to make bail; he'll be on personal recognizance."

Mercy sighed, "I'm glad to hear it, Cort. I've never seen anyone as sorrowful, remorseful, and depressed as Clay was yesterday after he told me about his brother. If he gets off easy…no felony charges…I plan on giving him his job back. He's a talented guy and I can use him."

I looked at her carefully before saying, "You're more forgiving than I could be, Mercy."

She dropped her gaze before asking, "How's Lindsey? How are the others? What's going to happen to Rockson and that despicable Akabile…and Clay's brother?"

"Linds will be fine; a few more days in the hospital and then some rehab. Same goes for Tom; he's got a hell of a concussion and is goofy as hell right now, but that's nothing new for him." I laughed as she grimaced at my tasteless joke.

"George Ivins is a different story. He's in bad shape. His whole right side was severely damaged; the doctors are optimistic but there's still a chance he could lose his arm. He's going to be in the hospital for a while and then is facing a long and painful recovery."

She raised her face and her eyes filled with tears. She glanced around like she wanted to escape to avoid any more conversation. "I'm so sorry for all of them, Cort. I guess I'm responsible for a lot of it. I--

"*That's bullshit, Mercy! You* are not responsible for anything! Everybody was just doing their job; just like I was trying to do mine…to protect you. Ask any of them and they'll tell you the same thing!

"This isn't over by a long shot. There will be years of trials and appeals before it's over and done with. You've got a company to run and a life to lead. You need to get on with it."

She put her hand on my shoulder. "Thanks for that, Cort. That makes the second time you've told me something to turn me around; you've been right both times." She turned to Janelle, "I want to set up a fund for everyone who was injured. I want to cover every dollar of their recoveries and rehabilitation…and I want it done anonymously. Will you coordinate it for me?

"I want to assemble an aggressive legal team to investigate filing suits against Rockson *personally* on behalf of anyone who was hurt."

"I also want to find the best defense lawyers available for Clay."

She pulled me around to face her and said, "Don't say a word, Cort. This is something I *have* to do."

# CHAPTER FORTY-ONE

It took five days before the hospital released Tom and Lindsey. Mercy accompanied me to Garland and during the flight, brought me up to date on what the lawyers thought of her idea about suing Rockson. I was surprised to learn there were precedents for law enforcement officers as well as private citizens like me to bring civil suits for injuries incurred during a police action. She said all of us, including Reynoso, could sue and expect to receive settlements commensurate with the injuries we suffered. In my case, it could go all the way back to my beating at the hands of Rockson's thugs.

I told her it would be welcome news--particularly for George. His doctors had said it would be several weeks before he could return to Denver. The good news was he would not lose his arm, although the doctors continued to warn him how intensive and lengthy his recovery would be.

After the paperwork and arrangements for Tom's and Lindsey's releases had been completed, I went to see George. When I walked into his dimly-lit room, he was propped up in bed and suspended like a circus acrobat. His right arm was in a cast with ropes and pulleys attached to a metal frame above the bed. His right leg was hanging in a similar contraption from the same frame. It didn't look comfortable.

I couldn't tell if he was sleeping or awake so I spoke as softly as I could. "Hey, George, are you awake?"

He stirred slightly and squinted in my direction which was directly into the light coming from the hall. "Who's there? Is that you, Cort?"

I walked to the side of the bed and took his left hand in a handshake. "Yep, it's me. How're you doing, pardner?"

"It's rough, Cort. Rough as anything that's ever happened to me; lots of pain, although it's getting a little better. One of my nurses said you're here to take Tom and Lindsey back to Denver." He seemed to straighten in the bed, although that would be impossible with all his straps and ropes. He asked the question I'd been dreading. "Did Laurie come with you?"

I'd been dreading it because Laurie was showing signs of delayed shock. She admitted to having no appetite, no energy, and was having trouble sleeping. She'd been frank in saying she didn't want to see George quite yet. She didn't know if she could handle seeing him in his current condition.

I'd considered several answers before settling on "No, she's in the midst of a deposition about what happened here. It's the first step in the feds' extradition process for Akabile. I've been at the federal courthouse for the last two days myself. She wanted to come, buddy; she *really* wanted to come. She asked me to tell you she'd definitely be here when you're ready to go back to Denver." I hoped he would buy into my answer.

George looked disappointed but understanding. "Makes sense; so what's happening with Rockson and Akabile now?"

I suppressed my sigh of relief. "They're both in jail here in Garland. As soon as we get Tom and Lindsey back, they'll be giving their depositions and the US attorney said he thought it would move quickly after that. You're going to have to do the same thing when you're able.

"You won't believe the laundry list of charges for the assholes! The feds are going with terrorism, weapons of mass destruction, espionage, and international bribery. Next in line will be Arapahoe and Denver counties for the murder charge and my assault.

"But, there's some other big news that'll interest you--she doesn't want you to know, but Mercy Drexler is funding an account to pay for *all* the medical expenses for everyone…you, Tom, Linds, and even Reynoso. It will include everyone's rehab too…no matter how long it takes.

"To top it off, she's also building a legal team to pursue civil cases against Rockson--that's where the money is--for everyone. I don't know how it'll all shake out, but it could mean millions."

George listened, took everything in, and was silent for several moments. "That all sounds great, but it doesn't mean squat if I lose my arm."

"You're not losing your arm, George! You know that! The doctors have already said you're not losing it. Having the chance--

He interrupted, "Maybe it isn't going to fall off if that's what you mean, but if I can't use it for anything what's the fucking difference?"

I hadn't anticipated this. "You've got to give rehab and therapy a chance; you haven't even started yet. It's going to take a while, but I'm sure you're going to be good as new." I *wasn't* sure of any such thing, but I didn't want George to know. "That's the great thing about what Mercy is doing: you can take as long as you need to get back and, what's more, if you don't make it all the way back, you'll never have to worry about money for the rest of your life. It means you and Laurie can have a future."

George grimaced as he tried to readjust his position, but I wasn't sure if it was physical or mental discomfort. "Laurie's not going to want to spend her life with a goddamn cripple. If I can't continue being a sheriff and a homicide investigator, I'm not going to be worth much of anything…to her…or myself."

Maybe it was time for tough love, "That's bullshit! You're the same man as you were a week ago and you'll be the same man next week, next month, and next year regardless of your arm. Laurie knows that and, what's more, she loves you. Get off the pity parade, George! I'm not buying it and neither is anyone else."

He remained silent for several seconds then slowly nodded his head. "Guess I needed to hear it from somebody; my thinking gets all scrambled being by myself all day." He raised his left hand again and I took it. The grip was stronger than before.

"I'll be coming back when you're ready to travel, pardner. Get your head on straight and we'll give 'em all hell soon as your able." He managed a weak smile as I backed out of the room.

Tom was ambulatory and showed no ill effects, at least outwardly, but both he and Lindsey had to be moved in wheel chairs, per doctor's orders. She used crutches to keep off her wounded leg. When we'd settled them in and were underway toward Colorado, Mercy said, "While I've got you as a captive audience, I want to tell you how much what you've done for me means. There's no way to adequately thank you for everything, but I need to say it anyway: *THANK YOU!*"

A few minutes later, she told Tom and Lindsey about the medical care and the legal team. She waved off Tom's protestations about "just doing my duty" and held Lindsey's hand while she explained how the lawsuits could bring millions.

I admitted I'd told George and explained I felt he needed some light at the end of what was going to be a very long tunnel. Mercy wasn't mad and actually thanked me.

Tom and Lindsey were literally speechless and we jetted along in silence for several minutes until Lindsey murmured, "I just wish George was with us. I'm worried about how he's handling his injuries and I don't mean just the obvious ones."

Again, silence filled the plane.

# CHAPTER FORTY-TWO

"I don't know, Cort. I appreciate the offer, I really do, but it feels like some kind of handout. Obviously, after two years in rehab, my arm is never going to be a hundred percent, but it's useable; probably seventy-five percent or so. The new sheriff hasn't pressed me to retire or take disability, but we've talked about it. I can stay on until retirement age if I want, although I'd probably have to ride a desk. He's been up front about everything, even came to the rehabilitation facility at Craig Hospital the week after he was elected.

"Both of the sheriffs have been great for me…and Laurie too! The old one, our boss at the time, gave her that extended 'leave of absence' and she spent almost a month with me in Garland. I was feeling pretty low when she didn't come with you when you picked up Tom and Lindsey, but she was honest and told me she wasn't ready. Truth be told, I probably wasn't either. But we made up for that in short order; seeing someone every day for a month leads to a lot of talk. It was good for both of us, and that's a fact."

George made a point of reaching across the table with his right arm to pick up the heavy glass margarita pitcher. He moved carefully, but he managed. Point taken. "This is nice out here; I envy your backyard. Every time Laurie and I come here, she goes home raving about the place. She keeps asking why we don't buy one nearby." He laughed and sipped his drink.

I was surprised by his admission. "Well, why don't you? There are at least three for sale in this area and a couple have better views than this one. And, it isn't like you can't afford it for chrissake! The settlement your lawyers got from Rockson has set you up for life--which is another reason I want you to throw in with me--you don't need the money!"

George gave me a lopsided grin, "You saying you do this for the fun of it? Getting threatened, beat up, shot at and God knows what else? Why the hell would I want to be a part of something like that?"

I was forced to return the grin, "Well, when you put it like that, I guess you wouldn't. I think I'll just keep all the fun to myself!

"But, seriously, George, I think Mercy's case just scratched the surface for what an international private investigation firm could do--and I'm going to get a lot of that work. I could really use your help, plus we'd have a chance at doing some real good. We wouldn't be in it just for the money, although it'll be huge. Didn't it feel good to watch the feds turn the key on Rockson? He's going away for the rest of his miserable life."

George shook his head, "But we didn't get everything we wanted out of those prosecutions. Akabile got what amounts to a fucking pass! Rockson was the only one who took a fall."

It was my turn to shake my head, "Not when you look at the big picture; Bre ended up dead--that's a pretty stiff sentence, wouldn't you say?"

He considered for a moment, "Good point, but it still galls me to think of Akabile being back in South Sudan *under house arrest!* How the hell did that happen? The son-of-a-bitch should be sharing a cell with Rockson in Super Max down in Canon City!"

"I agree, although I don't think the final chapter's been written yet. It does piss me off the US agreed to extradite the bastard. Having his bullshit claim of diplomatic immunity granted by the Justice and State Departments was a slap in the face of every federal prosecutor who worked the case, not to mention all of us and all the cops and district attorneys.

"I figure he had a bunch of South Sudanese government officials on the pad all along. I think they threatened to raise some kind of stink in the UN or against our State Department and it was enough to scare us into turning him loose. The government just didn't want to go through years and years of shit with an emerging third world country in that part of the world. Their government gets the oil deals they needed and ours gets rid of the problem."

George looked at me intently, "What did you mean by 'the final chapter's not been written?' You know something I don't?"

"No, I'm just thinking those guys change regimes like dirty underwear and almost as often. There've been three new 'governments' in the past eighteen months. Sooner or later, one of them is going to decide Akabile doesn't serve any purpose and could potentially be a problem. When that happens, I'm betting one of his 'guards' will put a bullet in his head--end of the story."

George slugged some margarita and said, "I hope you're right; couldn't happen to a nicer asshole and the sooner the better.

"But even Trey Worth got off a lot easier than he should. He was in it up to his eyeballs, wasn't he?"

I said, "That's a 'yes and no' answer. He was just a dupe for most of it; Bre set him up and used him. But once they had their hooks in him and threatened to implicate him in Mercy's car bombing and Dailov's murder, he jumped at the chance to not only walk away but to get rich doing it. He stupidly believed he could keep on being an environmental activist *while* getting rich.

"Still, twenty years of hard time for a terrorist conspiracy and espionage isn't an easy road, particularly in a federal pen like Super Max. He's probably already some lifer's bitch and he's going to get passed from one con to another until he's used up. What he's doing now is a far cry from carrying signs and protesting frack operations."

George stood and walked to the deck railing. He no longer limped and had resumed wearing western boots instead of the athletic shoes he'd been forced into for the past couple of years. "You know, when I listen carefully, I can *almost* believe what you're saying…*almost.*" He laughed bitterly.

"At least Rockson got the whole nine yards! Fifty years to life from the feds for espionage, terrorism, importation of weapons of mass destruction, conspiracy to commit fraud, plus some other shit. He'll probably die in prison. But even if he somehow gets out, he'll have a premeditated first degree murder, life with no opportunity for parole waiting for him courtesy of the State of Colorado.

"I couldn't believe it when the sniveling bastard started 'fessing up to everything in hopes of getting leniency. Jesus, he was holding Dailov's arms down when Bre stuck that cannon in his mouth for chrissakes! In a way, I guess he did get *some* leniency…he didn't get the needle. When you think about it, though, he didn't get anything for having you stomped or any of the other shit he did."

I joined him at the railing, "Oh, I don't know…life without parole, that's good enough for me. Plus, the money-grubbing asshole lost every dime he'd ever made. I mean, with you and Linds and Tom each getting something north of ten million, and Laurie, Reynoso, and me nearly half that, it wiped out his personal fortune entirely.

"The legit people who worked for his companies are damn lucky the corporations survived and they still have jobs.

"That's another place where Mercy helped out, you know. She and Marty Gear and Vada Benson, the woman who took over Wildcat Willie Davidson's company after he was murdered, combined and took control of Rockson International. They renamed it Colorado International Ventures and cut a deal with South Sudan *without* Akabile! They'll be 'womb to tomb' on most of South Sudan's oil development: drilling, completions using Mercy's frack technology, and then Marty and Vada will operate for the Sudanese.

"Frankly, everything's worked out superbly, including my original deal with Mercy Drexler and Frack Focus. My override rolled directly into Colorado International Ventures and, even though my percentage is super tiny, the operation and upside is huge. It's going to be worth a bucketful of money starting in a few years.

"So, like you, I don't need the money either, but I just can't get my head around having nothing to do. I've given it a lot of thought and decided I want--no, I *need*--to keep working. I like digging around in deals; you know what I mean, 'investigating' things. I think there'll be lots of chances to keep doing what I've been doing and I'd like you to be a part of it. It seems to me we've made a good team in the past, and I'd like that to continue."

George leaned back and stared into the distance. "Let me ask you something, Cort. And it doesn't have anything to do with the money--you know I was just ribbing you--but how 'satisfying' is the work? I mean, I've spent twenty-five years in the sheriff's office; I got to run down a bunch of bad guys, solve a lot of cases, and, to tell you the truth, I *love* it. How will working with you compare to that?"

It was a good question and difficult for me to answer. I'd never been in law enforcement, so I didn't have a basis for comparison. I *did* know how good it had felt to catch Mary Linfield's and Gerri German's killers…and George had been a big part of that. It had felt good to solve the murder of a Geological Survey geologist and break up a Chinese spy ring in the process. And, solving Denver's "murder of the century" when Wildcat Willie Davidson was assassinated had filled a need in me I hadn't been able to describe.

I finally said, "All I know is how *great* it feels when you get to the end of a case and *know* you've made a difference; that you've helped some people and put some asshole in prison.

"But the biggest thing, probably for both of us, regardless of the finances, is *neither* of us would be tied to a desk…*ever!*"

George drained his drink, set the glass on the table, and shook my hand. His grip was as strong as ever.

*****

# ACKNOWLEDGEMENTS

I admire every single author who has ever written and published a book and would like to acknowledge their effort. As my old friend Charles Hedges would have said, "If it was easy, anybody could do it." (That isn't "exactly" how Charlie would have put it, but he was not known for being politically correct!)

As with all my previous novels, my wife, Jan, has been my chief collaborator, editor, proof reader, and most importantly, cheerleader. Her support throughout the entire process has been instrumental.

I owe my good friend, Hugh Hebert, a huge debt of gratitude for providing his knowledge and experience to the sections dealing with airport operations and communications. He gave me a great deal of insight into an industry of which I know virtually nothing.

I appreciate and acknowledge over thirty-five years' worth of discussions with so many oil industry friends and associates who welcomed me to the industry and tried to keep me informed of its technical aspects. The new technologies, particularly in horizontal drilling and completing, would be mysteries to me without their continued help.

I would like to thank the Douglas County, Colorado, Libraries and, in particular, Lisa Casper, their coordinator of local author programs. The DCL system is one of the best in the nation and its numerous programs in support of local authors is invaluable in so many ways. The Local Author Showcases provide Colorado authors of all genres an unparalleled opportunity to get their work and their names in front of the most important audience of all…book readers.

Lastly, as always, I own all the mistakes.

## ABOUT THE AUTHOR

Lee Mossel was born in Eugene, Oregon, and grew up in the small logging and lumber mill town of Noti. He graduated from the University of Oregon with an advanced degree in geology and spent thirty-five years as a petroleum geologist in Denver, Colorado.

He is the author of three previous Cortlandt Scott mystery thrillers and the 2015 standalone biographical fiction novel *Bed of Thorns.*

He lives in Parker, Colorado, in a house and setting remarkably similar to Cortlandt Scott's.

## The Cortlandt Scott Series

The Murder Prospect
The Talus Slope
More Than 100% Dead
Fracked to Death

## Other Novels

Bed of Thorns

Lee Mossel's novels are available through amazon.com as either paperbacks or e-books and can be ordered online through bookstores everywhere.

Connect with Lee online: http://www.leemossel.com or at lee.leemossel.com

Made in the USA
Middletown, DE
03 April 2017